DARK SECRETS

DARK SECRETS

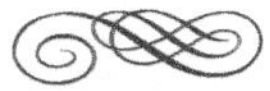

BRE ALLEN

Bre Allen

I

Ariette

The sun rose over the trees of the capitol city, Imperium. Summer wind rustled the leaves as men got up early to do their chores. Mothers roused their children, coercing them with food. The marketplace was doing its best to look as clean as possible for the inspection that day. In a two-story home on the outer edge of the marketplace, a young woman walked out of the back door. She had long, platinum blond hair and striking blue eyes. She still wore her nightgown with an apron and wooden clogs, lugging a bucket.

She took it to the well and yawned as she lowered it into the water. As she worked, she glared up at the palace. Her muscles strained as she cranked the lever to lift the bucket back out of the water, letting her hatred for the royal family be her strength. When it was finally resting on the side of the well, she did, too. It had only been less than a year and the wounds were still fresh. She gave it one final glare then stalked back into her home with the water.

She poured some of the water into the kettle and set it over the fire, hanging the apron up on the hook by the back door. She sat on the cabinet and watched the water. Upstairs, a door shut, and she swallowed thickly as her mother descended the stairs.

"Good morning, Ariette," her mother said, her voice stuffy.

Ariette sighed and hopped off the counter. The two women looked at each other before hugging.

"I'm sorry," Ariette said. "I didn't mean what I said last night."

"I know why you're upset," Elizabeth said. "I am, too. But we can't let our grief get in the way of our loyalty."

Ariette made a face as she prepared the breakfast and tea.

"I don't even know why they keep doing these," she said. "Nothing changes! It's always the same!"

"They're busy," her mother said with a shrug. "There's a war going on; they don't have a lot of time to come and visit their subjects. This gives them the chance to do so and get an update on the land."

"I hate it when you make a good point," Ariette pouted.

Elizabeth laughed. "I know. Now, I found the dress I want you to wear today."

"Ugh. Do I still have to-? I mean, yes, of course," she said quickly when her mother glared.

After a hurried breakfast of egg and toast, Ariette dragged herself up the stairs. She didn't bother hiding her contempt for what she had to do. A lump rose to her throat at the dress on the bed. It was the last gift her father had given her: Long and periwinkle blue, with sleeves that belled out at the elbow. She sighed and changed into it, trying to avoid thinking about the day they brought his helmet back.

Ariette had just finished putting her hair up into a bun when the horns sounded. She quickly put on her shoes and rushed downstairs. Her mother was in her wedding dress, obsessively making sure it was free of wrinkles. They walked out with the rest of the city. It looked as if a royal progression was arriving, but the lack of only increased Ariette's resentment. She whistled a tune to herself, looking around at her neighbors.

They were all dressed to impress, too. The children had been stuffed into hideously uncomfortable suits and dresses. Some were crying out of boredom and their fathers picked them up onto their shoulders, bouncing them. Ariette smiled as she remembered her father doing the same thing. They would make fun of the royal family together. Until he left to join the militia, that is....

"How long do we have to wait here?" she grumbled.

"Don't be so impatient," her mother said. "You know they like to discuss things with some of the marketplace vendors."

"So do it later. The rest of us have things to do."

Her mother arched a brow. "Really, Ariette? And what, pray tell, do you have that's so urgent to do?"

In a very unladylike manner, Ariette crossed her arms and slumped against the house.

"Nothing," she admitted grudgingly. "But still...."

She didn't have any other argument and her mother shook her head. Suddenly, she slapped Ariette's arm rapidly and she looked up from where she was tracing lines in the dirt. Despite her feelings, the three silhouettes at the top of the street snapped her body into attention. Elizabeth yanked at where Ariette's skirts had hitched up then straightened her own dress. Ariette couldn't hear anything; just a strange ringing in her ears. The family was getting closer, pleasant smiles on their faces as they spoke with some of the people. She hoped they'd keep walking after saying hello, but she knew better. The moment they stepped up to her and her mother, they stopped.

King Laurent hadn't changed in the few months since she last saw him. He still had black hair, speckled with white, and green eyes. His face was the same pale as it had been, the scar on his cheek as obvious as ever. The king had been in his fair share of battles and there were scars and a permanent limp to prove it. When he smiled at her and her mother, she could see the pity in those hateful eyes.

"Good morning," he said. "How are you ladies?"

"Just fine, your highness," they said in unison.

"And the farms?" he asked. "The harvest is coming in on time?"

"We believe so," her mother said. "I need to speak with Liam, of course."

The king nodded thoughtfully. "I admit, I was concerned about the two of you taking up what Robert had managed to do. But I can see- What was that?"

Elizabeth's eyes widened as the king stared at Ariette. She gulped. Even though she had done her best not to, a derisive laugh had escaped. She coughed to cover the noise but knew it was too late.

"Do you have something to say?" he asked.

"No, sir," she said. "My apologies."

He kept staring at her. She fidgeted with her fingers.

"So, the business has been keeping you busy?" the king asked her mother, though his eyes didn't leave Ariette's.

"Yes, very much so."

"And what of your daughter? Has she been keeping up with it easily, too?"

"You can just ask me, you know," she muttered, and Elizabeth glared at her.

"Yes, though I see perhaps some more tasks will help her keep more distracted."

Ariette scoffed and her mother elbowed her in the side.

"What's on your mind, Ariette?" the king asked. "I can see something's bothering you."

"Nothing," she lied blandly. "I'm perfectly fine, your highness, though I appreciate your concern."

He sighed and let go of his wife to put a hand on Ariette's shoulder.

"I know you miss your father," he said gently. "I do, too, and-."

"With all due respect," she interrupted, her voice shaking with emotion, "I ask you not mention my father. He was a soldier in your militia, you didn't know him."

"Ariette," her mother moaned, dropping pretense and covering her face with her hands. "Please, hold your tongue."

The king stepped back but didn't seem mad. He looked at his wife who was studying Ariette. Queen Stela was stunning, only a few inches shorter than her husband. She had long, flowing red hair and happy amber eyes. There wasn't a single sign on her face that hinted at her age.

For some reason, her warm gaze made Ariette feel both ashamed and uncomfortable. Queen Stela beckoned to her husband and he leaned closer to hear what she was saying. A smile spread on his face. Behind them, their son was openly glaring at Ariette and she returned it.

Prince Sorin was more of a recluse than his parents. He hadn't been down to see the village. The last time they saw him was when they had the mass funeral for his sister, Charlotte. Why he was there that day, Ariette couldn't imagine. He had his father's height and hair, but his eyes were the same odd amber as his mother's. She knew he was mad at her and she relished in the knowledge.

Finally, the king straightened.

"Come to the castle in three hours' time," he said to her. "Do not be late."

"Sire, please," her mother breathed, reaching out a little. "I'll talk to her about the way she speaks, but please don't punish her."

His eyes softened. He took Elizabeth's hands in his.

"Do not worry. I will not take another loved one from you."

He patted her hands once then looked back at Ariette.

"I regret it every day that I think about him," he said. "But I do know that he would be proud of you."

"You didn't even know him," she repeated. She was about to cry. "Don't speak as if you do."

Elizabeth groaned quietly again. The king didn't say anything, though. Instead, he offered his arm to his wife again and led the way onward. Prince Sorin didn't follow right away. He still glared at Ariette and she held her head high. Finally, he turned and followed his parents. Before Ariette could even take a breath, the door was open, and her mother shoved her through it.

"What were you thinking!?" she shouted once it was shut. "Are you trying to get yourself arrested!?"

"I'm sorry!" Ariette shouted back. "But I can't just- I tried but then he- He didn't even know him!" she cried, stomping her foot. Tears splashed down her face. "How dare he mention him like that!?"

"Enough!" Her mother was crying, too. "Enough! I can't keep going through this with you! I know that it hurts but you disgrace his memory by acting this way!"

Ariette gasped, taking a step back.

"Well," she sobbed, "if I'm such a mockery to his name, then maybe I should just leave!"

"You know that's not what I want or mean! Would he want you acting this way!?"

"I don't know because he isn't here! And it's because of him that he's gone! I'm not going to the palace!"

"Yes, you are," she said. "There is no question about it so don't even think about arguing! You will go and accept whatever punishment the king has in plan for you."

Ariette gawked at her. "Mother, you can't be serious!"

"Get ready. Three hours will pass quicker than you know."

With that, she went up to her bedroom and slammed the door.

II

Sorin

The royal family continued their walk, stopping to speak with a few of the other citizens. Imperium consisted of a main street with three more streets branching off from it. Nearest to the curtain wall surrounding the castle, was the market. Stalls of food, clothing, and other odds and ends were tended by the elderly while the younger people tried to catch passersby attention. After the market, the homes were for the wealthier of the citizens. One street broke off directly from the market district. This led to what the people had called the labor district. The smithy, the butcher, and the tanner set up shop. It would be they who the family would speak to last. After the homes, another street led to where the farmers slept.

Rosu was known for its wealth, a wealth that had been accumulated due to their farmlands. They grew several crops, corn and wheat being the more prominent. Their court wizard had made it possible to grow all sorts of food items in their climate, making Rosu one of the most desired allies. Three silos loomed in the distance at the far end of the fields. Each held the stores for the people when winter came.

The final street was the king's least favorite to go down. This housed the less fortunate; families who were hit hard financially from the war. They always had a kind word and gift for him, things that only increased his father's guilt.

As the family finished in the final district, Prince Sorin cleared his throat. His father sighed.

"Yes, Sorin, what is it?"

"I'm curious about what her punishment will be," he said, glaring at the home as they passed by it again.

Everyone was returning to their daily tasks, but both the girl and her mother were nowhere to be seen. He could hear raised voices coming from the home.

"Sorin," the king said.

"Far be it for me to tell you what to do," he interrupted, "but I think a good lashing would be enough."

"Sorin."

"Or a day or two in the dungeons. That ought to teach her to reign in that tongue of hers."

"Sorin."

"Of course, I've always been a fan of stringing people up by their thumbs. Perhaps-"

"Sorin!"

The prince stopped and smiled pleasantly. "Yes, Father?"

"There will be no punishment for Ariette Jones."

Sorin froze in the middle of the marketplace, gaping at his father. People scurried around him and he rushed to catch up.

"What!? But she was so disrespectful!"

Laurent sighed. "And she had every right to be."

"Don't be ridiculous, Father! She-"

"Enough," his mother said. Her voice was gentle but firm and he shut his mouth. "Let your father explain once we've returned."

"Fine," he grumbled.

The guards opened the gates leading to the palace keep. It was three stories tall and made of stone and brick. Three towers with parapets waved the kingdom's symbol on a flag: two golden daggers crossed at the hilt on a ruby red backdrop. Steps led up to the palace doors. Guards were sparring in the bailey and stopped to bow to the family. The king just raised a hand, his brow furrowed in intense thought. Sorin was frowning, too, but out of annoyance. He couldn't believe his father was going to let that wretch get away with how she spoke.

The foyer was large with a red carpet easing the eyes from the harsh stone. Tapestries and landscape portraits dotted the walls. The grand staircase went up then split into two directions. To their right, the door to the dining hall was wide open. The throne room door was closed, though, and his father paused to murmur something. The door opened on its own and he led his family through it.

This room served as both their throne room and ballroom. It was large and four thrones were on the far-right wall. Laurent helped Stela into her throne and Sorin stood before both of them, arms crossed and toes tapping.

"You're really going to let her get away with it?" he asked once his father was seated.

Laurent shook his head. "You don't understand, Sorin. I knew her father."

"Of course, you did. He was in your army."

Laurent fiddled with the sash on his hip. "Do you remember the final battle I was in?"

"Yes."

"Then you remember it nearly killed me." Sorin could only nod, waiting to see where this was going. "The reason I didn't die, was because a soldier took the blade for me. That soldier was Ariette's father."

"Just because her father's a war hero doesn't mean she can speak like that," he said.

"I never told them."

This gave Sorin pause. He lowered his arms slowly. The king looked guilty and pinched the bridge of his nose. Stela put a soothing hand on his arm.

"Why not?"

"Because that would mean revealing how close I was with Robert."

"Close? Why would you be close to a soldier?"

"Robert wasn't just a soldier," Laurent said. "He was my good friend."

"How good?"

"Good enough to know our secret."

Sorin took a step back in shock. "Father, you can't be serious! Do you know how dangerous that was!?"

"I never expected Ariette to feel so strongly about this, though," the king continued, ignoring Sorin. "Looking back, that's foolish."

"I can't believe you told him! He could've killed us all!"

"That's not the kind of man Robert was," he said. "But come sit. The people will be coming soon, and we must prepare for Ariette's visit."

"But-"

"Do as I say," his father snapped.

Sorin growled but did as he was told. He flopped onto his throne, trying not to look at the empty one beside him. If Charlotte were here, she would make his father see reason. The first villager came in, a young man who looked to be in his early twenties. He was large, his black skin marred with scratches.

"Good morning, Liam," Laurent said with a smile. "How are you?"

"Jus' fine, your highness," the man said with a clumsy bow. "You asked to see me?"

"Yes. Harvest time will be on us in just two months. Is everything prepared?"

"Aye. I've already got some men drawin' up a schedule so we can keep up with everythin'."

"Lovely. Any updates on the forests?"

"No, sir. The animals are still disappearin'. No one's too worried yet, though."

Laurent frowned in thought. "Where could they be going to?" he muttered. "Well, that's all I have. Dear?"

"I have nothing to ask."

He nodded. "Very well. You're dismissed." The man didn't move. "Is there something wrong?"

"I know Ariette has a knack for speakin' where she shouldn't," he said. "She's jus' hurtin'."

Laurent smiled again. "Thank you, I understand."

Liam bowed again and left, his hulky figure barely fitting through the door. A few more of the villagers came to give his father updates or to give requests. Those from the poorer district were bringing the gifts again. They were small trinkets, homemade jewelry or pottery. It certainly wasn't anything worthy of being in a palace, but Laurent appreciated the effort they put into them and had a special case in the throne room to display it all.

"Why do they keep bringing this stuff?" Sorin asked after the last of the families left.

"It's their way of thanking me," Laurent answered.

"What do you mean? They pay their taxes, that's all the thanks we need."

Laurent shook his head. "Loyalty isn't just about doing what is expected of you, son."

"Seems pointless to me. It's not like we're going to use these," he said, holding up one of the vases.

Stela pursed her lips and took it from him. "Just because an item isn't made of the finest materials, doesn't mean it does not have value."

"Whatever," he said. He walked to one of the large windows. It had a good view of the hunting grounds. "Animals are missing, Father?"

"Yes," he said. "It's been happening for about a year, numbers slowly falling. We're not sure what's causing it, but we don't have the time or manpower to do anything about it right now. Not with this bloody war going on."

Sorin frowned over his shoulder. "If you'd let me go to battle, perhaps we'd be able to do something about that."

A glare was his response and he huffed, looking out the window again. His father had been adamant about him not going to battle. It was starting to irritate him. How could he be the future leader of this kingdom if he had never tasted danger? How would he be able to look any of the soldiers in the eye, ask them to lay their lives down for him?

His mind drifted but was yanked back when the throne room door opened again. He glared from the corner as Ariette walked in. She had changed into a more casual dress, her blond hair pulled back into a braid. She stood in front of his parents, her head held high.

"Would it kill you to curtsy?" he snapped, and she yelped, spinning around.

"Do you always lurk in the shadows?" she snapped back.

His eye twitched. "A little respect is more than warranted here."

"Sit, Sorin," his father said before she could reply. He obeyed and sat down heavily; eyes narrowed on the girl in front of them. "Thank you for being on time, Ariette."

She lowered her eyes. He could feel her shame.

"I'm sorry for how I spoke to you," she said. "And I'm prepared for any punishment you may have for me."

"I feel your grief keenly," the king said. "Robert was a very good man."

"Please don't," she said wearily, closing her eyes.

"Come again?"

"You're talking of my father as if you knew him. Please don't. I get you're trying to make me feel better but-"

"Ah, you misunderstand me. I did, in fact, know your father quite personally." She looked up in shock. "I've asked you here, not to punish you, but to apologize. I realize that his death is still fresh on your heart, and I wish there were more I could do to lessen your burden. Tell me, what do you do during the days?"

She shrugged. "I do some of the bookkeeping with Mother. Liam and his family are the ones who handle the manual labor and farmers."

"I see. What of your home?"

"I don't understand."

"Do you like it?"

She shrugged. "It's a bit large for just me and Mother, but we make do. I'm sorry, your highness, but where is this going? If I'm not being punished, then why am I here?"

Laurent looked to Stela who nodded with a small smile.

"My wife is in need of a lady-in-waiting," he said. "And we'd like to offer you the position."

Both she and Sorin spoke at the same time.

"What!?"

Ariette's jaw dropped. "Come again?"

Laurent laughed. "Stela's previous lady-in-waiting had to leave us on short notice. I'd like to extend the offer to you."

"Why me?" she asked.

"Yeah, why her?" Sorin demanded. "Father, you know what happened to-"

Hold your tongue, boy.

Sorin clenched his jaw but stopped.

"I recognize that a young woman such as yourself needs more to do than bookkeeping," the king said. "And I wish to fulfill a promise I made to your father."

"What promise?" she asked. He didn't reply, just smiled more. "Well, I don't think I'm the right person for the job, sire. I don't know the last thing about being a lady-in-waiting."

"I'll teach you everything you need to know," Stela said happily.

"I don't know," she repeated, shifting on her feet. "I don't like the idea of leaving Mother alone."

"Oh, she'd come with you," the king said. "I'm sure she'll find plenty of things to do here. And the two of you can finally live in relative ease. At least, that's my hope."

She tugged at some loose hair. "Your highness, this is a huge honor. I don't understand why you're offering it to me, a girl who yelled at you in the street."

"Tell me about it," Sorin grumbled.

Laurent stood and put his hands on Ariette's shoulders. She flinched but didn't move away.

"Take some time to think it over," he said. "I do hope you accept the offer, though. I have many stories of your father I'd like to share."

Her eyes lit up. "What kind of stories?"

"It's getting late," Laurent said, glancing at the window. "Sorin, why don't you walk her out?"

"I know the way," she said.

"She knows the way," Sorin said at the same time and they glared at each other again.

Laurent rolled his eyes and pulled Sorin to his feet.

"Take her by the ground floor library," Laurent whispered. "Don't ask questions. Just go."

Sorin straightened his tunic and beckoned for Ariette to follow him.

"I look forward to hearing from you soon," the king said as Ariette curtsied.

"Yes, your highness," she muttered and followed Sorin out the door.

"Ah, not so fast," Sorin said, grabbing her elbow when she made for the castle doors.

"Oi, don't touch me," she said and pulled her arm away from him. "I know the way out."

"He wants me to take you somewhere first," he said and grabbed her arm again. "Just follow along. I'd rather not have to be around you more than necessary."

She glared but followed him through an archway by the stairs.

"For a prince, you sure are rude," she snapped.

"For a commoner, you sure are disrespectful. Honestly, how you're not in the dungeons I'll never know."

"Why *didn't* he punish me?" she asked, looking over her shoulder.

"If I knew, what makes you think I'd tell you?"

"Gods, you're insufferable," she said.

He opened the door to the library and pointed at it, glaring. She shrugged and walked in.

"It's a library," she said dryly. "How fantastic. I've never seen one before."

He made strangling motions with his hands behind her back as she strolled around. How could his father offer such an insolent brat like her the honor of being his mother's lady-in-waiting!?

"You have a lot of books," she said. "Seriously, some of these are even in languages I don't recognize!"

Sorin yawned dramatically but she wasn't looking. She nodded at some of the paintings then did a doubletake. Her body language changed entirely. Despite his feelings, he grew concerned. Her muscles were tense and her eyes wide. They filled with tears and a small sob escaped her throat before she fled from the room.

"Hey!" he yelled but she didn't stop. "What the?"

He walked over to the painting. He vaguely remembered his father commissioning one to be hung in this library. It was a man who looked awfully like....

"Well, damn."

III

Acceptance

Half an hour later, Ariette ran into the home, sobbing. Her mother was in a large chair by the fire, knitting. When she saw the tears on Ariette's face, she threw her work to the side and opened her arms. Ariette fell to her knees and dropped her head in her mother's lap. Elizabeth waited for the sobbing to subside.

"What happened, sweetheart?" she whispered.

"He- He- The queen needs- and then the stupid prince- and there's this painting and-"

"Ariette, calm yourself. You're not making any sense."

Ariette just dissolved into more tears. Elizabeth stroked her hair. When the sobs turned to hiccups, Elizabeth stood and helped Ariette to their dining table. Ariette blew her nose into a kerchief as Elizabeth made her a strong cup of tea. Ariette took long gulps with a relieved sigh.

"Okay, try again. What happened?"

"The queen needs a new lady-in-waiting," Ariette mumbled. "He offered the position to me."

"What? Really?"

"I know, right?" she said and sighed again. "I tried not to take it, but he says that he knew Papa personally. Ma.... Before I left, the prince took me to their library."

"So?"

"There's a painting of Papa in there," she whispered. Elizabeth gasped, her eyes watering. "I know. The king is hiding something from us."

Elizabeth swallowed the lump in her throat. "Are you going to accept the position?"

Ariette swirled the dregs of her tea in the cup. "I don't know. Part of me wants to, he said he'd tell me more about Papa. But... I don't know the last thing about royalty, much less how to serve them! I mean, what does a lady-in-waiting even do?"

"I haven't the slightest," she said. "But, Ari, I think you should accept."

"What?"

"I know you hate bookkeeping," Elizabeth said. "I also know that you hate this house."

"It's not that I hate it," she muttered and looked at the door. "It just has... bad memories."

"Exactly. Who knows? Maybe this will give you the closure you need about your father."

"Well, what about you?"

"I'll be just fine on my own," she said then Ariette shook her head. "I'm an idiot. I forgot. He said that you can come with me."

Elizabeth straightened her back. "Wait, go to the palace? To live there?"

"Yes. I don't know if you'd be working like me, but he did say we'd be able to live easily or something like that." Ariette rubbed her eyes. "You want to go, don't you?"

"It's every citizen's dream to live in the palace," Elizabeth said with a laugh. "I used to dream about it as a girl. Besides, I don't have the emotional attachment to this place that you do."

Ariette looked around the house again. It was true they hadn't been in it long. After her father was promoted to the head of the farmers' guild, they were provided this house. They lived in it for three years before her father was drafted into the militia. There were even still some boxes in the upper rooms that hadn't been unpacked. When she looked at her mother, her eyes were dreamy, and she looked like a girl again. Ariette knew she wouldn't be able to say no now.

"Okay," she said finally. "I'll accept. But we need to find someone who can take up the books. I'll go talk to Liam."

She finished her tea and went upstairs. The writing desk in her room had a pile of parchment and she scribbled a quick letter to the king. She rolled it up and put her boots on.

"I'll take this to the palace," Elizabeth offered, taking the letter. "Ask Liam and Isadora if they'd like to come to dinner."

"Of course."

They kissed each other's cheeks and her mother went right as Ariette went left.

It was nearing the evening time. She waved to some people who called out to her. One of her friends, Nicole, hastily put the wicker basket of laundry down and ran to walk beside her.

"I wasn't sure if you'd come out alive," she said and Ariette laughed a little.

"You and me both."

"Are you in trouble?"

"Nope. Quite the opposite, actually." As they walked, Ariette told her about the offer. "I talked with Ma and we both agreed I should take it."

Nicole laughed. "More like she wants to go, and you can't bring yourself to say no to her."

Ariette smiled and linked arms with Nicole. "You know me all too well."

"We did grow up together." They both laughed. "So, where are we going?"

"I'm going to talk to Liam about the move. Once we're in the palace, we won't be in charge of keeping up with the books anymore."

"We're going to Liam's?" she asked, her cheeks pink. "Why didn't you say so!? I would've changed my dress! This is covered in water stains!"

Ariette laughed loudly. "You're the one who decided to join me, silly. And stop worrying so much about impressing Liam. I told you: he'd rather have a woman who has a solid head on her shoulders. He doesn't care about the material things."

"Easy for you to say," she said with a pout. "How are you so calm around him?"

"He's like a brother to me, Nicky. I never really considered him that way."

"Speaking of," she said and tilted her head to the left. "Don't look now but I think someone's on his way."

"Please no," she groaned, and Nicole snickered.

"Ariette!" a voice called. "Ariette, wait!"

She took a breath and stopped, forcing a smile on her face. Ivan Tanner was running up to them, holding a bottle of polish in one hand and a brush in the other. Even though he was nearly ten feet away, she could smell the polish. She tried not to gag.

"Hi Ivan," she said. "I'm sorry, I can't stay to chat. I have to go talk to-"

"My pops is making some of his stew tonight!" Ivan said, grinning. "Would you and your mother like to join us?"

"As wonderful as that sounds, I'm afraid I'll have to decline." His smile dropped. "We already have dinner commitments."

"Again?" he asked with a hint of a whine. "You always have plans!"

"I'm sorry. But it seems we'll be moving soon anyway, so we want to have-"

"Moving?" he repeated. "Movin' where?"

"I really should get going," Ariette said, pulling on Nicole's arm. "Good day, Ivan!"

"Yeah, good day," he said and sulked off.

When they were out of earshot, Nicole collapsed into a fit of giggles.

"He's not so bad," she said. "He obviously likes you!"

"More like he likes the money we were left with," Ariette said. "No, I'd rather not have someone who interrupts me constantly."

"But he's really handsome!"

"That's true," she conceded. All of the Tanners had blonde hair and bright green eyes. "But good looks does not a man make."

"Eh, you're too picky," she said. "Where's Liam?"

"He'll be out by the cornstalks," Ariette said. "I think he and Gregory are planning out the harvest."

"It's hard to believe they're starting so early."

"Yeah, but they have a lot of work to do."

"No kidding," Nicole said.

They had reached the farmlands. They stretched in all directions, crops of all kinds swaying in the summer breeze. Out by the cornstalks, some of their livestock grazed in the new fencing. Ariette frowned.

"That fence," she said. "When was that put up?"

"I don't know," Nicole said, distractedly. She was craning her neck, obviously looking for Liam. "Really recent. Something about wolves coming in the night to take the cattle."

Ariette was about to speak when another call interrupted her. She beamed and let go of Nicole to rush into Liam's open arms. He chuckled as she hugged him tightly.

"Glad to see ya still alive," he joked. "I've never seen the prince so angry."

She puffed some hair out of her face. "He'll get over it. Anyway, that's kind of why I'm here. Do you have a minute?"

"Sure. Greg, ya got this?"

"You bet. Hey there, Ariette."

Ariette waved and walked off to the side with Liam, Nicole hovering awkwardly nearby.

"So, the king has offered me the position of being the queen's new lady-in-waiting." Liam's brown eyes widened. "Yeah, I know. He also has invited my mother to join me. So, we won't be living in our home anymore. I was wondering if your cousin is still wanting to learn the business side of things."

"Hmm. I think so. I'll have to ask him. When are you leavin'?"

"Not sure yet. Ma went to drop off the letter while I came to find you. She also wanted me to invite you and your mother for dinner."

He grinned. "Definitely!" He noticed Nicole and his smile grew. She turned red and spluttered a hello. "Oh! I'm sorry Nicky! Didn't even see ya there."

He offered a hug and she squeaked as she hugged him back. Ariette bit back a smile.

"It's good to see you," Nicole breathed, twirling her hair. "We haven't seen you up in the market lately."

"Ah, gotta get ready for the harvest," he said, pointing over his shoulder. "First year doin' it on my own." He swore as Ariette looked away. "Ari, I'm sorry. I didn't-"

"It's okay," she interrupted. "Really, it is. I should get back home. See you and Izzy soon?"

"For sure. Will you be there, Nicky?" he asked.

Nicole looked ready to faint. "Probably not," she said. "I have to help close down the stall."

"Ah, that's a shame. Maybe next time. You girls be careful now!"

"Bye," they said and waved as they left.

Nicole leaned into Ariette with a dreamy smile on her face.

"He hugged me, Ari," she said. "And he knows my name!"

Ariette giggled. "Of course he does! Your families do business all the time!"

"Yeah, but we've never really talked outside of that! Oh, he's so handsome."

Ariette laughed some more. "You know, you can come to dinner if you want. I'm sure Ma wouldn't mind."

"Thanks, but I really do have to help close down. Father still hasn't recovered from that sprain and Mum's close to her due date. We don't want her overdoing it."

Ariette smacked her forehead. "I completely forgot she's pregnant! Ugh, I'm a horrible best friend."

"Don't say that," Nicole said. They stopped outside of Ariette's home.

"You've been through a lot this year. Have fun and drop some hints for me."

She winked as Ariette laughed. "Sure. Say hi to your folks for me."

"Will do."

Her mother was already cooking dinner when she got back.

"That was long," she said. "Did something happen?"

Ariette groaned as she flopped in her chair at the table. "Ivan Tanner happened."

"Ah. He's still chasing after you, is he?"

"Yes! I've made it so abundantly clear. Anyway, Liam and Izzy will be here for dinner so I'm going to go wash up. He's also going to talk to his cousin about learning how to do the books."

"Oh! Wonderful!"

Ariette stopped at the stairs, inspiration striking her.

"Hey, Ma? What do you think about giving this house to them?"

Elizabeth stopped chopping some vegetables. "To Liam and Isadora?"

"And Freddy, yeah."

"I think that's a lovely idea," she said, her eyes softening. "I hate that they live in the Hala District."

Ariette grimaced. "So that's the official name now, huh?"

"Might as well be."

"We'll tell them at dinner. I'll be done in a few."

Five hours later, there was a knock on the door. Ariette hurried to open it, taking off her apron as she went. Her smile fell when she saw it wasn't Liam and Isadora.

"No thanks," she said and went to shut the door.

Prince Sorin shoved his boot in the crack, though. She pushed on it, but he easily opened it enough to get his head in.

"Relax," he snapped, "I'm not here for long. Let me in."

"Why are you here?"

"Let me in and I'll tell you."

"And if I don't want you in my home?"

His eye twitched. "Listen, minx, let me in."

"I don't have to- Hey! Did you just call me a minx!?"

"Ariette, who's at the door?" her mother asked behind her.

"No one important," she said and tried to close the door again.

Sorin stuck his hand in and waved at her mother. "Good evening, Mrs. Jones."

Her mother dropped the bowl in her hand. "Ariette, you brat! Let the prince in!"

"Ugh. Fine."

Sorin smirked at her and she resisted the urge to trip him as he walked in. She rushed to get a dustpan to clean up the shards as her mother curtsied and offered him everything under the sun.

"Thank you, but I can't stay for long," he said. "We received your letter and Father is ecstatic to hear of your acceptance. He wanted me to let you know he'll be sending men here in two days to gather whatever you wish to bring with you. The home will also be put on the market for-"

"No need," Ariette interrupted and pushed by him, carrying the large pot of stew. Her mother groaned and apologized. "We've already decided what to do with the house."

"It's not your choice to make," Sorin snapped. "This home was given to your father."

"And we inherited it," she said, slamming the kettle down. She turned and put her hands on her hips. "Therefore, it is our choice to make. We'll be giving it to Liam, Isadora, and Freddy."

His brow furrowed. "The farmhand?"

"Yes. Now, if you wouldn't mind, we're expecting guests so you can leave now," she said and made shooing gestures with her hands.

"Listen. Just because my father is willing to overlook your impudence, doesn't mean I won't. Hold your tongue and show some respect."

"Fine," she said. She opened the door and gave him an exaggerated curtsy. "Please, your highness, get the hell out."

"Ariette!" her mother gasped.

Sorin looked ready to snap. Instead, he cleared his throat and nodded to Elizabeth.

"We'll be in touch about the house." He paused at the door and his eyes met Ariette's. Something in them snuffed out the flame in her chest, her courage going with it. He lowered his voice. "I'm not joking, girl. Keep this up, and I'll personally make sure your tongue is fixed. Don't take my father's courtesy for granted."

He left, slamming the door behind him.

IV

Moving In

"I don't like this. I really don't like this. It's a bad idea."

"Oh, stop it and sit down."

Sorin stopped pacing but didn't sit.

"This is dangerous, Father. And the way she spoke to me! You should've seen it!"

"I'm no fool," his father said, looking through a scroll. "I'm very sure you brought some of it on yourself."

"I don't know why you're being so lenient with that brat."

"She's not a brat," Stela said. "Sit down, they'll be here soon."

"She certainly acts like one," he said and fell into his throne. "How old is she?"

"This is her twenty-fifth summer, I think," Laurent said.

Sorin grunted but didn't say anything else. The day before, his father had told him of the promise he made to Robert. It had stymied some of his arguments. To break a promise made to a dying man was the height of disrespect. He puffed his cheeks out.

"The meeting is today, right?" he asked his father.

"Yes."

"And I get to be there this time, right?"

He chuckled. "Yes, you get to be there. Why you're so fascinated by those meetings, I'll never know."

Sorin had been trying to sneak into every war meeting for the last year. Finally, his father had admitted defeat and decided to let him sit in on them. He was eager to get to know the four generals. He had only met them briefly at the balls they would do to honor the dead.

"Ah, I forgot," Laurent said, pointing at something on the scroll. "Did we get the sweets?"

"Yes," Stela said. "They finished this morning."

"Sweets for what?"

"We're going to host a ball for Robert," his father said. "It's long overdue."

"When?"

"Tonight, if the ladies are up for it."

Sorin only nodded. He knew how important the parties were to his parents. It was the only way they were able to honor those who were gone. He glanced at the clock. He still had an hour.

"I'm going to visit Peter," he said.

"Don't be gone too long. I want you here when they arrive to do the first screening."

"Of course."

Sorin left the throne room, rubbing his temples. Everything about this felt wrong. It went against what he was taught growing up. Having strange humans live in the palace was dangerous. Only one human per resident in the palace lived there. It was the only way they stayed safe.

If the citizens found out their royal family were vampires, they'd riot.

He went through the door to the servants' quarters. Maids scurried out of his way and he knocked three times on a door near the end. He heard the call to enter and poked his head in. Peter was on his bed, flipping through a book.

"Ah, your highness," he said and stood. "Is it time?"

"Another hour," he said. "May I sit?" Peter nodded and Sorin sat in the chair. "Peter, you once told me that I could always confide in you. Is that still the case?"

"Why wouldn't it be?"

He shrugged. "I mean, you're my main source of nourishment. I don't want to ask more of you than you already do."

Peter laughed a little and put the book to the side. "Listen, Prince Sorin. You saved my life. This is the least I can do. As for being a listening ear, I'd like to think I've earned your trust after all these years."

"Hmm." He paused. "Did you know Robert Jones?"

"I met him a couple of times, yes," he said. "I was the first one to meet him after your father told him the truth. King Laurent wanted me to be there in case Robert had any questions."

"Did he?"

"No, actually. He was very open to it. He did ask me what it was like being a human amongst everyone. I told him the truth: weird but pleasant."

"When you spoke with him, did he mention his wife and daughter at all?"

He thought. "Yes. He asked me how old I was then got disappointed."

"Why?"

"He was looking for a husband for his daughter," he said simply. "I was too young. Other than that, he just asked to be my friend. But I didn't see him much after that. Why are you asking?"

"I guess I'm just hoping they never find out the truth. I can tell Robert never told them."

"No one knows," Peter reminded him. "Not unless they're like me."

"Yes, I guess you're right."

Peter sat up. "This isn't just about that girl being a smart mouth, is it?"

Sorin looked at him. "You remember what happened to Guinevere. Am I supposed to just ignore the possibility of that happening again?"

Peter sighed and put a hand on Sorin's shoulder.

"You're worrying too much."

"We don't know who the target was, Peter. We don't know anything."

"Not true. We know that you got rid of the supplier, that's all that matters."

Sorin was about to speak but stopped.

They're early. Bring Peter with you.

"Ugh, of course," he said and stood up. "Let's go. The minx and her mother came early."

He nodded and quickly straightened his clothing. The plan had been to introduce Peter as Sorin's personal servant. That would make them being around each other often easier to explain. If they could avoid it, Sorin wanted to keep the truth hidden from Ariette and Elizabeth forever.

His parents were in the entrance, talking in hushed tones. They shook hands with Peter then Sorin took up next to his father. No one spoke. When the doors opened, the two women walked in cautiously. The men had already brought their belongings and put them in their rooms. Elizabeth was staring in wonder at the palace while Ariette curtsied to the king and queen.

"It's good to see you again," his father said, taking her hand. "Thank you for agreeing, once more."

"Thank you for offering," she said with a shy smile. "I hope you do understand I don't have the slightest idea what I'm doing."

Stela smiled and took her hand from his father's. "Don't even worry about it. Once we're done here, I'll take you to the room you'll be staying in. We'll talk more there."

"This place is gorgeous!" Elizabeth gushed. "Look at all of these tapestries!"

Laurent grinned. "I'm glad you like it!" She flushed and dipped into a sloppy curtsy. "My dear Elizabeth, you need not curtsy to me." She spluttered something. "Now, if you two will follow me, I want to show you something before you settle in."

"Can I go now?" Sorin murmured.

"No."

He sighed.

"This is Peter," his father said when he caught Ariette looking at him. "He is my son's personal servant, much like what you will be for Stela."

"Oh!" she said and shook his hand. "Nice to meet you! I'm Ariette!"

"Likewise," he said with a smile. "It's a pleasure to meet you. I've heard many things."

"Probably none of it good, judging by your source," she said.

Peter laughed as Sorin resisted the urge to snap at her. His father was leading them to the ground floor library. Sorin hoped he knew what he was doing. It was clear Ariette knew where they were going, for she began to slow down.

"It's okay," Stela said when she hung back. "You don't need to be afraid."

"I'm not," she muttered. "I'm worried about my mother. She won't take it well."

"Everything will be fine, I promise."

Ariette managed a smile as they got to the door. Laurent was holding a good conversation with Elizabeth. Sorin knew he was trying to keep her distracted. They all filed in and his father cleared his throat.

"I wanted to show you something, Mrs. Jones," he said.

"Please, call me Elizabeth."

He smiled. "Very well. I know Ariette saw this on her last visit, but I want you to know that it's here and you may come whenever you wish."

He stepped aside and pointed at the painting. The blood drained from Elizabeth's face and she looked ready to faint. Ariette rushed to her side. Tears were streaming down the older woman's face as she gazed into the eyes of her late husband.

"You really did know him well," she whispered. "You weren't lying."

"No, I wasn't," the king said gently. "And, if the two of you are willing, I'd like to host a ball in his honor."

"Really?" Ariette asked, eyes wide. "But those are only for high ranking officials or war heroes."

"And that's exactly why we'll be having it. Robert was more than my friend. He died to save my life. He is more of a war hero than anyone I have ever met."

It was too much for Elizabeth. She didn't faint, but she did weep. Ariette held her mother, tears of her own falling. Sorin felt awkward and edged to the door. He kept himself partially hidden and reached into the women's minds.

***

"This is where you'll be staying, Elizabeth," Laurent said, stopping outside of a room. "Ariette's room is just across the way there. She'll be staying right next to our room, as is tradition for a lady-in-waiting."

"Will you be all right while I meet with the queen?" Ariette asked as Elizabeth sat on the large bed.

She was still crying but nodded. "I'll be fine. Don't worry about me."

They embraced and Ariette left, shutting the door carefully. She sighed and wiped some of her own tears away.

"Thank you, King Laurent," she said, and he stared at her. "For what you said. But- Ah, never mind."

"Please speak plainly, Ariette."

"Why would you keep that from us?"

"I feared it would only increase your resentment."

"I guess that's a fair concern," she muttered. "Where is Queen Stela?"

"Waiting for you in your room," he said, pointing. "One last thing, though. I know Sorin is... hard to be around. But he only worries for everyone's safety."

"I understand, your highness. I'd be lying if I said it wasn't a little fun to get a rise out of him, though."

He chuckled. "Of course. I do have to leave, though. Good day."

Ariette just waved and opened the door to her own room. It looked much like her mother's, except there was an additional door. A large, four post bed sat between two windows overlooking the back gardens of the palace. The sheets were gold silk and the down comforter red. A fireplace was built into the right wall, two armchairs in front of it. There was a vanity, a door to a closet, and a small bookshelf. This was where the queen was. She smiled, putting the book back.

"May I sit?" she asked, pointing to the two chairs.

"This is your palace," Ariette said. "Why are you asking me?"

She laughed and sat, gesturing for Ariette to do the same. "This is your room, though. As of today, our home is yours."

"Oh, right."

They sat quietly for a time. Ariette wasn't sure if the queen was waiting for her to say something so she kept silent. It looked as if the queen was trying to think of where to start. Finally, she got comfortable.

"First, I want to tell you the truth about my previous lady-in-waiting," she said quietly. "Sorin was against the idea of you knowing, but you must if you're to truly understand the extent of your job."

"I don't understand. Didn't she just move on to a different post?"

"No. Guinevere was poisoned at the dinner table one night, six months ago."

Ariette gasped, covering her mouth in shock. The queen's eyes were remorseful.

"Poisoned? But why?"

"We're unsure. We're not even positive if the poison was meant for her. For all we know, it could've been meant for me. We never caught the one responsible, just the one who helped supply the poison. They've been dealt with, though. Ever since then, we've been doing extensive searches on anyone who comes into the palace."

"But we weren't searched," Ariette said. "Is that why Sorin is so nervous about us being here?"

"What do you mean?"

"I can tell it's not just because he doesn't like me. Something's bothering him."

She smiled. "You're very astute. It's one of the reasons he's nervous, yes. And you were searched. When the men brought your belongings yesterday, they looked through them. As for anything you might have on your person, our staff have been trained on what to look for. Different tells, if you will."

"I had no idea it was that serious. Am I... going to be safe?"

She reached over and held her hand. "I promise you that you're safe. Now, let's discuss what you'll be doing as my lady-in-waiting."

V

The Palace

"Your mornings will start one hour before mine," Stela said and Ariette began to commit everything to memory. "You and my husband's personal servant, Anton, will prepare our baths. As we bathe, lay out our outfits. Unless we're having guests, anything will do. Then we'll go to breakfast. Afterward, you will join me anywhere I go. If I have to use the washroom, you'll come. If I want to go to the music room, so shall you. Lunch is at midday. Once we've finished dinner, you'll return me to my room. The rest of the evening is free for you to do as you please."

"What of my mother? Is she going to be a servant?"

"Not at all. She has free reign of the palace."

"Okay. I noticed the servants wearing uniforms. Will mine be the same?"

"No," she said and stood, beckoning for Ariette to follow. She opened the walk-in closet. "We put all the clothes you sent on the right side. On the left, is your uniform. Usually, the female servants would wear a crème colored dress with a black apron. You are not the usual worker, though. While not a noble, you still have a higher social status than you did as a commoner."

She took out a dress and passed it to Ariette. It was black and red with no outstanding traits. A belt hung loosely on the waist and Ariette noticed what looked like little slots to put things in them. She nodded and passed it back to the queen.

"The last part we have to cover is... of a sensitive nature," the queen said and sat back down. "As I told you, my previous lady-in-waiting was poisoned. For this reason, my husband and I agreed that we will have all the staff learn basic self-defense. Nothing strenuous, just enough to get you out of a situation if someone does try to attack you."

Ariette shifted nervously. "Okay, I suppose that makes sense. Who will be teaching me? King Laurent?" Stela smiled and Ariette groaned. "No, don't tell me."

She laughed. "Sorin is the best at teaching people. He's also very gentle with the female staff so you don't have to worry about him being too rough."

"Sure," she said sarcastically. "When will the training happen?"

Stela actually huffed and glared at the barren fireplace. "Not for a while. In three days' time, my son will be riding into battle." Ariette gulped, not sure what to say. "I have a request, Ariette. This isn't part of being a lady-in-waiting. Far from it."

"Anything."

"It's no secret that Rosu is the ideal ally to have in these times. It also means that, to our enemies, we are a large threat. Therefore, I don't have many confidants. It's unorthodox, I know, but if you would be willing to indulge me, I'd be forever grateful."

"This is a tremendous honor," Ariette said after a few minutes. "But I would be more than happy to."

This got a smile from the queen.

"I'm not fond of Sorin going to battle. Truth be told, I'm not fond of this war at all. But I understand it's necessary."

"If you don't want the prince to go, why not ask the king to stop him?"

"We've made up excuses to stop Sorin from going to war for many years now. I fear that, if we keep forbidding it, he'll act rashly. Ever since his sister passed away, he's been more adamant about proving himself, even though he doesn't need to."

"I understand," Ariette said. "When Papa died, I focused on fixing everything around me. I took care of the house and expenses so Mother could rest and grieve. I felt like I had to fill the spot he left, if that makes sense."

"It does." They sat in silence for a while. Then Stela smiled and stood. "Let's go on a tour of the palace."

Elizabeth was waiting in the hallway and Ariette hugged her. She had freshened up and now looked around the hallway in interest.

"We'll start on the ground floor," the queen said. "You've seen the foyer and throne room. This is the dining hall. Mornings we have breakfast at eight, dinner at six in the evening. At each meal, I sit on the king's right, Sorin on his left. Ariette, you'll sit beside me."

"Do I eat with the servants?" Elizabeth asked.

"Of course not. Why would you think that?"

Elizabeth shrugged. "Ariette was the one offered a position. I assumed I would just be part of the staff."

"Not at all. This palace is yours to roam. If you do find yourself wanting to help with anything, our seamstress has been struggling to keep up with the demands for armor. I'll take you to see her later."

"That would be wonderful!"

Stela smiled and they followed her out. The grand staircase was flanked by two doors. They went through the one on the left first. This led to the back of the palace. Ariette and Elizabeth gasped. Hedges formed a sort of maze, little pink flower buds dotting the dense green. A fountain bubbled merrily somewhere in the depths of the maze. Stela led them behind it to where flowers grew in long, even rows.

"We have every flower we could manage to grow in our climate," she explained. "Unlike the crops, our court wizard cannot use magic to aid in growing other kinds."

"Why not?" Ariette asked.

"Flowers carry an energy of their own," Stela said, stroking a rose.

"They have strength, beauty, none of which can be replicated with magic. For many herbs, magic would only ruin them."

"I don't see any herbs."

Stela took them to a greenhouse nestled in some trees. Inside, servants were tending to rows of herbs. Some trimmed, some watered. They all stopped to curtsy to them.

"Many of these we use for medicine," Stela said. "When the war began, our ancestors hurried to have this planted; that way we would always have something to rely on."

Ariette frowned at the herbs. "I don't understand," she said. "You say ancestors. To have this many plants, it must have taken several generations."

Stela nodded grimly. "What do you know of the war, Ariette?"

"Just that it's been going on for a while but has gotten worse in recent years."

"This war started one thousand years ago." They made their way back inside. "Rosu only got involved about three hundred years ago when the enemy forced our hands."

"How?"

"They destroyed a city that my husband's ancestor was building."

"Why is the war going on so long, though? Has no one tried to bring peace?"

"Believe me, we have. But no one can come to an agreement. Large battles happen and the two armies leave to recover. Then, five to ten years later, another battle begins. This vicious cycle has continued. This is why...."

"You worry the one Sorin is going to will be one of those large battles?" Ariette asked gently.

Stela sighed as they climbed the stairs. "Yes."

The hallway to the left was their rooms, but a heavy door opened to a spiraling staircase.

"This leads to a nice view of the kingdom's capitol, and our gardens. The council room is also there. I don't go up there normally. I'm not ashamed to say that heights make me uneasy. Here is the Hall of Royals," she said when they got to the other side of the stairs. Portraits lined the walls. "We honor the living and the dead here."

"Where does that door go?" Ariette asked, pointing to the one at the far end.

"Our court wizards workroom," she said. "He's in the middle of something important, though. I'd rather not disturb him." She opened a door near the one leading to the workroom. Another staircase, less extravagant, gave them passage to the third floor. "The third floor isn't used as much as it used to."

When they got to the top of the staircase, Ariette was a little underwhelmed. No lavish tapestries or carpets decorated the hall. The midday sun cast rays of lights through the windows, dust swirling as the queen walked. The doors were all open, showing furniture covered in sheets.

"I'll take you by the seamstress," Stela said to Elizabeth. "I know she'll be happy to have another set of hands."

The three made their way back down the staircases. They went through the second door on the ground floor. Ariette recognized the door to the ground floor library. A few other doors branched off, but the queen strode to one at the end. She knocked and entered.

"Oh, my lady," a woman said. She was tall and looked rather young. Her brown hair was falling out of its bun and her blue eyes were cloudy with exhaustion. "I'm sorry, but I've only just finished the dresses. I've run out of leather for the armor."

Stela smiled kindly. "Worry not, Misha. I've come to bring you some helping hands."

Misha nearly started crying when Elizabeth introduced herself.

"You must be Elizabeth and Ariette Jones," she said. "This is good timing for I have finished your dresses."

"Our dresses?" Ariette asked.

"The queen requested these the day we learned you would be joining us," Misha explained and pulled a curtain, revealing two mannequins. "I wasn't sure of your sizes, so we'll need to do a fitting and- Oh!"

Elizabeth hugged her and Ariette gazed at the dresses. They were identical: black with gold trimmings. She touched the sleeves. It was a very thin silk, while the bodice and skirts were velvet.

"They're beautiful," Ariette breathed. "But why?"

"For the ball that we'll be throwing for Robert," Stela said. "I wanted you to have something special. Misha, can I leave Elizabeth with you? It's time I take Ariette to my study."

"Yes, of course."

Ariette hugged her mother tightly then followed Stela back up the stairs. In the Hall of the Royals, there were three additional doors. They passed by one and she jumped when something crashed inside. Stela grimaced.

"Sounds like another one of their lively conversations," she said and opened a door three rooms down.

"That was the war room?"

"Yes. So, this is my study. Whenever we're not in the throne room, this is where we'll be."

A desk sat right in front of the windows. Ariette grinned at the view; it was right over the capitol. She could see the crops and the bustling market. She had three bookcases filled with tomes of all sizes. A fireplace sat barren to the left and two armchairs were by one of the bookcases.

"It's lovely," Ariette said. "But what kind of work do you do? Forgive me, but I assumed everything was handled by King Laurent."

She sat elegantly behind her desk. Ariette looked around until she found a wooden chair and dragged it over. Stela opened a drawer and took out some thick parchment.

"It's up to me to plan our banquets," she said and passed Ariette lists. "I also handle all guests to our palace. If a citizen wishes to have our help with matters anywhere in the kingdom, I review them first. I then show them to my husband in order of importance."

"That's a lot of work," Ariette said, thumbing through the papers. Each one had a title and the date they were received. "How do you manage it all?"

"The days get long sometimes. But they'll be easier to bear now that I have you here."

"So, what do we do today?"

"Tomorrow is the ball for your father. Then, the day after, is when my son leaves for battle. Let's go over the list for the ball, first."

VI

The Ball

Tensions were high the moment the king and prince walked in. The fighting ceased and they all stood and saluted them. A servant began to pour wine and Sorin looked around at the generals. The generals each had their strengths and had been awarded their positions after great feats in battle.

The eldest was Dragos Dalca and Sorin's least favorite. Standing about a head taller, Dalca could be heard regularly expressing his displeasure with how the war was going. Though he never said it, Sorin wouldn't be surprised if the general would defect. Beside him, Antoine Alexei was polishing his sword, a look of embarrassment on his face. By their standards, the general was nearing his late adult years. Where Dalca excelled in sword fighting, Alexei had a head for strategy. Many of their successful battles were led by him. On the other side of the table, Constantin Marin sat beside his protegee, Ipan Vasile. Constantine was Sorin's favorite and the only one he addressed by first name. He had been in the militia for over sixty years. His mind was sharp and free of prejudice. Sorin didn't know much about General Vasile, but Constantine sang his praises.

"Dare I ask what the shouting was about?" Laurent asked.

No one spoke for a while. Finally, Dragos sighed loudly.

"A rumor has spread that you've brought two humans into the palace."

His dark eyes flashed as Laurent nodded.

"Their names are Ariette and Elizabeth. Ariette will be my wife's lady-in-waiting while her mother will work with the seamstress."

"So, Ariette will become the queen's personal source?" Alexei asked.

"No. We haven't told either of them of our nature."

All the generals looked at one another.

"Is that wise?" Constantine asked. "Lady Ariette will be under constant scrutiny. Surely you'd want the truth to come from you."

"The staff have been ordered to keep their silence. An order I'm sure I don't need to repeat here," he added.

"And what of you?" Dalca asked Sorin. "Are you truly comfortable with this?"

"I trust in my father's judgment," Sorin said. "When they arrived, I did the customary examination. They harbor no ill will or malicious intent."

"But-," Dalca began.

Laurent interrupted him. "They are also the widow and daughter of Robert Jones."

They stared at him, mollified.

"Why didn't you say earlier?" Alexei asked.

"I shouldn't have to," the king said. "Now, to the more important matter."

He leaned over the table, studying a map. It was a complete layout of their kingdom and the ones surrounding it. Rosu was on the western side, a ring of forests acting as a natural barrier. The main province, Imperium, was directly outside the castle gates, also surrounded by the forest ring. Behind the forests west of the palace, the coastline faced the biggest mystery: the wall of mist several leagues into the ocean. In the northern lands, the kingdom of Vin sat at the base of a mountain range. They were Rosu's ally and their main source of minerals. They only had two provinces. What they lacked in size, though, they made up for with the power of their nomadic tribes.

Their enemies took up most of the eastern and southern parts of Tărâm. Namhai was the largest of the two. Their armies were plentiful. No matter how many were cut down, there seemed to be two to replace them. Jende was roughly the size of Rosu. For the better part of the war, Jende was neutral. However, Namhai's army invaded and claimed the territory for themselves. For a long time, Sorin didn't understand the conquering but his father quickly explained it. By taking over Jende, they secured more land and more men to fight for them. Namhai also benefited by getting access to crops and animals their kingdom hadn't been able to maintain.

Red flags marked battles and small silhouettes dotted the places troops were currently camped. A patch of land, several miles wide, had yet to be touched. At the moment, it was dubbed simply as No Man's Land.

"This is our next objective," Alexei said, pointing to the land. "Troops are already moving in from the north and the west." He moved the markers. "They will arrive in a fortnight. Our scouts say no one is there yet, from either the enemies."

Laurent nodded. "Dalca, prepare a group of men. You will be joining the battle. You and Sorin."

Sorin coughed, wine spilling down his chin.

"Are you serious?" he asked.

The king's eyes were somber. "Yes, Sorin. You will journey with them on this campaign."

"May I speak?" Dalca asked, his eyes burning.

Laurent sighed heavily. "There's no need. I already know your concerns."

"But, sire-," he began.

"Make sure we have enough supplies," the king said. "Now, here's my plan for the battle. Our troops will arrive and stay within these trees. Do not attack right away. Tell them to wait for Dalca and Sorin. Once they get there, set up for battle. There's no telling how long it will take for the enemy to realize our plan to claim the land. It's my understanding there are no cities or people living in this area. It's a good place to set up a military camp. Bring enough supplies to build a wooden fortification."

***

Sorin stared at his reflection. The ball for Robert would be starting soon and Peter was helping him get ready. The attire was slightly different, muted reds and black.

"You'll meet everyone in the foyer," Peter was saying. "I'll leave you to check on the food and then return. My understanding is that you will lead the widow in the dance. Also – Sorin, are you listening to me?"

"Sorry," he said, jumping to his feet and putting his crown on his head.

"Thinking about your mother?"

"I haven't seen her that upset in a long time."

"Can you blame her?" he asked gently.

"Of course not. She was always more protective after Charlotte died. I just wish I could put her at ease."

"Just come home safe," Peter said. "I wish I could journey with you."

Sorin shook his head. "Father has ordered that the majority of the soldiers be vampiric on this mission."

"It must be dangerous, then."

"It is. But worry not, dear friend. I'll return safe and sound."

Someone knocked and his father poked his head in.

"Are you ready?"

"Yes," he said and put the decorative sword on his hip. Peter brought over the fur cape and Sorin wrinkled his nose. "Must I wear that? It's summer!"

Laurent laughed. "It's not for long. If I must suffer, so do you."

Sorin grudgingly let Peter put the cape on him and followed his father out into the hallway. Neither of them spoke. Both were thinking of earlier that afternoon when Laurent had reminded the queen Sorin would be leaving the morning after the ball. She had shed more tears than ever and screamed that it was too dangerous. Finally, Ariette had managed to calm her and usher her out to the gardens. This would be the first time Sorin saw her since the outburst and he was trying to think of ways to bring her peace.

"It's as Peter said," his father said suddenly. "Just return home safe and sound."

"You make it sound so easy," Sorin said. "I'd be lying if I said I wasn't worried, too."

"This is your first time going into war," Laurent said. "Of course you're scared. It's normal."

"I'm not scared," he said, and Laurent scoffed.

"You're fooling no one, son."

Sorin was about to argue, but they had reached the stairs down to the foyer. His mother was standing with Ariette and Elizabeth. The latter was wearing a black veil over her face and wasn't speaking. Through the veil, he could see her skin was pale and she seemed ready to faint. Ariette, for her part, had her back straight and her face set. Sorin couldn't help but admire her resolve.

"You ladies look beautiful," his father said, kissing both of the women's hands.

"Thank you," Ariette said with a curtsy.

Elizabeth made a choked sound as she curtsied, too.

"Are you sure she's up to dance?" Sorin mumbled to his father as they took their places for the doors to open.

"I don't think so," he mumbled back. "I'll have you dance with Ariette."

Sorin wrinkled his nose but he didn't have the chance to argue. The doors opened, bringing in both nobility and commoners alike. They were all dressed similar to the rest of them: blacks and somber colors. Each guest stopped to be greeted, curtsied and bowed, then filed into the ballroom. Once everyone was in there, Laurent escorted Stela and Elizabeth, leaving Sorin to escort Ariette. She didn't respond right away, but eventually gave in and accepted Sorin's arm.

The ballroom was packed. Buffet tables lined the walls, laden with food and drink. Servants were positioned throughout the room, ready to walk among the guests with platters. A long table at the head of the room was set for the five of them. Once Sorin and Ariette had joined them, the king cleared his throat and the low chatter died down.

"Thank you for joining us this evening," he said in a clear voice. "Tonight, we come together for an event that should have happened many months ago. Robert Jones was an honorable man, fierce and unwavering in his loyalty. If it weren't for his sacrifice, I would not be here." To his right, Elizabeth started to cry. "He was a dear friend of mine and I ask you all to raise your goblets in a toast to the memory of Robert Jones."

On cue, the servants walked through the guests, passing around the drinks. Everyone lifted their goblets and murmured Robert's name then drank deeply.

"And now we celebrate his life," his father finished. "We celebrate the joy he brought to his wife and daughter, the happiness he gave his fellow citizens. The devotion he showed all of us."

Laurent sat and the three of them followed suit. Different goblets were placed in front of the family and Ariette and Elizabeth. An orchestra in the back struck up some music and guests began to talk.

"Normally, I'd have Sorin lead you in the dance, Elizabeth," Laurent said. "However, would you be all right if Ariette opened?"

Elizabeth nodded, dabbing at her tears. "I'm sorry I'm so emotional."

"You have nothing to apologize for," Stela said, patting her on the shoulder.

Sorin stuck his hand out and Ariette frowned at it before accepting and let him lead her to the middle of the dance floor. Everyone made room for them as they danced slowly on the spot. It was incredibly awkward and Sorin kept his eyes over her head, occasionally seeing the generals watching her. He knew they were reading her mind. He also knew they wouldn't find anything that he hadn't already found.

"I can't believe our fathers knew each other so well," she said suddenly. "Did you know?"

"No," he said honestly. "I knew he was close with one of his soldiers, but never who it was. I was busy trying to learn."

"What do you mean?"

"My parents haven't been keen on me learning about battle and going to war," he said. "Not since my sister died."

"How did she pass? No one knows."

He looked at her. For once, her eyes weren't filled with contempt. He saw her grief and knew she was trying to connect with him. In her mind, he understood it would bring her comfort. Comfort he wasn't ready to provide.

"That's a secret that I'd rather stay with my family," he said.

"I understand."

Their eyes broke as he twirled her. When she was facing him again, her walls were back up. They spent the rest of the dance in awkward silence, neither looking at each other. Finally, his father came and danced with Ariette instead.

~~~

Ariette let out a sigh of relief as the king swept her into a quicker dance.

"Both of you looked like you wanted the world to open up and swallow you," he said with a chuckle.

"I'm sorry," she said. "I'm trying, I really am."

He smiled. "I know you are, and that's what matters."

"May I ask you something?"

"Anything."

"Where is my father buried?"

His smile dropped. "Namhaian soldiers set fire to the battlefield," he said. "I wasn't able to get to him in time."

"Oh."

Ariette felt like a small balloon of hope had been popped inside her. Her eyes stung with tears and she gulped, suddenly finding great interest in the war medallion on the king's chest. People had joined them and
~~~

soon the room was full of happy chatter. Ariette couldn't bring herself to join in, though.

"Excuse me," she said when the song ended.

"Of course," he said sadly, bowing to her.

She returned to the table. Her mother was talking to a few of the villagers that ran the market. Ariette took a sip of her tea, wondering if Nicole was there. She stood to go look for her when a strange sensation took hold of her. Her body became flushed, sweat breaking out over her forehead. She gripped the edge of the table and clasped her throat. She couldn't speak or even breathe. She fell to her knees, trying to get some-one's attention.

The dishes falling to the floor disrupted the dancing. Everyone turned to see Ariette go down and Sorin pushed himself away from some of the noblewomen who were clinging to him. Elizabeth was pan-icking, trying to get Ariette to respond. Sorin rolled Ariette onto her back and forced her mouth open.

"What are you doing?" Elizabeth demanded when Sorin touched Ariette's chest.

"Trying to find her heartbeat," he said. He shouted over his shoulder to his father. "Is he on his way?"

"Yes."

"Who? What happened to her? Is she going to be okay?"

Elizabeth shook Sorin's shoulder when he didn't answer. His eye twitched and he tried not to get angry. Finally, his uncle burst into the room and joined him by Ariette.

Lucian was his mother's brother and had been the one to teach Sorin. He abdicated the throne to study medicine and was the official physician for the palace.

"Don't let anyone leave," Sorin said to one of the guards as he left Ariette to Lucian. "Not until she wakes up."

"We can't just hold them hostage," the guard whispered. "What do we say?"

Sorin glared. "That someone has tampered with Lady Ariette's drink."

The guard understood and silently passed the message along to the others. They took up stations in front of the doors as discreetly as possible. Sorin watched as Lucian inspected Ariette, Elizabeth becoming more hysterical with each second that passed.

VII

Battle

Ariette's throat was sore and her head pounding. She tried to open her eyes, but they were heavy. Someone was holding her left hand while two cold fingers were on her other wrist. She finally groaned, a cough making her wince.

"Ari!" her mother cried. "You're awake!"

Ariette groaned again at the loud noise. She managed to open her eyes and looked around. She was in her room, still in the gown from the ball. Her mother was in bed with her, stroking her hair. Her eyes were swollen from tears. The king and queen were talking in quiet voices at the foot of her bed. The person on her other side, though, she didn't recognize. He looked a lot like Queen Stela, though, and was currently looking at a pocket watch.

"Who're you?" she croaked out.

The man smiled and gave her some water to sip.

"My name is Lucian, Queen Stela's brother. I'm the physician for the family and residents in the palace."

"Oh. Am I dead?"

He laughed. "No, of course not. Judging by your mother's reaction, I'd wager you didn't know you're allergic to honey."

"Allergic?" her mother repeated. "No, we had no idea. She wasn't much of a sweets child, so it never occurred to us."

"Just allergies," Lucian said when the king and queen rushed over. "I've made up a tonic for her to get back on her feet in no time. We'll just have to make sure the servants and cook know that her meals can't have honey in them from now on."

"Not a problem," Stela said immediately.

Suddenly, loud voices were heard from in the hallway and the king sighed.

"I'll go calm him down," he said to Stela. "You stay here."

Stela nodded, her face also a mix of exhaustion and exasperation. She sat beside Ariette. When the door opened, Ariette could hear the prince's shouts.

"Don't worry about it," the queen said and passed her the tonic. "Sorin's just pretty overprotective after what happened."

"What do you mean?" her mother asked.

"Ah, I assumed Ariette had told you."

"I wasn't sure if you wanted it to be a secret," Ariette said, her voice still hoarse.

"I appreciate that, but I think it's fair to let her know." Stela gave some water to Elizabeth. "It's about my last lady-in-waiting."

Out in the hall, Sorin had General Dalca up against the wall, fangs out and snarling. Laurent quickly shut Ariette's room to avoid her seeing the two. Dalca was also snarling at Sorin. Both men's irises were red.

"Enough!" Laurent ordered. "What's going on?"

"This *cretin* has said he hopes the girl dies," Sorin snapped. Laurent pulled him off the general.

Laurent gaped at Dalca. "Is this true?"

"A human doesn't deserve the honor you're giving her," he spat. "Besides, since she was poisoned, we'd have a better chance at finding the killer. After all, Sorin killed the only lead we had."

Sorin tried to lunge at the general again, but Laurent held him back.

"First, she wasn't poisoned," he said. Sorin relaxed a little but his eye twitched at the disappointed look on the general's face. "She's allergic to honey. They didn't know about the allergy. We'll just make sure no more honey goes into her drinks and food. Second, don't you *ever* speak of anyone in this palace like that again, Dalca."

"But, Sire–"

"If you do, I will remove you of your station!" Laurent said. That got the general to stop talking. "Now, both of you go and rest up. You leave tomorrow at morning's first light. Ah, ah, ah, not yet," he said, grabbing both of their arms when they tried to storm off separate ways. "I can't have you two going into battle with bitterness in your hearts. Apologize and put this behind you."

"You seriously want me to ignore the fact that he hopes Mother's lady-in-waiting dies!?" Sorin cried. "Are you out of your mind!?"

Laurent glared. "This battle is incredibly important, Sorin. We cannot afford to lose. Now apologize! Both of you!"

The two men glared at each other before begrudgingly shaking hands.

"Sorry," they said in unison through clenched teeth.

"Rest up. I'll wake you when it's time to go," his father said.

Sorin was still fuming but did as his father instructed. He slammed his door and plopped onto his bed. He was sure sleep would evade him. After the events of that evening and the upcoming battle, his mind was racing. As if she had heard his thoughts, his mother knocked on the door.

"Come in," he said, not getting up.

"I brought you something," his mother said, closing the door with her foot. She was carrying a tray with steaming hot cocoa. "I heard your argument with the general." He sat up so she could sit beside him and accepted the mug. "Your father is right. A heated temper only leads to mistakes."

He took a long sip of the cocoa. Immediately, his shoulders began to relax.

"You always made this for me when I was young," he said, watching the marshmallows slowly melt in the hot liquid. The calming effect was immediate. "Mother, you didn't hear the way he was talking about her. He wanted her dead."

"I'm not sure that's what he meant," she said. "He's worried about us, just like you are. Make amends tomorrow before you leave."

"We already did."

She chuckled, also drinking the cocoa. "A handshake is not what I mean."

Sorin was about to retort, but his eyes started to drift. "You put something in this," he murmured.

She kissed his forehead. Peter walked in with a set of nightclothes.

"I know you, sweetheart. This will help you sleep. Sweet dreams, love."

"G'night," he slurred and slipped into the darkness of sleep.

***

The next morning, Peter woke him. It was still dark out and his armor was waiting for him. He stared at it before rolling out of bed. Peter had a bath ready and he rushed through it. He knew General Dalca wouldn't wait for him. As Peter helped him into the armor, he adjusted the straps. A black tabard was placed over the cuirass with the kingdom's emblem. His helmet he kept tucked under his arm. Peter strapped the sword onto Sorin's hip for him.

"Looks like you're ready," he said.

"Yeah, ready," he muttered.

He stared at himself in the mirror. He looked like a completely different person. His hair was slicked back, and he knew that, when the helmet was on his head, he'd look just like the other men. The only part that would give him away was the sword. He followed Peter out of his room. His mother was waiting in the hallway, tears in her eyes. She immediately threw her arms around him, crying into his neck. He passed his helmet to Peter then embraced her back.

"It's going to be fine, Mother," he soothed. "I'll be back before you know it. The trip is only a week or two at the most."

"I can't stand to lose you!" she cried.

"And you won't," he promised.

As he comforted her, Ariette came out with Anton. Her face was also ashen, probably a relic of the allergies from the previous night. She kept her eyes fixed on his shoulder as Anton peeled the queen off of Sorin. Ariette walked forward and thrust something out.

"What's this?" he asked, taking it.

A hook shaped jade was tied to a rough rope.

"A charm," she said. "It was my father's."

"I can't take this," he said, feeling immensely uncomfortable. Why would she be giving him something so personal? "If it belonged to your father-"

"It's not like we don't have other parts of his belongings," she interrupted, her cheeks bright pink.

He hesitated then reached into her mind.

"I see," he said. She was remembering the night her father left and she hadn't given him anything. "Thanks."

She nodded then turned away, her discomfort mirrored on his own face.

He walked downstairs where his father was waiting with General Dalca. The latter looked a bit disappointed when he saw Sorin. He obviously hoped the prince wouldn't show up.

"Are you ready?" Laurent asked, his eyes full of emotion.

"Almost," Sorin said. He tucked the opal necklace into the breast pocket of his armor. "General Dalca," he said. The general drew himself to his full height. "I know we've had our disagreements. But I hope we can see past those. Our mission is one of importance and should be treated as such; including having level heads."

To his surprise, Dalca smiled a little.

"Spoken like a true leader," he said and shook Sorin's hand. "I agree to put it behind us. Are you prepared?"

"Yes," he said. He turned to his father and they embraced. "Keep an eye on Mother."

"I will. Come home safe."

Sorin smiled at him. "I promise."

The king watched as the two walked out into the early morning air. A group of one hundred men were lined up in front of the palace. Dalca grabbed Sorin's arm to stop him from walking on to the stables.

"A speech," Dalca whispered. "This is usually when you'd give them an uplifting talk, get them in the right state of mind."

"Oh. Right." He cleared his throat and lifted his voice. "Good morning, men. Today, we begin a two week-long trip to the land that will help bolster our numbers. This land is unclaimed by our enemy and is believed to be a source of gold. The battle will be dangerous, but I know you're the best of the best. Let's go and know that, despite what happens, you are all valued men in this army."

They all clapped. Sorin nodded to them then led the way to the horses with Dalca.

"That was awful," Sorin said.

"No, it was short and to the point," Dalca said. "You stated the objective, the location, and reminded the men they are valued. It's everything we could've expected from you."

"A compliment from General Dalca?" Sorin said, smiling a little. "How rare."

Dalca chuckled. "True, they are few and far between. But your father has told me how nervous you are about this battle. If I'm honest, that's why I wasn't sure you should be here."

"I need experience," Sorin said but Dalca interrupted him.

"I want it to be clear: the reason I'm here is not to lead the charge. It's to prepare you to do it."

Sorin nearly tripped on the uneven ground. They were almost at the stables. Fifty of their horses were getting ready, saddles and armor being placed on them. Some had saddle bags with their food and water.

"I see," he said, his voice shaking slightly.

"It'll be fine," Dalca said, and they mounted their steeds. "I know how you feel about me."

Sorin sighed as he was passed his helmet. "It's not personal, Dalca," he started but the general interrupted him.

"That's your first mistake, Prince," he said. The people who were getting the markets ready scurried out of the way as the troop started their way through the city. "When you're the king, everything is personal. Who you hire, who you trust, who you confide in, and even who you have to expel from the staff."

"Trust me, no one is stepping into this palace without my permission."

"Yet the humans were welcomed with open arms," he said. Sorin glared at him but the older man just held his hands up in surrender. "Just a statement, your highness. This is your first battle and I want you to be prepared for anything."

Sorin finally understood and looked over his shoulder. Though it was simple to read a human's mind, reading that of a vampire's was more difficult. The only way to do so was with the vampire's consent. It hadn't occurred to him that there were people in his army who didn't have the crown's best interests at heart.

"I've already interviewed each of them," Dalca said when he saw the unease on Sorin's face. "But it's an important lesson to keep in mind."

Sorin nodded. He hadn't heard Dalca speak this much outside of arguing with him and his father. It was a different side that Sorin was starting to appreciate.

"My first battle, I was about your age," Dalca said suddenly.

"Which age?" Sorin asked with a slight smirk and the general laughed.

"I was twenty-two."

"Eh, close enough."

"I had been in the same campaign as your father. It was my duty to watch over him. Every soldier is trained to know that our number one priority is the crown. No matter what. Deadly arrow shooting towards the king? We jump in front of it. We need to fall back and regroup? We force the king to abandon his stubbornness and retreat."

"Like Robert," Sorin said.

"Exactly."

"Were you at that battle?"

Dalca heaved a sigh. "Yes. It happened at night. We were all resting, eating. We didn't anticipate the attack until the morning. It was your father, Robert, and me. Robert was talking about his wife and daughter. Between you and me, I think Robert knew he was going to die soon."

Sorin did a doubletake. "What makes you say that?"

"He kept telling Laurent about his family. It didn't really occur to either of us what he was really doing. During the battle, Robert took the blade for Laurent. I was able to follow up and kill the man. I stood by, defending them as Laurent tried to save Robert; he even offered to turn him into a vampire. But Robert only had one request."

"What was it?"

"That your father take care of Robert's family."

"So that's why you stopped arguing after Father mentioned Robert," Sorin said.

"Yes. I'm still not thrilled that both of them were welcomed so easily but, at the ball, I did read their minds." He chuckled. "I will say, that Ariette is no fan of yours."

Sorin shrugged. "I don't care."

"But you do," Dalca said, watching him.

"Not in the way you're implying," Sorin said quickly. "I've never had someone speak so disrespectfully to us. It's... intriguing. I didn't know about Robert's request; now a lot of what Father has done makes sense."

Dalca nodded. "That's what you're going to have to do when you take the throne, Sorin. You're going to have to make decisions, ones that those who follow you won't agree with. They'll argue with you, tell you that you're making a mistake, but you have to stand with what you know is right."

Sorin didn't respond. They rode in silence for a long time, watching the sun rise among the trees. Once they exited the forest, they veered north. It was his father's orders that they take the longest route to get to the camps set up by the scouts. They camped for the few nights. At first, Sorin kept to himself in his tent, pouring over the battle plans. Then, as he was passing by a group of men, one of them spoke up.

He was a young man, one Sorin hadn't met yet. He was also one of the few humans trusted with the secret. He looked nervous as he stood to attention, his food in one hand.

"If it's not too bold, would you like to join us?" he asked, gesturing to the other men.

"You need to know your soldiers. Perhaps not as well as Laurent knew Robert, but these men are willing to fight and die for you. They deserve your respect."

Dalca had coached him on that not even three hours earlier. Sorin hesitated before smiling and nodding. All of the soldiers' relaxed and Sorin sat cross legged beside the one who invited him. They had a simple meal of meat and potatoes, the real source of nutrition in the special wine skin on each man's hip. As Sorin looked at him, he realized he had no idea what their names were.

"So, gents, tell me about yourselves," Sorin said, getting more comfortable on the forest floor.

They all looked at each other.

"Like what?" the one who had invited him asked.

He chuckled. "Let's start with names."

They laughed, too, albeit nervously.

"Well, I'm Ian," he said and pointed to the other three in order. "Holms, Trent, and Gerald."

"It's a pleasure to meet you men." They grinned. "I'm ashamed to say I don't know how long you've been in the army."

"We all started at the same time," Trent said, sipping from the wine skin. He stored it carefully back on his hip. "My wife," he added when he caught Sorin looking.

"I'm sorry. I wasn't trying to intrude."

"Don't apologize!" he said quickly, his face flushed. "Please, of all the people who apologize, you're not the one who should do so."

Sorin frowned but covered it by taking a small drink of Peter's blood. Even on the way to battle, they saw him as the prince, someone who should be respected and treated differently from others.

"Of course, they do," Dalca said as they continued their march the following morning. "They don't know you well enough yet. But that will change. I was glad to see you sitting with them."

"I'll sit with more of the men tonight," Sorin said with a firm nod.

Sorin missed the proud smile on Dalca's face.

It took them two weeks to get to the forest lining the last bit of land. They set up camp and some of the men called out to Sorin as he walked to the large tent. He waved back. It had taken a while, but they finally felt comfortable enough around him to be casual with him. In the tent, Dalca and some of the more senior officers were bent over a table with a map of the area. The air was grim.

"What's wrong?" Sorin asked.

"Our scouts haven't returned," Dalca said. "We have no idea if there's anyone there."

"I can go check," Sorin said.

"Absolutely not," the officer named Jensen said. "We need you here where it's safe."

Sorin frowned. "With all due respect, sir, I didn't come here to be safe. I came here to lead my men into battle. That's what I plan on do-ing."

Jensen sighed. "Your Highness," he began.

"Sorin," he interrupted. "We're about to go into battle. In my eyes, we're all equals."

Dalca took the officer's shock as a chance to speak up.

"I agree with the officer, Sorin. We have no idea what's on the other side of these trees."

"To be fair, we don't know what's on this side," Sorin said. "If our scouts haven't returned, then they haven't reported what's around us, ei-ther." Neither of the men had an argument for that. "I'll take some of our best archers. If there's anything we need to be worried about, we'll fall back immediately."

"I'm coming with you," Dalca said. "Who else do you want to bring?"

Sorin thought for a few minutes, going over the list of people he had met.

"William, Scott, and Jeremiah," he said finally.

"Let's go tell them," Dalca said.

"You three," Sorin said to the officers. "Hold down the fort. We'll return within the hour. If we don't, prepare for battle and set up sentries around the perimeter."

"Yes, sir."

Sorin nodded once then found the three men standing by a tent together. They had elected to only eat cold meals while this close to unknown territory. Dalca pulled Sorin back before they reached them. The older man's face was a mixture of anger and concern.

"Those men have no family to go back to," he said in a whisper. "You don't think it's safe, do you?"

"No," Sorin whispered back. "I've had this feeling since we were about two days away. It's why I sent the scouts in the first place. What are you doing?" he asked as Dalca suddenly dug around in Sorin's hip pack.

"Wear this," he said and Sorin scoffed.

He was holding the trinket Ariette had given him before they left.

"Seriously?"

Dalca thrust it over Sorin's head and Sorin swatted at the general's hand.

"What's gotten into you?" he demanded.

"I have a bad feeling, Sorin," he said, frowning at the trees. "A very bad feeling."

Sorin swallowed but just went to the men. They all smiled.

"We're making a scouting party," Sorin said. "I'd like you men to join us. Just a quick reconnaissance then we'll come back."

"Yes, sir," they said.

Sorin took off his heavier armor, leaving on the chainmail and leather under armor. The men followed suit. He put his sword on his hip and a bow and quiver of arrows on his shoulder. While he waited for the others, he scanned the trees. He suddenly felt the same dread Dalca had mentioned earlier. It was heavy on his shoulders and he clenched his jaw. He took a deep breath, eyes closed. When he reopened them, they were red, and his fangs extended. With his enhanced sight, he looked around the trees again.

It was very rare to use his power. He had only done it one other time since it left him more vulnerable. Colors were more vibrant and the shadows less dark. At first, nothing caught his eye. The men joined him, following suit and activating their powers. They tiptoed into the trees, their light steps making no noise. Sorin followed the strange shape in the shadows. He had never seen anything like it. When they got to the cluster of trees blocking their view, each man hid behind a trunk. Sorin was the first to look around. He covered his mouth to prevent the gasp.

A huge contraption stood in the clearing of the woods. It looked like a sixty-foot spoon, diagonal with the scoop up in the air. Some of the enemy were going around the base of it. They were oiling something he could only assume was a metal mechanism. His knees went weak as a soldier shouted something to another and they pulled a rope. The spoon part went all the way down then launched into the air.

Sorin took a steadying breath and was about to turn around when he sensed it. Movement behind them. Before he could even warn the others, an arrow lodged itself in the tree by his head. He spun around. Thirty archers stood around them, horrible grins on their faces.

"Hello, Prince," the one who had shot the arrow said. "I was hoping you'd fall for it."

"What are you talking about?" Sorin demanded, willing his fangs to recede.

"Didn't you think it was strange that none of your idiot scouts made it back?"

Like a punch to the gut, Sorin understood. The reports they received were forgeries. The men who had been sent ahead....

"I'm glad you were able to see our trebuchet," the man continued. "Not that you'll be able to see it at work. Now you can die knowing your stupid kingdom has no chance."

The man loosed the arrow he had been preparing but Sorin dodged it easily. He drew his sword and ran at the man, the others doing the same. The archer dropped his bow and grabbed a dagger. Sorin smirked.

"Bringing a dagger? Really?" he taunted and swung his sword through the air. The man blocked it with the dagger. "That's the best you have?"

The archer leaned forward, sneering. "Are you all right, Prince? You're looking a bit... red."

Sorin refused to show his fear. They knew. Somehow, these men knew. He glanced at the dagger. It was silver.

The man took the chance to swipe at Sorin. He barely dodged it but could feel the burn through the armor. He swung again, this time leaving a deep gash in the man's chest. He yelled in pain, alerting the others who hadn't been part of the ambush. Sorin didn't even wait. He leaped over the man's body.

"Fall back!" he yelled to the others.

They obeyed and dodged arrows as they flew through the air. Sorin felt panic welling in his chest. The arrows were silver. How many of them knew about this? Was it just a lucky guess? Or had someone told them?

Dalca was shouting something when they were in range of the camp. There was a flurry of movement and the men were mostly prepared. As Sorin spun on the spot, ready to engage in battle again, he felt his hand go weak and he nearly dropped his sword. They were outnumbered three to one. He set his jaw. One of the soldiers was putting his armor on for him.

"Kill them!" the man Sorin injured shouted. "Kill them all!"

Sorin took a deep breath and yelled in response, rushing into the oncoming horde.

VIII

Worry

The day after the men had left for battle, Queen Stela didn't speak much. Ariette understood her concern and shared it. It wasn't easy watching a loved one go to battle. Even though she didn't care for the prince, Ariette also worried for him.

A day later, Anton woke her when it was still dark out. She hurried into her dress, yawning every few seconds. She wasn't used to getting up so early. She splashed some water onto her face and smiled.

"Good morning," she said.

"Morning," he said and gestured for her to follow him. "The queen said you're not used to doing things like this?"

"Right. I mean, I'm used to cooking and caring for a home, but not taking care of royalty."

"Luckily, the king and queen are pretty self-reliant," he said.

He put his finger to his lips then opened the door to the royals' room. They crossed the room on silent feet, Ariette glancing over at their sleeping forms. Even in the dark, she could see the king embracing the queen. Anton opened a door and ushered her through. The washroom was almost as big as the bedroom. A large washtub was in the middle of the room and Anton knelt in front of it.

"First we light the fire," he said in a quiet voice. "A lot of water goes in there so it's going to take a while to heat up. While I do this, you pump the water."

Ariette nodded and stood back up, looking in the corners. There wasn't a pump, though. She was about to ask Anton when she saw a pump just outside the far corner of the tub. Doubtful, she started to pump it. Nothing happened for a long time. Anton was gathering the soaps without correcting her, so she assumed she wasn't doing anything wrong. Then the pipe began to vibrate, and she gasped. Water gushed out of the pipe and into the metal tub.

"How?" she asked when Anton turned.

He chuckled. "Pipes. They run through the castle. Don't ask me how they get it all the way up here, though. It seems like magic, but David says he hasn't cast any."

"Who's David?"

"The court mage. Now, while that fills up, we select their outfits."

They slipped into the bedroom again. The king and queen were stirring in their sleep, obviously slowly waking up. Anton went into the king's closet and Ariette into the queen's. Dozens of luxurious dresses lined the walls. Some were more elegant than others, a few even being nightgowns. Ariette decided on a dress that fit somewhere between, making a mental note to ask the queen the difference between the dresses so she wouldn't make a fool of herself. They put the clothing on the bed and Anton gestured for Ariette to follow him out of the room.

"They'll bathe themselves," he said. "The king will go first then I will help him get ready as the queen bathes. When she's done, you'll help her dress. Once all that is done, we'll go down to the dining hall for breakfast. Don't worry about the water in the tub; the other servants will take care of that."

"How long have you been the king's personal servant?" Ariette asked.

"Oh my," he said and pursed his lips in thought. "Fifteen years?"

"That's a long time."

"My family has always served the royal family," he explained. "From the age of eight, we are taught how to care for them. When the time comes, they assign us to a member. It's not always king and queens, though. Sometimes we're assigned to dukes and duchesses."

Ariette was about to speak but the door opened, and the king nodded to Anton. She stood in the hallway, feeling awkward. Servants were starting to bustle around the hallways, waving or bowing to Ariette. She returned the gestures. It was strange to see how many people it took to run the castle. When the door opened again, Anton stepped out.

"She's ready for you."

The queen was sitting at her vanity, dabbing at her hair with a towel. She smiled at Ariette.

"Feeling better?" she asked.

"Very much so. Thank you."

The queen stood, letting the robe she wore fall. Ariette felt her face go bright red when she realized the queen was completely naked. She hurried to grab the queen's undergarments. The king snickered from where he was waiting.

"Hush," the queen reprimanded. He beamed. "Honestly. Okay, Ariette," she said as Ariette dropped the dress. The queen held her hands. "Take a deep breath."

"Sorry," Ariette said in a small voice. "I didn't think you'd- I mean, of course you would be but- I'm not-"

Now the king was laughing until Stela glared at him. He cleared his throat.

"I'm sorry, I should've warned you. Now, about that deep breath." Ariette obeyed. "There you go. Let's start again."

Ariette unlaced the dress and helped the queen into it. As she tightened it, she asked about the dresses in the closet.

"Ah, yes. A side effect to being royalty. I have an overabundance of dresses. You were right: the ones on the left are nightgowns and the ones in the front and to the right are for formal events. This is perfect."

"Do you wear makeup?"

"Definitely," she said and sat down at her vanity again. "What is it?" she added when she saw Ariette's shoulders drop.

Ariette glanced at the king. "I- Well, I've never worn makeup before. I don't know how to apply it."

The queen turned in surprise. "Never? But what about when gentlemen callers came?"

"I only ever had the one," she said. The king opened a drawer in the vanity. "And, even then, he only waited until I was in the market. He never got a chance to talk to my father. Not that it would've mattered to him."

Stela frowned. "No others, though?"

"No. Some were too intimidated by my father. The others didn't like that I'm more independent than other women."

"Well, that's just silly," she said. "They'll rue the day you marry and learn they were wrong. For now, I'll show you how I do it."

She took a few things from the drawer the king opened. Ariette watched carefully as the queen applied the makeup. It looked easy enough. Ariette took the queen's crown from where it sat on a velvet cushion and placed it on her head. Stela smiled and stood again.

"And that's all there is to it," she said. She took her husband's arm as they left the room. "Don't worry, it'll get easier with time."

Ariette fell into step beside Anton. He continued to instruct her under his breath.

"Always three steps behind them," he said. "We want to be close enough should they need anything, but we must also show respect. You'll sit beside the queen while I go taste the meals."

Ariette nodded. King Laurent helped Stela into her chair and Ariette sat down, as well.

"I owe you an apology," Laurent said as they waited. Ariette started to brush it off, but he kept talking. "No, I was insensitive."

"Really, it's fine," Ariette said, uncomfortable with the king apologizing. "I know it's... odd for a young woman to not know these things."

"Did you work with your father often?" Stela asked.

"Yes. Mother did the bookkeeping while I helped organize the men.

The fields are vast, after all, and Father couldn't keep track of them all. There were many times Father wished I spent more time doing things like Nicky."

"Who?"

"My best friend Nicole. She aspires to be a housewife. Not that there's anything wrong with that, of course, but I can't stand the idea of being stuck up in a house. I admire her. She's content with supporting her future husband and bearing his children."

"And what of you? What do you wish to do?"

Ariette thought about it. Servants brought in food and set it in front of them. Anton held a gold platter with goblets.

"Tea," he said. "Without honey," he added as he placed Ariette's in front of her.

"Thank you, Anton," the king said. "Please, sit. We were just learning more about young Ariette here."

"I'm not sure what I want to do," she said, waiting for the king and queen to eat first. The king bit into some toast and the rest of them started to eat. "I'd like to live an adventurous life, but I think I've gotten too old to pursue that."

"Nonsense," the king said. "You're only twenty-five, correct? Look at Sorin: He's having his first adventure and he's twenty-eight!"

Stela put her fork down, suddenly looking pale. Ariette bit her lip. She knew that look. Both her and her mother had worn that look many times. The king hadn't noticed.

"I'm eager to hear of how the battle goes," he continued. "This is a monumental step in his life. I only wish I could be there with him. I know Dalca will keep him safe, though. When I went to my first battle, I was barely a man. My father insisted I go, but my mother wasn't keen on it. I guess I have that-"

"Your highness," Anton interrupted gently. "Perhaps now isn't the time."

The king finally looked up from his plate and saw Stela's face. He sighed.

"I'm sorry, dearest," he said and held her hand. "I wasn't thinking."

"No, you're right," she said. Her voice was higher than normal. "This is something he must do. I kept him from it for too long. After Charlotte, I can't bear the thought of...."

Her voice trailed off but Ariette knew what she was thinking. She was reminded, once again, of the day her father left for battle.

"Don't worry, cel mic,*"* he had said. *"No matter what, just remember I'll always be there for you."*

The queen stood. "It's time for our duties," she said. Her eyes were misty, but she smiled, nonetheless. "Come along, Ariette."

"Yes, your highness."

They left the dining hall and went up to the second floor. The queen didn't speak as they walked, the smile still on her face. Servants bowed to them, and a young man opened the door for them. The curtains were drawn, blocking the sun from heating the room. The queen sat at her desk and Ariette shut the door. The moment she did, the queen dropped her head into her hands and cried quietly.

Ariette hesitated. Then she remembered what the queen had asked; for Ariette to be her confidant. She approached the queen and put a hesitant hand on Stela's shoulder. She didn't push it away so Ariette kept it there.

"When Papa left," Ariette said, "Mama was beside herself. She didn't know what to do. We had to continue his work, though. Liam was great and took up the task of working with the men. But it still felt like there was a hole in our family. We cried a lot. His last letter.... Looking back, I know now he spoke of the king, but he said something that's stuck with me: 'I'm with a good friend, one who I would gladly lay my life down for, and he would do the same. I love you two, very much. I will be home soon.' Prince Sorin isn't alone. He'll be safe. No matter what, your son will return."

The queen hiccupped and accepted the handkerchief Ariette found on the desk.

"Thank you, Ariette," she said. "I needed to hear that." She cleared her throat, dabbing at her tears. "Now, if you would be a dear and bring me that box, we'll get started."

Ariette had thought the queen was simply there to support her husband. She was very wrong. The queen's duties were more numerous than she imagined, lasting all day. First, they each penned booklets for the new servants that they planned on hiring. After that, they went to the ballroom to plan the welcome home reception for Sorin and the battalion. Once that was done, they went to the servant's quarters to check in with the woman who watched over them. Then they went to the study after lunch, this time to look over any letters that had been received.

"Not again," she groaned, tossing a piece of parchment to the side.

"What is it?" Ariette asked.

"We have a duke who is... insistent about Sorin getting married," she said. She opened the next letter. "He has a daughter that is at the age of marriage."

"Why is that a bad thing? Forgive me, but Sorin has been ready to marry for seven years now. Assuming you go by the same traditions we do."

"We do, but Sorin refused to even entertain the idea of marriage before going to battle," she said with a weary sigh. "He has it in his mind that, if he doesn't go to battle at least once, he's not worthy of the crown."

"That's ridiculous. Sorry," she said quickly. "I don't mean to speak ill of the prince."

Stela laughed. "I'm very aware of your feelings about my son, don't worry. Sorin can be... difficult to deal with. I'll be the first to admit it. He means well, though. Our safety is his number one priority. As for why he feels like he has to prove himself, that's thanks to my useless brother."

Ariette frowned, thinking of Lucian. "I don't understand."

Stela puffed her cheeks. "When Sorin became a man, we had a celebration. My youngest brother came. Duke Theodore from the Liat province. You see, Charlotte was supposed to be the successor, not Sorin. So, he focused on his studies instead. But, when Charlotte passed away, he pushed Sorin to follow my husband's footsteps. Not that there's anything wrong with that," she added. "But Sorin was still young and impressionable. He took Theo's words to heart and I fear it's too late to fix that."

Ariette wasn't sure what to say. The queen had shared more than she had expected. Did the queen really have so few people to talk to?

Before she knew it, it was dinner time. The queen stretched.

"That's it for today," she said and stood, gathering her skirts.

"Goodness, you do a lot," Ariette said. "I didn't imagine there was so much to this!"

She laughed and they walked down the hall. "Yes, many think the queen is there to make her husband look good. It's so much more than that, though."

Elizabeth was in the dining hall when they arrived. Ariette rushed to her and hugged her tightly.

"I was starting to think I'd have to hunt you down," Ariette said with a laugh.

"I'm sorry I haven't come sooner," her mother said, sitting beside her. "It's been insane down there. We've been getting orders for more armor and other clothing."

"I appreciate you helping Misha," the king said. "We've been trying to get some more assistants for her, but we're stretched thin as it is."

"I'm going to turn in a bit early," Stela said. "After you've helped me, feel free to spend some time with your mother. I'll call should I need you."

"Yes, your highness."

Ariette went upstairs with her. As she helped her out of the dress and into a nightgown, she noticed a darkness fall over the queen. Her face was once again pale, and there were dark circles under her eyes. Once the queen was in bed, Ariette left quietly. A bad feeling settled in the pit of her stomach and she prayed Sorin would return home soon, for the queen's sake.

IX

The Truth

The army was gone for a month. Queen Stela had stopped getting out of bed after two weeks. Ariette sat in her room with her all day, trying to convince her to return to her duties. But the queen wouldn't even speak.

"Any word?" Ariette asked Anton as they walked to the king and queen's room.

Waking before dawn had become habit for Ariette finally, and Anton no longer had to wake her. He looked just as haggard as she did.

"None," he said. "Not a peep. Laurent is frantic."

"She still won't get out of bed," Ariette lamented after they had prepared their bath and were in the hallway again.

He sighed. "The king is the exact opposite. He throws himself into his work. He hasn't fed in days. I know he's regretting sending Sorin."

"I'm worried he-"

Before Ariette could finish her thought, the door flew open. The king and queen were both still in their nightclothes. Ariette and Anton tried to speak, but both of them ran down the hall. They shared a look then followed.

Ariette froze at the sight in the foyer.

The room was full of clamoring voices and groans, one rising above the others. Lucian was shouting orders. Men, soaked in blood, were carrying others. Many of the bodies weren't moving. A few men were being treated right there in the hall, their blood staining the stone. It was complete chaos. Ariette came back to her senses as the queen dashed among the men to get to her brother. Ariette hurried to her side, shaking. Lucian's face was pale and his eyes sad.

"I'm looking for him," he said before the queen could ask. "There are a lot of bodies, though, and- Stela! No!"

Eyes wild, Stela pushed by him and out into the evening air. Laurent did the same, both shouting for their son.

"Gods curse it!" Lucian groaned.

"Can I do anything to help?" Anton asked.

"I'm trying to organize men by need," Lucian said. "But I need to get below to begin working on the medicine."

"I can help with the medicine," Ariette said. She was wishing she had brought a kerchief. The thick smell of blood was starting to bring bile to her throat. "I used to make salve for the farmers, so I have some knowledge."

"And I'll organize everyone," Anton said.

Lucian hesitated then nodded, grabbing Ariette's arm. He led her through a door that branched off the hall that led to the seamstress. The shouts faded as they passed through a door at the bottom of a flight of stairs. Lucian snapped his fingers and torches lit up around the room.

"Get started on a salve for burns," he instructed.

"Burns? Were there many burned bodies?"

"We'll have to treat the men upstairs, there's not enough room for all of them here," he said, dodging her question.

Ariette went to the cabinet holding all the ingredients. She grabbed a few that she recognized and was about to turn away when an herb caught her eye. She didn't recognize it but, something pulled her to it.

"Very good," Lucian said when she dumped the herbs onto a cutting board. "Wait. Moonglow Flower?"

"Is that what this is?" she asked. "I saw it and it felt like the right thing."

She expected him to argue. After all, this wasn't cooking. He only nodded, though, and helped her prepare.

"What happened?" she asked.

"It was a trap from the very start," Lucian said heavily. "They knew and ambushed them. The fight lasted days but they had the upper hand. Finally, Dalca called for them to retreat."

"How do you know all of this?" she asked but he didn't answer. "Where's Dalca?"

Lucian's eyes closed in pain. "Dead. Took the killing blow for Sorin. Last I heard, Sorin was still with the retreating party."

"They were gone for a month. I wonder why."

"They stopped to treat the more immediate wounds. But they kept coming. They knew the routes they would take. They had to improvise and go a different way. The last fight happened early this morning. It's where we lost Dalca and Sorin went missing."

Ariette gulped, a lump forming in her throat. "Lucian, how do you know this?" she repeated.

Before she could get an answer from him, the door opened. The king entered, his son's body limp in his arms. Lucian cried out in relief and rushed to his nephew. Ariette gathered the herbs into the mortar, her hands shaking. She tried not to vomit when she brought the paste to the table Sorin was laid out on. The prince was covered in slashes. Five were on his bare torso alone, the blood shining in the light from the candles. His breathing was shallow, and Lucian got to work right away.

"Stela fainted," Laurent said. "Lucian, I've looked at the wounds. They were made from silver."

Lucian's hands were shaking as he cut Sorin's trousers. Tears jumped to his eyes.

"I don't understand," Ariette said, cleaning the wounds. "What's so bad about silver?"

Neither answered. Then Sorin coughed and his eyes opened a little.

"Father," he said in a hoarse voice. "Never thought... I'd see you again."

"Shh," Laurent soothed. "Rest. You're safe now."

"They tricked us," Sorin managed to say. "Knew we were-" He coughed, blood spilling out of his mouth. "They have a- Argh!"

Ariette grimaced as the prince screamed, his back arching. She had hoped he was too distracted, but the medicine touching the inflamed skin was stronger than she thought.

"Sorry," she said, keeping her hands steady. Laurent pinned Sorin's hands down when the prince tried to push her away. "The pain will pass soon and... and...."

Ariette dropped the bowl of medicine onto the top of the table. Sorin had screamed again and clenched his jaw. A set of ivory fangs were in Sorin's mouth. And not just canines. Long fangs. His eyes had turned an unnatural red. Someone was saying her name and she turned to Lucian in a fog. He slapped her lightly.

"Focus," he said.

"He's a vampire," she said, pointing with a shaky hand.

"Ariette, I need you to focus. Please."

"You know already," she said. "You- Wait." *The king hasn't fed in days.* "No," she breathed and tried to back away. "You're all vampires, aren't you?" No one denied it and she started to hyperventilate. "Let me go!"

"Ariette, please," Lucian begged. "We'll explain, I swear it. But if you don't help us, he will die."

Ariette's mind was a mess of emotions, tears streaming down her face. So much made sense now. Her ears began to ring, and blackness started at the edges of her sight.

"P-Please."

The voice was weak and pulled her out of her panic. Ariette stared at Sorin. He was reaching to her, tears mixing with the blood on his face. It made her own blood run cold. He was begging her for his life. She gulped and picked up the medicine again. With great effort, she calmed her hands enough to finish applying the salve. Sorin had fainted again, but his breathing was steady.

"He'll recover," Lucian announced shortly after.

"Get cleaned up and meet me in the throne room," the king said to Ariette, his eyes sorrowful.

Ariette wrapped her arms around herself, ignoring Sorin's blood still on her. She backed out without a word.

A little part of her had always believed in the supernatural. To see an actual vampire, though, frightened her. Were they all vampires? And what of the staff? Did they know?

Anton was waiting outside of her room.

"I'll wait for you to be ready," he said sadly.

Ariette felt her face go white. "How did you-?"

"The king will explain. Go clean."

Ariette edged around him. A servant already had a bath going. The young girl stayed close and Ariette gulped, stripping down. Of course, the king would have her watched. He couldn't risk her running and betraying his secret.

Sorin's blood ran off her body and tears stung at her eyes. Seeing all those dead bodies made her body shake. How many had died? Is that what her father looked like? Her father.... Did he know? He had never believed in the supernatural, preferring to pretend it didn't exist.

Once she was cleaned, she walked into the room with a towel around her body. The girl was still there with a new gown.

"Are you one, too?" she asked, not moving to take the dress.

"His highness has asked you to go straight to the throne room," the girl said.

Ariette's eye twitched. She couldn't blame the girl too much. She was just doing as she was told. She dressed quickly, an escape plan forming in her mind. She wouldn't be able to run right now, but she could do it while the royals slept. She'd grab her mother and leave for safety.

Anton was still in the hallway.

"I don't need to be escorted," she snapped when he followed her.

"That's not why I'm here. I figured it would help to have a friend."

"Are you my friend, though?" she asked, glaring.

"Of course, I am."

"Then why didn't you tell me the truth?"

"I was under orders by the king. Please don't be too harsh on him when you go in there," he said. He stopped outside the throne room. "Whatever you might think right now, he and the queen have thought only of you and Elizabeth. They've done everything they can to keep you safe."

Ariette didn't respond. Anton opened the door, ushering her in.

"Ari!" her mother cried in relief and rushed to her.

"Mama, we have to leave," she whispered into her mother's ear. "They're vampires. We're not safe."

"Just let them explain," her mother said with a sigh.

Ariette pushed her away, anger starting in the pit of her stomach. She tasted bile and glared at her mother.

"You knew!?"

"Yes. Please, Ariette, just hear them out."

"Why didn't you tell me!?"

"It wasn't my story to tell and-."

"I'm your daughter!" she shouted. "I could've been in danger!"

"Ariette, please," the king said from his throne. She recoiled as he stood and walked to her. "Just let us explain. If you still loathe us at the end, I will gladly let you leave."

She laughed humorlessly. "Yeah, sure you will! And then you'll kill me!"

"We'd never harm you," he said. "I'm begging you to listen to me."

She balled her hands into fists. "Fine."

A chair was brought in from the dining hall and she plopped onto it, not taking her eyes off the king and queen. Stela was awake but pale as a sheet. Her eyes were red with tears and she only cried more when she saw the hateful look on Ariette's face.

"I don't know where to begin," the king said. "I guess we'll start with vampires. What do you know of them?"

"Just that they're bloodthirsty animals," she snapped. "All of them deserve death."

The queen closed her eyes, gripping her chest as if Ariette's words had physically wounded her. The king looked resigned.

"Yes, many believe that. And it's not without reason. It's true there are renegade vampires out in the world, ones who kill for sport or just for the thrill of killing. Here, though, it is forbidden. You see, vampires are not born. They are made. In the case of the Rosu kingdom, the vampires are turned at the age they become men and women, twenty-one. Some can survive the turning, some don't. Those who do receive the bite, stay here, and live with us. They become either servants or guardsmen. There are some, though, who aren't vampires. They are what humans call thralls. Vampires can eat human food, but we require human blood for nourishment.

"Anton is mine, Peter Sorin's. Stela had a personal servant, but she was killed for reasons unknown. Some of the vampires here came because there are rumors in certain circles, rumors that we take in those without a master. It's true. I've become the master of many vampires this way. My daughter, Charlotte, did not survive the turning. It's why Sorin is so bitter. She was hesitant about the affair and Sorin offered to go first, to show her that it wasn't so bad."

"You're going to force us to become vampires, aren't you?" she asked.

"Goodness, no," he said. "No, this is a choice you will have to make. We are perfectly fine with you living in the palace as humans until the end. Normally, that is a requirement. But for you, we have decided to overlook it."

"Why?"

"Because of your father."

"Did he know?"

"Yes. He knew from the start. He reacted much like you did but, over time, we became friends. I trusted him with my life, and me with his." He paused and looked at her mother. "How long have you known?"

"A while," she admitted, her eyes downcast. "I noticed Misha's fangs and kept a closer eye on everyone. I eventually put two and two together."

"I see."

"That's how Lucian knew what happened, isn't it?"

"Yes. Vampires can communicate with one another telepathically."

Ariette didn't know what to say. She bent over, groaning into her knees. This was a lot of information to take in all at once. They had lost the battle; many men were dead, General Dalca included; Sorin was on the brink of death; and over half of the people in the castle were vampires. The worst of it all, though, was that her father knew and hadn't told her.

"I made Robert promise he wouldn't say anything," the king said as if he read her mind. Chances were that he did. "I begged him to keep it a secret. If our enemy learned the truth, we would all be dead. You see, the legend is true about silver. It's fatal to us. Or, it was."

"What do you mean it was?"

"I don't know how you managed it, but the Moonglow Flower added some kind of added benefit to the medicine. Sorin and the other men will have those wounds forever, but they won't die."

"Are you all right?" Elizabeth asked Ariette who was still doubled over.

"I don't know," she mumbled. "I think- I need to rest. I have a lot to think about."

"Before you go," the king said. "As I said, you're more than welcome to stay but, should you choose to leave, you cannot tell anyone of our true nature. We will know if you do."

Ariette stood up, a wry smile on her face.

"Do you think they'd believe me if I did?" she asked dryly. "It's well known that I don't care for your family. Well, didn't, that is."

"Rest well, Ariette," he said.

Elizabeth wrapped her arms around Ariette as they walked up the stairs. Sorin had started to scream and Lucian dashed across the hall, Peter close behind. They stopped to let them pass and Ariette felt the color drain from her face. Even though their rooms were several doors away, Ariette could hear the prince screaming even when the door was shut. She fell to her knees in the middle of her room.

"It's okay," her mother whispered, rubbing her back. "Let it out."

The sob that had been building in her chest finally escaped. She wailed, her mind playing images of her father's helmet being returned to them, the blood running off her body, the dead men downstairs, and an imaginary vision of Sorin thrashing in his bed. She couldn't stop the tears and eventually fainted, falling into her mother's arms.

X

Please Stay

Ariette didn't go down for breakfast or dinner the next day. The king and queen respected her choice, not that they had time to worry about that. Sorin had fallen into a sort of coma, waking every few hours to scream for General Dalca and his father, then slipping into unconsciousness again. Ariette spent the day with her pillow wrapped around her head. She wanted to flee.

On the third day, someone knocked on her door. She peeked out from under the blankets as her mother opened it. She let out a small sob as Nicole ran into the room, the queen behind her. Nicole tackled her, letting Ariette sob into her bosom.

"The queen wrote to me," she said when Ariette asked why she was there. "She said you needed a friend."

"All I can think about is Papa," she cried, and Nicole made a pitying sound.

The queen and her mother left, leaving the girls together. Nicole cried for her, stroking her hair. Finally, Ariette's hiccups died away.

"I was out when they came back," Nicole said. "Ma and I were doing the wash. It was a nightmare; bodies piled up on carts. It was impossible to tell who was alive and who was dead. Is it true that the prince hasn't been found?"

As if on cue, the prince started up again. Nicole grimaced.

"It's been like that ever since he returned," Ariette said.

"The poor man. I mean, I know he's not the kindest person out there, but still.... Other than that, how has your time in the palace been?"

Ariette was tempted to tell Nicole everything; about the vampires, the silver, and the way the prince would speak to her. She couldn't bring herself to do it, though.

"Turns out the king and my father were best friends," Ariette said, fiddling with the blankets. "Papa's last words were that he asked the king to take care of me and Mama. They've treated me well. Everyone calls me Lady Ariette which is weird. I'm thinking about leaving," she confided.

Nicole frowned. "Why?"

"I thought coming would give me some closure, but all it's done is leave me with more questions and heartache. Father kept a lot from us, deciding to keep the king's secrets over being honest with us."

"Ari, that's not fair," she said gently. "I know you miss Robert, we all do. But he swore to protect the royal family at all costs. Whatever secrets he kept, he did it out of devotion for his friend. Can't you honor that friendship?"

Ariette stared at her. "I hadn't thought about it that way." Nicole smiled. "What about you? Any progress with Liam?"

She tugged at her hair. "Not really. Tanner has decided to try and come after me now that you're here." Ariette curled her lip. "That's what I said. It's hard to find a reason to spend time with Liam without you, though."

"I'm telling you, Nicky. Just go to him and be honest. I love Liam, but that man can't pick up on subtle cues whatsoever."

"Easy for you to say! Have you met any cute guards?" she asked, wiggling her eyebrows suggestively.

Ariette laughed for the first time since the army's return.

"No. I've been too busy helping the queen. Nicky, the amount of work she has to do is insane! I thought she was just there to support the king. But it's so much more than that."

They spent the rest of the day catching up on each other's lives. It wasn't until she left around dinner time that Ariette realized she hadn't heard the prince. She felt immensely better after Nicole's visit and splashed some water on her face. She changed into her usual dress and sought out the queen.

She didn't have to go far. She was outside of Sorin's room with the king and Lucian, talking in low tones. Ariette hovered down the hall, wondering if she should just go back and wait until dinner was announced. The king saw her out of the corner of his eye, though, and held up his hand. He whispered to the queen then beckoned for Lucian to follow him into Sorin's room. Ariette met the queen halfway.

"How is he?" Ariette asked after some tense seconds.

"Better," she said. "His fever finally broke. He's been going on and on about some kind of weapon. I'm hoping Lucian's new tonic will get him to calm down long enough to make sense." Ariette just nodded, at a loss for words. "Was Nicole able to help?"

"Yes," she said. She curtsied. "Thank you for sending for her."

"Anything to make it easier for you. I know that this has all been–"

"I can't," Ariette blurted and gulped at the pain in the queen's eyes. "I mean, I can't be your personal servant. Not that way."

"Oh, Ariette," the queen said with a sigh of relief. "I was never going to ask that of you."

"But the king said you need human blood."

"Come with me," she said. They entered the king's study, going over to the portrait of her father. The queen pulled out a thick, old book from the shelf. "We didn't really get a chance to discuss it yesterday; it wasn't exactly a priority."

She opened it and passed it to Ariette. She read out loud.

"The blood of a human is our lifeblood. For, we were once humans, and require that humanity to remain sane. However, when human blood is not an option, the blood of your master will suffice." She handed it back. "So, who is your master?"

"Laurent," she said, putting the book back. "Our marriage was arranged. Even Lucian didn't know about vampires, in that sense. He came with me when I married Laurent, wanting to share his knowledge of medicine. Long story short, we both became vampires. I had many questions and this book answered the ones Laurent couldn't."

"Does it hurt?" she asked.

Stela looked at her for a long time. "I don't think you want to know the answer to that question."

"I suppose that's fair."

Stela sighed and reached for Ariette's hands. When she didn't pull them away, the queen looked relieved.

"Please stay," she said. "I know this life is dangerous, I know that it's frightening. But I've come to care very much for you and your mother. It would break my heart if you left."

Ariette bit her lip. "I don't want to be a vampire."

"You don't have to be," she said. "I swear to it."

"Then it's settled. I'll stay."

The queen beamed and embraced her. Ariette was surprised but hugged her back.

"Is this why you don't have many close friends?" Ariette asked. "Because of the vampire thing?"

"Yes. We learned the hard way that we cannot share this with others until they've proven they can be explicitly trusted."

Ariette was going to ask her something else, but the door opened. The king leaned into the room.

"Sorin's asking for you, Ariette."

"Me?"

"Yes. He's out in the gardens."

"Go ahead," the queen said. "I'll be fine."

"Very well. Oh, one more thing," she said before leaving. "I'm very sorry for what I said that night. If there are two people who don't deserve to be killed, it's you. And I guess Sorin, too," she added, and they laughed.

"Thank you," the king said. "It means a lot to hear you say that."

She nodded and went downstairs, her mind heavy. Even though she had been considering leaving ever since that night, her talk with Nicole helped her realize this is where she had to be. She may not agree with the lifestyle they lived, and she was afraid of what it entailed, but she couldn't imagine herself being somewhere else. When she walked out, the sun was high in the sky. She was musing about whether the rumors of the sun being deadly when she found Sorin standing in front of a rose bush, one arm in a sling.

"Just a myth," he said as she approached him.

"But the mind reading isn't," she said.

"If it bothers you so much, I won't do it. I'll have the others do the same."

She was surprised at his kindness. "Thank you." They stood in awkward silence for a while. Sorin didn't take his eyes off the roses, caressing the petals. "Erm... the king said you wanted to speak with me."

He plucked a rose from the bush with his free hand. He studied it carefully then walked up to her. She leaned away when he reached for her and she saw something in Sorin's eyes that she couldn't quite place.

"I won't hurt you," he said and tucked the flower behind her ear. "I owe you both an apology and my thanks. If it hadn't been for you, I would have died that night." Ariette wasn't sure what to say as he took something out of his pocket. It was her father's necklace. He put it in her hand. "Are you going to stay?"

"Yes," she said. She put the necklace on, tucking the charm under the front of her dress. "Oi, my face is up here," she added when Sorin's eyes lingered on her chest.

He rolled his eyes. "Don't flatter yourself, minx," he said and sat down on the stone bench, gesturing for her to do the same. She sat as far from him as she could. "I was thinking about that necklace. It was your father's?"

"Yes. He gave it to me before he left."

"Why would you give me such a precious item?"

She met his eyes. "I think you know why."

"That doesn't mean I understand. You hate me."

She sighed, watching a butterfly land on the roses across from them.

"I don't hate you, Prince," she said finally. "It's true you're not my favorite person here, but that doesn't mean I want you to die. My father made this necklace for my mother, you see. It was too big, though. So, he wore it when he came here to learn how to fight. He didn't have it with him when he went to battle and died. Call me foolish, but I didn't want to risk it again."

"Well, regardless, I owe you my life."

She squirmed. "No, that's okay. I'd rather you just accept it and move on."

Sorin shook his head. "That's not how this works. Perhaps among humans, a thank you would suffice. But, as you know, I am not a human."

"What are you saying?"

"I'm saying that I am in your debt until I am able to return the favor."

"Can't we just say you already returned it?"

"Of course not. Look, it's not like I have to follow you all the time. But, if the time ever comes for me to return the favor, I will do everything in my power to do so."

Ariette stood up. "Prince, please. I'm not comfortable with this."

"Trust me, I'd rather not be in your debt. If I could give you the most extravagant gift we own, then I would. But it still stands that you saved my life." She didn't know what to say. He stood up. "I'm pleased to hear you aren't leaving. My mother in particular cares much for you. As soon as my arm is healed, I'll teach you how to defend yourself. Elizabeth, too," he added as an afterthought. "I must go inside to the generals."

Ariette watched him walk away. He didn't hold himself with the same bravado as usual and it made her nervous. She followed shortly after and found the queen in the throne room. She went to her usual spot behind the throne.

"Sorin told us that you've expressed discomfort about people reading your mind," the queen said. "All the staff have been ordered not to."

"Thank you," she said in a small voice.

"What is it?" the king asked.

"Is there any chance Sorin can just... I don't know... forget the whole debt thing?"

"No," the king said. His voice was surprisingly firm. "This is ancient magic, Ariette."

"I figured you'd say that," she mumbled.

The door opened and a villager she recognized bowed before the king and queen.

"Thank you for agreeing to see me," he said. "My name is Richard."

"Welcome," the king said. "Your letter was vague."

"I.... Well, I was worried you wouldn't agree to see me," Richard said, still bowing. "We all saw the men return. Did we lose the battle?"

Ariette looked at the king out of the corner of her eye. His face was impassive.

"You needn't concern yourself with this," the king said.

"With all due respect, your highness, some of our friends were among those who did not return. I believe we have the right to know the outcome of the battle."

The king sighed. "No, we did not lose. But we didn't win, either. It was a stalemate on both sides. Our men are starting construction on a barrier to protect the capitol."

"I see."

"Is there anything else?"

"No," Richard said but he still didn't move.

Ariette frowned. Something was wrong. She looked at the king fully. He was staring intently at Richard and she understood he was reading the man's mind. The king stood up and walked to him. Richard finally looked up, audibly gulping.

"Put it down, son," the king said in a soft voice. "It's not worth it."

Richard hesitated then produced a dagger from his side, swinging at the king. Ariette tried to go to him, but the queen stopped her. The king easily blocked the attack. His face was full of sorrow as Richard shook with rage.

"Who was it?" the king asked. "Your father? Brother?"

"My son," he said. "He was going to be celebrating his fifteenth year this winter. How could you take him from me!?"

"I did not draft any younger than eighteen," the king said. "However, we do not turn away anyone who wishes to join. His name was Philip, yes?" Tears pooled in Richard's eyes. "He came to me claiming he had your permission. I am truly sorry for your loss, Richard. I will do what I can to make amends. But never try something this foolish again. I'm assuming you have a wife. Would you really subject her to losing a husband and a son?"

Richard's chin quivered then he started to cry. He dropped the dagger and the king let go of his wrist, using his foot to push the dagger behind him. Richard just shook his head and left.

"You're just letting him go?" Anton asked.

King Laurent sighed as he picked the dagger up, returning to his throne.

"I know the pain of losing a child," he said. "If I could have, I would've done the same the night Charlotte died. I do not begrudge him of his actions."

"Can I make a suggestion?" Ariette said after a long silence. The king nodded. "You usually host balls when soldiers die. Perhaps... perhaps inviting all of the village instead of prioritizing dukes and duchesses," she said in a rush before she lost her courage.

"That's actually a very good idea," the king said. "Love, can you write up the invitations?"

"Of course," the queen said and stood up.

They passed Sorin in the halls and Ariette avoided his eyes.

"Is everything all right?" he asked. "I heard shouting and was on my way."

"Just a grieving father," his mother said. "How was the meeting with the soldiers?"

"As good as it could be, under the circumstances. I'm on my way to see the generals now. I'm assuming we're still doing a ball?"

"Yes, I'm about to go write up the invitations with Ariette now. We'll be focusing on the villagers, though, at Ariette's suggestion. We'll invite some of the nobility, of course, but we wish to include the people to keep us in their favor."

Sorin nodded. "A wise idea. Please, excuse me."

"Something's different," Ariette said when they got to the study.

"War will do that to a person," the queen said sadly. "Sorin is suffering from survivor's guilt right now. I worry it will take him a while to move beyond it. All we can hope is that he'll recover quickly. Now, let's work on those invitations."

XI

The Moonglow Flower

The meeting with the generals was very subdued. When Sorin entered, arm still in a sling, they stood with grim faces. He motioned for them to sit, Ariette's suggestion still ringing in his mind. He sat beside his father who began to talk.

"We'll be having a ball in Dalca's honor," he said, and the generals nodded. "But not just his; we are doing it for the men who died in the battle, too. My wife and her lady-in-waiting are putting together all the necessary arrangements as we speak."

"Is it true that the human girl found a cure for silver?" Vasil asked.

Sorin stood and lifted his tunic. "It's not a full cure, but it's good enough in my opinion."

The generals stared in wonder at the scars.

"We should reward her," Constantin said. "To find something that can bring this kind of relief...."

They all thought for a long time.

"What about a seat on the council?" Sorin suggested.

"I don't know how that would go over with the council," General Alexei said. "You know our customs."

"Of course, I do," Sorin said. "But I also know that she saved my life, even though she was horrified."

"What woman wouldn't? War is terrifying."

Laurent shook his head. "Not just that. She knows now; both of them do. She found out that night and still helped my son. I agree with Sorin. A seat on the council is the least we can do."

Vasil sighed. "You're the only one who can make that choice," he said. "We, of course, will stand by your orders. I can't say the same for the council members."

"Leave that to me," Sorin said. "Now, I do have a report to make." He stood and drew a crude sketch on some parchment. "This is their new weapon. It stands about sixty feet tall. They pull a thick rope and this part launches projectiles at least a mile wide."

"By the gods," Alexei gasped. "What is it?"

"I don't remember the name. But we need to start construction around Imperium. A solid wall, reinforced with David's magic." He pulled over a map of the capitol city and pointed. "We'll build it here. Sixty feet high, all the way around the city. Enlist the guards and some of the stronger men of the village. We must start now. They've added silver to their weapons and that concerns me deeply."

"As you order," the generals said.

***

That evening, the queen told them of the invitations.

"We got them done in one day," she said. "Ariette is a hard worker."

"You did most of the work," Ariette said, waving to her mother as Elizabeth joined them. "We should be able to get them out tomorrow morning."

"Once you've sent them out, come by the throne room," Laurent said.

She fiddled with her fork. "Did I do something wrong?"

"Not at all," he said. "Just trust me."

She nodded. Sorin walked in shortly after, looking exhausted. His sling was gone, though.

"I've just got done talking with the guards," he said as Peter put his food in front of him. "Construction will begin immediately."

"Good."

"Ariette, I need a favor," Lucian said, poking his head into the dining hall. "May I borrow you for a moment?"

Ariette looked to the queen who nodded. She followed Lucian into the foyer.

"I've run out of the Moonglow Flower," he said. "My usual servant can't go to get it tonight. Can you go for me?"

"Does it have to be tonight?"

"Yes. It only blooms under the full moon."

"Where is it?"

"In the forests beside the castle gardens," he said. "At the base of the cliff that leads to the ocean."

"The forest?" she asked, her voice higher than normal. "In the dark?"

"Is that a problem? We need it for the men who haven't been treated yet."

Ariette remembered the angry gashes and scars on Sorin's torso. She couldn't just leave these men to the same fate. She sighed.

"Not a problem at all. Can you make me a map of where they are?"

"Ask Sorin to take you. It'll be good for him to be out of the palace."

"Right," she said, her heart dropping a bit. "Lucian needs more Moonglow Flowers," she said when she returned to her seat at the table. "He's asked me to get some, but I don't know where the flowers are."

"They're in the forest, about twenty yards in," the king said.

"You shouldn't go alone," the queen said. "Would you like me to join you?"

Ariette wanted to accept but remembered Lucian's words.

"Lucian suggested the prince," she said and Sorin frowned over his goblet.

"Me? Why?"

"Something about you getting out of the palace."

The prince rolled his eyes. "Let me guess, it has to happen tonight."

"That's what he said."

He put the goblet down and dabbed at his mouth. "Well, there's no time like the present."

"Are you all right with me going now?" Ariette asked the queen.

She smiled. "Of course, I'll be just fine."

"Will you be okay?" Elizabeth asked, looking nervous as well.

"I should be," Ariette said.

"There's nothing too dangerous in these parts of the forest," the king said. "It's just easy to get lost, that's all."

"I promise," Ariette said when her mother still looked nervous. "I'll be fine."

Elizabeth sighed and nodded. Ariette went with Sorin into the foyer again. A servant was holding a wicker basket that Ariette accepted and perched on her hip. Out of the corner of her eye, she saw Sorin putting his sword on his hip.

"I thought the king said there wasn't anything dangerous out there."

"There isn't," he said and led the way into the night. "But it doesn't hurt to be prepared."

"I guess," she muttered.

They hooked around the back of the palace. A wall separated the forests from the gardens and Ariette lingered outside the tree line. She bit her lip at the darkness in the trees, the sun having gone down long ago. Her mouth went dry and Sorin finally noticed after he had made it a few feet into the trees.

"Oi," he said. "Are you coming or not?"

She gulped a few times until she found her voice. "J-Just give me a minute," she said, her knees knocking.

He stared. "What is it?"

"Nothing," she lied.

Her palms were sweating, and she wiped her free hand on her skirts. Sorin seemed to understand finally. He walked back over and held out his hand.

"Come on," he said in a surprisingly soft voice. "You'll be safe."

"C-Can't we take a torch?" she asked.

"No. The flowers won't bloom if there's artificial light."

She whimpered but accepted his hand. Ever since she was a child, Ariette had feared the dark. Nothing her parents did made it better, so she learned to cope with it. The forest seemed to press in around them and she involuntarily stepped closer to Sorin.

"Why are these flowers so far away?" she asked, her eyes facing forward.

"It's the only place they can thrive. Mother has tried to grow them in our gardens, but they only wilt."

"Typical," she mumbled.

"Have you always been afraid of the dark?"

"Yes."

He just nodded. They walked for a while longer before they reached a clearing. The trees parted for the moonlight.

"We're early," he said and immediately let go of her hand. He leaned against a tree trunk. "Should be any minute now, though."

"What do you mean?"

He pointed to the ground and she looked. She could make out the shadows of flower stems, buds closed. She frowned and knelt down among them. The stems were dark green and, when she touched them, the texture was coarse. The moonlight crept further into the clearing as they waited. She didn't know what to expect but felt better now that they weren't in the pitch darkness.

Finally, the moon reached above the clearing and Ariette gasped in wonder.

Hundreds of flowers bent their buds towards the sky. The pedals curled open, reaching for the moon. The pollen in the center glowed bright enough to light up the forest for several feet. Ariette reached for one, almost afraid to touch it.

"They're beautiful," she whispered.

The pedals were deep purple triangles, fading into white until they got to the center. The idea of plucking them to have them ground up into medicine pained her. Sorin knelt beside her and plucked one. She watched, waiting for the glow to dim, but it never did.

"Lucian's been doing research since that night," he told her as they plucked more. "He believes its healing properties are tied to our... nature. The full moon is more than just a phase."

"What do you mean?" she asked but he didn't answer. Once the basket was full, she held it in both hands. "Will the flowers grow back?"

"Yes," he said. "They aren't your ordinary plant. They're magical."

"Right," she said. Her eyes lingered on the remaining flowers for a few more seconds. "I hope I can come back here."

He shrugged and led the way back into the trees. "I can't imagine why you wouldn't be able to."

"Are you okay?" she asked.

He frowned, stepping over a root. "I'm just fine."

"I know we're not on the best terms," she said, "but if you need someone to talk to...."

"I'm fine," he repeated.

"It's just... I know what it's like to lose someone and-."

"I said I'm fine," he snapped, and she looked at the ground, clenching her jaw.

"Fine," she snapped back.

They didn't speak until they had left the forest. Sorin muttered something about going back to dinner but she didn't respond. She went to Lucian's workroom, slamming the basket on the table.

"There are your bloody flowers," she said.

"Hey, what happened?" he asked.

"Nothing."

"Ah," he said and put a leather pouch down. "You had another argument with Sorin."

She glared at him. "I thought the king and queen had ordered you not to read my mind."

He chuckled. "I didn't need to," he said. "I know he's difficult to be around. Give him time. He'll open up eventually."

She rolled her eyes. "Why should he? I'm just a commoner."

Lucian frowned. "That's not true, Ariette. Never say that."

"Why not? It's what he thinks."

Lucian sighed heavily. "Sorin is hurting, Ariette. In more ways than just his wounds. Just.... Just give him time."

"Whatever," she said. "Is that enough?"

"Yes, thank you. Good evening."

She nodded again and left.

~~~

Lucian sought out Sorin later that evening. He knocked on his door and Sorin let him in.

"You could be a bit nicer to her, you know," Lucian said in a stern voice. "She did save your life, after all."

"Then maybe she should learn to keep her nose out of other people's business," he said stubbornly. He took his nightshirt off so Lucian could reapply the medicine. "She dared to compare my life with hers. Ow!"

Lucian had put pressure on one of the larger scars on Sorin's back.

"Stop being ungrateful," he snapped. "Your pride will be the end of you, Sorin. I know you're struggling right now, but you have to be aware of the other people around you. You are the only one who can teach her the self-defense she needs to know. Make amends. Apologize."

"I don't apologize to commoners."

To his surprise, Lucian clapped him upside the head. He spun on the chair, gawking at the older man.

"She's not a commoner anymore," Lucian said, pointing at Sorin. "She is your mother's lady-in-waiting, a member of the council after to-morrow, and the woman you owe a life debt to. Start treating her with the respect she deserves, or I'll pull your mother into this."

Sorin squirmed. "That's not necessary. I'll apologize to the minx."

Lucian rolled his eyes. "I guess that's the best I can hope for tonight. Now, your father wanted me to remind you to be in the throne room by midday. That's when you'll be presenting her with the sash. We're keep-ing the affair small to avoid... tension."

"Let me guess: the members didn't agree."

"Not at all. But I'm just a doctor, I keep my nose out of politics.
~~~

Okay, this should be the last time I have to apply this," he said after wrapping more bandages around Sorin. "Let me know if you ever start to experience pain, though."

"I will."

"And think on what I said," Lucian said before leaving. "She may have started off as a commoner, but Ariette has made herself much more in the two months she's been here."

Sorin just nodded.

Ariette and the queen left after breakfast to deliver the invitations. The ball would be in one week and the nobles would have their invitations mailed to them. The market was alive with shoppers who stopped to bow and curtsy to the queen. Ariette happily greeted the people she recognized, giving them the invitation. There were a few house calls they planned to make, though. Ariette had the list tucked under her arm. They approached the first one and the queen sighed a little before knocking.

"Your highness," a woman said, her eyes wide. "And Ariette! How wonderful to see you. Please, come in!"

"Thank you," the queen said as they walked in.

Ariette knew the woman as the shoemaker's wife. The shoemaker himself was sitting in their small dining area, frozen in place when he saw them.

"Your highness," he said. He didn't stand, though. "I wondered when you'd come by."

"Johnathon," the wife said but he shot her a glare.

"Come to give us some mediocre apology for my son's death?" he asked. Ariette gulped. She knew the man's anger, understood it deeply. In fact, she had held the same thoughts towards the family not long ago. "Regardless of what it is, you can turn around leave right now."

His wife grimaced. "I'm sorry," she said to the queen. "He's just-."

"Don't apologize to her," he snapped. "And you two, get out. I have no interest in speaking to either of you."

"What did I do?" Ariette asked.

"I thought you'd understand! They took your father from you! And what do you do? You go and work for them! I heard what you did! You made some kind of special medicine! You healed the prince! Why would you do that!?"

Ariette began to shake. "What you're saying is borderline treason," she said in a dark voice. "It's true that my feelings for the royal family were... not good. But I've learned a lot since then. And no matter how much I dislike the prince, I would never, and I mean *never*, just let him die like that. My father wasn't forced to draft into the king's militia. He did it because he wanted to protect us all. The same is true for your son." She slapped the invitation on the table in front of him. "You're still welcome to come, but I would watch your words when you arrive. Many men were lost, and we want to honor them."

"Let's go," Stela said quietly, and the wife led them back to the door.

"I'm so sorry," she said in a mortified voice. "He's just...."

"I understand," Stela said. "I'm sure it won't be the first time we encounter that. Have a lovely day."

"You do the same. And thank you," she added. "I personally didn't expect anything to be done for those of us here in the village."

The queen smiled and held the woman's hand. "I am sorry our family has been... out of touch. I'm hoping to change that."

"Good day."

Ariette huffed when the door shut. "Now I know how Sorin felt."

"I appreciate you sticking up for us," she said. "But, as I said, that won't be the only time we'll run into that. Let's go; we have many more to go."

They didn't return to the palace until just before lunch. Ariette sat down at the table, rubbing her eyes.

"How did it go?" the king asked.

"You won't believe the amount of people who yelled at us," Ariette grumbled, stabbing at her lunch.

"Actually, I can," Sorin said with a pointed look. She glared at him. "What did you expect?"

"A little understanding! We're doing more than sending them provisions!"

"They're grieving," Elizabeth said. "Be patient with them."

Ariette sighed. "I know. I'm just frustrated."

After they were done eating, the king stood.

"Come with us to the throne room," he said. "There's something I want you to see."

Sorin excused himself and rushed out.

"Where's he going in a hurry?" she asked.

"To get ready," he said and offered his arm to her.

She took it, still thinking about her interaction with the shoemaker. She knew he was upset and understood why. She also felt ashamed. She had been the same way with the king not too long ago. The memory made her face go warm and she tried to push it away. After whatever the king had planned, she and the queen were to start working on preparations for the ball. It was only a few days away, after all.

"Wait here," he said. "A guard will come get you two when we're ready."

Ariette frowned at her mother. "Do you know what's going on?"

She shook her head. "I'm just as in the dark as you are. Are the Moonglow flowers as beautiful as I've heard?"

"They're beyond description," she said with a longing sigh. "Next full moon, I'll take you with me. It's a beautiful sight."

The door opened and a guard smiled, beckoning them in.

XII

The Council

The throne room was full of men, some in slings like Sorin had worn. Others had bandages and a few with canes. The royal family were all by their thrones. The king took her hand and helped her up the few steps. She hesitated when he took her to Sorin. She was still mad about the previous night but saw a folded cloth in his hands and her curiosity won out.

"Lady Ariette Jones," the king said in a voice that carried. "Today, we wish to thank you for your discovery. Because of your actions with the Moonglow flower, you were able to save my son's life. Not only that, we took that medicine to our soldiers. The men you see before you are the ones you saved."

Ariette looked at all the men, blushing as they grinned at her.

"As a way to thank you," the queen picked up, "we want to make you a member of the council."

Ariette did a double take. "What!?"

Stela laughed and motioned for Sorin to step forward. Ariette tensed but he unfolded the cloth in his hands. It was a sash and he reached up to drape it over her left shoulder, the other side resting on her right hip. The sash was made of fine red silk, not the cotton it originally looked like. The Rosu symbol, etched into gold, was pinned to the left side of the sash and she touched it in awe.

"Thank you," Sorin said, though he didn't meet her eyes. He took her hand, bowed, and kissed it. "Because of you, our lives were spared."

She remembered the life debt he mentioned, and she felt heat creep up her neck. He took her back down the steps to the group of men. One by one, they took her hand and kissed it, some even going so far as to hug her. A young man hugged her tightly. He couldn't have been older than seventeen years, making her wonder how he ended up in the war. She asked him.

"My parents are old and ill," he said, wiping at a tear. "I went to earn the gold to care for them. They'll be at the ball in two days. I'd be honored if you'd meet them."

"Sure," she said with an awkward smile. "Really, this isn't necessary," she added when the men kept coming to thank her.

"Don't be rude," Sorin hissed at her under his breath.

"Look who's talking," she snapped back.

He glared but didn't say anything. When everyone returned to their spots, they looked at her expectantly. She realized they were expecting her to say something.

"Thank you for this honor," she blurted. "I'm humbled to know that so many of you were able to benefit from the medicine. I hope this can help at least give our militia the advantage they need. Erm... I hope you and your loved ones will all be at the ball and that we can move on from this tragedy the best we can."

She fidgeted and turned to the king, her eyes asking for help. He smiled and put a hand on her shoulder.

"Return to your homes," he said to the men. "Thank you for coming today."

They all bowed and smiled at her once more before leaving. Once the door shut, she relaxed her shoulders.

"You could've warned me," she said.

Laurent chuckled. "My dear, if I had, you would've declined."

"Yes, I suppose you're right. Thank you," she said again. "This really is a tremendous honor."

"I'm so proud of you," her mother said, crying. "Oh, this is what Misha was working on! She wouldn't let me see!"

"I wanted it to be a surprise for both of you," the king said. "Look on the other side of the pendant."

She took the sash off carefully and turned the pendant over. At first, she didn't see anything. Then the light caught on a perfect, albeit small, carving of her father. Impulsively, Ariette hugged the king. He chuckled and patted her on the back.

"Now, I believe Sorin has some things to teach you while we wait for the rest of the council," he said.

Sorin gestured for her to follow him to a table. She gave the sash to her mother and followed. The table was holding several daggers, all of different sizes and shapes. He picked up one and put it next to her hand, turning it every which way.

"I owe you an apology," he muttered as he did so. He tested another dagger. "I didn't mean to be as rude as I was. There's no excuse, so I hope you'll be able to forgive me eventually."

"I appreciate it," she said. "But what in the world are you doing?"

He laughed a bit. "Trying to find the dagger that will best fit your hand. This should do." He handed her one with a small hilt. The blade looked incredibly sharp and she felt nervous just holding it. "All right, the first thing we'll cover is attacking."

"Shouldn't we start with defense?" she asked as he pulled her back to the center of the throne room.

"No. Better for you to know how to attack, that way learning how to defend will be easier."

"Okay...."

"Now, the important thing to remember is that you should always keep the dagger below your shoulders," he said. "This gives you better control and you can rely more on your center of gravity. Try and hit me with the dagger."

"I don't know," she said anxiously. "What if I hurt you?"

He shook his head. "You won't. Trust me," he added.

She arched a brow. "Seriously?"

For a second, he looked like he was going to smile.

"Just attack me, minx."

She took a deep breath but did as he said. She lunged forward, thrusting the dagger at his stomach. He easily blocked her and shook his head.

"Never go for a stab," he said. "Swipe in a direction. Try again." She swiped from left to right, but he blocked it again. "Notice my stance. My right arm was up, making it easy to block. One more time." She groaned but tried her best. He grabbed her wrist and knocked the dagger away with his free hand. "Better."

She picked the dagger up and gasped when, suddenly, he was behind her. His dagger was near her throat.

"That's not fair!" she said. "I wasn't ready."

"Your attacker won't care," he said and stood beside her. "Watch my motions." Miffed, she obeyed. He showed her different ways to attack, including feinting. "By all accounts, feinting is your best way to get in a successful hit. Okay, time for defense." He straightened his tunic and she tried to get ready. Once again, he was behind her. This time, though, his other arm had her arms pinned to her sides. "Break free."

"I can't!" she said, her heart racing. She didn't like the feeling of being confined, and this was worse. "If I move, your dagger will cut me! Why do you have it so close to my throat!?"

"Calm down," he said, and she felt a surge of anger. "I'm serious. Calm yourself. My dagger is this close because so will your assailant's. I'm not going to go easy on you just because you're a woman. Now, take a deep breath." She gulped and did so. "Very good. First thing you need to do is try and get your arms free."

She wiggled her arms, but they didn't move. Frustrated, she acted on impulse and stomped on his foot. His hold loosened in surprise and she took the opportunity to elbow him in the gut. The dagger moved away from her throat and she dropped, ducking away from him. She spun on the spot, breathing heavily. She held her dagger in front of her, her hands shaking. He nodded.

"Very good," he said. "I'm impressed." She yelped when he ran at her, his dagger stopping a foot from her chest. She dropped hers in fear. "Grab my wrist with your dominant hand," he said. She obeyed and he used his other hand to tighten her fingers around his wrist until it hurt. "The goal is to apply enough pressure to loosen their hold on the dagger. Once you see it go slack, slap it away the way I did."

She watched until it was loose and smacked it. It clattered to the floor and she let out a sigh of relief. It quickly turned into a small scream as he grabbed her arm, spun her around, and pinned it behind her.

"Gods curse it!" she shouted and, without thinking, she threw her head back. Sorin staggered back in shock, his nose throbbing. "I am so sorry!" she said in a mortified voice. "I didn't- I was just- You scared me and I-."

Sorin shook his head, touching his nose tenderly. "No, you did well. It seems you have the instincts of a soldier, something I'm sure you got from your father." He was about to continue but stopped, his head turning to the door slightly. For some reason, his expression turned sour. "We'll have to stop here. We've covered all the basics, so I'll have a dagger specially made for you. I was going to teach Elizabeth, but they're here."

He took her dagger and put it on the table. He strode quickly to his throne, narrowed eyes on the door. His demeanor made her nervous as the king beckoned her over. She stood behind him as the door opened.

Four men walked in, each looking pretty old. They seemed to glide; their hands hidden in the folds of their robes. They all bowed before the family then turned their eyes to Ariette. Three of them had skeptical looks on their faces. The fourth was beaming at her.

"Your highness," the first one said, his voice deep. "Why did you send for us? We were deep in discussion, as you know."

"Yes, and I'm sorry, Sir Tobias," the king said. "I wanted to introduce you all to your new council member."

Their lips went thin as he gestured to Ariette.

"So. You went through with it after all," the second man said. "Despite our feelings. I wonder, what's the point of a council if you ignore our advice?"

"That's rude," Ariette said and flushed.

"Silence," the third said. "You have no say in this."

She felt her heart speed up. "Excuse me," she said. "I don't even know who you are."

"I am Sir Tybalt," he said. "The man responsible for the pipes that run through this castle."

Ariette loathed the way he put emphasis on the word man.

"And I am Sir Tobias," the first said with an unnecessary flourish. "You can thank me for the home you lived in before you came here."

"You may call me Sir Carlisle," the second man said. "I have been with the royal family since the very beginning."

"I'm David, the court mage," the last one said with a grin. He grasped her hands. "I'm so pleased to finally meet you. I'm sorry I couldn't sooner; I've been doing important research."

"Each of us have advised our respective kings," Tobias interrupted, brushing against David to move him away from her. He leaned down to be closer to Ariette's level. "Sir David is also the advisor for King Laurent. Tell me, *Lady,* what have you contributed? What gives you the right to call yourself our equal?"

"Gods, I've never met such a misogynist," she said when she found her voice. Tobias's eyes widened in anger. "Seriously, not even the prince is this bad!" On his throne, Sorin coughed but it sounded more like a laugh. "My name is Ariette, as you already know. And, if we're comparing contributions, as you seem so keen to do, I'm the reason the prince is still alive. I was the one who found out the Moonglow flower could be mixed with other herbs to heal silver wounds! I'll agree with you on one thing: I'll never be a royal advisor." She stepped closer, her eyes challenging. "But I can't help but notice that, despite being immortal, none of your kings have survived."

The council members inhaled sharply. Tobias's eyes were burning, and she feared he would hit her. Instead, he straightened and looked at her with contempt.

"I had heard you had the tongue of a disrespectful whelp," he said snidely. "How disappointing to find out it's true." He gestured to his fellow men. "Come. I've had enough of this. You may wear the sash but know you will never be one of us."

Three of them left, noses turned up in dismissive anger. Only David remained. The door closed and, with it, the adrenaline. Panic set in and Ariette turned to the family.

"I am so sorry. I don't know what came over me," she said, eyes wide. "I never meant to disrespect your ancestors. I just- They were so rude and I-."

"Ariette," Sorin interrupted. She gulped, expecting one of his many reprimands. "We knew the council wouldn't agree with us from the beginning. They fought against it, but they are only advisors. They've become complacent in their old age. It's refreshing to see someone put them in their place for once."

"Let me just say, I do not agree with them," David said, walking over to her. "I knew your father. You remind me of him very much. Speaking of which, may I borrow that pendant?"

She hesitated and looked at the family again.

"Go ahead," the queen said gently. "You can trust him."

She took off the jade pendant and passed it to him slowly. She kept a hand on the cord, though. He didn't object.

"The family told me of your concerns," he said as he turned it over in his hands. "While the staff have been ordered to not read your mind, I regret to say the councilmen probably won't follow such a decree. One of the things I've researched is a way to put up a kind of block." He put the pendant between his hands and whispered a few words. Light pulsed between his hands and faded when he stopped. "There you go! So long as you wear this, none of us will be able to read your mind."

"Thank you," Ariette said earnestly. She put it around her neck. "Does it work?"

King Laurent stared at her. "I haven't a clue what's on your mind," he said.

"I do need to return to my workroom," David said. "I just need to do a few more things for my research. Good day."

"Thank you," she repeated and waited until he was gone. "Are you mad at me?"

"No," the king said. "It's as Sorin said: they've always been like that. It might take some time for them to come around to having you on the council, but I don't doubt you'll manage to make them see you have as much to offer as them."

"If not more," the queen said gently. "Now, are you ready to go do the preparations or do you need a moment?"

"I'm ready," she said, tucking the pendant under her dress. "Mother, would you like to come?"

"I need to help with the dresses," she said and hugged her. "I'm very proud of you."

Ariette hugged her tightly and waved as she left.

XIII

Confrontation

Ariette was still shaken for the rest of the day. She did her best to keep track of everything, but her mind kept going back to what that horrible man had said.

The morning of the ball, she noticed Peter walking out of Sorin's room, a bandage on his neck. She gulped.

"Did he…?"

"Just a nightmare," Peter said with a smile. "Nothing you need to worry about."

"Does it help?" she asked, pointing awkwardly at her neck.

"Yes. I'll explain more later, if you'd like," he said.

"I am a little curious," she said. "In a weird, morbid way."

He laughed. "I heard you gave the council quite the talking to."

She groaned as Anton walked into the room to help the king get ready.

"I was sure he was going to smite me where I stood," she said. "But I couldn't stand the way he was talking to me. So pompous."

"I've only ever met them once," he said. "I didn't care for them, either."

"Can I ask you something?"

"Of course."

"Why are you doing this? Being a... whatever it is?"

He smiled. "The technical, yet outdated, term is thrall. Sorin prefers to call us personal servants, though. Thrall gives the impression that I am under Sorin's complete control. About ten years ago, I became ill. I came to the palace, seeking help. Sorin had just become a vampire and they needed someone to be with him. After swearing secrecy, I accepted the position."

"I thought personal servants had a higher constitution. If you were ill, wouldn't that make you more prone to dying?"

His smile turned sad. "It wasn't that kind of illness," he said. "In truth, I.... I wanted to be sent to the front lines. My fiancé had died, and I didn't have the courage to take my own life."

She reached out to him. "I'm so sorry, Peter. I had no idea."

"It's better to let people think I was deathly ill," he said, patting her hand. "I'm ashamed of the man I was. I'm grateful that the family has given me a second chance."

"You don't look older than twenty-five, though."

"When you become a personal servant, it slows the aging," he said. "It's to make sure the vampire you serve has someone they can rely on."

"Convenient," she commented, and the door opened. "Ah, she's ready for me. Thank you for being honest with me."

Peter bowed and she went into the room to help the queen dress. Laurent was yawning sporadically, looking as if he hadn't slept. Ariette wanted to ask what was wrong but stopped herself. The queen sat at the vanity, also looking exhausted.

"Are you all right?" she asked as she began to apply the makeup.

"I won't lie, last night was unpleasant," she said with a sigh. "Sorin has decided he will be the one giving the speech tonight."

"Why is that a bad thing?" Ariette asked.

"He hasn't taken time to heal," the king said, frowning out the window. "I know he had several nightmares; I heard them form here. I worry what will happen if he gives the speech tonight."

"You don't have someone to help with this kind of thing?"

"We've never needed it," the queen admitted. "I don't know what we'll do if he has more nightmares tonight; Peter won't be able to help him again. He may have a high constitution, but even he has his limits."

"Is there anything I can do to help?"

"Yes, actually," Stela said. "Normally, the one giving the speech would lead the honored one's wife or daughter in a dance. Dalca didn't have any surviving family; we were all he had. As for the villagers, there are too many for him to dance with."

"You want me to open the dance with him again?"

"If you don't mind," Laurent said.

"If it helps, I will," she said. "What's on the schedule for today?"

"Laurent will stay in the throne room while we finalize everything," Stela said. "Sorin is going to work on his speech. We'll start in the kitchens."

Ariette curtsied to the men once they were in the hall and they bowed back. Ariette was given a list from the queen who had one of her own. She was surprised at the number of tasks they were to accomplish by evening.

"As usual, we'll have Anton test the food," the queen said as they walked. "He has built up tolerance over the years. Normally, Peter would join him. In light of the circumstances, though...." The doors to the kitchen opened. The staff were in full swing, preparing their breakfast and the start to the meals. "Hello, Chef Quinton. How are you fairing this morning?"

A plump man with a chef's hat on his bald head bowed to them.

"Queen Stela, Lady Ariette," he greeted. "I'm just fine, thank you. I wasn't expecting you until after breakfast."

"I was hoping we could eat it as we worked," she said and Ariette lifted the list for him to see. He grimaced. "Yes, as you can see, we have quite a day ahead of us. I've just come to confirm the menu."

"We've done everything as you've requested," he said and led the two of them through the kitchen. "These are the desserts. We made sure that the ones going to Lady Ariette are free of honey."

"Sorry," she said, embarrassed.

He tossed a pudgy hand. "There's no need for you to be sorry, my dear. It's not your fault you're allergic. As for the remaining food, here are the recipes I'll be following."

He passed them a stack of parchment and Ariette groaned quietly. This would be a long day.

~~~

In his room, Sorin was scribbling furiously on a piece of parchment. He made a frustrated noise and crumpled it up, tossing it into an overflowing wastebasket. He couldn't understand why words weren't coming easily to him. It should be simple. But nothing seemed adequate. He remembered Ariette's fury when they first met, the pain she felt at the loss of her father. How could he possibly calm dozens of hearts when he couldn't even calm hers?

"Sorin?"

He turned from his writing desk. Peter had walked in, an outfit draped over his arm. He was shocked at the state of the prince. His hair was on end, ink splatters on his nose.

"Is it time already?" Sorin asked, looking out of his window. The sun was starting to set, and he swore. "I'm not ready! I don't even have the speech written!"

"Maybe that's not a bad thing," Peter suggested and gave Sorin a damp cloth for his face. "We both know that, sometimes, the best words are the ones from the heart."

"You're such a poet," Sorin said.

Peter laughed. "I'll take that as a compliment. King Laurent wanted me to let you know you'll be opening the dance with Lady Ariette."

"I assumed as much," he said as he took the tunic from Peter. "I heard you talking to her this morning. What was it about?"

"She just had some questions about being a personal assistant," he said. "I didn't tell her anything you wouldn't want me to."
~~~

"I'm surprised she asked," he said. "She was so horrified when she learned the truth."

"Maybe she's more like her father than we thought."

They finished getting ready and waited for the others in the foyer. He fidgeted with the new medallion on his chest: two swords crossed at the middle of the blade. It was given to those who fought in a major battle. He didn't feel the pride he normally would have, though. They lost, after all.

When his family joined, Ariette and Elizabeth were with them. At his father's insistence, she wore the sash. The other council members would be there this evening, and Sorin knew he wanted Ariette to be as involved as possible. They took their places as the doors opened.

Everyone was somber, just like before. But it was more this time. Wives, children, and siblings all dressed in black stopped to say hello. They then followed the servants leading to the ballroom. David had used his magic to increase it and elevate it slightly, erecting a balcony. As the family filed in, Sorin considered telling his father to leave it like it was. It was very appealing.

As usual, tables laden with food and drink lined the walls. A separate table was made for the family and their servants, though. Sorin swallowed thickly as he took his place beside his father. All eyes were on them and Laurent nudged him with his elbow.

"Good evening," Sorin blurted, clearing his throat when his voice cracked. "Thank you for coming tonight. Not long ago, we lost many great men. Fathers, brothers, uncles, sons, and friends all went to protect us." He lowered his eyes, thinking of Dalca. "One such friend, General Dragos Dalca, saved my life. Because of him, and those who fought that day, I am still alive. I can't express my grief adequately. I wish I could turn back time, do things differently. All I can do, though, is make sure we keep his memory alive. But not just his; all of your loved ones' as well." He lifted his goblet and everyone in the room did the same. "Tonight, let us be equals in our grief. To all those who could not be here tonight."

Everyone drank and then clapped politely. He took a long breath then took Ariette out to the dance floor one again.

"That was very beautiful," Ariette said.

"Thank you."

He wasn't sure what else to say, but it seemed she didn't, either. He saw the council members watching her with great scrutiny. He was glad she wasn't facing them. Tobias leaned in to whisper to Tybalt, though, and he clenched his jaw.

~~~

Ariette felt the prince tense and tried to follow his gaze. He swept her into an elaborate spin, though, and she lost sight of her surroundings for a moment. The crowd was watching them, waiting for the cue to join in. Many were still dabbing at their eyes, moved by his speech. Ariette was confused, though. The last she knew, Sorin and General Dalca hated each other. What had happened while they were away?

The song ended and Sorin bowed while she curtsied. People joined in finally and Ariette made to return to the queen. Before she could, someone took her hand and pulled her into their arms. She looked up and frowned.

"The polite thing to do is ask a lady to dance," she said, trying to get away from Ivan Tanner.

He held her tight. There was a gleam in his eyes she didn't like. She tried to find one of the royals, but she was blocked by the crowd of dancers.

"I've missed you," he said. "I couldn't risk someone else taking you from me."

"Last I saw, you weren't on the list," she said. When she couldn't find an escape, she resorted to dancing stiffly with him. "How did you get in?"

"It's good to see you, too. I've heard you're rather close to the royal family."

"What does that have to do with anything?" she asked. She tried
~~~

to scream in her mind then remembered the hook pendant under her chest. *Damn.* "I'd really like it if you'd let me go."

"Well, that's rude. Don't you need manners to be a lady-in-waiting?"

She glared. "Why can't you just take no for an answer?" she snapped, abandoning pretense. "I have no intention of ever marrying you."

"Perhaps," he conceded. "But it's not your choice to make, is it? The answer is to come from your father. Oh wait," he said, laughing nastily. "He's dead."

An anger Ariette hadn't felt in a long time surged in her chest. She raised her hand to slap him, but a hand stopped her. It was the king. The queen and prince were close behind, her mother coming from the side with General Vasile. The look on King Laurent's face was furious and Ivan gulped audibly.

"You weren't invited," Laurent said, gently pushing Ariette to her mother. The others stood between them. "Normally, I would overlook this. We are all grieving for our friends and family. However, I will not tolerate harassment, especially towards my wife's Lady."

Ivan found his voice. "I meant no disrespect," he stammered. "I just wanted to ask Elizabeth for Ariette's hand, that's all!"

"So this is the tanner's son," Stela said. Her voice was uncharacteristically cold. "The one you told me about, Ariette."

Ivan paled.

"Leave," Laurent said. "You are hereby banned from these grounds. I'll be speaking with your father about his future business with us."

"And Ariette speaks for herself," Elizabeth snapped.

"But-."

Sorin stepped closer to Ivan, easily towering over him.

"I'll be more than happy to show you the way out," he said.

Ivan gulped again. "Fine," he said and glared at Ariette. "You're a fool for saying no. It's not as if any other man will want you. Maybe it's best your father isn't here to see the disappointment you've become."

"Guards!" Laurent shouted as Ariette saw red. "Get him out of here."

Before they moved in, Ariette lunged for Ivan. Sorin caught her around the waist and Ivan looked scared for a brief moment before following the guards out. When he was gone, Ariette stopped struggling. People had stopped to stare, even the musicians. With a pointed look from the king, though, they started up again.

"Are you all right?" Stela asked anxiously.

Ariette just pushed Sorin's arm off of her and stormed out to the balcony, hot tears threatening to pierce through her eyes.

~~~

"I'll talk to her," Elizabeth said.

"But the uniforms," Vasile said but stopped at the look on her face.

"Let me," Laurent offered.

"Your highness, Duke Ingvar is here," a servant said. "He wishes to speak with you and the queen."

"Gods bless it," Laurent groaned quietly. "I'm sure I can guess why."

"I'll go," Sorin said. "Anything to avoid the duke."

They nodded and he slipped between the dancers. Ariette was one of several people who were seeking fresh air. Autumn was swiftly approaching. In the distance, he could see the bones of the battlements. He tried to rehearse what he'd say as he stood beside her. She didn't react to his presence and, to his discomfort, he heard her sniffle. He put his hands behind his back, fiddling with his fingers as he tried to think of something to say.

"He's wrong," he said finally. "Robert would be proud of you." He felt her start to tremble and put an awkward hand on her shoulder. "You've come a long way since the day you yelled at my father."

"I said sorry," she said, her voice threatening to break into sobs.

"That's not what I mean. Ever since Dalca.... Well, I've learned a thing or two about grief and resentment. I know now the seed it plants in one's heart, the darkness that spreads from it. To overcome it in just six months is admirable. I doubt my anger will be so easily tamed."

"That's different," she said, trying to wipe her tears away surreptitiously. "Your anger is toward our enemy; it's justified. Mine was not."
~~~

Sorin fished in his breast pocket and passed her a kerchief. She mumbled her thanks.

"Yes, I loathe the man who killed Dalca and those who took the lives of my soldiers. But it's more than that. Not long ago, you offered to help, but this rage is not one you know. This anger.... It's also towards myself."

Ariette looked at him in surprise. He hesitated, but also turned to her. Tears were still falling, and he took the kerchief, wiping them away.

"But why?" she asked.

She had taken the kerchief back, obviously uncomfortable with his kindness.

"A story for another time," he said and looked back over Imperium. "My point is, don't listen to that coward. Your father would not be disappointed, and I'm sure even a minx like you will find love."

That got a small giggle from her.

"Thank you," she said. "And, for what it's worth, I'm not the only one who has matured. You're not as arrogant as you used to be."

"Was that a compliment?" he asked, dramatically putting a hand over his heart.

She laughed. "Don't get used to it."

He smiled. "Well, I appreciate it. Death has a way of opening a man's eyes."

"I'll wash this then return it," she said, folding the kerchief and tucking it carefully into her sash.

"Keep it," he said. "Do you feel better?"

"Yes," she said.

They smiled at each other again. He was about to ask her to dance when a shout came from the ballroom. He grimaced.

"I knew it!"

Sorin cursed under his breath as the duke stormed over, Sorin's parents hot on his heels. Ariette watched in surprise.

"I knew I picked up on your scent," Ingvar snapped. "You can't keep avoiding me, Prince!"

"Scent?" Ariette repeated and took a step back at the glare he shot at her.

"Who the hell is this?"

"Come on," Sorin said, grabbing Ariette's hand. "We need to discuss the burials."

"But-."

He gripped her hand harder and she seemed to understand.

"Oi!" Ingvar called but Sorin ignored him.

His heart hammered in his throat the rest of the night. Ariette had been approached by Liam and a boy who looked a few years younger. He left them to catch up, dodging every once in a while, to stay out of Ingvar's line of sight. Finally, the night came to an end and he rushed to his chamber, feigning illness to get away from the duke.

"Your highness," a voice said as he halted outside of his room.

"Ah, Orin," he said. The castle's blacksmith was holding a box. "Are those the daggers?"

"Yes, sir. Crafted to your specifications." He opened the box and Sorin looked them over. "Would you like me to deliver these to Lady Ariette?"

"I'll place them in her room," he said. "Thank you."

Orin bowed and Sorin opened Ariette's room. He wasn't sure what he expected, but he was surprised at how clean and orderly her room was. He had instructed all the servants to leave the royal family's rooms alone, the cleaning done only by two select servants. As far as he knew, no one had been assigned to her and Elizabeth's room yet. He put the box on her bed and was about to leave when a picture frame caught his eyes.

It was a painting of the three of them. Robert stood beside his beaming wife, a large grin on his face. Ariette sat in front of her parents, back straight and smiling. The name of the artist and a date was scribbled in tiny script in the bottom corner of the page. He squinted at it.

"He had it commissioned before he left." Sorin yelped a bit and turned. Elizabeth stood in the doorway, smiling sadly. She held a box, too. "It was his gift to us. We each have one."

"I wasn't trying to snoop," he said. "Her daggers were finished, and I was just delivering them."

"It's okay," Elizabeth said. She put her box beside his, opening them to look. "Whether the two of you want to acknowledge it or not, you're friends now. It's normal to be curious about her past."

"Friends might be pushing it slightly," he said. "What's in the box?"

"It's Robert's birthday tomorrow," she said quietly. His heart dropped. "To celebrate it, we get each other gifts; something he would have bought us."

"That's a wonderful way to celebrate," he said. "I'm very sorry. I'll speak with Father; perhaps we can have a special meal in his honor."

Elizabeth dabbed at her eyes. "Thank you. We would appreciate it very much."

He made to leave then hesitated again. "Elizabeth, may I ask you something?"

"Of course, your highness."

He opened his mouth but heard Ariette saying good night to his mother in the next room.

"Never mind," he said. "It sounds like she's finishing up. I'll see you in the morning."

"Thank you for calming her down," she said as they bowed and curtsied. "Good night, Prince Sorin."

XIV

The Mist

Ariette closed the door quietly and found her mother waiting. There were two boxes on her bed, one tied as a gift and one in a smooth, polished box. She hurried to her vanity and got her gift out of her drawer. Normally, the gift exchange wouldn't happen until the next evening, but both of them were too busy.

"Happy birthday, Papa," she said and passed the gift to her mother.

"I miss him, too," Elizabeth said.

Ariette opened her gift and let out a watery laugh. Nestled in silk lining was a pink rabbit, complete with a crooked ear. It looked exactly like the one she had loved to death as a little girl. Elizabeth laughed, too. While Ariette was passing around invitations, she told the queen about their tradition. They visited a jewelry stand where she found a gorgeous golden ring that resembled her mother's first wedding ring. At first, she couldn't afford it, but the queen insisted, telling her to consider it her first pay stipend.

"Thank you," they said in unison, hugging each other tightly.

She put the rabbit up against her second pillow with a fond smile.

"Is this from you, too?" she asked as she took the second box.

"No, the prince delivered it just a few moments ago."

She opened it and whistled quietly. Two daggers were placed in grooves of velvet. A scrap of parchment explained that one was for her calf and the other her upper arm. Holsters were under the daggers. The handle was made of marble and the blade double-edged.

"They're beautiful," she said. "I never thought I'd say that about a dagger."

Her mother laughed. "I said the same thing. I'm going to go to bed. I love you."

Ariette hugged her tightly. "I love you, too."

~~~

Shouts of battle filled Sorin's ears. He had lost his helmet long ago, his cuirass discarded long ago so he could run faster. They were trying to retreat, but their enemy was relentless. Just before they reached cover, the monstrous weapon launched a boulder ahead of them, making them skid to a halt. He yelled in frustration and turned to fight. The two armies clashed, and he quickly found himself on the ground, gasping for air. Pain flared throughout his body as a silvered sword slashed at his torso. Suddenly, a body barreled into his attacker. Dalca did his best to fight them off, shouting for someone to get Sorin to safety. Sorin screamed as a sword was thrust through Dalca's throat. He tried to get to the general, but he was being dragged away.

"Sorin!"

A sharp slap on his cheek woke him. He sat up, safe in his bed. Sweat dripped from his body and he felt tears on his face. Peter stood beside him; his eyes concerned.

"Sorry," Peter said. "I've been trying to wake you for nearly five minutes. Was it the battle again?"

"Yes," he said, voice hoarse. He heard voices outside his room. His mind was still cloudy from the nightmare, making it hard to hear. "Did I wake everyone?"

"Not exactly. Ariette is missing."
~~~

"What?"

"Queen Stela had noticed Ariette was missing from her room. No one can sense her, even though the necklace she's wearing only masks her thoughts."

"Meaning she's not in the palace," Sorin finished with a sigh.

He got out of bed, struggling into a pair of loose trousers. His parents were in the hallway, talking to the servants.

"No one's seen her," his mother said anxiously. "Elizabeth said she's probably walking in her sleep. She took a few guards into Imperium to find her."

"I'll check the grounds," he said.

"Let me know as soon as you found her," his father said.

Sorin nodded and ran outside. She wasn't in front of the palace. He hooked around to the side, remembering her infatuation with the Moonglow grove. The grounds were lit by a full moon, meaning she wouldn't be too afraid, even if she were awake. He didn't know anything about sleepwalking, but it was the first place he thought of. He was at the trees when the sea air carried a scent that could be only one thing. He changed direction immediately.

The gardens were lit by the moon and the occasional firefly, making navigating it easy. He dashed through the plants and trees, following the scent to the other side of the trees. He cursed under his breath.

Ariette stood at the cliff, facing the sea.

"Ariette?" he called over the sound of the crashing waves. "What are you doing out here?"

She didn't respond. He approached her carefully. Blood on the ground led to a wound on her leg. The closer he got to her, the more he realized how close she was to the edge. He grabbed her arm, pulling gently.

"Step back," he said. "You'll fall if you're not careful." She didn't answer. "Why aren't you-?"

He was able to turn her finally. Her eyes were glassy and out of focus. She had one hand gripping the jade necklace, her other arm extended as if reaching for something. He looked behind her, but all he saw was the mist in the distance.

"Ariette," he tried again. "You're hurt. We need to get you inside. Can you walk?"

Still no reply.

I found her. She's behind the gardens but something's wrong.

We're coming.

"Let's go," he said. He pulled again but she didn't budge. "Damn it, Ariette. Snap out of it!" He shook her slightly. "Forgive me," he said and slapped her.

That did the trick. Her eyes blinked rapidly, pupils expanding. Her breath came in hitches as she looked around. When she saw his hands on her arms, she screamed. She tried to fight, stepping dangerously back towards the cliff's edge.

"Stop!" he yelled over her screams. "Stop fighting me! You're about to-!" She slapped him and he ground his teeth. "For gods' sake, stop you minx!"

Somehow, that got through to her. She stopped fighting him, her chest heaving. He moved the hair out of her face, trying to get a good look at her eyes.

"Prince Sorin?" she whispered. "Where am I?"

"Behind the gardens," he said, relieved. "Your mother said you were probably sleepwalking. Are you all right?"

She gulped. "I-I think so. But how did you find me?"

"You're bleeding," he said.

She looked at her leg then yelped, gathering her hair in bundles, and clutched it to her chest. Her cheeks were red. He couldn't blame her; he was mildly embarrassed, too.

"Can you walk?" he asked again.

"I'm not sure."

She took a few cautious steps but tripped. He caught her, making a mental note to have Misha make night gowns that were a little more modest.

"I'm sorry," she said as he helped her walk. "I haven't done that since my father died."

"Don't be sorry. I'm just glad I found you before you fell. What causes sleepwalking?"

"Nightmares," she muttered. "I must have been dreaming about him." They were in the gardens now and Elizabeth and his parents were running to them. "I guess we're even now."

"Not quite," he said.

"Ari!" her mother cried. Sorin let her go so that Elizabeth could embrace her. "Are you all right!?"

"Yes," she said. "Sorin saved me. I hurt my leg, though."

"Let's get you inside," his mother said, her voice shaking slightly.

"She almost fell off the cliff," Sorin told his father once they were alone. "She said it's caused by nightmares. It was strange, though. She was reaching for the mist."

Laurent frowned. "Really? That's odd. Are you all right? Your nightmare sounded awful."

Sorin just shrugged. "It's the same one as always." He paused in the foyer, trying to avoid looking at the red stains not covered by the rug. Ariette was being half carried up the stairs, her foot now covered in blood. "I guess we both have our demons."

~~~

"The mist?" Ariette asked the next morning at breakfast.

"Yes," the king said. "You were reaching for it. Do you remember what you dreamt?"

"No," she said as a frown creased her forehead. "It's strange. In the past, I would only go to familiar places."

"Is that why you went to the city?" the queen asked Elizabeth.

"Yes. But I agree with Ariette; why would she go there?"

"I'll keep some guards posted out of your doors for a few more nights," the king said. She tried to object, but he shook his head. "I don't want to risk anything."
~~~

"Very well," she said with a sigh.

The dining hall door opened, and a man walked in. He wore very peculiar clothing that made Ariette tilt her head. He wore what looked like a kilt made of the hide of a wolf. His calves were also wrapped in the hide. He didn't wear anything to cover his torso. He carried himself with a pompous air, not bothering to bow. He was holding a scroll.

"Your highnesses," he said, his tone clipped. He thrust the letter to King Laurent. "From Lord Ingvar."

The king's eye twitched. "For the hundredth time, he is a duke, not a lord. I assume you're here to ensure a reply?"

"My lord has asked me to tell you his patience is at its end. If I do not return by morning, he'll follow through with his plan."

Laurent sighed. "You might as well sit and eat. I've no doubt you ran here."

The messenger sat beside Ariette. He smelled strongly of musk and pine. It was very unpleasant.

"You should remember that my lord has a great influence with the nomads."

"If you call him lord one more time," Sorin began.

The king cleared his throat pointedly, not looking up from the letter. A scowl quickly replaced his neutral face. He gestured to the guard by the door.

"Assemble the council," he said. "And set up our guest in a room so he may rest. Come with me," he said to the rest of them. "Elizabeth, I believe Misha was looking for you."

"Yes, your highness," she said.

Ariette had a strange sense of foreboding as they climbed the stairs. They stopped by her room, the king telling her to get her sash. He then led them up a spiral staircase to the western tower. The council members were already there, scowling at Ariette as the king helped her to her seat.

"Are you sure you should be out of bed?" Tybalt sneered, glaring at David when he greeted her enthusiastically. "I'd hate for your delicate frame to hurt."

"I appreciate your concern," she said coolly. "But I am a member of the council; I would be remiss in my duties if I wasn't here."

"Keep believing your fantasy," Tobias said.

"That's enough," the king interrupted. "We're here to address an ultimatum." He put the letter on the circular, wooden table. "Duke Ingvar from Vin's province has said that, if Sorin does not marry his daughter, he will no longer mediate."

Angry words filled the room as Sorin glared at the scroll.

"Who is he to make such demands?" Tybalt spat.

"The brother of the nomad's chief," David said.

"We can't let that harlot onto the throne."

Ariette inhaled sharply.

"That's crass, even for you, Sir Tobias."

"Silence, girl," he hissed. "You have no right to give input on things you don't understand."

She made to stand but Sorin stopped her.

"Vin's nobility is, sadly, important to us," the king explained to her. "They have great influence with the nomadic wolf tribe."

She did a doubletake. "Wait. Wolf? As in werewolves?"

"Yes."

Her jaw dropped. "They're real?"

Sorin rolled his eyes. "You're in a room full of vampires and werewolves seem farfetched?"

"I didn't say that," she said with a glare. "And don't be so condescending; I get that enough from them. It's not my fault you kept me in the dark."

"It was for your safety," he argued. "By the gods, I was wrong. You're still as-."

"Enough," Laurent said again. "Lady Ariette, I understand your frustrations. I will personally explain everything later. For now, all you need to know is Duchess Sigrid has tried, on multiple times, to worm her way onto the throne through malicious means. Her latest attempt has led to her temporary restriction from the palace."

"What did she do?"

"She tried to use a spell that would seduce me," Sorin said, his face twisted with disgust.

"Oh." She looked at the letter. "And this nomadic tribe; we need them for the war?"

"Obviously," Carlisle said. "It wouldn't be an effective threat if we didn't."

She glared at him but didn't rise to the bait.

"So you can't afford to say no, but to say yes means putting people at risk," she said. "Is there no third option?"

"Like what?" Tybalt asked. "Do you have a better idea, girl?"

"Stop calling me that," she snapped, her voice rising. "At least I'm trying instead of moping in my seat! I've not heard one suggestion from any of you!"

Sorin got to his feet, eyes wide with realization.

"We have until tonight to give our answer," he said, his voice breathless. "I have an idea, but I need to check something first."

He left without any warning. No one spoke for a while. The queen's back suddenly straightened, and she whispered a word of surprise.

"We'll go into remission," the king said, also looking distracted. "Return in two hours."

The men left. When the door closed, Ariette slammed her fist on the table, regretting it immediately. She rubbed it as the pain vibrated up to her wrist.

"They're insufferable!" she yelled.

"Sorin wants to see you," King Laurent said. "He's in the ground floor library."

"Me? Why?"

"I'll let him explain; you should go."

"You'll be all right?" she asked the queen.

"Yes, of course."

Ariette curtsied and left the tower, still fuming. Who did those council members think they were? She may be a woman, but she was just as capable as the rest of them!

The door was partially closed, and she walked in. Sorin was looking up at the portrait of her father, a book in his hands.

"Close the door," he said. "I don't want to be overheard."

"Okay," she said slowly. She stood beside him. "Are you all right?"

He didn't answer right away.

"Tell me something," he said. "What do you think the duties of a royal are?"

She thought about all she had seen the queen do.

"Many things," she said finally. "Keeping people happy, enforcing laws, signing treaties, that sort of thing."

"And what about our duties to ourselves?"

"I don't know. I believe you all deserve to be happy, at the very least."

"Dalca told me this might happen," he said. "He warned me that many wars have ended by marriage. With that in mind, do you still believe that?"

"Yes, but I'm not royalty. I have no way to relate."

"I refuse to marry Sigrid," he said firmly. "Her attempts to ensnare me only strengthen my resolve."

"So what can you do? Surely you're not thinking of running."

"Of course not," he said with a frown. "I'm talking about marrying you."

Ariette stared at Sorin. He had stopped looking at the portrait and was now facing her. His face was completely serious.

"You're out of your mind," she said, shaking her head and starting to walk away.

"Just hear me out," he said. "Let me explain. If you still think it's a bad idea, then I'll drop it."

She sighed. "Fine."

He put the book on a lectern and opened it.

"This is a book of Rosu's laws," he explained. "I've looked through it and nowhere does it say I must marry a noble. Not only will this keep Sigrid away from the throne, it will also help you."

"How?"

"The council," he said. "They'll have no choice but to respect you."

Ariette tagged at her sash. "Vin is our ally, right?"

"Yes."

"I don't understand. Why would he make this demand now?"

"Like my father said, he has great influence with his brother, the chief of the nomads."

She ran a hand through her hair. "I understand," she said. "But this is a big risk. I'm sorry, Prince, but I don't love you."

"Nor I you," he said honestly. "We don't actually have to wed. It will be a façade. We'll invite them here to meet you, see that we're engaged. Once the treaty is signed, we'll go back to normal."

"And if they further demand we marry?" she asked. "We can't just end the marriage. For all we know, this could drag on until I die. What's to stop Ingvar from waiting that long?"

"I haven't thought that far," he admitted, and she scoffed. "Look, I'll have my father use his influence to push for the treaty signing."

Ariette still wasn't sure.

"Why is this tribe so important?"

"Wolves are strong and fast. They will turn the tide for us. Unlike vampires, they are impervious to silver. Just as people like Peter have a higher constitution, they can take more hits than we can. Once Ingvar is satisfied, we can get in touch with his brother."

"And if he isn't satisfied?"

"Wolves are honor bound. He cannot refuse."

Ariette wrung her hands. Sorin watched her patiently. She had heard of political marriages, of course, but never thought she would be part of one. It didn't appeal to her at all. However, she had long since passed the age of marriage. If what Sorin said was true, then no one else would have to die. A centuries year old war would come to an end. All she had to do was pretend. It couldn't be that hard, could it?

"Okay," she said finally.

Relief washed over Sorin's face and, to her shock, he embraced her.

"Thank you. I will repay you; I swear it."

"First we need to convince the council," she said, patting him on the back.

XV

Getting To Know You

They returned to the council room an hour later. They had spent the hour with Sorin's parents and Elizabeth. All of them were as anxious about it as Ariette. By the end of it, though, they agreed it was their best option.

"So," Tobias said once everyone was seated. "Did you get the answer you needed?"

"Yes," Sorin said. "We'll send the messenger back with an invitation for the duke and his daughter to join us. They'll want to meet my fiancé."

All members but David were confused. The latter was slowly starting to grin.

"And who is this woman?" Carlisle asked. "I don't recall meeting a princess or duchess you actually cared for."

"That's because she isn't a princess," he said and reached over to hold Ariette's hand. Their eyes all grew wide. "Not yet at least."

Tobias was red with rage.

"This peasant!? She is who you have chosen!?"

"Absolutely not!" Tybalt and Carlisle shouted.

"This isn't up for you to decide," King Laurent said. "Nowhere in our bylaws does it say Sorin must marry a princess or duchess. Would you rather Sigrid be your future queen?"

"She lacks the training, the proper etiquette! Look at her! She knows nothing!"

Ariette got to her feet. Her body was shaking, but she locked her eyes on Tobias.

"As you've constantly reminded me, you are advisors to the king. However, that doesn't give you the right to dictate every decision he and the prince make. We have all discussed it and believe it to be the best option."

"Silence!" he shouted, his face apoplectic with rage. His fangs had grown, scaring her. She refused to back down and show her fear, though. "I am done trying to remind you of your place!"

"Just admit it! You're objecting it because then you'll have to accept me!"

"I will never accept you as one of us!" Tobias shouted, taking a menacing step towards her.

Sorin blocked him. His irises had gone red and Tobias seemed to shrink.

"We're betrothed," he said in a cold voice. "This is not a choice you have any say in. I would strongly suggest you treat her with more respect. To speak so horribly to her means disrespecting me and my parents. Now, if you'll excuse us, we have a messenger to speak with."

David joined them as the others glared. Once in the hall, Ariette let out a long breath. She took her sash off and followed everyone to the foyer. A servant went to get the messenger. Ariette chewed on the inside of her cheek nervously.

"So, you've finally seen reason?" the man asked once he was in front of them.

"Yes," the king said.

"Wonderful. I'll let my lord know to prepare for Sigrid's marriage to the prince."

"Sorin will not be marrying Lady Sigrid," the king said. The man's eyes widened. "He has chosen his bride. I extend an invitation for him to join us for the engagement celebration."

"I see," he said, his eyes narrowing. "I'll deliver the message now." He paused at the doors. "Expect them in two weeks. Both my lord and his daughter."

King Laurent nodded. "I'll have the necessary arrangements made."

Once the doors closed, Sorin shouted, "He's not a lord!"

"What's the difference?" Ariette asked.

"The only person worthy of the title 'lord' is a king. Dukes are just nobility, hardly more important than a commoner. To call him a lord is an insult to my father."

"Now's not the time for this," the king said. "We only have two weeks to prepare. First, we must begin preparations for the engagement ball."

"I'll meet her highness in the study."

"No, Ariette," he shook his head. He pointed to the two of them. "You have to be able to convince them of your love for each other."

"What?" she asked, her cheeks hot. "Can't we just say it's political?"

"No. It won't be enough to explain away Sorin's rejection. You both have to be comfortable enough around each other. No arguing, no avoiding. Wolves can pick up on lies, even if they can't read minds."

"But then who will be helping the queen?"

"Don't worry about me," Stela said. "Laurent is right. This is more important. Now go and spend time together."

Ariette wanted to argue further, but Sorin took her arm. They went through the door to the gardens and walked among the flowers.

"I don't even know where to begin," she said with a sigh as they entered the hedge maze. "How are we supposed to convince him? It's no secret among anyone of our feelings for each other. What if someone talks?"

"We'll worry about that later," he said. He was frowning at the ground as they turned a corner. "For now, we need to know everything about each other. We also have to be able to be... outwardly affection-ate."

"Care to elaborate?" she asked, her voice cracking as color creeped up her neck.

Even Sorin's cheeks had turned pink.

"Do you really need me to?"

"I guess not. It's just.... I've never...."

She groaned in embarrassment.

They stopped at a fountain in the center of the maze. Several stone benches surrounded it. It made sense now why they came here. There probably wasn't anywhere more private. He sat, indicating the space beside him was for her.

"Never?" he asked, watching the water fall serenely from the tips of the stone. "I thought you and the farmer, Liam, had history."

"Not that kind. We grew up together. He was my father's apprentice. The only man to approach me was Ivan. You saw how that worked out."

"Hmm."

Ariette also looked at the fountain. This hadn't been part of the plan. It was supposed to be purely political, a fact known by everyone. Pretending to be in love was one thing, but being affectionate?

Suddenly, Sorin took her hand. She twitched her arm but relaxed.

"Just trying to get used to it," he said. He still wasn't looking at her. "Wolves have a different standard than ours. They don't have weddings as we know them. From the start of their relationship with their mate, affection of all kinds is displayed without shame." He coughed awkwardly. "Tell me about your past."

She sighed. "It's not that exciting. I was born in the midway through the winter. My father was just a farmer at the time, but quickly worked his way up. I learned all the usual tasks for women: cooking, sewing, dressing wounds, and such. It was meant to prepare myself for my husband. But then Father taught me to read."

He finally looked at her. "You say that as if it's a bad thing."

"It is. At least, in the city it is. Among my peers, a woman's only job is to care for her husband and rear his children."

"That's ridiculous."

"I couldn't agree more." She sighed, looking at their hands. It looked stiff so, heart beating faster, she laced their fingers. He hesitated as she did but closed his fingers around hers. "Ivan started trying to court me about a year before Father left. He mostly did it in secret, though my father knew about it. He wanted to wait, though, until Ivan approached him. I think Ivan purposely waited until Father went to war to be more aggressive about it. I'm not sure why he came to the palace. Last I heard, he had turned to Nicole."

"He craved power," Sorin said. "He heard about you saving me and correctly guessed it gained you more favor. He thought he could become nobility by marrying you."

"How do you know?" she asked, and he arched a brow. "Oh. Right. I forgot." She tried to get more comfortable on the bench. "Your turn."

"Well, I was born...." He groaned suddenly, covering his eyes. "This is awkward."

"What's wrong?"

"I'm older than you. Several years older."

She rolled her eyes. "I know. Peter told me you're about thirty-one. That's only six years. No need to be so uncomfortable."

"I guess you're right. My sister and I were set to be turned when we became twenty-one. As you know, she didn't survive."

Something in his voice made her look at him.

"You feel responsible?"

"How could I not? I went first to convince her it would be okay. It resulted in her death."

"It's not your fault."

He just shrugged. "Mother didn't want me to go to battle because they couldn't conceive another child. Our birth was... violent. Lucian believes it resulted in damaging her. That's the other reason people want me to marry as soon as possible. If I don't produce an heir, centuries of the first vampire's bloodline dies."

"That's a huge responsibility."

"No kidding. Anyway, the best I can do right now is prepare."

"If Charlotte died ten years ago, why was her funeral eight years after?"

"We hoped Mother would be able to pose as Lottie. That's how it has been in the past: when a king or queen had to step down, they faked their death and took on the persona of their child. To cover the mystery of why the child was only revealed now, they were said to be at war if they were a man, and constantly in lessons if they were a woman. That hope was diminished when they found out they couldn't have another child."

"I see."

"I thought being a war hero would compensate my lack of a wife. Obviously, I failed on both accounts."

"You're being too hard on yourself," she said. "Enough of that, what do you do for fun?"

They spent the rest of the day learning about each other. It was a lot of information but talking was at least easier. At dinner, Ariette plopped into her seat between the queen and her mother. She put her head on her mother's shoulder.

"So much," she said. "I don't know how I'll remember it."

"You and me both," Sorin said with a sigh.

"Tomorrow, you need to teach her etiquette," the king said. "Stela needs to interview the servants, find a lady-in-waiting and a personal servant for Ariette."

Sorin just nodded, looking as tired as Ariette felt. The next day, she met Sorin in the dining hall after breakfast. The table was set.

"So, I know you already know how to eat when nobility is around," he said. "But this is different. When we're hosting for the wolves, we won't have greens as often. So no salads." He took away the salad fork. "There will be a lot of meat, so be ready for that. They prefer their meat as rare as possible." He also took away the desert fork. "The only other thing we'll have that they're used to is soup. Very meaty soup, but soup nonetheless. When you introduce yourself, do not curtsy. It's an insult to them."

"Why?"

"Wolves pride themselves on not conforming to the ways of others. We took on the concept of bowing and curtsying as a way to blend in with humans. They will greet us with the salute of their pack. We'll simply nod to them. Now, if we were part of their pack or another one, we'd return with a salute of our own. This is the part you'll probably struggle with: Women are meant to be seen, not heard."

"So pretty much what the council members think," she said and kicked at a chair a little.

"Yes. I know it's a pain, but we need you to watch your tongue. Don't argue with him, don't speak out of turn. It's a deep insult to them."

She puffed her cheeks out. "Fine. What else?"

"They don't dance much. Even if they did, you and I are both off limits."

"Why?"

He took her to the library again. He found a book and showed it to her. She squeaked as her face turned red.

"Sorry, I know it's graphic, but it's the only book we have," he said. The page had a drawing of two humans in a naked embrace under a full moon. The picture slowly transitioned into them being wolves on the ground together. "Wolves mate for life. They're assigned a mate by their goddess, who they call the Moon Mother. Even though we don't have anything like that, it's the same as everything else: they have to respect that you and I are in love. They'll hate it, but they don't have a choice; it's in their nature."

She flipped the page to get it off the graphic picture.

"How are we supposed to pretend to love each other?" she asked. "I'm not a good actress."

"Well, I have good news and bad news," he said. "The good news, is they don't see love the same way we do." He turned back to the image and she averted her eyes. "This is the way they see love. Emotions are rarely tied to it at the beginning. The bad news is-."

"That's how we're going to convince them," she finished, and he nodded. "Oh boy."

"I'm not going to force you to do anything you're uncomfortable with," he said, putting a hand on her back. "It won't be for long."

"All right," she said. "What do we do now?"

He shrugged. "Spend time together. Tomorrow, I'm going to check on the battlements if you wish to join me."

"Can we visit Nicole? I'd like to tell her personally."

"Yes."

***

They left the palace close to midday. While they walked, they bounced between holding hands and lacing arms.

"Holding hands is more comfortable," she admitted. "But it's not the way things are done."

"We have to be at ease with each other," he said. "If holding hands is how we need to do it, then that's what we'll do."

People called out to her then hesitated when they saw her holding hands with the prince. She was embarrassed but did her best to look as if it were a common thing. He asked where Nicole lived, and she took him there. She knocked on the door. It took a few seconds until Nicole's mother, Pamela, opened the door. She beamed when she saw Ariette and pulled her into a tight hug.

"It's so good to see you, Ari!" she said. She held her at arm's length. "You look lovely. Are you here to see Nicole?"

"If she's free. I need to introduce her to someone."

Ariette stepped to the side and Pamela gasped.

"I'm so sorry, your highness!" she said, dipping into a curtsy. "I didn't see you there!"

"Worry not," he said.

"Nicky is in her room. I'll go get her. You can wait here."

She ushered them into the waiting area. The home was smaller than the one Ariette shared with her mother before they went to the palace. It was comfortable, though. Even Sorin was nodding in approval as he looked around. Ariette heard a squeal then her best friend hugged her. Ariette hugged her just as tightly, glad to see her again.

"Oh!" she said when she saw Sorin. She curtsied, too. "Your highness, welcome."

"Are you thirsty?" Pamela asked. "I'll make us some tea."

"That's not necessary," Ariette began but Pamela had already disappeared into the kitchen.

"What brings you here?" Nicole asked, pulling Ariette to the couch as Sorin sat on the armchair stiffly. "Shouldn't you be with the queen?"

Ariette looked to Sorin who nodded.

"Erm... Prince Sorin and I are engaged," she said quietly. Nicole's jaw dropped. "It's a secret right now, so please don't tell anyone, even your mother. There will be an engagement ball in two weeks, though, and that's when it will be public. I just wanted you to know now and not through an invitation."

Nicole gawked between her and Sorin.

"But you hate him."

Both of them laughed a little.

"Not anymore," she said honestly. "I...."

"Go ahead and tell her the truth," Sorin said. "She deserves it."

Ariette studied him for a second. He was looking at Nicole intently and understood what he was doing. With a deep breath, Ariette told Nicole everything, excluding a few key details. By the end of it, they all had teacups, Pamela excusing herself. Nicole gulped hers down.

"So, let me get this straight," she said. "You two are engaged, but not really, and some important dignitaries are coming. But the only reason you're 'engaged' is because one of the dignitaries is a cow and you don't want to marry her?"

"A good summary of it, yes," Sorin said. "It is of the utmost importance you keep this to yourself, Miss Nicole. If this gets out, Ariette's life is on the line."

Nicole's eyes grew wide. "It's that serious?"

"Yes."

He held her gaze until she finally looked at Ariette again.

"Do I get to be your maid of honor?"

Ariette let out a relieved laugh and hugged her tightly.

"Thank you," she whispered, and Nicole squeezed her.

"Are you going to tell Liam?"

"I'll tell him we're engaged, but I won't tell him everything I told you," she said. "Not because I don't trust him, far from it. But he's likely to beat Sorin to a pulp if I do."

Nicole giggled as Sorin shifted in his seat.

"Yes, I can see him doing that."

"We should go," Sorin said after checking the time. "Thank your mother for her hospitality."

"I'll see you soon," Ariette said to Nicole.

Nicole saw them out and Ariette looked to Sorin.

"Why did you let me tell her the truth?"

"She was devastated," he said as they walked. "She felt betrayed and it hurt her to know you had kept it from her."

"Oh," she said, shoulders dropping. "Well, hopefully she feels better now."

"She does."

They walked in silence the rest of the way. At the edge of the main street, the stones ended, and dirt began. Men were gathered around, going over a piece of parchment. The battlements were tall, already nearing twenty-feet high. Wood and stone were integrated into a wall that went as far as Ariette could see.

"Your highness," a man said, bowing.

"Hello, Mikael," Sorin said. "I see you've made great progress."

"We had to send the commoners back home," he said. "They couldn't keep up without us giving away some... information."

"She knows, you can speak openly."

Mikael saw their clasped hands and looked at the prince in surprise. Sorin didn't address it, though.

"Er... right." Mikael cleared his throat. "Anyway, they should be finished in a fortnight."

"Just in time," Sorin said. "We'll be having visitors. The duke and duchess from Vin's province."

Mikael wrinkled his nose. "That wretch again?"

Ariette frowned. "You know her, too?"

"Mikael is the head of construction," Sorin explained. "He was there during one of Sigrid's more aggressive attempts."

"Tried to scale the walls," Mikael said. "Little did she know, we were prepared for that. I had them slicked with oil."

"Well, I'll be back later," Sorin said. "Keep up the good work."

They bowed.

"Why has Sigrid been allowed to get away with all that she's done?" Ariette asked as they headed to the farms.

"Because of her uncle. As soon as that's taken care of, she won't be setting foot into this city or palace again."

Liam was among the corn, holding a clipboard with the harvest schedule.

"Working hard?" Ariette asked.

Liam grinned and scooped her into a hug. "What're you doin' out here? Ah, 'ello your highness."

"Good afternoon," Sorin said politely. "Is there a place we can speak in private?"

"Aye," he said and finished giving directions to the farmhand before leading them to the silo. The doors were opened, and he told the men in there to take a break, closing the doors. "We're cleanin' it out, gettin' ready for this year's harvest. How can I help ya?"

Sorin gestured with his head to Ariette.

"Sorin and I are engaged," she said in a rush.

Liam blinked, arms slowly uncrossing from his chest.

"Come again?"

His voice was low and Ariette took a deep breath. She had expected this.

"We're going to be married," she said again. "We.... We love each other."

Liam looked between the two of them and balled his hands into fists.

"Is he forcin' ya to do this?"

"Of course not!" she said. "No, it's nothing like that, Liam!"

"I know ya hate the man. Now ya expect me to believe ya've fallen in love in the last two months?"

Ariette looked to Sorin for help. He sighed heavily and eyed Liam, wondering if he could risk the information he was about to give.

"I'll be honest with you, Liam," he said, and the farmer glared daggers at him. It was enough to intimidate Sorin, painfully aware that the man's biceps were the size of his head. "This marriage is political. We're telling people we're in love, though, to ease the news. In fact, it may come to pass that we won't have to marry."

"I don't understand," he said. "Why do ya have to do this, Ari?"

Sorin tried to read Liam's mind, but it was hard to keep up with all of his thoughts.

"Are you in love with her?" Sorin asked and Liam's jaw dropped.

"No, 'course not," he said. "No offense," he added to Ariette. "But... this doesn't make any sense. Aren't there other women out there?"

"There are," Sorin agreed. "But none that would be able to do as good a job as Ariette. To those outside of the palace, it shouldn't be too hard to believe. Everyone knows she saved my life. A love could blossom from that easily."

Liam nodded slowly but advanced on Sorin. Sorin took a small step back.

"Hurt her and you have me to answer to," he said in a low, rumbling voice.

"Liam!" Ariette groaned.

Sorin held up his hands in a surrendering gesture. "I wouldn't dream of it."

Liam's nostrils were flaring, but he nodded. He embraced Ariette, whispering something in her ear. Sorin let out a breath and, interested, reached into Liam's mind now that it had quieted.

"What did he say to you?" Sorin asked as they headed back for the palace.

"Just that he wishes me the best," she said, but he knew she wasn't saying everything.

Nicole waved to them, a laundry basket on her hip, as they walked by. They returned her wave.

"He loves her," he said.

She frowned at him. "What?"

"Liam. He loves your friend."

Ariette's eyes lit up and she grinned. "Wonderful! She loves him, too! Maybe at the ball sparks will fly."

He chuckled. "Just as long as they're between Liam and Nicole, not you and the duchess."

XVI

The Duke And Duchess

"It's not that hard!" Sorin said, frustrated. "All you have to do is nod!"

"I've been curtsying ever since I got to the palace!" Ariette snapped back. "And I'll have to keep doing it tomorrow night anyway! It's not an easy habit to break!"

"I told you! Curtsying to a wolf is insulting! Do you really want to jeopardize all we've done!?"

"Don't you dare put this on me! It was your idea!"

"Please, both of you," the king said wearily from his throne. "They'll be here in less than a day. This arguing has to stop."

Sorin sighed. "You're right. I'm sorry, Ariette. I know it's a lot, but it has to be flawless."

"I'm tired," she said, trying to keep from crying.

"Dinner will be ready soon," the king said but she shook her head.

"I've lost my appetite."

Sorin groaned as she left. He collapsed onto his throne, rubbing his temples.

"She's right, too. This was my idea and I'm taking all my anger out on her."

"It's never too late to say you're sorry," his mother said delicately.

"Take her some food; Sylvia told me she hasn't been eating. You two have come a long way. Don't let one argument ruin all of that progress."

"And Sorin," his father said before he left. Laurent's eyes were sad. "I understand how both of you feel about this. However, I know you haven't been practicing the more physical part of this." Sorin gulped. "You need to tell her tonight."

"I'm already taking her future from her," he said. "I don't want to upset her more."

"It's not as if you'll have to engage in intercourse. She may be nervous at first, but I know she'll understand."

Sorin's shoulders fell. "Very well."

He went to the kitchens, palms clammy. In the past two weeks, he and Ariette had become good friends. But, aside from being able to embrace each other comfortably, they hadn't gone beyond holding hands.

Anton was in the kitchen, tasting the food as usual.

"I need a tray," Sorin said. "For two."

"Coming right up, your highness."

Once a platter was made, complete with two goblets of Elderwine, he made to leave. He noticed some floral arrangements on his way out, decorations for the next evening's ball. He took one of the red roses and placed it between the plates. When he reached her room, he knocked, feeling uneasy. How in the world would he tell her the truth without getting hit? Sylvia opened the door and looked relieved at the food in his hands.

"Can we have some privacy?" he asked.

"Of course," she said and left, shutting the door behind her.

Ariette was standing at her window, her back to him. He knew she was crying and tried to say something.

"I brought some food," he said finally.

"I said I'm not hungry. And open the door, this isn't proper."

He sighed and set the platter on the writing desk. He stood beside her, but she inched away from him. Swallowing thickly, he took her elbow.

"Ariette, we need to talk about something," he said.

"I know I'm incompetent," she interrupted, wiping at her tears. He frowned at her. "This isn't easy, though. I have no idea how to behave when they get here! I know all the formalities, yes, but what about in between those times? They're going to hate me, that much I know right away. What if I mess up? I don't want to get anyone in trouble and-."

Sorin made a rash decision and kissed her. She froze under his lips.

"What was that?" she whispered, breaking from the kiss.

"The only way to get you to stop," he said and led her to the food. "Please eat while I explain. Sylvia said you've been refusing food."

She scowled. "I thought personal servants were supposed to keep your confidence."

"Not when it involves you neglecting your health," he said. He brought one of the armchairs over to sit with her, also eating. "I know you're scared. I am, too. But we can do this."

She sniffled, picking at her dinner roll. "There's something you're not telling me. It's bad news, isn't it?"

"Not necessarily," he said awkwardly. "I guess it depends on how you feel about...." He took a deep breath and said the next part in a rush. "How you feel about sharing a bed with me."

She dropped the fruit she was eating and turned her head to him slowly. Her eyes were wide, jaw agape.

"I beg your pardon?"

He swallowed. "It's what they'll be expecting and-."

"To hell with that they expect!" she shouted. "What about how I feel? Has no one considered that!?"

"Of course we have. But this is how important it is, Ariette! I told you how they expect us to show our love for each other! We talked about this; that it was risky. But you agreed. We can't turn back now."

She started to cry again. "I don't want to sleep with you," she murmured.

He shook his head. "We won't be doing... that," he said, and her shoulders relaxed. "If it will make you feel better, I'll sleep on the floor."

"That's not fair to you," she said. "It's your room, I'll sleep on the floor."

"There's no compromising here."

She sighed again and continued to eat. Neither spoke while they ate. Sorin was feeling a little better now that Ariette knew everything. Her reaction had been what he expected, but it didn't make it easier. When they were both done eating, he put the plates on the platter and picked up the rose.

"I brought this here for you," he explained and broke the stem.

"Why?"

"Roses are some of the most difficult flowers to grow," he said. "They require plenty of attention, and their petals are very delicate. However, the further down the stem you get, you run into a natural defense: thorns. They're beautiful, but not nearly as fragile to the touch as people think; especially those focused only on the weaker parts of them." He tucked the rose behind her ear. "No matter what happens while they're here, remember: you're stronger than anything they can say and-."

This time, it was Ariette who interrupted him, leaning across to kiss him. He was shocked at first but kissed her back. She tried to break from the kiss, but he held her head in place with his hand behind her neck. Her lips were soft on his and he wanted the moment to last a little bit longer. He deepened the kiss and she shivered under his hands. They sat, kissing in silence, until she suddenly jerked away.

"Sorry," she gasped, getting out of her seat. "I- It was lovely, but I felt your fangs, and-."

"Hey," he said. He pulled her in for a hug. "It's okay. You should get some sleep, though. We don't know what time they'll be here tomorrow. Knowing them, they'll show up at the most inconvenient time."

"Good night, Prince Sorin," she said.

He stopped at the door then walked back to kiss her once more.

"Call me Sorin," he muttered and left, his face flaming.

Ariette touched her lips, feeling exhilarated. She had never kissed a man before. She wondered if all kisses felt that wonderful. It was hard to believe Sorin could be so gentle. Unbidden images of Sorin kissing her again flooded her mind. She squeaked and covered her face.

"Stop it," she chided herself. "It's not real."

Real or not, though, she definitely couldn't wait for him to kiss her again.

Sylvia woke her shortly after dawn. She groaned into her pillow.

"Are you all right, Lady Ariette?" Sylvia asked.

"I couldn't sleep," she mumbled. She burrowed under her covers, away from Sylvia. "Just five more minutes."

"I'm sorry, my lady. But Prince Sorin has arranged a breakfast with you, and I've been told to get you ready now."

Ariette's eyes flew open. Sorin had requested breakfast with her? She had spent most of the night reliving the moment and had finally convinced herself he was just practicing. But the thought of him below, waiting for her, made her heart flutter in a most unwelcome way.

"I- Tell him I'm not hungry."

She heard Sylvia sigh and, suddenly, the blankets were yanked off of her.

"Hey!"

"I'm sorry," Sylvia said. "But I've been given an order and I intend to see it through."

Ariette groaned. "Fine."

It was Sylvia's blunt nature that appealed the most to Ariette. The queen had given her the choice between three servants, and Sylvia was her favorite. She didn't hold back and, as last night confirmed, she wasn't afraid to do what was right in regard to Ariette. After a quick bath, Sylvia helped her into a dress her mother had made with Misha. She had been given several elegant dresses to wear while the duke and duchess were here. King Laurent was sure they wouldn't stay for more than a day or two, so she felt confident it would be enough.

Sylvia led her to the gardens where a wicker table had some breakfast foods and a steaming jug. Sorin was reading over a piece of parchment with a frown on his face. He stopped, though, when she cleared her throat.

"Thank you, Sylvia," he said, standing to take Ariette's hand and helped her into her seat. He pushed the chair in, his hand lingering on her shoulder. She felt goosebumps erupt on her arms and had never been more grateful for the necklace preventing him from reading her mind. "Go ahead and help yourself to some food from the kitchens. Will be done in about an hour."

"Your highness," she said and curtsied.

Ariette begged her not to go with her eyes but Sylvia did as she was told. She swallowed the lump in her throat and turned back around. Sorin had put some scones and eggs on her plate.

"I thought some fresh air would be good for both of us," he said when she asked about the location. "We've been cooped up in the palace the last two weeks."

"It is refreshing," she agreed.

He poured them each some tea. "Don't worry, I made sure there was no honey in it."

"Dying on the morning of our guests' arrival would put a damper on things," she joked, and he laughed.

"Yes, it would."

They ate in silence. Ariette looked around as she did so. The gardens were nothing new to her, but it was better than looking at Sorin. She couldn't stop thinking about their kiss. It had excited and frightened her; his fangs were sharp on her tongue. A shiver ran down her spine as she remembered it.

"Are you cold?"

Sorin was looking at her, concern on his face.

"No," she said. "Just a breeze."

"Huh. I didn't notice. But autumn is coming, so it's bound to cool off significantly." She nodded her agreement. He took a drink of his tea, watching her. "Look, Ariette. About last night. I'm sorry if I went too far."

She lowered her eyes to her plate, knowing that from her chest to her face she was blushing.

"You didn't," she whispered. "I just wasn't expecting it. I got so caught up in learning the etiquette that kissing had never really crossed my mind. Like I said, I have no experience."

"If it makes you feel better, nor do I."

This surprised her. "What? But what about the other women? Tobias said you've had princesses and duchesses come."

He chewed thoughtfully on his scone.

"Only a few of them knew of our true nature," he explained. "I won't lie, I read their minds. Those who knew had taken precautions to stop me from doing that. It felt like deceit, granted I wasn't much better. The others all just coveted my crown. Thanks to our crops, we're a valuable commodity. I only met one woman who I had any interest in."

"What happened?"

He seemed to choose his words carefully. "I wasn't what she wanted."

"Don't you mean who?"

"No, I mean what." When she still looked confused, he cleared his throat. "She was more interested in someone like you."

"What do you- Oh!"

"Yes, it made it hard for us to really click. She did confide in me eventually. She had several brothers and sisters, so the lineage wasn't in jeopardy. I told her to return home and pursue the person she truly loved. The last I heard, she was disowned, but she and her partner are happy in a home by the ocean."

"That's sad," Ariette said with a frown. "Her family should love her, no matter her preference."

"I agree. I offered to let them come live here, but she declined. She wanted a fresh start and I was more than happy to give her one."

Once they had finished eating, they met Peter and Sylvia in the front hall. Both looked anxious. His parents came out of the throne room when they heard Sorin's voice.

"Thank goodness," the king said.

"What's going on?" Sorin asked.

"They're here."

"What?" Ariette gasped. "As in... now?"

"Yes, now," the queen said. She held Ariette's hand. "Don't worry. You can do this."

She swallowed thickly and nodded, standing beside Sorin. He put his arm around her waist as his parents took up their positions beside him. The king made sure everyone's outfits were spotless then nodded to the guard at the doors. They opened slowly, the duke and duchess striding in confidently.

Duke Ingvar looked just as she remembered him: wavy brown hair and tan skin. Instead of the elegant robes he had worn to the previous ball, he was in clothing that looked like the messenger's wolf hide. His brown eyes surveyed the royal family, ending on Ariette. He curled his lip at her. His canines were sharp, and she inched closer to Sorin. Beside him, Duchess Sigrid stood, haughtily glaring at Ariette.

Gorgeous was an understatement for the woman standing in front of her. She was taller than Ariette by several inches. Her hair and eyes were the same as her father's, though her skin was darker. It glistened in the light from the candles and the sun that filtered in through the windows. She wore a skirt of wolf hide that reached the middle of her thighs, and a single stretch of hide to cover her chest. She was very muscular and Ariette immediately felt inferior.

"Welcome," King Laurent said. "I'm thrilled you were able to make it in time for the ball."

"I wouldn't miss it for the world," Duke Ingvar said, his eyes still on Ariette. "This is her?"

Ariette almost curtsied but remembered what Sorin said.

"Good morning," she said in as calm a voice as she could. "My name is Ariette Jones. It's lovely to meet you."

"A human?" Sigrid asked. Ariette bit her lip. Even her voice was beautiful. How in the world could Sorin possibly reject her? "Surely this is a joke."

"And why would you think that?" Sorin asked.

"Humans are fragile, unable to keep up with the power of a vampire," she said. "Tell me, Ariette." Her voice turned to a sneer when she said Ariette's name. "Do you really think you can keep up with Sorin? After all, I've heard vampires can be quite rough, if you know what I mean."

Ariette's face blossomed red and she smirked in success. Her blunt speech had thrown Ariette off.

"I'm more than capable of taking care of myself," she said finally. "As for your implications, I'll do what I need to. After all, isn't that the duty of a wife to her husband?"

She narrowed her eyes. "We'll just see about that."

"Is that a threat?" Ariette asked, anger starting to dominate her fear.

"What if it is?"

Before Ariette could retaliate, the king spoke up.

"You should go rest before the ball," he said. "I'm sure the trip was long. Where is your luggage? I'll have my men carry it to your rooms."

Ingvar turned and beckoned to someone. Ariette's jaw dropped. Four men came in carrying stacks of luggage. King Laurent looked stunned.

"I'm sorry," he said when he recovered. "I was under the impression you would only be here for a short visit."

"Well, I didn't want to limit ourselves. After all," he smirked at Ariette again, "who's to say everything will go as you planned?"

Ariette's jaw clenched but her fear of the man kept her from speaking. He gave her another contemptuous look then led his daughter up the stairs. When they were out of sight, Ariette felt faint. Tears stung at her eyes, but she didn't let them fall. The royal family were talking about the final plans for the ball, occasionally glancing at the stairs. Ariette thought to the tall, beautiful woman upstairs and felt her confidence deflate.

Her throat constricted and she left, ignoring everyone when they called for her. Sylvia hurried to keep up but, once outside, Ariette ran around behind the palace. She had seen a path that led down to the beaches during her first month there. She had to get away; to go where she could breathe freely. Clouds were rolling in, the sea a churning mass of grey waves. The sand was still warm under her feet, though, as she took off the heels that were becoming more and more in fashion. She set them on a rock and stepped into the water, ignoring how her skirts were sticking to her skin. She closed her eyes and breathed in the salty air.

Another smell drifted to her when the wind shifted. She sighed, knowing that cologne.

"You shouldn't run off like that," Sorin said. "Not with them here."

"Great. Not only are we risking the possible alliance with the nomads, but my life is really at stake."

"Come out of the water," he said. "You'll get sick."

She stepped backwards, not facing him, out of the water. She could smell rain in the air and welcomed it. Maybe the ball would be canceled if it stormed. Sorin took her arm and turned her to face him. She kept her eyes downcast, though.

"Hey," he said. "Look at me." She shook her head, tears in her eyes. "I can't read your mind, Ariette. Tell me what's wrong. This isn't like you."

"You must be blind," she said. "To reject a woman as beautiful as she is...."

"Ah, I see," he said quietly. "I figured that was the case." She could only shrug. "There's more to beauty than what's on the surface. That woman's personality makes her the ugliest person I know. Besides, why should I look at her when I have you to look at?"

"You're just saying that to make me feel better," she mumbled. "This marriage is a fake."

"Regardless, I still know beauty when I see it."

Ariette didn't know what to say. It didn't matter, though. Suddenly, a voice carried on the air. She finally lifted her head, frowning. Sorin had been about to kiss her, but she turned slowly on the spot, ears straining.

"What is it?" he asked.

"You don't hear that?"

"Hear what?"

"Just listen."

He stood still, listening as well. It was a woman's voice, whispering words Ariette couldn't make out. She walked in a small circle until she found the source. Her eyes landed on the wall of mist. The second they did, she felt her feet move on their own. Sorin was confused. She started to walk but then it turned into a sprint.

"Ariette!" he shouted. "What are you doing!?"

Sorin lunged for her, but she was already diving into the water. He cursed and dived in after her. It was clear she couldn't swim but she was fighting tooth and nail to get further into the ocean. He caught up to her and put an arm around her waist, pulling with all his might. She struggled against him, her elbow crashing into the side of his head. He cursed as sea water filled his mouth. It took longer than normal to get to the shore. Finally, he got back to the sand and stepped in front of her.

It was almost like the night he found her by the cliffside. But her normally blue irises were now the same color as the mist. She was fighting to get back into the water. Regretfully, he slapped her.

She gasped sharply and staggered back.

"What the-?" she began and coughed, shivering. "What happened?"

"You tell me," he said. "One second you're looking for a voice, and the next you're diving into the ocean like a mad woman."

"A voice? I don't hear a voice, though...."

He looked at the mist behind him. It was swirling as usual, but he felt like they were being watched.

"Let's get you inside," he said finally. "I don't want you getting sick."

She didn't argue. She was shaking like a leaf, her teeth chattering. He put his arm around her, rubbing her arm as they walked back up the path. His parents were waiting in the garden, looking anxious. His mother rushed to Ariette.

"What in the world happened?" she asked.

"I'm not sure," she said.

"We'll talk later," Sorin said. "Get her warmed up."

Sylvia went with his mother up to Ariette's room. Sorin turned to where he could see the mist between the trees.

"Son, what happened?"

"It was the mist again," Sorin said and told him everything. "Do we have any books on the mist?"

"I think we have a couple, yes. Do you want to read while we wait for Ariette?"

"One more thing," he said, and his father looked at him. "Did Mother ever compare her appearance to other women?"

"A few times; especially when she was pregnant with you and Charlotte."

"How did you convince her otherwise?"

"Mostly with gifts and reassurance. Why? What did Ariette say?"

"I think she's feeling self-conscious around Sigrid."

"Oh. I hadn't thought of that...." They both stood silently in thought. "Let's talk to Elizabeth. Maybe she can give us some insight into Ariette that you can use to help her feel better."

Sorin nodded. "Thank you."

"It's nice to see this," his father said.

"See what?"

"You care about a woman."

Sorin flushed. "It's not like that," he said quickly. "She's become a good friend. I don't want her to be upset; especially over someone like Sigrid."

His father clapped him on the shoulder. "Whatever you say, Sorin. I'll see you at lunch."

XVII

Acting?

Shortly after noon, the entire palace smelled of cooking meat. Ariette and Sorin met in his father's study to go over the plans for the evening. Her mother had panicked when she heard about her attempt to swim. Ariette had never been good at swimming.

"I don't know what happened," she said for the hundredth time. Sorin passed her a list of the guests. "Oh! Nicole is coming!"

"I thought having a friend would help make it easier," he said. "I also sent an invitation for Liam."

"Because you wanted him to support me or because you're afraid of him?" she teased gently.

He shuddered. "How can a human be so intimidating?"

"He wanted to go to war with my father," she said. "But, when we were kids, he hurt his leg. It never healed properly. I think he felt guilty about never going to battle, so he compensated by getting as strong as he could."

"He's an honorable man, that's for sure. What?" he asked when he caught her staring.

"It's just hard to believe you're the same man who threatened me three months ago," she said.

He just shrugged, looking uncomfortable. After confirming the last details, he left her to get ready for the ball. Misha and her mother had rushed to make her more dresses after finding out the duke and duchess would be around longer. Now, though, her mother was in her room with Sylvia. A dress of red and gold was laid out on the bed. Ariette gawked at it.

"This is beautiful," she said, running her hands over the silk.

"The prince asked us to make something a little more elegant," her mother said with a smile.

"Sorin? Why?"

"You'll have to ask him that," she said. "Let's get you ready."

"I hope you'll be able to come tonight."

"Of course I will. Misha took over the orders for me. I really enjoy working there, but I've missed spending time with you like we used to."

"So do I. It'll be nice to have a relaxed ball. For the most part," she added, thinking about the wolves in the other wing. "You know what they are, right?"

"King Laurent filled me in," she said. "He wanted me to know everything before we all agreed that your engagement was the right choice."

"Can you two keep a secret?" she asked and both of them nodded. "I'm afraid."

"They won't hurt you, my lady," Sylvia said, sitting her down to work on her makeup. She melted some black wax and traced her lids carefully. "The king has made sure of that."

"That's not what I'm afraid of."

Elizabeth mixed crushed diamonds into gold powder. "Then what is it?"

"I.... I think Sorin and I might actually have to get married," she mumbled, fiddling with her necklace. "They brought a lot of luggage, said they wanted to be here in case plans change."

"Oh."

None of them spoke. Ariette closed her eyes as her mother applied the powder. When she opened them again, Sylvia was busying herself on the other side of the room. Elizabeth knelt down in front of Ariette's vanity chair. Ariette tried not to cry as her mother caressed her cheek.

"I know I signed up for this," she said, her voice tight. "I knew that this was a possible outcome. But I already have to share a room with him. He told me that they'd be suspicious if we didn't. If we get married, that means- Everything has been moving so fast and-."

"Ari," her mother interrupted, and she gulped. "First of all, take a deep breath. There you go. Now, you're right. Things have gone very fast for you and Sorin. Just three months ago you two hated each other. You may not love each other, but even a blind man can see that you two care about one another to some degree. Did I tell you how your father proposed to me?"

"No."

"We were young, younger than you," she said. "Your grandparents were pushing for me to get married. They were worried I wouldn't find a man after I passed the traditional age. I was incredibly stressed. Robert and I were good friends, kind of like you and Liam. I told him of my concerns and fear that they would marry me off to the first man who came by, regardless of who it was. He suggested I wed him. I thought he was joking; neither of us had expressed feelings like that. Little did I know, he had loved me for years. Granted, he didn't tell me that until we had been married for a year."

"I had no idea."

"It's why we didn't push you to find a husband. Neither of us wanted you to go through that. My point is this may not be how you imagined yourself getting married. However, out of all the men I know, I would prefer you marry Sorin. Well, Liam was my first choice, but I have a feeling that's not an option."

Ariette laughed a little. "He loves Nicole."

"Oh, thank the gods," she said, laughing, too. "Those two have been like puppies for years now."

Ariette hugged her. "Thank you, Mama. I'm still scared, but it helps knowing you approve."

Elizabeth tightened her arms around Ariette. "Your father would be so proud of you."

"Please don't make me cry; we just finished my makeup."

They laughed together and she took a deep breath, standing and straightening the skirts. The dress looked beautiful on her. She did notice, with some trepidation, the front was cut lower than her normal gowns.

"Is this necessary?" she asked, tugging her hair in front of her.

Sylvia rejoined them. She put Ariette's hair up in an elegant bun, weaving gold thread through it.

"I think Sorin wanted to make a point," her mother said and gestured to a small box. "He brought that, too."

"What kind of point, though?"

"That Duchess Sigrid has nothing on you," Sylvia said with a smile. "Trust me, no one likes her. Sometimes, I think her father wants the prince to marry her so that he can be rid of her."

The three giggled and Ariette opened the box. A gold tiara with rubies glittered in the candlelight. The implication was clear, and she swallowed thickly. Her hands shook as she took it out of the box. Her mother made an approving noise. She placed it on Ariette's head and grinned.

"What a beautiful daughter I have," she said.

Ariette smiled back. "I get it from you."

Someone knocked and she jumped, her heart racing.

"Are you ready?" Sorin asked from the other side of the door.

Ariette whimpered quietly and Elizabeth pulled her in for another hug as Sylvia crossed to the door.

"It's okay," Elizabeth whispered. "No matter what, everything will be perfect."

Ariette could only nod and turned to the door. Sylvia checked her arm, making sure the long sleeves covered where her dagger was hiding. With a final look over, she opened the door. Ariette kept her eyes focused on Sorin's chest.

He was also wearing a more extravagant outfit. His tunic was red silk with gold thread. He wore the medal again, as well as other pins that she didn't recognize. He didn't speak and she finally chanced a look at him. His face was surprised, eyes looking her up and down. She shifted on her feet.

"You look magnificent," he blurted, and she blushed.

"Thank you," she said. Her voice was higher than normal. "You look very handsome, too."

He offered his arm and she accepted it, her body trembling. She knew he could tell, though he didn't say anything. He wore a crown on his head, similar to his father's but simpler. Ariette's mouth was dry. Down in the foyer, Stela clapped happily.

"You're a vision of beauty," King Laurent said, taking her free hand to kiss it. "I'm pleased to see Charlotte's tiara suits you."

"This was hers?" she asked and reached up to take it off. "You shouldn't have given it to me! It's not-."

"Ariette, relax. It was just collecting dust. Besides, I know Charlotte would have wanted you to wear it."

Before she could say anything else, a familiar drawl caught her attention. She tensed beside Sorin.

"Well, I personally think it's an insult to Charlotte," Duke Ingvar said, escorting Sigrid.

The duchess was in a beautiful dress, one that clung to every part of her body. Ariette flushed when she realized the top of her gown was even lower than her own. They really had no shame.

"I'd watch your tongue," Sorin said in an even voice. "Regardless of who your brother is, don't forget that this is the future queen."

"If you say so," he said with a shrug. "Are the guests here yet? I'm starving."

"They should be here any moment," Laurent said. "Now, the evening will be simple: we'll start off with a meal, then Sorin and Ariette will dance. We'll mingle for a while, then everyone will return to their homes."

"I'd hate for anything to go awry," Sigrid said with an unpleasant smile. "I'm glad you kept it so easy."

"Quite," Laurent said. "Our guests have arrived," he added after someone knocked on the doors. "Head into the ballroom, Sorin and Ariette. We'll join you after we've welcomed everyone."

Ariette gladly let Sorin lead her to the room. David had kept the room the same as last time. The tables were now further into the room with chairs, golden plates glittering. Sorin helped her into her chair at the head table and she took a few deep breaths. Was it just her imagination, or did he move his chair closer to her when he sat down?

"Are you all right?" he asked, taking her hand under the table.

"I think so," she said. "That dress, though!"

"I figured she'd pull something like that. Hence the outfit change," he added.

"I'm not used to it, I won't lie," she said, tugging at the bodice, trying to inch it higher.

"It's the newest fashion." He coughed a little and she looked to make sure he was okay. His cheeks were pink. "I'll be the first to admit it, though: it looks wonderful; especially on you."

"Oh," she said, her voice cracking. "Oh, thank you. I- I'm not sure what else to say."

She was spared, though, as people began to filter into the room. The colors were magnificent, and she grinned when she saw Nicole walking beside Liam. She wasn't sure if they had come together, but they both were smiling together.

"They make quite the pair, don't they?" Sorin asked, also watching them.

"If only they'd admit their feelings," she agreed.

Under the table, she laced their fingers.

"It can be hard to make such a big step," he said. "After all, you never know what such words could do to a friendship."

She looked at him again. He was watching her, and her heart skipped a beat.

"That's true," she whispered.

"Then you'd agree their hesitance is warranted."

"Sorin," she began but the servants filed in, carrying large trays of food.

She sighed as everyone took their seats. The duke sat next to the queen, leaning over to speak to Ariette.

"I do hope you'll do me the honor of dancing with me," he said over the sounds of people eating.

"After I've danced with my fiancé, of course," she said.

"I don't see why the order matters so much. After all, Sigrid has missed him; surely you'd let him dance with her first."

"Absolutely not," she said and met the duke's eyes. "I empathize with how the duchess feels, but this ball is to celebrate our engagement. Despite anyone's feelings, I intend to enjoy the evening with my future husband."

He made a sour face but sat back.

"Well done," Sorin whispered and she picked up her goblet of wine, taking a deep gulp.

The rest of the night passed in a blur to Ariette. She was nervous about the end of the night, but still enjoyed her time with Nicole and Liam. At one point, she caught them dancing and eagerly showed Sorin. He laughed and took her hand, leading her to dance beside them. For a few, blissful hours, she forgot about the duke and duchess. Sigrid and Ingvar would periodically try to separate them but Sorin, having had several goblets of wine, would sweep Ariette into a kiss and dance with her more. Each kiss made her face warm; that or it was the wine, she couldn't be sure.

There was a spring in her step as they walked down the hall after everyone had left. It really had been a fun evening. Nicole promised to visit soon, and they had successfully avoided the duke. When she tried to stop at her door, though, Sorin kept pulling her down the hall. She remembered what he had said the day before and, just like that, her mind sobered.

He opened the door. Peter and Sylvia were inside, getting the bed ready for them. Sylvia took Ariette into the walk-in closet to prepare her for bed.

"Peter and I agreed you weren't ready to change in front of him," she said in a quiet voice. "We tried to get a separate cot in here, but we were being watched."

"It's okay," she breathed. "I used to go sleep in my mother's room after my father died; I'd end up on the floor eventually."

"I highly doubt the prince is going to let you sleep on the floor."

Once she was in her nightgown, Sylvia checked that it was clear for her to come out. Sorin was standing by his mirror, reorganizing the medals he had worn to the ball. Sylvia left and Ariette fidgeted with her hands. She was desperately trying to say something when Sorin turned. Their eyes met. Before she knew it, they were kissing.

Goosebumps erupted on her arms. This kiss was different; more like their first one. No one was around to watch them, no eyes scrutinizing to find any fault in how they were acting. Spurred by the wine still in her system, Ariette deepened the kiss. Sorin's reaction was unexpected. He pulled her so close their bodies were touching. Ariette wondered why she had denied herself the feeling of such a wonderful thing like kissing. Now she understood why her parents would do it so often.

It wasn't until his lips were on her neck that she was brought back to reality. Her eyes snapped open. His hands were running up her sides, getting dangerously close to her chest.

"Sorin," she breathed. He didn't respond, pressing long kisses just above the vein in her neck. "Sorin, stop." She felt his fangs grow and pushed at him. "Sorin!"

He gasped and staggered back, eyes wide. He was panting and covered his mouth, his fangs down to nearly his chin. She shook, trying to catch her breath.

"Ariette, I'm so sorry," he said. "I don't know what came over me. I'm sorry."

"It's okay," she managed. "We both had a lot to drink. Maybe-Maybe we should just go to sleep."

"Right," he said. "I- Let me just get some pillows on the floor."

"I can sleep on the floor," she began but he shook his head.

"No chance."

She was about to argue but stopped. He was already moving the pillows, avoiding her eyes. She wanted to assure him that everything was okay; the guilt in his eyes made her uneasy. Instead, she got under the covers and tried to sleep.

~~~

Sorin woke what felt like just an hour later. He sat up, rubbing his eyes. His head was heavy from the remains of the wine. He looked around and tried to realize what had woken him. He stood. The room looked just like it always did; fireplace empty, doors closed, bed empty.

Bed empty.

He swore and pulled on his boots, hopping on one foot as he fell out of his room. Peter was already on his way to him.

"The beach," Peter said and Sorin cursed loudly.

He ran down the hall, ignoring his parents when they came out of their room. He took the stairs two at a time and went out through the back. He had to get to her before something horrible happened. What if she was mesmerized by the mist again? He prayed to whatever deity was watching them that she'd be okay.

The moon wasn't full, but the clear sky gave it the chance to illuminate everything around him. He sprinted down the path and scanned the beach for her. She wasn't near the cliff and he called her name, ready to run into the water if he had to. Thankfully, he found her. But she wasn't sleepwalking. She was very much awake and sitting on the rock, her knees pulled to her chest.

"Thank the gods," he panted, stopping beside her. She didn't look at him. "Don't do that. I was worried you had fallen in the water and-."

"I don't think this is a good idea," she said. He stared at her. "Let's just stop pretending and go back to normal."

"Why are you saying this?" he asked. He had been sure everything was going well. "What happened?"

"I got up for some warm milk," she said. "I ran into Sigrid. She told
~~~

me...." She took a deep breath. "Sorin, is it true you two had an affair when you were younger?"

Sorin's jaw dropped. "Come again!?"

She flinched at his raised voice. "She said that you two had an affair, that you had hoped to have a child so you wouldn't need to get married," she said in a rush.

He groaned and pulled her to her feet. He made her face him.

"You have to stop listening to her," he said. "No. I never had any kind of affair with her. Yes, I had hoped to never get married. I knew I'd have to once Charlotte died, though."

"I'm sorry," she said, tears glistening in her eyes. "I shouldn't listen to her, I know, but it's so hard."

He wiped her tears away. He remembered what her mother had said when he spoke to her earlier that day.

"Just be honest with her. Tell her the truth."

"Ariette, I need to tell you something," he said, taking her hands. "The truth is... I have been keeping something from you. Mostly because I didn't understand it at the time. Now, though.... Ariette, I'm starting to-."

Before he could finish, though, a strong wind blew around them. Ariette cried out in surprise as sand swirled around their bodies. They covered their eyes.

"What is this?" she yelled over the wind.

"I don't know!" he yelled back, looking around. "It can't be a spell! We're still in the barrier!"

"What barrier!?"

He didn't answer. He squinted his eyes, trying to see through the sand. He heard shouting from the palace and knew the guards had seen it, too.

What's going on? his father's voice echoed in his mind.

I don't know. It's down here at the beach.

We're coming.

Sorin pulled Ariette close. Had Ingvar and Sigrid set some kind of trap? Was this another attempt at trying to steal his heart? What if they had tried to kill Ariette?

"Sorin!" Ariette shouted suddenly. She was pointing out to the sea. "Look!"

He followed her finger and gasped, coughing as sand filled his mouth.

Something was emerging from the swirling mist.

XVIII

The Forgotten Kingdom

Ariette clung to Sorin, watching in fear as something long and dark made its way out of the mist. The wind kept blowing in every direction. Soon, her mother and the king and queen were standing by them. Guards, Ingvar, Sigrid, and the personal servants weren't far behind. People were shouting, pointing at the thing.

"It's a ship!" Ariette yelled.

The bow of a ship finally lit up in the moonlight. It was enormous; larger than any ship in Rosu's fleet. A strong gust of wind knocked everyone off their feet. Sorin caught Ariette before she landed on the rock, pulling her into his chest. They sat up and Sorin shouted.

"Move!" he ordered. "It's going to crash!"

People screamed and scattered out of the way. However, the wind around them suddenly ceased, the speeding ship slowing to a leisurely pace. It glided easily to the beach about twenty yards away. They held their breath. The sound of an anchor splashing in the water made Ariette jump. A long ramp slid out of the side of the ship, falling with a loud crash on the sand. She instinctively reached for her daggers, but they were still in Sorin's room and she gulped. Around her, the guards were pulling their swords and readying bows.

For a while, nothing happened. The vessel was made of a wood Ariette had never seen before.

"It's from a kingdom," she whispered to Sorin, pointing up at the mast. "Look, I can see a flag."

He squinted to look. An emerald green flag fluttered in the air, an ornate leaf in silver thread stitched into it.

"I don't recognize that signet," he said and held her close again.

The guards walked forward slowly, ready to attack. However, before they got close, a tall figure stood at the top of the ramp. Laurent put his hand on Sorin's shoulder.

"Get ready to run," he murmured.

"Please, put down your weapons," a deep voice called. "We've come peacefully."

"We?" Laurent shouted back.

The figure gestured beside him, and three other people walked to join him.

"I am King Taranis of Talameh, and this is my family."

Talameh? Ariette had never heard of it but, judging by Laurent and Sorin's sharp inhales, they had.

"What is it?" she asked.

"May we approach you?" the stranger asked.

"Slowly," Laurent said finally. "And with your hands up."

All four of the strangers did as he said. Once they were closer, Ariette gasped again. All of them were tall and slender. Their skin was fair, and they had long, flowing blond hair. As the wind moved it around their head, she could see pointed ears. There were two males and two females. They wore robes and dresses of silk and velvet, all green and silver in color. The older two had a crown and tiara on that looked like twigs and leaves dipped in gold. The guards all parted for them until they stopped in front of the royal family. As one, all four of them bowed.

"King Laurent of Rosu, please forgive our dramatic arrival," King

Taranis said as they straightened. "But I fear my family and I are in desperate need of your help."

Laurent seemed to be at a loss for words.

"Come inside," Stela finally said. "I'm... I'm sure you're tired from your journey?" she added uncertainly.

"I'm sorry, my lady," Taranis said. "But time is of the essence."

"Take them to the council room," Laurent said, finding his voice. "We'll be there shortly."

Again, the king bowed. A group of guards surrounded the strangers. They all watched as the family was escorted to the palace.

"What's Talameh?" Ariette asked once they were out of sight. "I don't understand what's going on."

"Talameh is a kingdom of legend," Sorin said, frowning at where the family had gone. "Long ago, when the war started, they disappeared. No one knows where they went. However, when they vanished, there were reports of a mysterious mist in the ocean."

"Let's go talk to them," Laurent said. "Everyone return to your rooms. Get some rest. I will inform you of their intentions in the morning."

"We'll be there," Duke Ingvar said, drawing himself to his full height.

"This doesn't concern you," Sorin said.

"I highly disagree! My king would be very interested to hear about a mysterious kingdom returning after all these years!"

"Don't," Laurent said when Sorin tried to argue. "Just let him. It's fine. But only them, Ariette, and the rest of the council."

"Fine," Sorin said and, arm still around Ariette, he walked back up to the palace. "Just a moment," he added when they were inside. He went into his room and came back with one of her robes. He helped her into it, glancing anxiously at the door at the end of the hall. "I need you to be careful, Ariette. I can't read their minds."

She did a double take. "But I thought you could read anyone's mind, even other supernatural beings."

"So did I."

"Are they elves?"

"I don't know," he said, grabbing her hand. "But I think we're about to find out."

She swallowed thickly and nodded. They walked together up the winding staircase. The council members were already there and pointedly looked away from Ariette. Sorin had a hunch they had gone straight to the council room the moment things had calmed. The family were looking around in interest. Sorin couldn't help but feel like the queen in particular looked familiar.

"I'd offer you refreshments, but I feel like we're beyond that point," Laurent said once everyone was seated. King Taranis nodded grimly. "Forgive me, but all of this is rather hard to believe."

"I understand." The king's voice was deep. "First, let me introduce my family. This is my lovely wife, Deidre," he said. The queen smiled, green eyes twinkling even in the dim light. "And my children, Eratos and Fiona." The prince and princess were obviously twins. Sorin noticed Prince Eratos's eyes lingering on Ariette. "Again, I'm sorry for our sudden appearance; especially this late at night. If it weren't so important, though, I would have sent an emissary."

"What's wrong?" Laurent asked.

"We have reason to believe your ancestor's... experiment has backfired," Taranis said.

"Experiment? What experiment?"

Taranis looked troubled. "You're unaware of it." It wasn't a question. "Well, this makes it much harder...."

"Just explain," Tybalt said. "Don't keep dancing around the issue."

"Many centuries ago, King Darius of Rosu tried to build a city called Osanda," Taranis began. "He filled it with vampires and humans alike. He hoped that, through trial and error, he could find a way to make the need for thralls unnecessary."

"Osanda was destroyed," Laurent said.

"Yes. That is when he reached out to me."

"How? People have tried to navigate the mist and never returned."

"Each king before Darius had been given the ability to contact us," Taranis said. "Darius told me about Osanda's ruin. I had been helping him, you see. I endorsed the idea of humans no longer being needed to keep vampires alive. We both thought it would cut down on the number of rogue vampires. When Osanda fell, I offered Darius something I have come to regret."

"What was it?" Sorin asked when Taranis hesitated.

"I let him, and a small group, come beyond the mist," he said. "They were allowed to continue their attempts in the safety of Talameh. About thirty years ago, though, something happened. An energy blast decimated their part of the island. Trees were dead, animals mere corpses on the ground. The community they had built was nothing but ash and rubble. I've sent several of my men to inspect what happened. None have returned."

"Why are you coming here now?" Laurent asked. "Why not when it happened?"

"Once Darius was with us, I thought he could still telepathically communicate with his family. I didn't find out until after his disappearance that it wasn't so."

"I thought King Darius died in battle," Sorin said.

"It's the rumor I had Darius spread," Taranis said. "Prince Sorin, do you know why we retreated behind the mist?"

"No."

"We elves never agreed with this war," he explained. "The father of our people had punished us and, to keep my people safe, I cast a spell to keep intruders out. I still wanted to keep in touch with my brothers, though. Darius's last report to me was that his descendent had just had a son, Laurent."

"Brothers?" Ariette repeated. "Does that mean there are more elves here?"

"No," he said. "I'm sorry, but I'm not aware of your name."

"Ariette," she said, eager to hear the rest.

"Ah, it's a pleasure to meet you, Lady Ariette. But to answer your question, the brothers I speak of are the ones created by my father."

"I don't understand," she said.

"Nor do I," Laurent said.

Taranis's eyes were sad. "You do not know of our father. That saddens me. I admit, I hadn't expected this.... Right. Long ago, a god descended on this realm. His name is Nezeu. Humans were already living here, and he wanted to perfect his children. I and two others were created: a vampire named Roland and a werewolf named Percival. The three of us were instructed to live in harmony with the humans. We were meant to expand our races, be at peace. However, Roland gave in to his bloodlust. He killed a human and began to turn humans without Nezeu's consent. Percival did the same with his wolves. I tried to stop them, to remind them of our father's orders. They wouldn't listen. Soon, my brothers were fighting each other over territories. That's when Nezeu returned.

"He wanted to see how his children were faring. To his despair, he found the world in shambles. War had destroyed the country, and I'm ashamed to say I had hidden with the few elves Nezeu had created. We were summoned to the island I am from, Talameh. There, Nezeu cursed us all. The vampires would never know true peace. At untold times, they would experience rebellion by the humans they ruled. The wolves would never gain the power they fought so hard for. And for the elves, we were banished to Talameh for my cowardice. The war was coming to a head and I created the mist."

His story ended and Sorin held Ariette's hand tighter. He couldn't believe what he was hearing, yet it somehow also made sense.

"As for why I'm just now contacting you," Taranis continued, "I had heard that major steps were being made. Steps to end the constant feud between our people. You see, Nezeu told us that, once we were able to put our differences aside, then we would be able to live in peace once again."

"You're referring to our meeting with the nomadic tribe?" Laurent asked.

"Yes."

"How did you know about that if you've not been in touch for thirty years?"

"Nezeu," Taranis said simply. "He had left after separating us. I hadn't heard from him since then. Two nights ago, I had a vision. It included the young prince and a young woman I didn't recognize. Looking back, I believe it was you, Lady Ariette. Nezeu told me that an alliance would soon forge, making it possible for us to come back to the mainland safely. I had intended to wait for another sign from Nezeu. Unfortunately, my people have begun to disappear again."

"Please forgive me," Laurent said, "but I don't have any proof that I can trust you and what you say."

"I assumed you'd say that," Taranis said. "And I take no offense. I expect such hesitance from a ruler faced with a potential threat. If it's proof you require...."

He trailed off and turned to his wife. The elven queen took off a necklace. One that looked exactly like Ariette's. She gasped and pulled hers out from her nightgown. Queen Deirdre grinned at her but didn't speak. She handed the necklace to Taranis. He laid it down on the table and hovered a pale hand over it. The jade pendant lit up with a blue light and Ariette gasped again as her pendant lit up, too.

"You asked how your ancestors were able to contact me," Taranis said. "This is how."

"But... my father made this," Ariette said, holding her necklace in her palm.

"No, he didn't," Taranis said gently. "These necklaces were made by my queen, Deirdre. She crafted them and used her magic to create a telepathic link."

"Then how did my father get it? Unless...."

Laurent pinched the bridge of his nose.

"Father, did you have something to do with this?" Sorin asked as Ariette's grip on his hand got tighter.

"Robert came to me," Laurent said. "He told me about how he was worried about his family. I thought it was just a random piece of jewelry. I gave it to him and said to tell his wife he had made it."

"The voice I heard," Ariette said, starting to understand. "Was that you?"

Deirdre nodded and finally spoke. "I knew something was happening even before my husband's vision," she said. The familiarity of her voice staggered Ariette. "My necklace had been silent all that time. But the morning before Taranis's vision, I saw a woman in distress. She stood by the sea, her heart reaching for us. I heard her speak of visitors that she feared. As I watched, I realized why her presence was strong enough to awaken the necklaces. Lady Ariette, you are one of the few descendants remaining on the mainland."

Everyone stared at her. Sorin looked between the two women.

"That's crazy," Ariette said with a laugh. "You said that you took all the elves to Talameh."

"Not all wanted to leave," Taranis said. "I warned them that they would die out. They had fallen in love and started families, though. It would seem that their bloodline made it longer than I thought it would."

"I- I need...." Ariette trailed off, putting the necklace back on. "I need to speak with my mother. Please excuse me."

"Yes, leave," Tobias said in a quiet voice. "Leave the men to discuss this."

Ariette stopped at the door. Sorin tried to intervene, but he wasn't fast enough. Ariette spun around to look at Tobias. His chair was near the door and she slapped him. Hard. Without another word, she stormed from the room. Sorin glanced at the family from Talameh. They all seemed surprised, but not upset.

"I'm sorry you had to see that," Sorin began.

Queen Deirdre shook her head. "Everyone has the right to stand up for themselves," she said simply. "And I have the feeling this was a long time coming."

Tobias glared at the queen but didn't have the courage to retaliate. Instead, he addressed Laurent.

"Are you going to let her get away with that!?"

Laurent arched a brow. "I've been telling you since the beginning to respect her. I know for a fact that you men have been in fisticuffs before, so this should be nothing new to you. Regardless," he said in a raised voice when Tobias tried to argue. "It's my understanding that you need more men to go back with you, King Taranis."

"Yes," he said. "It's my belief that, if one of Darius's children comes, there might be a spell that can be broken."

"Like blood magic?" Sorin asked.

"Yes."

Laurent sighed. "Unfortunately, this is very poor timing. My people are about to do negotiations that are pivotal for the war. I can't leave."

"I'll go," Sorin said. "I can take a small group of men and, afterwards, maybe we can come to an agreement to lower the mist," he added to Taranis.

"I don't know," Laurent said. "You've never been on a diplomatic mission."

"I can accompany him," Stela suggested. "I can guide him through it."

"That's actually not a bad idea," he said.

Suddenly, Sigrid leaned onto the table on her elbows. She winked at Sorin.

"I can go to keep you company," she said in a sultry voice.

"Thank you, but I'll be taking my betrothed," he said coldly. He stood. "Please excuse me while I let her know. King Taranis, are you able to wait until the morning so we can prepare?"

The elven king stood, relief washing over his face.

"Certainly," he said. "No need to put us in rooms. We will sleep on the ship."

"How did you sail it all the way here, by the way? If it really is just the four of you," he said.

Taranis's eyes twinkled as he smiled. "You'll see tomorrow."

Sorin hesitated but bowed, excusing himself to find Ariette.

~~~

"Mother?" Ariette said, poking her head into Misha's workroom. "Do you have a moment?"

Elizabeth looked up from the suit of armor she was fitting on a man-
~~~

nequin. At first, she looked hesitant. But, when she saw the look on Ariette's face, she rushed to her.

"What's wrong?" she asked and pulled her to a secluded corner of the room.

Ariette tugged at her hair, then stopped when she realized it was the same shade as the elven queen's. She wiped her sweaty hands on the bodice of her dress.

"What... What did my grandparents look like?" she asked.

Elizabeth frowned. "Ariette, what happened?" Ariette took a deep breath and told her everything, crying by the end of it. Elizabeth sighed. "I'm sorry, Ari, I don't know anything about it. It's true that neither your father nor I had your hair. I know my great grandmother had this hair if that helps you any. I don't see how your hair being that color matters."

Ariette sniffled and wiped her nose on the inside of her arm.

"She also did a spell that activated this," she said and took the necklace out from her robe. Elizabeth gasped. "Apparently, Pa didn't make it like he said he did."

"I see," Elizabeth sighed when Ariette told her where it really came from. "I had a feeling he hadn't made it. Your father was good with tools, not jewelry."

"I don't know what to think," she said. "What if your ancestors were elves?"

She shrugged. "So what if they were? That doesn't change who we are. In fact, it only makes you more special."

Ariette turned pink. "I don't think I need to be special," she muttered.

Elizabeth was about to argue but the door opened again. It was Sorin.

"May I speak with you?" he asked and Ariette nodded.

"We'll talk about it more later, okay?" Elizabeth said. "Just put it out of your mind for now and rest."

"Good night," she said, hugging her again. Sorin led her out to the back of the palace, the mist visible between the trees. "What did you want to talk about?"

"Mother and I will be taking a group of men to Talameh," he said. "We're going to find out what's going on, then Taranis will cast a spell to remove the mist."

Ariette looked at the mist. "Oh my. That's quite the risk, isn't it?"

"If what he says is true, we'll make it through safely. Father has to stay here to negotiate with the nomads. Ariette, I'd like for you to join me."

"Really?" she asked, eyes wide. "You want me to go?"

"Of course. Not only would you get to see where you came from, it would be less suspicious with Sigrid and Ingvar."

"Oh." For some reason, Ariette felt disappointed. "I see."

"It's not just that," he said quickly. "I mean, I also want you to be there so-."

"Don't worry about it," she interrupted with a smile. "It's okay. Of course I'll go. When do we leave?"

"In the morning. But, Ariette, wait." He took her arm before she could walk away. "Please don't misunderstand. I don't want to go without you. I need you."

At his words, Ariette's heart sped up. She met his eyes and swallowed thickly. She couldn't read his mind, but she could see he meant it.

"Okay," she whispered. "I'll see you in the morning, then."

"May I kiss you good night?" he asked.

Ariette smiled a little and nodded.

XIX

Voyage

Ariette was woken by Sylvia at the crack of dawn. She grumbled. It had been hard to sleep the night before. Something in Sorin's words made her heart race and her face heat up.

"I need you."

"The king and queen from Talameh have offered to feed you on the voyage there," Sylvia said when Ariette asked about breakfast while she bathed. "I have a favor to ask."

Ariette looked up from her vanity. She had been practicing makeup on herself, leaving Sylvia to dry and style her hair.

"What is it? Are you all right?"

"Yes, of course," she said quickly. "It's just.... Oh, never mind."

"No," Ariette said. "Tell me."

For the first time, Sylvia looked embarrassed. Ariette was reminded that the girl was only twenty years of age.

"I heard about who's going today," she said, mumbling and looking at her hands. "I-I was hoping I could come with you."

Ariette blinked. "I already thought you were. He and I are still technically engaged," she added in a whisper. "But who's going to make you want to join?"

Sylvia gulped audibly. "Raphael," she said. "He-He's a lieutenant in the militia."

"You love him, don't you?" she asked with a small smile.

"I don't think it's love exactly," she said. "But... I do enjoy spending time with him. I've not seen him much since I started working with you."

"I'd love for you to join me," Ariette said and Sylvia beamed.

"Thank you. I promise I won't make you regret it."

"The only way I'd regret it is if you and Raphael don't get some time alone," she said, and Sylvia blushed more. "I hadn't realized you put that aside to work with me. You should go pack. I need to speak with Sorin."

Sylvia curtsied to her and Ariette knocked on Sorin's door. It took a moment, but Peter opened.

"Oh, good morning," he said. "Sorin's just finishing his bath. Would you like to wait out here?"

Out of the corner of her eye, she saw a door further down the hall open. It was where Duchess Sigrid was staying.

"I think I should wait inside," she said, gesturing with her head.

Peter made a face and let her in. "Can't stand them," she heard him mutter.

He excused himself back to helping Sorin.

"She's what!?" she heard from the other room.

There was frantic splashing, something falling, and Sorin swearing. Ariette was concerned until she heard Peter laughing. Finally, the door opened. She blushed and fixed her eyes on Sorin's face. He was in just his trousers, hair still damp.

"I didn't think you'd come here so early," he said. "Are you all right?"

"Of course," she said and stood from where she was sitting. Peter was trying to dry Sorin's hair. "I'm fine. Surprised, actually, that I was able to sleep in my own room."

Sorin swatted Peter's hands away and took the towel. When his face was covered, Ariette took a bold look at his torso. Her heart ached when she saw all the scars. Though her medicine had stopped the silver from poisoning him, it didn't heal completely. She remembered Lucian telling her that Sorin would have those for the rest of his life. She didn't want him to catch her staring, so she looked back at his face. Peter, though, was smirking at her from behind Sorin and she glared. He just laughed, covered it with a cough, and went to get Sorin's traveling gear.

"I had to go over last-minute travel plans with Mother," Sorin explained and took the tunic from Peter, oblivious to Ariette's flaming red face. "I hope you didn't wait up for me."

"I was pretty tired," she said. "I honestly don't even remember falling asleep. Oh, Sylvia asked to join me. I said yes, I hope that's okay."

"I was going to suggest it either way. Peter will be coming, too. Mother's temporary lady-in-waiting will also be joining us."

"Oh. I guess I assumed I'd take that up now that we won't be around the duke and duchess."

Sorin's face twisted into a scowl. "They're coming."

"What? I thought they weren't!"

"So did I," he said with a frustrated sigh. "Somehow, Ingvar convinced King Taranis that wolves would be a good idea. Back up and all that."

"Great," Ariette said and kicked the vanity chair in frustration. "Oh, sorry."

"Don't apologize. I understand, believe me."

She puffed out her cheeks. "Well, I guess we don't have much of a choice in the matter."

Sorin suddenly held her hand. She blushed but looked up at him. He also looked slightly embarrassed.

"At least we can spend more time together," he whispered. Peter was loudly packing his trunk. "King Taranis said, once we pass through the mist, the voyage will take three days."

"That would be nice," she said, and he smiled. "But why three days? Didn't they get here in just one night?"

"Taranis said he'd explain once we set sail," he said. "Are your things packed?"

"Yes. Sylvia did so while I bathed."

"Good. We're meeting everyone in the gardens. I do have a surprise for you, by the way," he added as they walked out.

"Oh? Where is it?"

"In the gardens," he said with a smile. "Do you have your daggers?"

"Always," she said and showed him.

He nodded in approval. When they exited, Ariette gasped and kissed Sorin on the cheek. He couldn't help but grin as she ran into the arms of Nicole.

"But how?" she asked.

"Prince Sorin sent me a letter this morning," Nicole explained. "I know your mother can't come, so he asked that I come."

"Thank you!" Ariette said and hugged Nicole again. "Ugh, I've missed you so much. Will your parents be all right without you?"

"Of course they will. Besides, Liam's working the harvest," she added and blushed. "He.... Well, he spoke to my father last week."

Ariette gasped in joy. "Is he finally courting you?"

Nicole nodded and Ariette clapped happily.

"It's all thanks to you and Prince Sorin," she said as Sorin joined them.

"Us?" he asked. "How do you mean?"

"After you came by to tell us you're engaged, we were talking about it. We're both very happy for you, and he asked when I'd be getting married. I told him that no one was interested, and he seemed upset. We didn't really talk much about it after that, though. The next day, he came to me in the morning and asked to join me on my morning walk to the market. He told me he had spoken to Papa and gotten his blessing."

Ariette couldn't help but squeal. "Oh, finally! It took him long enough! Wait. But, if you come with me, what about Liam?"

"Like I said, he's in charge of the harvest. It starts in a week and he's been busy anyway. When we get back, we'll be able to have more time together."

"That's perfect. I'm so glad you're...."

She trailed off when the door to the palace opened again. Sorin looked over his shoulder and immediately pulled Ariette to him. Sigrid came out in her usual wolf pelt, sneering at Nicole.

"I didn't realize a commoner would be allowed on such an important mission," Ingvar said.

"She's my best friend," Ariette said simply. "And my maid of honor. I'd like for her to see where I've come from. Perhaps she can work that into any plans she wants to do."

Nicole opened her mouth but Ariette nudged her. She cleared her throat.

"I'm assuming you're Duke Ingvar and Duchess Sigrid," she said and curtsied. "How lovely to meet you."

"The feeling isn't mutual," Ingvar said, and Nicole glared.

"I'm sure Ariette would like to catch up with her friend," Sigrid said and tried to take Sorin's hand. "Let's go to the ship, they're waiting for us."

"He's fine, thanks," Ariette said and stepped between them. "But I appreciate you being so conscious about my friendship."

Sigrid just rolled her eyes and stomped down the trail to the beach. Sorin held her hand, lacing their fingers.

"Very well done," he praised.

"I wasn't sure if I overstepped," she said. "I don't want you to think I'm trying to control your actions or-."

"Trust me," he interrupted. "Remember what I said: wolves are territorial. What you did is exactly what a female would do for the male in their pack."

"Wolves?" Nicole asked. "Pack? What are you talking about?"

Sorin swore under his breath. He had forgotten she was there. He knew Ariette wanted to tell her and sighed.

It's okay, his mother's voice said. She looked over her shoulder from where she was talking to his father. *Once we're settled in, tell her.*

"We'll explain later," Sorin said, his shoulders relaxing. He had forgotten how tiring it was to keep it a secret. "Let's get to the ship. I'm very curious about how they managed to sail it on their own."

"Is it very big?" Nicole asked.

She and Ariette waited as Stela and Sorin said goodbye to Laurent.

"Yes," Ariette said. "I've never seen anything like it."

"Things are going well, aren't they?" Nicole whispered.

"What do you mean?" she whispered back.

"With you and the prince. I see how you look at each other."

"We're friends," Ariette said simply. "Remember: it's just a farse. Once the duke and duchess leave, everything will be back to normal."

"I wouldn't count on that if I were you," she said with a smirk.

"Are you ladies ready?" Sorin asked, coming back over, and taking Ariette's hand.

"I believe so," Ariette said. "Where are the other men joining us?"

"I had them, Sylvia, and Peter go to the ship with our belongings," he said. He offered his arm to Nicole, but she declined, walking beside the queen. "You'll have a chance to meet them there."

Ariette nodded. "I'm excited. It was kind of them to agree to join us. Oh, but I guess if the king ordered them, they wouldn't have much of a choice," she added.

"True, but Father did ask for volunteers. The men who are coming are either unfit for battle or needed the extra coin."

Ariette remembered the lieutenant Sylvia had her eyes on. She wondered which category he fell under. The ship soon came into view and Nicole gasped from behind them.

"It's huge!" she said.

In the early sun, the golden wood glistened. Ariette couldn't help but stare in awe. It looked even more impressive in the daylight. Men were carrying luggage and other supplies onto the ship. Standing with Sylvia was the queen's lady-in-waiting, Crystal. Ariette didn't care much for her but did her best to smile all the same.

It was clear Crystal coveted the position of lady-in-waiting. Many times Ariette overheard her telling the queen loudly that she'd be willing to stay on once the duke and duchess left. The queen would put her in her place, but Ariette still had to restrain herself from speaking. There was a reason Crystal wasn't the lady already, though Ariette wasn't sure what it was.

"Lady Ariette," a voice said.

She looked away from the ship finally to see four men gathered around her, all bowing. One of them she recognized right away.

"You were at the ceremony," she said, and he grinned. "You had a sling, though."

"Yes. My name is Raphael. I was a lieutenant in the militia."

"You still are," Sorin said gently. "Your position hasn't changed."

Raphael shook his head. "No, your highness. As much as I appreciate your insistence, lieutenant is a title I no longer deserve."

Ariette crossed her arms. "That's not true. You fought valiantly at that battle, Sir Raphael. Whether you can fight or not is irrelevant. If it were up to me, I'd give you a promotion."

Raphael stared at her then laughed. "I can see why you chose her as your bride, Prince Sorin!"

"She has quite the spirit," Sorin agreed and put his arm around her again. "Along with Raphael are Captain Orin Alexei, Lieutenant Gerald Albu, and Lieutenant William Luca."

"Alexei?" she repeated. "As in the general?"

"General Alexei is my brother," Orin said. "It's an honor to meet you, Lady Ariette."

"The honor is mine," she said. "This is my best friend, Nicole."

Nicole waved meekly and looked flustered when they bowed to her.

"That's not necessary," she spluttered.

"Any friend of Lady Ariette's is a friend of ours," Gerald said. "We owe her our lives."

Ariette laughed uncomfortably. "Shall we get on the ship? I'm eager to see it."

"We're just waiting for the king to grant us access," Stela said, joining them. "It would be rude to just welcome ourselves."

Ariette nodded in agreement and they waited. She was getting anxious, though, and bounced on her feet. Sorin chuckled but didn't say anything. Finally, King Taranis paused when he was walking by the deck.

"Why are you still down there? Come aboard!"

Stela laughed. "We didn't want to intrude, King Taranis."

"Nonsense!"

They walked up the ramp and Ariette looked around. She felt like a child in a toy store. Every inch of it sparkled, but it wasn't so bright it hurt the eyes. The masts were so tall she had to crane her neck to see the crow's nest. No one was up there, and she frowned, noticing the lack of any deckhands. A staircase in the middle of the upper deck led to the lower floors below. A door opened from the captain's quarters, and Prince Eratos came out.

"Welcome," he said. He took Ariette's free hand and kissed it. She felt uncomfortable when he kept holding it. "I'm glad you were all able to come."

"Likewise," she said and gently tugged her hand away, moving closer to Sorin. "This ship is gorgeous!"

"I'd be glad to give you a tour," he said.

"Your father already offered," Sorin said in a flat tone. "But thank you."

"Ari, look at the figurehead!" Nicole said. "It's a phoenix!"

Sorin let her go so she could go with Nicole. Once they were out of earshot, he turned to the prince.

"She's off limits, Prince Eratos," he said, his voice low. "I had thought that was more than clear."

"I know the reasons behind your engagement. I also know the terms. Besides, don't you have more important things to worry about?"

"Nothing is more important than my bride," Sorin said. "Keep that in mind."

Sorin didn't wait for an answer and joined Ariette and Nicole by the railings.

"But how are they going to get it to sail?" Ariette was asking. "There's no one else here! And I don't think any of the men know how to sail. I certainly don't."

"We have all that arranged."

King Taranis was nodding to Eratos. The prince climbed the ladder to the crow's nest.

"I don't understand," Ariette said.

"Do you know anything about elves, Lady Ariette?" Taranis asked.

"No."

"Elves?" Nicole gasped. "You're really elves!?"

"I'll explain later," Sorin said again. "Please, continue your highness."

"Each elf was gifted an ability by our father: an element to manipulate. For myself, it is the power to bend light to my will. My wife is able to control water. My son and daughter, as twins, share the ability to harness the wind."

Something clicked in Sorin's mind. "They were the ones who steered the ship."

"Exactly," Taranis said with a grin. "To get us here quicker, they used their powers together. For now, it will be just Eratos until we pass through the mist. From there, we'll let the winds take us home. Are you ready?"

"I believe so," Stela said, standing next to Sorin.

"Ready!" Taranis shouted. "I'd hold on to something."

Ariette gripped the railings just in time. They all exclaimed as wind gusted from behind them. The ship lurched forward, and she nearly fell. Sorin caught her and she gasped as the wind ripped through her hair. She couldn't help but laugh. It felt much better than riding a horse. They sped along the water, watching it splash up the sides of the ship. The mist was getting closer and, for some reason, she felt a building sense of urgency.

Queen Deirdre let go of her husband to stand closer to the end of the ship. She closed her eyes and took a deep breath. The necklace around her neck started to glow again, Ariette's doing the same. Moved by an unseen force, Ariette stood beside the queen. Both necklaces lifted as one and the blue light shot out in a beam to the mist. A large opening formed where it hit. Ariette felt as if it was coming from her very essence and started to get light-headed. Beside her, Queen Deirdre was joined by her husband. He took her hand and Ariette saw the queen straighten again, renewed. Ariette started to sway but two arms wrapped around her.

"Easy does it," Sorin whispered into her ear. "You can do this, my minx."

Ariette couldn't help but smile and gripped tightly to his arms. Nicole staggered over to her, looking seasick, and also held one of her hands. Their combined support gave her the strength she needed. They all watched in awe as the mist passed over and around them. It was thick but sparkled from somewhere inside of it and the air surprisingly cold. It stretched on for at least a mile and Ariette's legs trembled. Sorin tightened his hold on her, though, and they made it through. Once the sun shone again, Ariette let out a sigh of relief. As he stepped away, she was sure Sorin had kissed her neck.

"I don't understand," Ariette said, holding her now normal pendent. "You didn't need it last time."

"Last time we just navigated through the mist," Deirdre said, also looking tired. "I appreciate your assistance, Ariette. I wouldn't have been able to do this without your help."

"Can we still see the ship?" she asked.

"Of course," Taranis said. "Assuming you're up for it."

"I just need to walk a bit," Ariette said. "I'll be okay."

"Then follow me," he said with a smile.

XX

Shipwrecked

Sorin helped Ariette walk but she was quickly recovering her energy. Nicole kept asking her if she needed anything and Ariette finally put a hand over Nicole's mouth.

"If you ask me that one more time, I'll kick you," she said, and Nicole laughed.

"Sorry. I'm just worried about you."

"I'm fine, I promise. You can let go, too," she added to Sorin, his arm still around her waist.

"I'm fine like this," he said then cleared his throat. "Unless you want me to let go."

"No, that's okay," she breathed.

Beside her, Nicole snickered. King Taranis took them down the stairs where the duke and duchess were gripping their stomachs, leaning against the walls.

"Still getting your sea legs?" Taranis asked, his eyes twinkling.

"We weren't made for the water," Ingvar groaned.

"It was your idea to join us," Stela said.

"I'm well aware," he said and glared at her.

"A little respect," Ariette began but Stela smiled.

"Don't worry about it."

"This level holds the bedchambers, dining area, and kitchens," Taranis said, looking moderately uncomfortable. "I hope it's all right that you and Lady Ariette share a room, Prince."

"Of course it is. We're due to be married, after all," he said, glancing at Eratos. He met Sorin's eyes but didn't say anything. "It doesn't seem like there's enough room for everyone, though. Where will you and your family sleep?"

"In the rooms above deck," Taranis said with a point. "My daughter is a wonder when it comes to cooking. She'll have dinner ready shortly."

"May I help you?" Ariette asked and the princess looked surprised. "I enjoy cooking and haven't had a chance to do so."

The princess looked to her father.

"That would be lovely," he said. "If you'd like, she'll start preparing in about two hours."

"Sounds perfect."

"Down below is just where we store luggage and other supplies," Taranis said, pointing to the second set of stairs. "You can go below if you'd like, but there's really nothing of note to see there."

"I hope you don't mind that I go down there," Sorin said. "I mean no disrespect, but-."

"No need to explain," Taranis interrupted with a smile. "I'm very pleased to see you being cautious."

"Thank you," he said and passed Ariette's hand to Nicole.

"Will you be all right?" Ariette asked.

"Of course. It's just a lower deck."

Ariette watched anxiously as Sorin descended the stairs. Prince Eratos stood beside her.

"There's nothing to fear, Lady Ariette," he said. "I must admit, I'm surprised he left you here."

"As you said, there's no threat," she said with a shrug, still keeping her eyes on the dark square at her feet.

"He said you were his primary concern. I would think he'd send one of his men to do the job."

"I am," she said. "But so is the safety of all of our people."

The prince just made a noise in his throat. Sorin came back up the stairs just a few minutes later, nodding to his mother. He saw Eratos and his eye twitched slightly.

"Let's go sit for a while," he said, brushing by the prince and taking Ariette's arm. "Nicole, if you'll come with us?"

"I'll meet you in the kitchens soon," Ariette said to the princess who nodded with a smile.

They entered the room that she was sharing with Sorin. Nicole sat in the chair by the table and Stela put a hand on the door, whispering a spell. The door glowed then went back to normal.

"I don't want someone listening in," she explained when Ariette asked.

"I'm confused," Nicole said. "I didn't know you could do magic."

Ariette sighed, sitting next to her pillows. Sorin sat beside her, Stela next to him.

"There's a lot you don't know," Ariette said and grabbed one of the pillows, cuddling it to her chest. "Before we tell you, though, please don't be angry with me. I was sworn to secrecy."

"First, we'll start with the palace," Stela said.

An hour later, Nicole was crying. Ariette started to cry, too, gripping the pillow so tight it was crumpling under her fingers. Nicole got to her feet and got on her knees in front of Ariette.

"Are you safe?" she whispered.

Ariette swiped at her tears. "Nicky, I've never been safer in my life. Nothing that's happened since I came here was forced. I agreed to everything on my own. I knew the risks; I knew what was expected."

Nicole searched her eyes. "I believe you, but if you ever feel threatened...."

She trailed off but Ariette didn't need her to finish. She threw her arms around Nicole and cried into her neck. Nicole cried, too. Ariette's worse fear was that Nicole would hate her. She was glad that wasn't the case.

"I'll keep your secret," Nicole promised. "I hardly think anyone would believe me, even if I decided to tell."

Stela smiled wryly. "You'd be surprised what people would be willing to believe."

Nicole sighed, wiping away her tears, too. "So, about the duke and duchess. They're really werewolves?"

"Yes."

"And Sigrid wants to marry Sorin, so she's trying to sabotage everything?"

"We're not sure if she'll really go that far," Stela said. "But she certainly hasn't been holding back."

Nicole's eyes darkened. "Let her try and touch Ariette. I'll make her regret it."

Ariette laughed through her tears.

"Admirable, but unwise," Sorin said. "A wolf is not to be trifled with."

"With all due respect, your highness, neither am I."

Someone knocked.

"It's the king," Sorin said and Nicole opened the door.

"If you still want to join my daughter, she's ready."

"Oh! Yes, I do. You'll be all right?" she asked Sorin and Stela.

"Of course we will," Stela said. "I need to check in with Sylvia, Peter, and Crystal anyway. Nicole, you can rest if you'd like."

"I'll stay with Ariette," she said.

"Before you go in," the king, "you should know something about my daughter. You see, twins are very uncommon among elves. Unfortunately, that means that certain disabilities can happen. Fiona, as a result, cannot speak."

"I assumed as much," Ariette said. "She hasn't said a word."

"Please don't treat her differently," he said.

"Don't worry," she promised. "I wouldn't do that."

"Thank you, Lady Ariette."

He opened the door to the kitchens. The princess had an apron on and offered ones to Ariette and Nicole. She smiled as they put them on, the king bowing out.

"What are we making?" Nicole asked and Fiona gestured to the open recipe book. "Oh! I guess I thought elves didn't eat meat."

Fiona picked up a quill and scribbled a quick message on some scrap parchment.

We don't eat as much as others, that's true. But Father wanted to make sure you were all comfortable.

"That was very kind of him," Ariette said and opened the package of salted pork. "Shall I start chopping the meat?"

Fiona nodded with a grin.

~~~

"She took it surprisingly well," Sorin said, laying on his back.

"She doesn't really trust us, though," Stela said.

"I know. We'll win her over, I'm sure. She only cares about what's best for Ariette."

"Speaking of Ariette," his mother said and closed the door. Sorin averted his eyes, knowing that tone. "You're both doing well, yes?"

"Of course we are. We're friends."

"You know what I mean."

He groaned. "Mother," he began.

"Don't you 'Mother' me. Answer my question."

"You know the answer, why is it so important?"

"Because I heard what you said to Eratos," she said sternly. He finally looked at her. "And I can also tell he's interested in Ariette." Just the thought made Sorin angry, and he gripped his hands into fists. "Exactly. Sorin, I don't understand. Why haven't you just proposed to Ariette?"

"I already have," he said, rolling onto his side to put his back to his mother.

"Sorin. Stop dodging the answer. I know you love her."

He groaned, putting a pillow over his head.
~~~

"It's not love, Mother," he said, his voice muffled. "I don't know what it is, but it's not love."

"If you don't know what it is, then how can you be sure it isn't love?" she asked. He had no answer. He heard her get up and sit beside him, putting a hand on his back. "Sorin, I know you're worried about everything and this isn't helping. But I know you. I know that, if you haven't already, you're falling in love with Ariette. Tell her. It will help her, I promise."

"I need to rest before dinner," he lied. "Can I have some privacy?"

She sighed. "Yes. I'll come get you when it's ready."

"Thank you."

The door closed. Sorin groaned. Did he love Ariette? He knew he already was starting to. It was how he had hoped to get her to stay, after all. But, faced with the possibility of actually telling her, he was having doubts. He shut his eyes and willed himself to sleep.

Unfortunately, the next time he saw his mother was not for dinner. His door burst open less than an hour later. He sat up. Peter was pulling Ariette and Nicole in against their will.

"But Queen Stela!" Ariette cried.

"Is not your responsibility right now," Peter said. "Sorin, the ship is under attack."

"What!?"

"I was above deck with the king, learning about the area. We saw a ship come from the distance. It was moving fast; faster than it should be against the wind. Something about the flag set Taranis off. He told us to get the women and be prepared to abandon the ship. We have to-."

Before he could finish his sentence, the ship lurched. Splintering wood and rushing water filled their ears and Ariette cried out.

"We have to find the queen!" she screamed. "Where is she!?"

Mother. Mother can you hear me?

Get Ariette and Nicole to safety! Now!

Sorin didn't need to be told twice. He grabbed the two women and Peter followed him out. Two large wolves were at the top of the stairs, growling at their enemy. Sorin didn't risk taking a look. Ariette was fighting him, trying to get to Stela and Sylvia, but he pressed on.

"This is their job!" he shouted over the sounds of another cannon being launched towards their ship. He nearly lost his footing as it slammed into the side of the ship. "Hold on tight!"

He didn't give them a chance to argue and leaped into the water, Peter close behind. The water was ice cold even in the midday sun. Ariette clung to him as Nicole tried to tread water. Peter grabbed her and they started swimming.

"We don't even know if there's land near!" Ariette said. "Please, Sorin! We have to go back!"

"No," he said, kicking his feet furiously.

Ariette must have realized it was futile for she stopped fighting. Sorin reached out to his mother but everything was moving too fast. He could see them being tied up and moved to the other ship. Anger burned in his chest and he turned just in time to see the ship blow into pieces. Ariette screamed as a large wave of water rushed at them. Before he could react, a piece of wood hit him in the head, knocking him unconscious.

***

"It's going to be okay. Just take a deep breath, I promise it'll be okay."

Sorin woke, coughing up sea water. He heard someone breathing heavily and Nicole whispering soothing words. He sat up and his blood ran cold. Peter lay in the sand of a beach, a large plank of wood sticking out of the center of his chest. His mind went numb as he crawled to him.

"I-I'm sorry," Peter panted. "Thought I could-."

He grimaced as he coughed.

"Don't apologize," Sorin said automatically. "We're safe."

Hurried footsteps announced Ariette. She was carrying a bundle of herbs and a large leaf. He moved, knowing to let her do what she had to. He kept holding Peter's hand as his eyes scanned their surroundings. They were on the beaches of an island. He had no idea if Talameh was just one island or multiple. He had to believe it was just the one, though. Ariette's hands were shaking as she tore the herbs, smashing them the best she could in her hands and Sorin grabbed hold of the wood.

"On three," Ariette said and Nicole also grabbed the wood, her face pale. "One, two...."

They pulled and Peter screamed, his back arching. Ariette moved quickly to stop the bleeding and applied the paste she had made. Peter sobbed in pain. Once it had been spread in a thick layer, she took the large leaf and wrapped it around, using a strip of her skirts to make a tie. When she was done, she went to rinse her hands in the ocean and Peter had fainted.

"What happened?" Sorin asked, watching his friend sleep.

"You were knocked out," Nicole said. She looked at the trees around them. "Peter got us on land. I didn't even know he was hurt. Ariette saw, ran to the trees, and then you woke up."

"I'm not sure what all of those herbs were," Ariette said when she returned. There were dark circles under her eyes from stress. "I recognized a few and went with my instinct, just like that night. Sorin, I have a serious question to ask you."

"What?"

"If it comes to it, are you able to turn Peter into a vampire?"

His head snapped to hers.

"Why are you asking me that?"

She flinched at his harsh tone but pushed on. "Because that wound is deep. I cleaned it and dressed it the best I could. But he's human. He may have a higher constitution, but we have to be prepared for the inevitable."

"No," he said. "I'm not going to turn Peter into a vampire. He'll live. I'm sure he will. We just need to get him to the palace."

"We don't even know where it is," Nicole said, her eyes filling with tears.

Sorin closed his eyes and focused on his mother.

"I can't see much," he mumbled. "I see... another beach. They're being taken in by more elves. Everyone's tied up, even the royal family. They're headed north."

"But north on this island or another?" Ariette asked.

He opened his eyes again and looked at her. "I don't know."

She sighed. "We can't move Peter. Not yet. His wound is too large; I had no way of stitching it. If we move him then- Sorin!"

Sorin lifted Peter carefully.

"We have to keep moving," he said, glaring at her. "Peter needs to be treated. No offense, but he needs a real doctor."

"Sorin," she said again. "If we do this, you have to know that you're risking his life. He could bleed out. He needs at least a few hours of rest."

"We don't have a few hours! Everyone's been taken prisoner! It's a miracle we survived! If you can even call that for Peter!"

She walked up to him and grabbed his face.

"He's going to live," she said, her eyes on fire. "No matter what, he's going to live. But he needs rest. His body needs to recover the blood it's lost. This will give me time to gather the herbs and more leaves. If there aren't any, we'll need to make bandages. He's a human, Sorin. He doesn't have the advantage you do. Please. Just five hours. That's all I ask."

Fuming, he nodded.

"Good," Nicole said with a sigh. "Now, where are we going?"

"This way," Ariette said and gathered her sopping skirts. "We'll go where the herbs were."

Sorin carried Peter with great care. The moment they entered the trees, he felt calmer. He wasn't sure if that was all the attackers; what if there were more on their tail? It would seem Ariette had the same thought; she reached where she had gathered the herbs, but took a ser-pentine route further in, keeping an eye out to make sure they still had herbs wherever they rested. A small clearing with a tiny stream caught her eye and she pointed. He put Peter in the shade of a large tree and took off his shirt to bundle it under his head. Peter made a face in his sleep and groaned but didn't wake up.

Ariette was gathering wood and throwing it into a bundle as Nicole looked for leaves.

"There aren't anymore," she told Ariette.

"We'll make our own, then," she said, and, to Sorin's slight horror, she took off her outer dress.

Even Nicole looked scandalized until they saw the slip she wore under it. She ignored them and started to tear her dress into bandages. Nicole joined her while Sorin watched Peter sleep. He had to live. Sorin couldn't do it without him.

He stood and tested the nearest trunk. It was thick and sturdy.

"Don't leave the area," he told them.

They just nodded and he began to scale the tree. It was a tall red oak. His fingers slipped a few times and he swallowed thickly. When was the last time he had fed? He couldn't remember. They had to get to safety soon.

He reached the top of the tree and gave his eyes a chance to adjust. To the west, he saw the remains of the battle. He turned to the north, though, and sighed in slight relief. The top of a crystal castle could be seen. He judged about a day or two's walk from where they currently were. Be it divine intervention or pure luck, Talameh really was just one large island.

He scaled back down the tree. The women had finished with Ariette's dress and Nicole was washing the fabric. He didn't see Ariette, though.

"She's collecting herbs," Nicole said when he asked. "She promised to not take more than ten minutes. That was seven minutes ago."

"Okay."

He sat down beside Peter. He was tense, they all were. Peter started to groan in his sleep, muttering Sorin's name several times. Sorin put a hand on Peter's until the younger man calmed. Ariette returned only a few minutes later. Her arms were full of herbs.

"I just wish I had a bowl," she said with a sigh.

She grabbed a piece of her bodice that still had the skeleton of a corset. She dumped all the herbs in it and plopped to the ground, exhausted.

"Did you see anything?" she asked, and he nodded.

"Two days, maybe three," he said. "We'll rest up and we'll only stop so you lot can rest."

"What about you?"

"I don't know what you mean."

"Did you... you know? Feed?"

"Yes," he lied. "Now get some rest. I'll keep watch."

She and Nicole shared a look but both of them laid next to each other. He watched as they fell asleep. His ears were straining for noise of any kind. Peter moaned beside him and Sorin gulped, gripping his hand.

"Don't worry, Peter," he whispered. "I'll find whoever did this and kill them."

XXI

Desperation

Sorin woke the girls promptly five hours later. The sun was starting to set.

"Shouldn't we wait?" Nicole asked nervously. "We don't know what kind of creatures live in these woods."

"I'll be able to fight off whatever might come," he said as Ariette checked Peter's wound.

She ran a hand through her hair. "If we could just find something to continually put pressure on it...."

"Put him on my back," Sorin said as he got on his knees. "The pressure can come from me."

He knew Ariette wanted to argue, but she did as he said. He then pointed to a vine near the tree.

"Tie him to me."

"Oh," she said in surprise. "That's actually a good idea."

He just nodded and waited. She and Nicole worked to loop the vine around the two of them until they could tie it around his chest.

"Is that too tight?" Ariette asked when he grimaced.

"No," he said. "The vine is just uncomfortable, that's all."

"All right," she said and sighed. "Now, which way?"

He pointed. "Stay close to me. If I tell you to run, by hell you better run."

Ariette picked up the makeshift bowl of herbs and Nicole picked up two sharp looking branches. The three of them set off. Sorin felt blood soak through the bandage but did his best not to panic about it. Peter's skin was hot on his with obvious fever. Ariette was right: If Peter didn't get care soon, he would die. The thought pushed Sorin forward.

Under normal circumstances, the forest would be beautiful. Trees were covered in moss and brightly colored flowers. He had no idea what was poisonous and what was safe, though. He didn't even know if the herbs in Ariette's arms were actually helping Peter and not making it worse. Night fell quickly and his fear of being blind was quickly diminished.

"It's beautiful," Nicole gasped.

As soon as darkness fell on the forest, insects lit up the area. They looked like fireflies, but they were bigger and different colors. Some were blue, some were orange, some yellow, and even a few red ones. They blinked around them peacefully. He could hear water running but saw no signs of predators. He heard the sounds of critters, though he wasn't sure what kind they were. If they were crickets, they weren't like any he had heard.

They made it to about one in the morning when Sorin's legs gave out the first time. He played it off as missing a hole in the ground. Ariette didn't seem convinced, but he wasn't surprised. The woman was sharp as a tack. Regardless, both were getting exhausted. He hadn't realized their hike had been an uphill trek.

"Just a little bit further," he said. "Once the sun starts to shine."

"That could be hours from now," Ariette said wearily. "We're hardly any use to you now. It's even less if we're exhausted."

"I know you're worried," he said. "But we can do this. Come on. Peter needs us."

Ariette bit her lip then nodded. As they climbed a small grouping of rocks, Sorin's hand slipped. Ariette grabbed it, though.

"Are you sure you're okay?" she asked when he was on his feet.

"I'm fine," he panted, wiping at the sweat. Peter mumbled in his sleep, trying to struggle. "Need to get Peter to safety."

Ariette's concern was only getting more and more strong when the sun finally rose. She expected Sorin to argue when they'd ask for a respite, not be the first to drop to their knees.

"We'll camp here," he said. "A few hours of sleep then we move again."

Ariette was about to say something but, once he had Peter in a safe spot, Sorin passed out.

"Something's wrong," Nicole whispered. "I think he lied to us."

"I know he did," Ariette whispered back. "We can't force him, though. Let's get some sleep. When we wake up, we'll find food."

"Ari, are we going to be okay?"

Ariette laid down next to Sorin, Nicole next to her. She faced Nicole and nodded.

"Yes, we will. Not sure how we're going to get out of this, but we will. I'm just worried about the others...."

"Me too."

Ariette sighed and closed her eyes, thinking of Queen Stela.

Her dream was filled with the sounds of fighting and rushing water. She opened her eyes and stood in front of a purple crystalized palace. In front of her, she could see the elven family, Queen Stela, and the others all grouped up. A rough looking elf stood in front of them, a murderous look on his face as he yelled at Taranis. Ariette tried to move closer to hear what he was saying, but her legs wouldn't respond. She watched desperately, wishing she could go and help them. As if sensing her presence, Queen Deirdre looked at her. She was mouthing something and Ariette strained her eyes to see.

Hurry.

Ariette woke with a gasp. She was still in the small clearing with Nicole, Sorin, and Peter. Nicole was cooking something. The food made Ariette's stomach growl, and she joined her.

"They have rabbits," Nicole said. "I didn't want to add any seasoning, though. I don't know what's safe, so it'll be bland."

"It's food, and that's the best we could hope for," Ariette said. "Where did you learn to do this?"

"Liam," she said. "I asked him to teach me so I could be of more help. He didn't want to at first, but I insisted. Thank the gods I did."

"I'm going to check on Peter. Good job, Nicky."

She walked quietly to Peter, trying to let the prince sleep. She got on her knees and checked the wound. It had stopped bleeding, thankfully. It looked like her herb mixture was helping, but his skin was on fire with fever. It made her anxious. She didn't have anything that could help with that. Just as she was wrapping the wound in fresh bandages, a hand gripped her wrist painfully.

Sorin was glaring at her, fangs down below his lips. Ariette was stunned, terrified of the look in his eyes. The irises were red.

"Sorin?" she choked out. Nicole looked up, startled at her tone. "Sorin, let me go."

"Don't touch him," he snarled.

She tried again, prying at his fingers. "It's me, Ariette. Please. You're scaring me." His only response was tightening his fingers. At this rate, he'd break her wrist. She thought of a way to bring him back. "Snap out of it. It's Ariette, your minx."

She hadn't planned to say it, but it worked. Sorin blinked a few times, his eyes returning to their usual amber. Ariette let out a sigh of relief. She worked her wrist free and rubbed it. He saw the bruise and regret filled his eyes as he sat up.

"I'm so sorry," he said in a hoarse voice. "I don't know what came over me."

"It's okay. Are you all right? I'm worried about you."

"I'll be fine," he said. He saw her fingers on Peter's neck. "How is he?"

"His pulse is erratic, and he has a fever, but he's no longer bleeding. I think the herbs are working. The wound isn't as inflamed as it was yesterday. I had a... vision," she added, and he looked at her again. She told him what she saw. "I think it was the necklace. It's the only reason I can come up with."

"Let's go," he said. "Once you've eaten."

"What about you? You haven't fed in a while. Don't lie to me," she said when he started to speak. "I know you. Tell me the truth. When was the last time you fed from Peter?"

He sighed, clearly irritated. "Before the ball."

Her jaw dropped. "Sorin, why didn't you tell us!?"

"It's not important," he snapped. "Now come on. Eat and help me get Peter on my back again."

She wanted to argue, but the look on his face scared her. She accepted some rabbit from Nicole and tried to feed some to Peter. He seemed to be in some kind of coma, though. He wouldn't wake. She tore it into small pieces and told Sorin to hold Peter's mouth open.

"Now rub his throat," she said after putting the rabbit in his mouth. "I don't know if he'll be able to stomach it, but it's better than him not having anything at all. Nicole, is there any water nearby? There isn't enough water in this small stream," she added, dipping her finger in the inch deep water.

"Yes," she said. "We'll have to take him to it, though. We don't have anything to carry it in...."

Ariette dumped the herbs onto the ground. "Use this."

Nicole did as she was told. While she was gone, Sorin took Ariette's injured wrist.

"I really am sorry," he said again. She flushed as he kissed it. "I don't have the energy to heal it right now, but I swear I'll make it up to you."

"Stop apologizing," she said. "I understand. I'm worried about him, too." She shivered. The island was warm, but her slip did little to prevent the occasional breeze from hitting her skin. "I just want to get to the others. That elf looked different from the others."

"How?" he asked.

Her blush deepened as he pulled her to him, rubbing her arms to warm her up.

"He was more muscular," she said, remembering the way he looked in her dream. "And he had a lot of scars on his arms. I wonder if he's one of the elves sent to the village, but he made it out."

"It's hard to say."

They sat in silence, the only sound the cracking of the small fire Nicole made. Her back was against Sorin's chest, and she leaned into him. He stopped rubbing her arms and wrapped one arm around her waist. Her heart quickened as he took her chin and tilted her head. She closed her eyes, waiting for his lips to rest on hers.

The kiss was short, though, as they heard Nicole's careful steps. The bodice was filled to the brim with water. They all drank gratefully, tilting what was left into Peter's mouth. Sorin rubbed his throat again, waiting until the water was all the way down his throat. Once they were done, they put him on Sorin's back again. She tied the vines tightly and paused. She stood on her tip toes and kissed him briefly on the lips.

Nicole smirked at her, but it changed to a frown. She saw Ariette's wrist.

"I'm okay," Ariette promised. "Let's go. I feel like we're close."

"The dream?" Nicole asked.

"Yes. Are you all ready?"

Both of them nodded and they started their hike. The sun rose slowly. Normally, Ariette would stop to admire it. But Peter was dying, as much as she wanted to believe otherwise. And Sorin....

It didn't come to a head until after midday. They came to a higher grouping of rocks.

"We can't climb this," Ariette said. "Stay here. I'm going to look for another way around it."

She walked quickly along the rocks. It took about five minutes, but she finally found a slope and called to the others. They climbed up but Sorin kept slipping. They both grabbed each of his arms and pulled. He pushed them away when he got on level ground.

"Oi," Nicole snapped. "I get your tired, but the least you could do is treat us with some respect!"

"Nicole," Ariette began.

"I'm worried about Peter, too! But this attitude isn't helping!"

Sorin's head was down, hands balled into fists. It seemed like a dark cloud was gathering around him.

"Nicole, stop."

"No, Ariette! I'm tired of the way he's treating us! Look at your wrist! He hurt you!"

"You're going to make him mad," she whispered.

"Are you listening to yourself!? You sound like you're defending his behavior!"

"That's not what I'm doing!" Ariette argued. "He's a vampire, Nicole!"

"You said you were safe! Were you lying to me!?"

"We don't have time for this! I am safe! But he hasn't had blood since before the ball! He's weak and compromised!"

"Watch who you're calling weak."

His voice was a low growl. Even Nicole looked frightened. He still hadn't looked at them.

"Sorry," Ariette said quickly. "I didn't mean-."

"If any of us are weak, it's you two. Peter's dying and all you care about is resting and eating."

Despite her fear, Ariette walked over to him, reaching out nervously.

"You're not thinking straight," she said. Her voice was breathless. "Come on, Sorin. We need to keep going."

"I know!" he shouted. He finally looked at her. All four of his fangs were showing, and his eyes red. Not just his irises anymore, but the whites of his eyes, too. "What do you think I've been saying for the last two days!"

"You're scaring me," she said.

"Good!" His voice had reached a roar. "Then maybe now you'll take me seriously for a change!"

"I always have," she snapped, her anger overtaking her fear.

"You've never been respectful!"

He advanced on her, snarling. She took a step back and tripped on a rock. She fell back painfully. Nicole ran to her side. She tried to shield Ariette, but her body was shaking with fear. Ariette looked around for a weapon. Her eyes landed on the branches. She saw the sharp point and finally understood what she had to do. She scrambled for it and pierced her arm. She cried out in pain.

"What are you doing!?" Nicole cried.

"He needs blood," Ariette said in a shaking voice. "Please, Nicole. This isn't him. I don't know what it is, but that's not Sorin."

"You're mad! What if you become a vampire, too!?"

"Peter was able to do it," she said and looked at Sorin. He was still snarling and walking to them. "Maybe I can, too."

"Ari," Nicole said. She was crying. "Please don't do this."

"I'll be okay. I can't explain it, but I know I'll be okay."

Before Nicole could stop her, she stood in front of Sorin. He grabbed her arm, his eyes on the blood running down it.

"Go ahead," she whispered. "Please, Sorin."

He didn't need telling twice. He brought her arm to his mouth and drank deeply. She gasped. Though his fangs didn't pierce her skin, the feeling of her blood leaving her made her panic. Nicole grabbed her when her knees gave out.

"You're taking too much," Nicole said, shaking Sorin. "Stop!"

As if in a trance, Sorin dropped her arm. He swayed on the spot as Nicole quickly bandaged Ariette's arm. His eyes slowly returned to normal.

"What-?"

He looked around him. He brought his fingers to his lips and stared at the blood on them.

"Ariette, what have you done?" he rasped.

"You needed blood," she said, leaning into Nicole. "You were about to attack us. You weren't thinking straight and-."

"You don't get it," he said. To her shock, his voice trembled with emotion. "You gave me your blood."

"I had to."

"Risks aside, you're now just like Peter."

"What do you-? Oh," she whispered. She swallowed thickly. "I mean, you have Peter. You don't necessarily need me, right?"

"I honestly don't know. But something's woken up in him."

"In who?" Nicole asked.

"I'm sorry," he said. "I didn't mean to scare you. It's a defense mechanism; that's the best way I can explain it right now."

Ariette's strength was returning to her already.

"Come on," she said. "We need to get to the palace now more than ever."

Sorin couldn't look her in the eyes but she didn't care anymore. She led the way further north, praying they'd reach it soon.

~~~

They stopped at nightfall. Sorin put Peter down, using his shirt for a pillow as usual. The two girls were talking about finding another rabbit. Guilt gripped him when he saw Ariette's arm. He couldn't stand it.

"I'm going to see where we are," he muttered and climbed the nearest tree before they could speak.

He couldn't believe what Ariette had done. She clearly hadn't thought it through. Nothing would have been able to stop him from killing her, or worse – turning her into a vampire. He refused to do that to anyone. The process of being a vampire was painful and had to be monitored carefully. When he reached the top of the tree, all thoughts of resting were gone. They were only a stone's throw away from the palace. He slid down the trunk.

"Wait," he said when Nicole left to find some food. He struggled to get Peter on his back. "We're close. The palace is on the outside of the trees."

"We're really that close?" Ariette asked, her eyes hopeful.

"Yes."

Ariette helped him get Peter on his back as Nicole regathered the herbs, just in case. They walked as fast as they could without disturbing Peter. The trees were thicker, but they managed to finally break free from the tangles of branches. It took Sorin a minute to take it all in.

The palace was made of a purple crystal. There was a large chasm
~~~

around it, bridges connecting the two land masses. He squinted and a welcome sight was outside of the palace steps.

"Mother," he gasped and grabbed both girls' hands.

He pulled them with him, desperate to get to safety. He could hear her voice. She was talking to someone about sending people to find Sorin and the girls. He tried to call out to her, but his heart was in his throat. The events of the last few days were catching up to him. Finally, he managed a shout and his mother spun around. Her face broke into a relieved smile, tears streaming down her face.

"Sorin!" she screamed and ran to them. "Ariette, Nicole! You're alive!"

"But Peter almost isn't," Ariette said, hugging the queen back. "He needs medical attention."

"Come inside," his mother said. She was still crying. "They have a good doctor who can help him."

"Where's the man who abducted you?" Ariette asked.

"I'll explain once we get Peter inside," his mother said. "I can feel his life slipping."

Sorin carried him inside. The inside of the palace was also crystal. There were no doorways, just arches. The king and queen were in the foyer, also talking about sending someone to find them. Deirdre gasped and rushed to Ariette.

"You got my message," she said.

"Yes, but it seems the danger has passed."

"The elves responsible are in the dungeons," Taranis said. "Oh no. Come with me; we'll get your servant cared for."

They followed him through a side arch. Taranis walked with brisk steps to a side room. Inside, an elf was bent over a book. He looked up when they entered and immediately cleared some space for Peter. Sorin set him down carefully. Behind him, Nicole gasped, and he turned. Ariette had fainted. Nicole caught her.

"I think she's exhausted," she said. "She didn't rest to get her blood back."

Her eyes were accusatory and Sorin was filled with remorse.

"I'll take her to her room," Deirdre said.

"I'll help," Sorin said.

"You've helped enough," Nicole snapped.

Sorin's heart sank as an elven guard picked up Ariette, following the queen and Nicole out of the room.

"What did she mean?" his mother asked.

"Ariette gave me some of her blood," he muttered. "He took over and I lost control."

"I'll talk to Nicole, explain everything. Stay with Peter."

Sorin nodded miserably and looked to the doctor.

"My name is Sorin," he said, extending a hand.

"It's a pleasure to meet you," he said and shook his hand. "I'm, ironically, Peter. Did you dress his wound?"

"No, it was Ariette. Why?"

"She did a wonderful job. Peter will live, but I need to keep him under observation for a few days. His body has given in to the fever and is in shock."

Sorin's body went weak with relief and he fell into a chair.

XXII

⸿

Recovery

Ariette woke up to a whispered argument.

"I don't care if it was defense or not. He could have killed her. And he said some really horrible things."

"I understand, Nicole. Believe me, I do. It wasn't him, though."

"You keep saying that, but you refuse to explain! Tell me or I'm taking Ariette and leaving!"

She heard Queen Stela sigh. "Very well. But Ariette's awake."

Ariette had finally opened her eyes and sat up. Her head was pounding, and she felt groggy. Nicole ran to her, hugging her tightly. She passed her a vial.

"The doctor made this for you," she explained. "It's to help you get your strength back."

Ariette accepted the medicine, looking at the room. She was in a feather bed. The sun was low in the sky and she could hear music in the distance. It was a soothing sound, and she felt a burden lift from her shoulders slightly. The room didn't have much decoration, but it was still beautiful with the purple crystal making up the walls. Two female elves walked in and bowed.

"We're here to prepare a bath for you," one said.

"If you ladies will go to your rooms, baths await you, too," the other said.

"Are you going to be okay?" Nicole asked.

"Yes. Go, you're exhausted, too."

Nicole hesitated but nodded. Stela followed and Ariette watched the two elves work. A clawed tub had been brought into the room. The first elf held out her hands and beads of water materialized.

"How are you doing that?" Ariette asked in awe.

"I can control water," she explained. "I'm taking what moisture is in the air and I'll be able to expand it."

"And I have the power to make fire," the other said and showed Ariette.

She put her palm out and aimed under the tub. A flame floated independently under the tub and, soon, there was steam floating up from the water. They turned so Ariette could get into the water.

"You don't have to help me," she said as the two elves started to put soap in her hair.

"It's our honor," the first elf said. "We haven't met another elf from off the island before."

"I'm not a full elf," she said. "An ancestor of mine stayed on the mainland, apparently."

"Still, though, it must be interesting there."

"I suppose so. It's nowhere near as beautiful as Talameh. I saw some beautiful flowers and other plants as we traveled here."

"I'm sorry you were attacked like that," she said with a sigh. "We've had some elves try to rise up against the king. They're not happy he reached out to outsiders."

Ariette frowned at the water. "That seems foolish. If we can help, why not ask?"

"Elves are proud creatures."

"I see."

Once she was done bathing, they gave her a towel to dry off and gathered some clothing. It was a green dress decorated with gold stitched leaves. The sleeves were made of tulle and she put reached for her daggers before remembering they had been lost when they abandoned the ship.

"Are you hungry?"

"No thank you," Ariette said. "Is there somewhere I can get some fresh air, though?"

"Yes. Our gardens are to the left of the palace. Would you like me to take you?"

"Please."

Ariette followed the two down the hall. A door at the end led to a staircase that ran along the outside of the palace. In the setting sun, Talameh was even more beautiful. She remembered their first night in the woods and how the lightning bugs lit up the world. As they walked, the bugs showed up again.

"We simply call them lightning bugs," the first elf said when Ariette asked about them. "Here are the gardens. I'll come get you when the feast is ready."

"Feast?"

"Yes. King Taranis has ordered a feast to celebrate your arrival."

Ariette watched them leave, a flurry of thoughts and emotions running through her mind. It made her head hurt and she sighed. The gardens around her were unlike any she had seen. Where the ones at Rosu were ordered, sectioned off, and decorated sparsely, the ones in Talameh could only be described as chaotic. Plants and flowers she couldn't identify grew wherever they wanted. Trees stretched across the dirt pathways, their roots winding around each other. Fruits hung from their branches that looked like some she had contemplated eating while they were making their way to the palace. Perhaps they were edible after all. The music she heard in her room continued outside and she meandered among the greenery. A fountain trickled somewhere nearby, and she sought it out. After a few turns through trunks, she came upon a beautiful sight.

The fountain was of three men, all positioned in brotherly camaraderie, standing proudly in front of the large moon slowly ascending the sky. The lightning bugs were in abundance here. One of the statues was clearly Taranis. The man beside him vaguely resembled Laurent and Sorin, while the third was shorter but muscular.

"The original three."

Ariette yelped and spun around. Sorin was in the shadows and she clutched her heart.

"You scared me," she accused.

"Sorry. I thought you heard me."

He joined her and she looked at his clothing. It wasn't his usual suit; instead, he had green silk trousers with a golden belt wrapped around the lower part of his torso. In place of a tunic, he wore one of the robes the king and prince had. She blushed when she realized she was staring and quickly looked back at the fountain.

"You mean the three brothers Taranis spoke of?"

"Yes. That's my ancestor, Roland. I'm assuming Percival is the third person, the first werewolf."

"I see." Suddenly, Sorin took her hand and moved the sleeves. "I lost the daggers in the attack or I'd be wearing them."

"It's not that," he said and traced the scar on her arm and the bruise on her wrist. His eyes were full of regret. "Those can be replaced. This, though...."

She watched as he passed his hand over the injuries. Her skin tingled as he did so and, when he lowered his hand, they were gone.

"That's amazing," she said. "I didn't know you were able to use your healing properties like that!"

"The scars are gone, yes. But the regret lingers."

Ariette sighed and held his hand. "Sorin, stop. I may not understand what happened, but I know it wasn't you."

"Nicole was right," he said. "What I did is unforgiveable."

Ariette couldn't handle seeing him feel so guilty.

"Maybe explain it to me," she suggested. "Then that can help you feel better."

He sighed and thought for a long time. As he did, he laced their fingers and she felt goosebumps erupt on her arms. She was used to his tender touch when they were around others, but they were completely alone.

"Father explained that vampires aren't born," he started. "At twenty-one, our bodies are fully developed, and it was deemed we were ready to begin the transition. When it happens, a part of our humanity dies away. It's replaced with a different life essence. We call it our inner vampire. Think of it as a conscious with nefarious intentions. It takes a lot of training and self-discipline not to give in. The vampire feels things strongly. Anything they want or need; they feel it more extremely than humans do. When I was low on blood, my life was at risk. I was trying to fight him off, but he eventually overpowered me. He acted in my stead. So, in a way, you're right: it wasn't me that hurt you. But, because I was too weak to fight him, he was able to do what he did."

Ariette wasn't sure what to say. She wrapped her arms around his torso, and he hesitated before returning her embrace. They stood in silence for a while. She couldn't imagine having to fight off a second part of her mind, constantly battling while trying to hide the fact they were vampires to the public. It had to be exhausting.

She kept holding him until she felt his body relax. His arms tightened, hands running up her back. She closed her eyes and listened to his heartbeat. It was faster than her own.

"I don't blame you for what happened," she said finally. "The thing about Nicole, is she's always been protective of me, and I her. Think of how you feel for Peter. Let me talk to her, I'll explain what you told me. But I do have one thing I have to ask of you."

"Anything."

"Don't lie to me anymore. If you haven't had any blood, tell me. I don't mind being there for you if Peter isn't capable of it."

"It's too risky, Ariette. I'd sooner take blood from Sigrid than you."

She wrinkled her nose. "Yeah, no."

He chuckled and she smiled at the feel of the vibrations through his chest.

"Are you jealous, Ariette?" he teased.

"There would have to be competition for me to be jealous."

He laughed again.

"Oh!" She looked up at him, too comfortable to leave the hug. "How is Peter?"

"He'll survive," he said, tucking some of her hair behind her ear. She smiled a little when his knuckles stroked her cheek. "The doctor said we got him there just in time. He'll be down for at least a week, but he's going to live. Thanks to you."

"I'm just glad we got him here in time," she said. "What about the others? I haven't seen anyone since I woke up except for your mother and Nicole."

"Relaxing, mostly. I'm not aware of what happened while we were separated; King Taranis promised to explain tomorrow."

She nodded. "Good. I expected to come back to some kind of rebellion or war."

"As did I, though I'm glad we didn't. Peter probably wouldn't have lived."

They didn't speak for a while. Ariette was having a hard time looking away from Sorin's eyes. In the light, they looked more gold than amber.

"When your eyes go red, does that mean your vampire is about to take over?"

"Yes."

"I see."

"Ariette," he said after another lengthy silence. "I want to take advantage of this time to tell you something."

"Of course."

He took a deep breath. For some reason, she felt anxiety gathering in her chest. Could it be what he had wanted to tell her the night the Talameh ship arrived?

"Ariette, I'm starting to-."

"There you are!" a voice said and Sorin growled, glaring at who came from the trees. Prince Eratos smiled. "The feast is ready, but we can't start without our honored guests."

"We'll be there in a moment," Sorin said.

"Surely you must be hungry," Eratos said.

Ariette could hear Sorin grinding his teeth in agitation.

"He's right, Sorin," she said. She tried to step away, but his arms tightened on her. "It would be rude to keep them waiting."

"Fine," he said and finally let her go. He put his arm around her waist, though, and seemed to glare daggers at the prince. "Lead the way."

"Gladly."

"What's gotten into you?" she whispered as the elven prince led them around to the front of the palace. "You're never this rude."

"It's nothing," he said, kicking at some dirt.

She wanted to argue, but she was surprised by what she saw. Long, wooden tables had been laid out on the land in front of the palace, just before the large chasm. They were laden with foods of all kinds and elves were gathered around, talking merrily. She could still hear the music, but no one was playing an instrument. When Eratos got his father's attention, Taranis grinned and pulled them over to the rest of their party.

"Are you okay?" Nicole asked her, looking sideways at Sorin.

"I'm perfectly fine, Nicky," she said. "Look what the prince did for me."

She moved her sleeves again and Nicole looked at the healed skin.

"Wow. Thanks, Prince," she added, sounding genuine.

"It's the least I could have done," he said.

"Yes, it was."

"Nicky," Ariette hissed but Sorin shook his head.

"Don't worry about it, Ariette," he mumbled.

Suddenly, a small body barreled into Ariette and she staggered, laughing a little.

"I'm so sorry!" Sylvia wailed. "You trusted me, but I couldn't help you!"

"Don't apologize," Ariette said, rubbing the young woman's back. "We were all taken by surprise. It's not your fault."

"We all owe you an apology," Raphael said.

He had joined them with Orin, Gerald, and William. They got on their knees in front of her, Sorin, and Nicole.

"Because of our negligence, you were put in great peril," Orin said in a grave voice.

"Please stand up," Ariette said. When they didn't, she nudged Sorin with her elbow. "Help me out here."

"Ariette's right," he said. "None of this is your fault, you shouldn't feel guilty."

"No, the one who should apologize is me," Taranis said. "I should have told you about the rebellious elves before we left."

"Will you tell us now?" Ariette asked, still comforting a crying Sylvia.

"I'd like for it to wait until morning, if that's okay," he said. He gestured at the assembled elves. "We've made this feast for you and would like to enjoy our time."

"Where's Stela?" she asked.

"Getting ready with my queen. As a fellow royal and, hopefully, future ally, I had something special prepared. Just as I did for Prince Sorin."

"I'm not used to apparel like this," Sorin said honestly. "But it's surprisingly comfortable."

Taranis beamed in pride. "And don't worry, Ariette. I haven't forgotten about you and your friend. You'll both also receive clothing worthy of royalty."

"That's not necessary," Ariette said as Nicole blushed. "I'm not royalty."

"Not yet," Taranis corrected. "And any friend of yours is just as much royal to me."

Ariette was about to tell him the truth, but the doors opened again. Ingvar and Sigrid walked out, still in their wolf's pelts. Ariette had almost forgotten they were there and wondered what had happened to them during the attack. Not far behind, the two queens walked out to uproarious applause. Ariette grinned.

Queen Stela was in an elegant dress of gold and red. It was simple, yet still had more extravagance than anything Misha had made for her in Rosu. Deirdre wore a similar dress, though hers was in Talameh's kingdom colors. Sylvia had finally let go of Ariette, so she rushed to Stela once the applause had died down.

"I'm so glad you're okay," Ariette said, and the queen hugged her.

"As am I. I was so worried when we couldn't reach you. I didn't know at the time that Sorin was weakened."

"Does that block the telepathic bond you share?"

"Yes. Thank you for taking such good care of him and Peter."

"It was my honor."

"Of course, I'm the one who got you to safety on the ship," Crystal said from behind Ariette.

Ariette's eye twitched as she turned around. Crystal was looking at her with thinly veiled disdain.

"Thank you," Ariette said. "I appreciate the fact that you were able to protect the queen."

Crystal lowered her voice. "Just because you've discarded your duties to play around with the prince doesn't mean we all will."

"Crystal," Stela snapped, and the woman looked shocked. "Watch your tongue."

"But it's true!"

"You know it isn't," Stela said. Her voice was firm and angry. "Even if it was, this is not the time nor the place. We are guests here and should behave appropriately."

Crystal sulked but didn't say anything else. Ariette was angry and Sorin, who had been catching up with Captain Alexei, did a double take.

He had been getting their side of the events as Taranis got everyone gathered in front of them.

I think you should do something before Ariette attacks Crystal.

The message hadn't made any sense until he looked over. Ariette's hands were clenched into fists and she was glaring at Crystal. Confused, he excused himself.

"Are you all right, Ariette?" he asked.

"Just fine," she said and crossed her arms. "Are we starting soon?"

"I think so," he said slowly. "What's wrong?"

"Nothing," she snapped. "Now's not the time. Queen Stela's right: we're guests here and shouldn't be arguing."

"Who's arguing?"

No one answered and he frowned at his mother. With a slight jerk of her head, she motioned to Crystal. Sorin sighed. He knew Crystal would do what she could to take over Ariette's position. He was weary of the drama and politics surrounding the lady-in-waiting slot. It was too much for him and was glad he didn't have to deal with it. Ariette was fiddling with her pendent, eyeing the elves around them.

"I still can't read their minds," he said, correctly guessing the question on her face.

"I wonder why," she said. "You can read Ingvar's and Sigrid's, right?"

"Yes. Why?"

"I thought maybe it had something to do with all the races having the same father or something to that effect," she said with a shrug.

"That's actually a very good guess," he said. She smiled a little. "I plan on asking Taranis tomorrow."

Finally, Taranis raised his arms to get everyone's attention. All eyes turned on them and he felt Ariette stiffen beside him. He returned his arm around her waist and pulled her close to him. Slowly, her body relaxed, and she put her hand on the one he had resting on her hip. His heart swelled at the contact.

"Thank you for coming tonight," Taranis said in a voice that carried over the assembled crowd. The elves all clapped. "I would also like to thank all of you who came to check on us. We are all just fine and hope to spend this evening in merriment. Please, join me in welcoming our esteemed guests from the kingdom of Rosu."

More applause then Taranis led them to one of the tables. Once they were seated, all of the elves did the same. Most of the food were of their local flora and fauna. Sorin let Taranis put food on their plates.

"These are much like your potatoes," Taranis explained as he did so. "Many of our flowers, while delicate, have wonderful nutritional benefits. We don't eat much meat, but we did try to provide enough for all of you."

"You didn't have to do that," he said and took a bite of what the king said was a root. "Oh, this is wonderful!"

Taranis grinned, taking his seat across from them. Deirdre sat to his right, the twin siblings to his left. Eratos was directly across from Ariette and engaging her in conversation, explaining the other dishes on the table. Sorin was irritated and held Ariette's hand where it was resting on top of the table.

Was this how Ariette felt about Sigrid? And how did the king not notice what his son was doing? His furious thoughts were interrupted, however, when Ariette laced their fingers, still listening to Eratos. It calmed him and gave him hope that, no matter what the elven prince said, she would still pick him.

He almost dropped the spoon he was holding, though, when that thought occurred to him. He looked over at his mother who was smiling at him, a mixture of pride, happiness, and the hint that she was rubbing it in his face.

Sorin had fallen in love with Ariette.

XXIII

Feast

"This food is delicious," Ariette said. "Do elves not need the same things humans do?"

"What do you mean?" Eratos asked, leaning closer presumably to hear her over the chatter.

"King Taranis said you don't eat meat that much. Meat has many nutrients we need; protein for example."

"Oh! Yes, we do. We just get it from other sources. Many of our plants have it. What we can't get from the plants, we do get from meat once in a while."

"A mostly vegetarian diet," she said in awe and looked at Sorin. "Can you imagine?"

"Probably not," he said with a small smile. "After all, I am a vampire."

She laughed. "You know what I mean."

"Try this," Eratos said and put a goblet in front of her. "It's our famous honey wine."

"Not a chance," Sorin said and grabbed the drink. Eratos looked offended. "She's allergic to honey."

"I had no idea. I'm sorry."

"Don't be," she said quickly. "Of course you didn't know; we hadn't told you." Taranis got his son's attention and Ariette leaned in to whisper to Sorin. "Why are you being so rude to him?"

"Not right now," he whispered back and took a sip of the wine. "I hate to say it, but Eratos is right. This wine is exquisite."

After the meal, Taranis brought the royal family to the front. Sorin insisted on bringing Ariette and she waved to Nicole. She stood beside him as three elves approached them.

"We come bearing gifts," a male elf said. "To thank you for agreeing to help us."

"Thank you," Stela said with a curtsy. "We accept gladly."

Stela was given a beautiful mirror made of the same golden twigs as the crowns. Different jewels adorned the handle. It also came with a brush that matched. An elf held out a sword for Sorin. The blade was strong steel, and the hilt pure gold, diamonds and rubies embedded in it. Ariette was given a tiara. She marveled at it in her hands. It looked exactly like the one the queen and princess wore. Sorin put it on her head and smiled.

"It matches you perfectly," he said, making her blush.

"Thank you," Ariette said. "These gifts are beautiful."

"Tomorrow, I'd like to take you on a tour of my kingdom," Taranis said once he had dismissed the elves. "You're all welcome to join, of course. This is our first time having wolves in our province."

"Well, I'm sure that's why you didn't have gifts prepared for us, too," Sigrid said, sneering at the tiara on Ariette's head.

For some reason, Taranis laughed. Sigrid looked offended.

"My dear duchess, you're just like Percival."

"What's that supposed to mean?"

"You should all return to your rooms," he said to the group at large. "I'll have servants come to wake you."

"You'll tell us what happened, right?" Ariette asked.

"I swear to it," he said. "Rest well, my friends."

"Good night."

Sorin took Ariette to a different room than the one she woke up in.

The bed was larger, and several dresses were hanging on the wall. There wasn't a wardrobe or even a closet.

"I'm so used to what we have in Rosu, this is so foreign," she said, walking to the window. It overlooked the gardens. In the distance, she could see the mist. "I wish we hadn't lost all of our belongings.... Mother made me that dress and- Oh!"

Sorin wrapped his arms around her from behind and kissed her shoulder. The warmth she had come to associate with his touch spread from the spot.

"I need you to do me a favor," he said.

"What is it?"

He didn't answer right away. He put his chin on her shoulder, also looking out the window.

"It's about the prince," he said in a low voice. "Be careful around him."

"He won't hurt me."

"I know he won't. It's the exact opposite I worry about."

Ariette couldn't understand what he meant. She turned in his arms and frowned.

"Sorin, be honest with me."

His jaw clenched a few times. "He's trying to take you for his own."

"I mean, so are you," she said. "But that doesn't necessarily mean-."

"Exactly," he interrupted. "Our engagement may be political, but that doesn't mean you're not spoken for. Eratos being this forward is disrespectful."

"Maybe it's different here," she said. "Even in Rosu it's not uncommon for a woman to have more than one suitor."

"This is different. If we were commoners, then I would say you're right. But we're not. I'm the prince."

"You don't even want to marry me," she pointed out. "So why are you so upset?"

He frowned at her. "Is that really what you think now?"

She didn't know what to say. She was even more confused. He didn't wait for an answer, he just let her go and took off his robe. Without a word, he got into the bed. For a while, she stood by the window, staring out at the lightning bugs. There wasn't another bed, but there were some chairs that looked comfortable enough.

"Just get in bed," Sorin said suddenly.

"I-."

"Don't argue. You're exhausted."

"I don't know what I said to upset you, but I'm sorry."

"It's late. We have a long day ahead of us."

Her shoulders fell but knew he was right. She took off the dress, standing in just a slip. There weren't any nightgowns, so she quickly dashed to the blankets. She slid in, trying to leave as much distance between her and Sorin as she could. After several fretful hours, she finally managed to fall asleep.

***

Sorin woke feeling very warm. There was a steady brush of air on his chest and he blinked open his eyes. It looked to be early morning. His arms were wrapped around something. It was Ariette. She was deep asleep, her forehead pressed to his chest. He remembered what she said the night before. She still thought he saw her as a political game piece. Granted, he hadn't had an opportunity to convince her otherwise. He pushed some hair out of her face, and she stirred a bit, mumbling his name. He couldn't stand the thought of Eratos taking her from him.

There was a light knock on his door then a female elf poked her head in.

"The king has asked I waken you and your fiancée," she said. "A tub will be brought in."

"Can you make that two?" he asked and felt Ariette start to wake up.

The elf looked confused. "But you are engaged to be married."

He gave her a pointed look and her cheeks went red as she understood. She bowed out and Ariette yawned, stretching. His eyes landed on her chest, and he forced them up. In the night, the top of her dress and pulled down. Very low.

"What time is it?" she mumbled, rubbing her eyes like a child.

It was oddly endearing.

"Around dawn," he said. "Did you sleep well?"

"Mm," she said with a nod. She kept her eyes closed and put her head back on the pillow. "I don't want to get up yet."

"Nor do I. I'm rather comfortable."

"Me too," she said.

Suddenly, her eyes shot open. She saw their bodies touching and squeaked. Sorin snorted as she scrambled away from him and landed on her back on the floor. He edged to the side of the bed, smirking down at her. She squeaked again and grabbed the edge of the blanket, tossing it over his body.

"What's wrong?" he teased.

"Shut up," she grumbled, using one of the throw pillows to cover her chest.

He laughed. "You're too easy to tease."

She mumbled something but didn't respond. The door opened and two tubs were carried in. Ariette only grew redder as they were placed right next to each other. The elves used their powers much like before then bowed out. A final elf brought in soaps. Sorin watched with a grin as he saw the internal debate going on in Ariette's face.

"You get in first and shut your eyes," she said, pointing at one of the tubs.

"Why me?"

"Because I don't trust you."

"I'm hurt," he said, feigning pain.

"Just get in the tub, Sorin."

He laughed again as she covered her eyes. He stripped down and got into the steaming water.

"Are your eyes closed?" she asked behind him.

"Yes, yes, they're closed."

He heard her moving around and resisted the urge to turn and look. He opened an eye when he heard the water beside him slosh. He couldn't stop a loud laugh. She was so hunched into the tub that the water came up to her nose.

"How do you plan on bathing like that?" he asked, still laughing.

He stopped when she brought her face out of the water. From her mouth, she spat a stream of water at him. He blinked a few times in surprise. She giggled shyly.

"Is that how we're going to be?" he asked.

"You deserved it," she said and grabbed one of the soaps on the floor. "You teased me."

He shrugged, watching out of the corner of his eye as she rubbed the soap on her arms. He felt a stirring near his groin and fumbled with his soap.

"If you weren't so easy to tease, I wouldn't do it," he said matter-of-factly.

"I'm not used to you being like this," she said. "And stop staring."

He shook his head and finished bathing. He leaned back onto the side of the tub, looking at her fully now.

"Need I remind you: I'm the prince, but I'm also a man."

She stopped and stared at him.

"What are you saying?"

Before he could answer, someone knocked on the door.

"Gods bless it!" he growled and slid down into the water.

At this rate, he'd never get the chance to tell her.

Peter and Sylvia had arrived to help them dress. Peter was carrying a screen.

"King Taranis wanted you to have this," he explained, setting it up between the two tubs. "He apologizes; he assumed you two were... closer."

"It's not a problem," Ariette said and let Sylvia help her out of the tub.

"Maybe for you," Sorin said under his breath.

"Are you all right?" Peter asked him.

Ariette and Sylvia were talking on the other side of the screen. Sorin kept his voice low.

"Just five minutes alone with her. Is that too much to ask?"

Peter's eyes were sparkling. "So your mother was right. I assumed it was true, especially since you haven't said anything to me."

Sorin paused as he finished putting on what Taranis said were pants. He did a double take then gripped Peter.

"Peter! I'm so sorry! Are you all right!? They said you wouldn't be better by now!"

Peter laughed as Sorin embraced him.

"I'm perfectly fine, Prince Sorin. A bit fatigued, but I've healed quicker than they thought. The doctor wasn't aware I was your thrall."

"I hate that word. I'm so glad you're okay, though."

"Peter!" Ariette gasped, coming around in a new gown. She threw her arms around him. "Thank the gods! Shouldn't you be in bed!?"

"I've been given the go ahead to rejoin you," he said. *Do I have your permission to hug her back?* Peter was staring at Sorin and he nodded. "Though the doctor has said I can't do anything too active."

"Luckily, it's just a meeting then a tour of the kingdom," Ariette said. She held Peter at arm's length. "Are you sure you're well enough?"

Peter took her hands and patted them.

"It looks like the prince isn't the only one in your debt. I promise that I'm just fine, Lady Ariette."

"Okay," she said, crossing her arms. "But if you start to feel too tired, then say something."

"I will," he promised. "The king is waiting in the dining area."

A few elves were waiting in the hall, bowing to them all. Nicole hurried to walk next to Ariette.

"These beds are amazing," Nicole gushed. "I've never slept so well in my life!"

"We used to use phoenix feathers."

They were in the dining area and Sorin helped Ariette and Nicole into their seats. He was doing his best to get into Nicole's good graces again. Across from him, Eratos was looking upset. Perhaps Taranis had finally spoken to his son.

"Unfortunately, the phoenix hasn't been seen in centuries," Taranis continued once they were all sitting.

"What happened?" Sorin asked.

"The war," he said sadly. "After it reached Rosu, the phoenix seemed to just disappear. All of them did."

"That's terrible," Ariette said. "Is there no hope of them coming back? Isn't that the cycle of the phoenix, after all?"

"I pray to Nezeu every day that it happens," Taranis said. "For now, though, I owe you all an explanation." Ariette straightened up. "I consult my people on everything I do. After all, it is their lives that are affected, just as much as mine. Many didn't agree with me reaching out to you. I never thought Ezekial would take it to such extremes, though."

"Is he the tall, muscular one?" Ariette asked.

"How did you know about that?"

"Queen Deirdre," she said and pulled the pendent out from under her gown. "I had a vision."

"Yes, it was Ezekial."

"Where is he now?"

"In the dungeons."

"I want to talk to him," Sorin said immediately.

"I'll give you a chance," Taranis promised. "Today, though, I want to show you Talameh."

"It'll be okay," Ariette said when Sorin tried to persist. She put her hand on his leg and his body eased. "Let's just have a good day today. We've had enough going on the last three days."

He smiled and held her hand. "You're right."

She blushed and returned to her food. His mother grinned at him as he clumsily ate with his left hand. Ariette tried to take her hand back but he held tighter to it.

"Will the duke and duchess be joining us?" Eratos asked.

"They've decided to stay in their quarters," Taranis said.

"Was that their decision, or someone else's?" Stela asked.

Taranis smiled at her. "Does it matter?"

"I see you share the feelings of others," she said.

"A polite way to put it, but yes. Percival and I never saw eye to eye. I was not surprised when I heard how he died, though I was saddened by it. It seems his ideals didn't perish with him, though."

"How did he die? If you don't mind me asking," Ariette added quickly.

"Not at all! You're to be the future queen of Rosu, you should know its history."

"Actually," she said but Taranis kept talking.

"Roland and Percival were fighting, as usual. I was already gathering my people to return to Talameh. I heard Percival roaring and Roland screaming. When I got to them, Percival had ripped Roland's throat out and Roland had beheaded him."

Ariette dropped her fork, jaw agape. Everyone else looked just as shocked and Taranis grimaced.

"Probably not table talk," Deirdre said gently. "Regardless, let's finish breakfast so we can see the village."

XXIV

Talameh

Ariette finished her meal quickly. She was still jarred by what the king said but did her best to see beyond it. It was the past, after all. As everyone was standing, Princess Fiona approached her with a letter in her hands.

"For me?" Ariette asked and the princess nodded, pointing to herself. "Oh, from you."

She unrolled it and smiled.

Thank you for keeping everyone safe. After the tour, I'd like to teach you how I speak with my family.

"I'd love to," Ariette said with a smile and Fiona grinned. "Will you be joining us?"

Fiona shook her head.

"But don't worry," Eratos said, appearing next to her. "I'll be there."

"How wonderful," Sorin said dryly. He pulled Ariette gently to him. Fiona laughed into her hand. "Are you sure you don't wish to join us, Princess?"

She curtsied in response and he frowned. Taranis swept them to the door, explaining in a lowered voice.

"Fiona prefers to stay indoors. While my people love her, they don't necessarily like her. It breaks my heart, but she's accepted it."

"That's a rotten behavior to have towards their princess," Ariette said angrily. "Do you want me to talk to them?"

Taranis laughed. "You have a fiery temper, dear Ariette. Thank you, but we've already done all we can."

"You're too peaceful," Ariette grumbled.

Sorin snorted. "Ariette, what do you expect them to do? Throw everyone in the dungeons who don't like her?"

"Isn't that what you tried to do to me?"

This time, he laughed loudly.

"Fair point."

"You had her thrown into the dungeons?" Queen Deirdre asked, eyes wide.

"That was before," Ariette said. "And I probably deserved it."

"Doesn't sound like your fiancé was looking out for you," Eratos said.

Ariette frowned as they walked out into the morning air. It was heavy with dew and the sky was a clear blue. She wasn't sure what was going through the prince's head but, before she could find out, her mind was turned to something worse. Sorin tried to lead her to the bridge, but Ariette dug her heels in.

"I don't like heights," she stammered.

"But when we got here," Sorin began.

"I was more worried about Peter than heights!"

Taranis shared a look with his wife. "That might be a problem," he said.

"It's okay," Sorin said and stood in front of Ariette. "Look at me." Nervously, she obeyed. "Take a deep breath and focus." When she did, she noticed his eyes seemed to swirl much as the mist had. "You can do this. One foot in front of the other. Just hold onto me."

She could only nod. He held her hand then put his other arm around her. She kept her eyes focused on the sky, crying out when the bridge creaked under her feet.

"This reminds me of the night we gathered the Moonglow flower," Sorin said.

"Trust me, I know. The urge to vomit is just as strong as it was then."

He laughed. "All I'm saying is, the walk through the dark was worth it, wasn't it?" She remembered the flowers opening up to the moon and nodded. "This will be just like that. You'll see."

Finally, her feet landed on solid earth again and she let out a long groan, bending over double. Sorin rubbed her back with an amused smile. Taranis, though, still seemed sheepish.

"What is it?" Sorin asked.

"Perhaps we should get something soothing for Lady Ariette," Queen Deirdre suggested.

Ariette straightened, pushing her hair out of her face.

"I don't like the way you said that."

Taranis gestured behind him and she groaned.

At first glance, there was nothing behind him but the forest. But then she saw the ladders. Ladders that went up at least fifteen feet into the trees to platforms. All of Talameh was suspended over the ground.

"No," she moaned. "Really?"

"It'll be okay," Sorin said. "Think of it this way: If you fall, it'll only be about twenty feet instead of eternity."

Ariette glared and shoved him a little. "Thank you. That makes me feel so much better!"

Sorin laughed again. "Relax, minx. You just crossed that chasm. What's stopping you from this?"

She huffed. "I guess you're right." She grabbed Nicole's hand. "Come on."

"You're just going to let him insult you like that?" she asked as they followed behind Taranis, Deirdre, and Eratos.

"What do you mean?"

"He called you a minx. That's rude."

"Oh." Ariette shrugged. "It's not really an insult. It's just... something he's called me for a while now."

"A nickname?" she asked and Ariette nodded. Something passed over Nicole's face and she turned slowly to look at Sorin. "I see."

"I'll let you go first," Taranis said when they reached the closest ladder.

"That way you can all watch my failure," she said. "Look at this wood! How can you be sure it's secure!?" She poked it and it swung. "See!?"

Sorin shook his head and shouldered his way up to the front.

"I'll go first," he said.

"No, I can go," Eratos said suddenly and took the ladder from Sorin. "After all, I'm the prince of this kingdom."

"As much as I appreciate you willing to do that, I'm sure having someone she knows up there will help Ariette climb."

Ariette stared between the two of them, jaw open, as they continued to bicker. Stela was snickering into her hands, but King Taranis didn't look as amused.

"Boys," Ariette said loudly. When they didn't stop, she clapped her hands and yelled, "Oi! Children!" They finally looked at her. "I'll go first. Move."

When neither did, she shooed them with her hands. Sorin was the last to let go. He held the ladder steady for her, and she closed her eyes, taking a deep breath.

"You've got this, Ari," Nicole said behind her. "I'm right behind you."

Her shoulders relaxed and Sorin glared at Eratos. The prince returned it. Before he could speak, King Taranis pulled him to the side. Sorin helped Nicole onto the ladder after Ariette had managed a few rungs. He felt disheartened. Even now, after he got her over the chasm, she still reached out to Nicole and not him.

"Don't worry about it," his mother said as she gathered her skirts. "But please try to stop fighting with the elven prince. The last thing we need is for our possible alliance with them to go up in smoke because of a girl."

"It's not just any girl, Mother," he murmured. "It's Ariette."

"Even so, you don't have to fight for Ariette's affection. I know you have it."

She kissed his cheek then climbed up the ladder. He followed her, feeling a small bit of hope. When he got to the top, he looked around in surprise. He stepped to the side so the royal family could join them, marveling at what he saw.

Bridges connected every grouping of trees. Elves had built huts on top of the platforms, some extending all the way to the next tree, eliminating the need for a bridge. Elves were trading goods but, when they saw the family, some bowed. The others just stared. Sorin remembered what King Taranis had said. How many of the elves were unhappy with their appearance?

"This is where my people live," Taranis said once everyone was standing. Ariette was pale and clinging to Nicole. "Their homes and bridges are made with dead wood that elves gifted with earth have reinforced."

"There's no marketplace," Ariette said.

"No. Unlike on the mainland, we have no use for that. Anything that an elf might need, they can get from the forest."

"Why so far up in the trees?" Sorin asked, craning his head to look over the side of the platform. Ariette groaned and pulled him away from it.

"Predators mostly," Taranis said. "As you can tell, elves are not made for war or fighting. We are hunters, gatherers. Such a passive lifestyle doesn't do well on the ground."

"That makes sense," he agreed. "You had made it seem that the tour would be a day long occurrence, though. Is there more?"

"Yes, actually. Follow me."

Sorin looked around in interest while they followed him beyond the huts. Elves hurried out of their way. He tried to smile at a few of them, but they only scampered away. The line of homes seemed to extend for several miles. When they finally reached the end, Taranis was helping a quietly swearing Ariette down to the top of a ladder.

At the base, Sorin hesitated. Ariette and Nicole also looked uneasy.

"What's wrong?" Taranis asked, noticing their concern.

"I didn't realize we had been so close," Ariette said sadly.

Not more than ten yards away was the spot Sorin had almost attacked the girls. He saw her rub the arm she had cut, and guilt settled on his stomach again. Stela tried to give him a reassuring smile, but he shook his head. He looked behind him. The ladder was cleverly hidden; if he hadn't been looking for it, there was no way he could've seen it.

"Wait," Sorin said as a thought struck him. "We were this close, and no one noticed us?"

"I hope that's the truth," Ariette said. "I know they're not happy we're here, but they wouldn't just leave us, would they?"

Taranis didn't have an answer.

"This is something we'll need to discuss after we're done investigating," Stela said to Taranis as gently as she could. "You know my family and I would love to become allies, but your people aren't making it look like a possibility. If there's one thing I've learned, it's that you have nothing if you don't have the faith and support of your people."

"Believe me," Taranis said. "I will make sure they understand the importance of it all. No matter what, they will be behind us. Now, this is what I wanted to show you."

He took them further into the forest on a path. The flowers and plants were plentiful here.

"It's our main hunting route," Queen Deirdre explained as they walked. "It's also where we gather much of our greenery for eating."

"You must not have been here recently, then," Nicole said.

"Talameh is brimming with magic," Taranis said. "The plants around you grow back at a quicker rate than on the mainland."

"Is that magic you can teach to our wizards?"

"No, I'm afraid not. This magic is in the land."

The path wound through the forest for a while. Taranis would explain different points of interest. Before long, a heavy feeling settled in Sorin's stomach. He slowed down with a frown as his mother and the soldiers they brought with them did the same. Ariette turned when she noticed.

"What's wrong?" she asked.

"Something's wrong," Sorin said, his hand going to the sword he had been gifted.

Taranis looked sad. "We're near the city that Darius had built here. What you're feeling is the same presence that's been taking my people."

Sorin's eyes searched the trees. His sense of paranoia increased. He rushed to stand in front of Ariette and Nicole, the soldiers taking up around them. Stela's nails were growing, as were her fangs. Even Taranis had felt the malicious intent from the invisible intruder. They waited for several tense minutes. Just as quickly as it had come, the feeling disappeared. Birdsong he hadn't noticed was missing returned, and they breathed a sigh of relief.

"You weren't wrong," Sorin said. "There really is something here."

"Yes. And it's not something my people are equipped to handle."

"Very well," he said. "We'll need weapons. Food won't be necessary."

Taranis nodded. "For now, let's return to the palace to plan."

<p style="text-align:center">~~~</p>

Ariette and Nicole joined everyone in a library. Like the rest of the palace, its walls and floor were made of crystal.

"Where did you get all of the crystal to make this?" she asked, sitting beside Stela and Nicole.

"I actually created it with Deirdre," Taranis said. "We combined our powers to make it."

"It's very impressive," Nicole complimented.

Eratos took down a large, rolled up parchment. He laid it out on the desk and Ariette got up to look. Stela stopped her, though, with a small shake of her head. All of the men bent over it.

"This is a map of our island," Eratos said. "Here is the palace, and here is the city. It's not large, hence the reason we're so worried."

"What did your search party find when they came back?" Sorin asked.

"None of them have returned."

Ariette bit her lip nervously. She fiddled with the pendent around her neck. She yearned to know what else they were saying, but they had lowered their voices to deliberate.

"I'll just go ask," she said.

Stela stopped her again.

"I know you're curious, but Sorin will tell you later."

"Why can't I go now?"

"Sorin has asked you not go up there right now," she said. "I don't know why, but I think we should just wait patiently."

Ariette sighed. "I hate being patient."

Nicole giggled. "Not as much as you hate heights."

"Ugh. That was so terrifying. Queen Deirdre," she said, and the queen looked up from the book in her lap. "Why is that chasm all around the palace?"

She closed her book and said, "It's a relic from when we were banished here. Before Taranis put up the mist, we had a few invaders. They had horrible weapons and tried to take over the palace. We gathered all the elves in front of the palace. Those who could manipulate earth then created the chasm. It was enough to scare the men off, though I'm sad to say a few did die. We had to fell a few trees to make the bridges, but sometimes sacrifices have to be made."

"Is that why the bridges in the village are made of dead wood?" Nicole asked. "So you don't have to harm any more trees?"

"Exactly."

Ariette sat in silence, thinking about what the queen had said. She had never met such a passive group of people before. Yet, despite their desire to uphold those beliefs, there were still elves out there willing to destroy to stop strangers from coming into their land. Although, knowing about the chasm's creation explained the extreme measures somewhat.

After an hour, the men all agreed on a course of action. Ariette was doing her best not to fall asleep. All the books were in Elvish and she had given up trying to read it. Chairs were brought over to where the women were, and an elf came in with some food to pass around.

"So, we have a plan," Sorin said at the same time as Eratos.

"Technically, it's Sorin's plan," Taranis said before the two could start to argue. "We'll let him explain."

"Tomorrow morning, I and the soldiers will go to where the city is," he said. Ariette frowned. "We'll inspect the area. It's small and shouldn't take more than a few hours. From what you've told me, it sounds like a powerful spell is at work here. I took several lessons from David and, hopefully, I can figure out what to do to break it."

"And what are we supposed to do?" Ariette asked. "Just sit here and wait for you to get back?"

"It won't take more than a day," Sorin said. "Don't worry."

"There's no way I'm just staying here," she said. "I'll go with you."

"It's too dangerous," he argued. "We don't know what's waiting there. You felt that presence."

"Let me get this straight: because I'm a woman, I'm too fragile?"

"No," he snapped. "Because you're a human."

Her eyes flashed. "Need I remind you it was with my blood we got here in the first place?"

Sorin matched her glare. "I told you not to do it. If you're that worried, we can bring Ingvar and Sigrid with us."

"Like hell you're taking her! If they can go, so can I!"

"No!"

"You're not the boss of me, Sorin!"

"That doesn't mean I can't stop you from doing something stupid!"

"Enough," Stela said when Ariette and Sorin got to their feet to shout more. "Ariette, I know you're worried, but Sorin is right. This is too dangerous for a human to go to."

"I'll be surrounded by vampires, though! Honestly, is there any better defense?"

"She has a point," Stela said. "There are five of you."

"Ari," Nicole said, standing beside her. "Maybe, just this once, you should listen to them. I don't want you getting hurt."

"I won't get hurt," she promised. "Sorin taught me how to fight."

He pinched the bridge of his nose. "I taught you how to defend yourself, Ariette. It's not the same thing."

"I can help," she said. "I'm not just going to sit here!"

"And I'm not just going to let you go somewhere you can get hurt!"

Stela stood up, too, and grabbed Ariette and Sorin by the arms. She marched them out through the palace. She didn't let them go until they were in the gardens.

"I'm so ashamed," she snapped. "We're guests here. If you want to argue, do it somewhere private. Do not come back until you've sorted this out."

Ariette deflated immediately. Stela walked off briskly. The fight had left both Sorin and Ariette for a while.

"She's more frightening than my mother," Ariette muttered.

"Imagine growing up with that."

Ariette sighed and stared at the fountain.

"I know you're trying to keep me safe, Sorin," she said. "But there's something in me telling me I have to go. I can't explain it, but I know I have to be there."

"I understand. But look at this from our point of view," he said. "We're not only vampires, but soldiers, too. On top of that," he added when she tried to argue, "I can't risk you getting hurt."

"I'm not as weak as you think I am," she said.

"You're not understanding me." He took her face and kissed her. Before she could respond, he stopped. "I can't live with myself if something were to happen to you."

She shook her head. "Sorin, you don't need to keep it up here. We're alone and-."

"I'm not acting," he said firmly. She stared at him, her heart beating faster. His eyes were locked on hers. "Ariette, the reason I don't want you to go is.... It's because I love you and I don't want you to get hurt."

XXV

The City

Ariette couldn't think of anything to say. She took his wrists and stood on her toes to kiss him. He let go of her face to pull her close, deepening the kiss. Time seemed to freeze. So much made sense now. The tenderness even when they were alone, his hostility when Eratos would get too close to her, and his stubborn refusal to let her go.

The question was, though, did she love him, too?

She broke from the kiss and he pressed his forehead to hers, breathing heavily.

"Now you definitely aren't leaving without me," she whispered. "Sorin, don't make me wait here for you after telling me that."

"Do you understand what you're walking into?"

"No," she said honestly. "But do you?"

His shoulders dropped. "No."

"Please, Sorin. Let me go with you. If you make me stay, I'll sneak out and follow after you anyway."

This managed to get him to smile.

"You know, I wouldn't be surprised if you did." She bit her lip, waiting anxiously. "Fine. You can come with us. But you have to stay with me, no matter what. I don't care what you see or hear. I'll tie you to my waist if I have to."

"I promise," she said immediately.

"I'm not done," he said. He let her go to pace. "If I tell you to run, you get your ass out of there. If we do have to fight something, you will in no way try to help. You'll get somewhere safe and wait for me to get you. Am I understood?"

"Crystal clear."

"Don't make me regret this, Ariette."

"I won't," she said and held his hands. "I swear."

<center>~~~</center>

They returned to the palace a few minutes later. Everyone was still in the library and Ariette sat down, her cheeks pink.

"Ariette will come," Sorin said once he had returned to his seat.

"You're out of your mind," Eratos blurted. "You can't let her go!"

"She's an adult and her own woman," Sorin said, barely containing his anger towards the prince. "At the end of the day, the only way to stop her is to lock her in the dungeons."

"If you have any love for her, you wouldn't let her go," Eratos said.

"It's because he loves me that he's letting me go," Ariette said. Sorin's stomach flipped at her words. Despite everything, he had noticed she hadn't said if she loved him, too. "Thank you for your concern, Prince Eratos, but I'll be safe."

"You know, if this doesn't prove to the duke and duchess this is all a lie, I don't know what will," Eratos snapped.

"What's a lie?"

Sorin clenched his jaw. Of all the times to show up....

Ingvar and Sigrid had shown up in the archway, frowning at the assembled group.

"Nothing," Sorin said with a sigh. "We're going to the place Darius made his city tomorrow morning."

"And when were you going to tell me?" Ingvar demanded.

"As soon as we were done here," Sorin said. "You're welcome to join us."

Sigrid smiled at him. "I'll gladly join you, Sorin."

"Knock it off, Sigrid," Ariette said in a tired voice. Everyone gawked at her. "Seriously, this is getting exhausting. If you're coming tomorrow, then fine. But stop trying to take my place as Sorin's wife. It's not going to happen."

"She's going?" Sigrid demanded. "The human is coming!?"

"My fiancée is coming, yes," he said. "She's more than you think she is. We'll wake at dawn for some food then we'll go."

He grabbed Ariette's hand and gestured to Nicole and their personal servants. His mother followed. No one spoke until the seven of them were in the room he was shaving with Ariette. Once the door was closed, his mother put her hand on the door, whispering the words to the spell that muffled sound. When she was done, she turned to Ariette.

"Do you have to do this?" she asked.

"Please don't," Nicole said. "Let me come if you're going!"

"I need you to stay here," Ariette said. "There's something you can do while we're gone."

"Me?"

"Yes." She walked to their window and pointed at the mist in the distance. "Taranis says he can lower this mist once we finish at the city. But it makes me wonder: why hasn't he done it already then? What's stopping him? We're clearly going."

"You don't trust him?"

"It's not that. I'm just not sure he can really do it. You've always been the fastest reader. Look through their books. Maybe there's something there."

"I don't want you to go," Nicole groaned. "It's so dangerous."

"I'll be with Sorin," Ariette said but Nicole just shook her head again. "If that's not enough, I'll also be with Orin, Gerald, William, and Raphael."

"Maybe she's right," Sylvia said. "Orin is the captain; he's very experienced in battle. And, out of them all, I would put my faith in Raphael more in making sure Lady Ariette gets out safe."

"His orders will be to drag her out if he has to," Sorin said, digging through the outfits they had given them. "I know you don't care for me, Nicole, but I swear to you she'll be safe. I won't let anything happen to her."

"Just like you did when we were on our way here?" Nicole snapped.

Sorin lowered the robe he was holding and took a few deep breaths. Clearly, his mother hadn't had a chance to explain it to her.

"Sit down," Sorin said, pointing to the bed. "I'll explain it to you."

"Just listen," Ariette said as she sat beside Nicole. "Let him tell you and it'll make sense."

Nicole just glared at Sorin. He knew she was listening, though. He told her about his inner vampire, explained how it acts when he's in immediate danger.

"What's to stop all of your vampires from attacking her, then!?" Nicole demanded after he was done.

"That's where Raphael comes in," Sorin said. "Raphael was chosen because he's done something very few vampires, myself included, have been able to do."

"And what's that?" she asked.

"He has... what's the best word?" he asked his mother.

She thought for a few minutes. "Fused is the only one I can come up with."

"It's as good as any. He's fused with his vampire. They work as one. So, under the extreme circumstance that we're all incapacitated, he can and will get Ariette out." Nicole still didn't look convinced, but she had relaxed a little. "I know why you're worried, and it brings me peace knowing that someone cares about Ariette as much, if not more, as I do. Think what you will, but know I'm telling the truth when I say I love her."

Nicole whipped her head to Ariette who nodded.

"I thought your relationship was just to stop what's-her-name from being queen," Nicole said, whispering.

"It was," Sorin said. "However, when we get home, I hope to change that. For now, though, we need to focus on this city. Ariette is right: I'm not convinced that Taranis knows how to lower the mist. I don't think he's trying to deceive, just that he hasn't thought this through all the way."

Nicole heaved a sigh. "Fine. I'll stay and look through their books."

"I'll do the same," his mother said. "Will you be taking Peter?"

"The doctor said I shouldn't go," Peter said sadly. "Even if Sorin doesn't need my blood, I still risk reopening my wound."

"That's not a concern," Sorin said. "I really do believe this will only take a few hours. We will need to see if they have different kinds of clothing for us. We're not going to be poking around some ruins in silk."

"I'll go talk to Queen Deirdre," Ariette offered.

Sorin nodded. "Sylvia, I'd like for you to stay here. Sigrid and Ingvar are coming."

Sylvia was clearly disappointed but agreed. They spent the rest of the day getting ready. Thankfully, the queen was able to provide clothing for them that was more appropriate for what they were doing. After a quick dinner, they went to bed early. Sorin was particularly nervous. It was his first time alone with Ariette since he told her the truth.

"We have everything ready, I think," Ariette said, dumping out their rucksack to repack it. "I'll wear this in the morning, that way I won't have to change." She laid out what looked like a riding outfit: tight pants and a loose cotton shirt. "They've added extra rations in here just in case we're there longer or if you guys start to need food. Here's the small flask with Peter's blood; poor guy will have to spend a day in bed. Remind me to get him something nice when we get back. Ah, here's the-."

"Ariette," he interrupted, and she stopped. She didn't look at him. "Are you really packing or trying to stall?"

"I don't know what you're talking about," she lied, folding a shirt for the tenth time.

"I'm sorry if I said it too soon. I just needed you to know."

She sighed. "I'm not upset that you told me, Sorin."

"But you're still upset."

She fiddled with the shirt and, when she next spoke, he heard the lump in her throat.

"I feel bad," she mumbled. He walked over to her, trying to get her to look at him. She refused. "I care about you, very much. But I'm not sure if...."

"I'm not expecting you to love me back," he said, though his heart dropped. "I know I haven't made it easy. I meant what I told Nicole. When we return home, I'll do it right this time."

"But I'm a human. Sigrid was right about that."

Finally, he got her to turn. He gently forced her face up so he could kiss her.

"To me, that just makes you more precious," he whispered and wiped at a stray tear on her cheek. "We should sleep, though. You have a bridge to cross in the morning."

She groaned. "Don't remind me."

~~~

Ariette didn't sleep well that night. She kept thinking about Sorin had said. Did he really love her? After all they had been through, was he really sure it was love and not just appreciation for what she had done? And what about her feelings for him? She definitely cared about him; she couldn't stand the thought of him going to that city and possibly dying. But that could simply be affection, not love.

When the sun did finally rise, it took Sorin threatening to dunk her in cold water to get her out of bed. The screen Peter brought in was still up and she changed into the outfit the queen had given her. It was very comfortable. She stepped out to model it for Sorin.

"Queen Deirdre said the women here wear this more than dresses," she said, rotating. "Maybe Stela and Laurent will consider doing the same! This is so comfortable."

"You look lovely," he complimented, shouldering the rucksack. "But I don't know if Rosu is quite ready for that."
~~~

"Well, we'll just have to make them ready."

He laughed as they walked out. Ingvar and Sigrid were in the hall, bags of their own slung over their shoulders. Ariette frowned, forgetting they had wormed their way into the party once again. Sigrid gave her a once over then turned, nose up in the air. Sorin gave Ariette a piece of ribbon and she tied her hair up. Breakfast was waiting for them in the hall. Nicole hugged her tightly.

"Please, please, please be safe," she whispered and Ariette hugged her back.

"I will be. If nothing else, I have Sorin."

"I'm still not sure how I feel about that," Nicole grumbled.

Ariette laughed. "Just remember to take notes."

The king was holding a platter of scones and she took one with a word of thanks. Queen Deirdre passed around waterskins and Ariette attached it to her hip. Sorin tied a sword onto her other hip, using the action to hide a quick kiss on her shoulder that made her heart flutter. He made no mention of it, though, as he passed around the other swords. Stela gathered them all in a group before leaving.

"I'd like to say a prayer over you," she told them.

Ariette felt a little uncomfortable. She didn't really have a deity to believe in. Though, if what the king said about her Elven heritage was true, perhaps she should learn more about Nezeu. After a quick prayer, Stela hugged her and Sorin.

"Stay safe and come back," she said.

"We will," Sorin said and kissed her forehead.

They waved to them and Sorin and Ariette took up the front of the group. When they got to the bridge, she was about to shy away until she remembered Sigrid behind her. She squared her shoulders and started to walk. Then she looked down and squeaked.

"I've got you," Sorin said from beside her. He put his arm around her. He pointed to a tree. "Do you see the flowers on that tree?" She nodded. "Focus on those."

"I'm going to vomit," she moaned.

"You'll be fine. Remember: one foot in front of the other."

Ariette gulped and did as he said. They took it slow and, when they reached the other side, her knees went weak. She leaned into him for support.

"Well done," he said. "Take a second to breathe."

"Thank you," she said. "I'd rather get to the city as soon as we can, though. The sooner we get this over with, the sooner we can go home."

"I agree." He made sure everyone had caught up and began their walk. "Any ideas on why you're so compelled to come?"

"I've thought about it. I'm half elf, after all. Perhaps it's something from my ancestors."

Sorin nodded, though he doubted that was the case. He followed the route the king had suggested. Once they reached about a mile from the ruins, everyone slowed down. The malicious aura was back. Ariette nervously gripped the hilt of her sword, eyes darting. Behind them, everyone else was doing the same. The two wolves' teeth were showing, waiting for the first sign of danger. Even the sky seemed to have darkened. Eventually, they reached the edge of the ruins.

It was smaller than Sorin anticipated. It had just a few buildings, all but a few burned down to the foundations. From what he could tell, there wasn't much order to the way things were laid out.

"Okay," he said once they had all grouped around the front gate. "Remember the plan: stick with at least one person. By the looks of it, we should be done within an hour or two. Meet back here then."

"Yes sir," they all said in unison.

"All right."

He put his hand on the gate and hesitated. He felt something shoot up his arm, like a tiny bolt of lightning. He ignored it, though, and pushed the gate open. Ariette took his hand and they walked in together.

XXVI

Trapped

The ground under their boots was hard. Ariette was surprised by what she saw. Beyond the stone walls that surrounded the city, everything was burnt. The grass was charred and the trees all dead. She sniffed a couple times and held her hand out. Ash fell onto her hand.

"How is that possible?" she asked, showing Sorin.

He frowned, too. "Maybe the wind is kicking up some old ash," he said. "There's a building there we can look through."

He took her into the nearest one. The lower half was one big room, a staircase in the back leading to the second floor. Most of the walls were still standing. They climbed the stairs carefully, pausing every time a stair creaked. The upper floor was also open, but she saw sheets crumpled on the floor. Stepping carefully, she inspected them. The ceiling above each sheet had small holes in them. She picked up a sheet and gasped in pain.

"What's wrong?" Sorin asked.

She showed him her red hand.

"There are metal hooks on the sheets," she explained as he pressed his hand on hers, healing the burn. "I'm guessing so the sheets can create a wall. I touched one and it burned me. It's like it was still hot from fire."

"That's impossible," he said and kicked the sheet around with his foot until the hooks were visible.

"I don't know...."

"There's nothing else up here," he said. "Looks like it was just a home."

"I didn't see any kind of structure on the way in. Just a bunch of buildings wherever they wanted to put them."

He nodded and they explored a few of the other buildings. Not many had other floors, just the one. They saw one that looked like it had once been a shop. Another home was only a single floor, and Ariette felt a lump form in her throat. Sorin was inspecting some rubble in a corner and she approached a piece of furniture in the back of the home. She recognized it immediately.

A small crib was pushed into the back corner. Charred remains of wood gave her the impression that whoever lived there had tried to hide the crib. Her hands shaking, she reached out and moved the blanket. She let out a small sob and Sorin rushed to her.

"What happened? What is- Oh," he whispered. He pulled her to him, making her face his chest. "I'm sorry you had to see that."

"It's just a little baby!" she wailed.

"I know."

"What in the world happened here?"

"Let's go look for the others," he said in a somber voice, walking away from the crib. "It's been about an hour and-."

He didn't get to finish his sentence. Somewhere in the distance, they heard a piercing scream.

"Luca," he said and ran out into the street, listening.

She did the same, gripping her necklace. They heard it again, somewhere to the north.

"Prince! Please!" Luca's voice carried to them. He was sobbing in pain. "Please help me!"

"Where are you!?" Sorin yelled back, running blindly.

"Please! Oh gods! I don't want to die!"

Ariette's tears doubled as she chased after Sorin, gripping his hand tightly. Sorin's irises were red, his free hand on the hilt of his sword.

"Tell me where you are! I'll come save you!"

"The chapel!"

Those were his last words. With a final, blood curdling scream, his pleas for mercy faded into the distance. Sorin screeched to a halt, panting. Ariette couldn't stop crying. She only had a few minutes to register that she didn't recognize where they were. Before she could say something to Sorin about it, they heard something shuffling from the corner ahead of them.

"Luca!" Sorin panted.

"Wait," she began but it was too late.

He pulled her around the corner, and she screamed in horror.

In front of them, a figure stood in the gloom cast by the wall of the building. It was at least eight feet tall, its body grey and emaciated. It was impossible to tell the gender, but it had elongated hands and feet. The hands only had four fingers that were stretching out in front of it. The head is what horrified her the most. It had a large mouth with rows upon rows of sharp teeth. Blood and drool stretched between very thin lips. Its nose was simply two slits. Where the eyes should have been, there was a stretch of clammy skin. Two holes on either side of the head is all it had for ears.

The creature's movements were slow and calculated. Sorin drew his sword and its head snapped in their direction again. Ariette stifled another scream. It moved quicker and Sorin broke through his shock, swinging his sword. The creature let out a high-pitched shriek as its hand fell to the ground with a squishy thud. Black blood squirted out of the stub and the creature retreated into the shadows. Ariette edged away from the disembodied hand.

"What the hell was that?"

Sorin's voice was hoarse and she gulped.

"I-I don't know," she said, trembling. "We need to find the others and get out of here."

"Luca," Sorin said as if just remembering. "We have to find Luca."

"Sorin."

"He was this way," he said, dragging her. "We just have to catch up with him."

"Sorin."

"If we can find him, we can still save him."

"Sorin!" she said loudly, and he finally stopped. Her eyes were sad. "Sorin, I don't think we'll be there in time. I'm sorry." His eyes flickered with panic and he gulped a few times. "We need to find the others."

He managed to nod, and they continued walking, Ariette drawing her sword, too. Every corner they reached, Sorin checked it before giving the all clear.

"Something's wrong," she whispered. "We should have been to the gate by now. None of this looks familiar and-."

She stopped. There was another sound coming from ahead and she quaked. She couldn't handle another one of those monsters. Sorin regripped his sword then dashed around the corner, bringing his sword down. Ariette cringed but, instead of the agonized scream of a demon spawn, she heard the clang of steel on steel.

"Sorin," Captain Alexei panted. "Thank the gods it's just you."

Ariette cried in relief. It was the rest of the group. At first, she thought the wolves by them were from the village. Then she recognized the pattern of their fur and their eyes. Both of them were snarling, their hair on end as they constantly looked around them.

"You heard it too," Alexei said. "Luca...."

"Of course I did," Sorin said. He sheathed his sword. "We need to get out of here. We'll go back and tell Taranis to find a way to conjure magic flame and burn it down. I don't care how; we just have to-."

"Your highness, I'm afraid that's not going to be possible," Alexei said.

"What do you mean?" he snapped.

"We tried to leave," Albu said. "We can't find the gate. There's some kind of spell going on here."

"I don't understand," Sorin said.

"This city has turned into a kind of labyrinth," Raphael said. "We can't find the exit. We're trapped in here."

~~~

Sorin found a building with all walls still standing. There were still a few wooden furniture pieces intact and the men worked on barricading the doors and windows. Sorin checked the upper floor for any of those creatures. All he saw was an open floor and a few shattered windows. When he got back to the lower floor, Ariette was crouched in front of a small fire. She hadn't stopped crying. He sat behind her and let her cower into him.

"Who was the last person with him?" he asked finally.

"He went off on his own," Albu said grimly. "I told him to stay with me, but he was sure it was safe. I saw him suddenly fall and ran to help him. That's when he started to scream."

"I chased after it," Ingvar said, shifting back to a human with Sigrid. Both were covered in dirt, scrapes on their arms. "It was fast, Prince. Even in our wolf form, we couldn't keep up with it. It-It doesn't just walk on two legs like us. It scrambles around on all fours."

He felt Ariette shiver in fear.

"I lost it when we came to a dead end," Sigrid picked up the story. For once, her voice wasn't haughty. It sounded defeated and scared. "It leaped up the wall with Luca hanging from its mouth."

"He said something about a chapel," Sorin said. "Did you see one?"

"No. But he was facing behind the creature. I imagine that was the last thing he saw."

Sorin clenched his jaw, guilt ripping at his chest. He dropped his head onto Ariette's back, taking deep breaths. She was still trembling, and he tried to comfort her.

"Raphael," he said, and the lieutenant looked from where he was standing guard by a crack in the window. "Can you tell what the time is?"

"No, your highness. In fact, the sun hasn't moved at all."
~~~

"It wasn't old ash we saw," Ariette said in a hoarse voice. "We're in a time lock."

"How do you know about time locks?" Ingvar asked.

"The books in the queen's library back in Rosu," she mumbled. "A few talked about them and blood magic."

"She's right. But why would someone lock this city at this point in time? For what purpose? And why the labyrinth?"

Sorin rubbed his eyes. "We need to find the chapel. But first." He grabbed the rucksack and started to dig through it. "Oh gods. Please no."

Ariette turned in alarm. He dumped out the sack. All of their food had spoiled somehow. Even the bread was hard as a rock. Sorin tried to keep his hand steady as he opened the flask and held it upside down.

It was dry.

"We're doomed," Sigrid whispered, also rooting through her sack. "All the food. It's gone. Spoiled. But how?"

"We have to break this curse," Alexei said, his face paler than normal. "It's the only way we can leave."

"I need to rest," Sorin said. "We all do. We'll take turns keeping watch."

"Don't worry about being the watch," Ingvar said. "You should take care of her."

He gestured to Ariette who had fainted when she saw their destroyed rations. He was surprised at Ingvar's sudden concern. It must have shown on his face, for Ingvar sighed.

"I hate to admit it, but it's clear," he said after everyone had figured out who would be next to guard their hiding place. "And I commend her for coming here."

"Thank you," Sorin said and looked to Sigrid.

She just turned her back on him and laid down. Ingvar also laid down beside his daughter. Sorin laid Ariette out in front of him, letting her use his arm as a pillow. He bundled up the rucksack under his head and shut his eyes, holding Ariette as close to him as possible.

He woke what felt like just a few minutes later to Ariette thrashing in her sleep. His eyes shot open. The first thing he saw was Sigrid's hand on Ariette's face and he swiped at her. She hissed at him, though, and he took a closer look. Ariette was clearly having a nightmare, her screams muffled only by Sigrid's hand. Everyone was gathered around her.

"How long ago did this start?" he whispered.

"Just now," Sigrid said. "I heard it coming."

Sorin pushed Ariette's hair away and kissed her cheek then neck. He whispered into her ear.

"It's okay, Ariette. It's just a nightmare. You're safe. Wake up. Come on, wake up, my minx."

Her body continued to squirm, but her screams had died out. Finally, she went limp and Sigrid timidly removed her hand.

"I didn't do it for her," she snapped when Sorin thanked her. "I did it so she wouldn't get us killed."

He rolled his eyes but, with a loud gasp, Ariette sat bolt upright, her head knocking into Sorin's chin. He grimaced, rubbing his jaw. Ariette was looking around in terror.

"Easy," Sorin said, rubbing her arms. "It was just a nightmare."

"No," she panted. "I-I know what happened here." She wiped at her sweaty face. "And I know why I had to come." She took a few gulps from her waterskin and leaned into Sorin. They waited for her to catch her breath. "It was Darius, kind of...."

"This should do it," Darius said, holding up a vial of blood. "Are you sure you're fine with this?"

"Anything for my king," Ishmael said.

Darius passed him the vial, watching intently. Ishmael swallowed the blood. At first, nothing happened. Darius was about to celebrate but, before he could, Ishmael fell to his knees. Blood was pouring out of his eyes and ears. He opened his mouth to scream but all that came out was blood. He fell face down on the stone floor. Darius growled and kicked at the table.

He thought that, if he came to Talameh, he would find an answer. This place just breathed magic! There had to be something! He paced around in the home he had built. He looked through his books for the tenth time, praying to find something new. Nothing showed up. He threw the last book over his shoulder and something caught his eye.

A large, black book was in the back corner. He frowned. He didn't recognize it. He took it out and opened it. It was written in a script he had long since thought was dead. He propped it open on the lectern. The book spoke of eternal life. He gripped the lectern, eyes wide. Eternal life not just for humans, but for vampires, as well. Without the need for human blood!

The spell seemed easy enough. It mentioned a name, one he hadn't heard before.

"Diav," he muttered. The room went dark and he jumped. "Who's there!?"

"I see you've found my book," a voice echoed through the room.

Darius tried to find the source of the voice.

"Who are you?" he demanded.

"The one you need," the voice said. "I have the solution to what you seek."

"You know the spell?"

"I know the component it needs. I have it. Here."

"What is it? I'll pay you. All the gold you want."

Cold laughter. "I have no need for petty things like gold. No, what I need is more refined. I need your soul."

Darius frowned. "My soul? Why?"

A gush of wind made him duck. When he straightened, he saw nothing. He felt breath on the back of his neck but couldn't bring himself to turn.

"The soul of a vampire is a powerful thing indeed."

Darius gulped. "Do you swear to it?" he asked. "It will free my people from this curse?"

"Yes."

"Then I accept."

A stone fell in front of him, etched with runes.

"Cast the spell in the temple," the voice said as it started to fade. "It will begin immediately."

The room and everything in it faded. Suddenly, Darius was running through the street, headed for the temple. Blood was pouring from a gash in his arm. He kept looking over his shoulder. The screams of his people echoed in his ears. Screams that quickly turned into the shrieks of the hell spawn. He *slammed the doors of the temple, dragging a pew to block them. A statue he had erected for their god, Nezeu, sat in the far back corner. He staggered to it and fell to his knees.*

"I'm sorry," he said in a hoarse voice. "I didn't know." A loud crash from the door made him jump. "I-I'm going to fix it, though. No one will be able to get out. I'll lock this here. But please. Help us."

The door opened and he closed his eyes, lips trembling as he spoke out a spell.

"Whatever spell that demon gave him turned the citizens into those... things," she finished, sniffling. "He sacrificed himself to lock everything in the village. That's why we can't get out."

"Gods," Orin said. "How do we get out?"

"We do what Darius asked," Sorin said. He got up, pulling Ariette up with him. "We're going to help them."

XXVII

Nezeu

"I'll go first," Sorin said, standing in front of the door. "Ariette, behind me. Don't let go of my hand. Alexei, you bring up the rear. Have your sword at the ready. We don't move until I say."

Everyone nodded. Ingvar gripped Ariette's other hand as the rest filed in line. When they were all ready, Sorin moved the barricade. He inched closer to the doorway, eyes searching. He waited for a few moments, but nothing happened. He started going north, the direction Ariette had seen in her vision. At every corner, he stopped.

It was quiet for a while, but then he heard a different sound. At first, he could hear the shuffling. But another sound accompanied it: a rattling and gasping. He pressed his back against the building, everyone else doing the same. He looked around the corner and clenched his jaw. It was another creature. It hadn't noticed them yet. He gestured with his head and Alexei seemed to understand. Without breaking the link, he walked on silent feet. The line curved with him. Once he was level with Sorin, they swung at the same time. Sorin's sword went through the creature's neck, not giving it the chance to make a sound. Alexei's cleaved it in two.

Ariette gagged behind him but didn't make a noise. He knew it was a mistake to bring her.

They continued their slow journey. It was impossible to know how long it took. He was worried they were going the wrong way and looked to Ingvar. He mouthed, "Check," to him and Ingvar shifted noiselessly into a wolf. With deft motions, he scaled the nearest building. He hunkered low onto the roof, just in case, and swiveled his head. He did a doubletake and returned to them. He pointed to the north east before taking Ariette and Sigrid's hands again. Sorin gave him a nod and they turned down a new alley.

Sweat was building on his neck and forehead. Ariette's hand was clammy in his. Each corner brought more anxiety. But then he reached one that gave him a sliver of hope.

The chapel was about sixty yards away. What worried him was the open space. There was a lot of it. They had about two more buildings of cover before they would have to make a mad dash for the entrance. Sorin led them along it before sheathing his sword. Alexei did the same. Sorin motioned for them to group around him and spoke in an almost imperceptible whisper.

"I'm going to run to the door. Ariette, follow me after you get the signal. Only go one at a time."

Before he could go, Ariette grabbed him and kissed his lips.

"Just in case," she began but he stopped her.

He kissed her lightly before sprinting for the front of the chapel turned temple. It hadn't been touched by time nor fire. There was a large sign with a small amount of space for them to hide behind. He beckoned for Ariette and she flew to him, her feet making no noise on the ground. She clung to him, shaking, as he silently called for the next person. Soon, everyone had made it across.

The handles, though old, also seemed to be immune from decay. He turned a knob and opened the door. Stale air rushed over their faces and he gagged. His senses were heightened as he ushered everyone through. Just as he was going to run in, he heard a horrible sound behind him.

The creatures knew. Their shrieks and the odd padding of their feet filled the air. He ran in and slammed the door shut. Raphael and Ingvar wedged pews into the doors. Sigrid and the others were doing the same to the stained-glass windows. Ariette, though, was slowly walking towards a statue at the end of the room. He ran to her, trying to pull her away. She wouldn't move.

He looked at her face. Again, her eyes were glazed over. They were fixed on the statue, though. Sorin didn't stop her, but he did walk close in case she fell. Her steps were slow, and he had time to study the floor as they got closer to their destination. His blood ran cold when her feet finally stopped.

At the foot of the enormous statue, a corpse lay face down in a puddle of blood. The body of his ancestor was perfectly preserved. Ariette snapped out of her trance.

Her back lurched and he jumped out of the way in time. She vomited on the floor, gripping her stomach. She was panting and swayed on the spot. Behind them, bodies were thudding against the chapel door. The shrieks sounded desperate. A creature tried to throw itself through the window but rebounded off the pew.

"What do we do?" Ingvar asked, looking afraid.

"The stone," Ariette said. "We need to find the stone."

She looked fearfully at the body. Sorin passed her to Raphael and approached the body nervously. He knelt down.

Darius looked exactly like the paintings back in Rosu. His face was lined, though, and he had grey streaks in his hair. He was clutching something in his left hand.

"I'm sorry," Sorin muttered and forced the frozen fingers open.

A perfectly smooth stone clattered to the floor. He picked it up.

"It's an anchor," Ariette explained. "We have to-." She screamed as the chapel doors splintered under the weight of the creatures. Raphael backed her into the statue, holding his sword at the ready. "We have to destroy it!"

"How?" Sorin asked, slamming it against the stone floor.

"I don't know," she sobbed. "I'm sorry!"

Grey arms were straining for the pews. Ingvar and Sigrid had shifted and were biting off arms. But a new creature would just replace the one they mauled. Sorin felt his vampire start to stir. He was panicking. He looked closer at the stone.

He didn't recognize the script. Nothing he had studied with David had looked like this. How was he supposed to break it? And how did he know that breaking the stone would stop this all? This was a fool's errand. He never should have let Ariette come!

Ariette. He looked at her over his shoulder. She was sobbing into Raphael's back, crying for someone to help them. She had said it was a time lock. A time lock made with blood magic.

"Please," he said, gazing at the statue. "Please let this work."

He cut his hand on his sword and drenched the rock in it. It started to glow and pulsate. In his uninjured hand, he brought the blade down on the stone. Time seemed to freeze. An energy pulse knocked him off his feet. There was the sound of glass shattering. When he opened his eyes, the stone was in two pieces. The creatures had stopped, and, for a blissful moment, he thought it was over.

"Move!" Raphael shouted suddenly.

He grabbed Sorin by the scruff of his neck and yanked him to his feet. Sorin turned to see the back of the temple starting to cave in on itself. He scooped up the remains of the stone and grabbed Ariette's hand. She stumbled as they raced for the door. Albu and Alexei were scrambling to move the pews. The floor behind him shuddered and he chanced a look behind him.

"Forgive me," he said to Ariette.

He picked her up and threw her as carefully as he could, jumping out after her. He felt a piece of the roof knock into his boot, making him fly further than intended. The air was filled with dust and the sound of falling rubble. His ears were ringing. When the chaos passed, he lifted his head. The dust was thick, and he winced at the pain in his foot. Where the creatures once were, all that remained were piles of ash. But something much worse caught his attention.

"You're going to be okay," Raphael was panting. "Just hang in there. We'll get you back."

"Sorin," Ariette gasped.

He rushed over to them, swiping at the dust in the air to get it to move. His knees gave out. There was a large piece of shrapnel in Ariette's side. She was bleeding profusely, and he knew she was struggling to breathe.

"It may have pierced a lung," Raphael said. "Sorin, I don't think she'll-."

"I can see the gate!" Alexei shouted from a few feet away. "Does that mean the spell broke?"

"We have to get her to the palace," Sorin said, picking her up as he stood.

"Sorin, you have to be careful. If she loses too much blood-."

"I'll take her," Ingvar said. "I can run faster than you."

"I'm not letting her go," Sorin said. "I'll get her there."

He started running for the gate, but he was still disoriented from the fall. Ingvar grabbed him, helped him steady, then shifted. Sorin understood that the wolf wanted him to get on his back. Glad that Ingvar was a large wolf, he did so and held tight to the back of his neck. As soon as he had settled, Ingvar took off at full speed.

"We're almost back to the palace," Sorin said to Ariette. "Don't worry. You're going to be okay."

"Sorin," she said again, her voice weak. "I don't think- I'm sorry. I-I shouldn't have-."

She coughed, blood running out of the corner of her mouth.

"Stop," Sorin said. "Don't speak. You're going to be okay. I can see the bridges now."

"I'm sorry," she said again, and her eyes closed.

"No!" he yelled and shook her, stumbling off of Ingvar when they were across the bridge. He was vaguely aware of people around him. His eyes were blinded by tears and exhaustion. "Please! Someone!"

"I'm here!" a familiar voice called.

He couldn't place who it was but fell to his knees.

"Save her," he managed before fainting.

***

Sorin's body was numb at first. Then he felt water wash over him. It wasn't hot, but it wasn't cold, either. It passed over his face and he opened his mouth to scream. The water rushed in and he feared he would drown. He was being sucked down into something. Then, his body was rocketing through the air until he was on his feet. He staggered, looking around.

All he could see was the marble floor, a few marble columns, and a statue. Everything else was a swirling mass of black and purple, stars blinking in the distance. The statue in front of him was what looked like a man. He had two wings, long hair, pointed ears, and a wolf's pelt. He almost fell over when the stone shattered. He raised his hands to protect his face but didn't feel anything hit them. He chanced a peek and was overcome with fear. He fell to his knees, immediately trying to placate the god standing before him.

"Rise, Prince," the god said. "You need not kneel to me." Sorin was too afraid to move, though. "Do you know who I am?"

"Please forgive me, but no."

"No apology is necessary," he said. "I am Nezeu, father of your kind."

"You're real," he rasped.

"Yes, I am. You and your love have done me a great service."

"The stone?"

"Your ancestor wanted to make life better for everyone. He prayed to me, but I told him the truth: this is part of your punishment. You must sustain yourself on either the blood of your master or a human. He got desperate and reached out to an old enemy of mine."

"Diav?"

"Yes. If he had not sacrificed himself, I would not have agreed to spare them."

Sorin finally got the courage to look the being in the face. He had fangs and Sorin gulped.

"Is she okay?" he whispered.

"Yes. She will live. But her recovery will be hard. She will need you by her side."

"Why her?" he asked desperately. "Why did she have to be there?"

"Ariette comes from a long line of seers. Oracles, if you will. Only she could reveal the way to end the curse. I have planned this since the beginning."

Sorin was having trouble comprehending everything.

"Why am I here?"

"As a reward for your actions, I am giving you very important information. What you do with it is up to you." Sorin waited. "The secret to the mist lies in the elven princess."

The world around him started to fade.

"Wait!" Sorin called. "What do you mean? She can't speak!"

"Keep close to Ariette, Prince. You are her only chance at life."

"What does that mean!? Don't go! Please! Wait!"

He tried to get to his feet, but a force was keeping him down. Soon, everything was black.

XXVIII

Recovery

Sorin woke in a cold sweat. He was in the room in Talameh's palace. He staggered to his feet, vaguely aware of someone saying his name.

"Ariette," he said, pushing their hands off of him. He tried to get to the door. "Take me to Ariette."

"You need to wait, son," the person said.

Sorin stopped, swaying on the spot. He turned and blinked until his vision cleared.

"Father?" he asked.

Laurent caught him before he fell and helped him to a chair. Without preamble, he cut into his arm and let Sorin drink from him. Sorin drank until he regained some strength and fell back into the chair, grimacing as he felt the wounds that had yet to heal due to lack of blood.

"Why are you here?" he asked when his father sat down. "You should be in Rosu."

Laurent's face was pale. "Sorin, how long do you think it's been since you left?" he whispered.

"Just a week or so. Why?"

His father shook his head. "It's been a month."

"What!?"

Sorin tried to get up again but Laurent pushed him gently into the chair again.

"You were in that village for almost a month," he said. "King Taranis sent an envoy with the queen after you were gone for a week. I came with Seamus, the nomad's alpha, and some of our men. None of us could get close. There was some kind of barrier that Taranis had said wasn't there before." Laurent rubbed his face. "We haven't slept in days, trying to get you back. Nicole is beside herself. I was about to find a spell to break the seal when we felt a small earthquake. I came out to find what it was to see you running with Ariette barely alive in your arms. What happened?"

"I need to see her," Sorin said, standing with a groan. "How long was I out?"

"Three days."

"Take me to Ariette. I'll explain once everyone's together."

Laurent sighed but nodded. He helped Sorin walk through the halls and down the stairs. He had never seen wolves, elves, and vampires together, but they were all merging in the antechamber. Everyone bowed to him as Laurent kept walking through a back door he didn't recognize. They went down another hall. Finally, they came to an archway. Sorin pushed away from his father and rushed to a table. Nicole was holding Ariette's hand, lips trembling.

"She won't wake up," Nicole whimpered. "This is all your fault, Sorin! I told you not to take her with you!"

Sorin ignored her. He caressed Ariette's face. It was pale and cold.

"He said I'm her chance at life," he whispered. "I hope he didn't mean what I think he did."

"Who said that?"

"Nezeu."

"Who the hell is Nezeu? You better fix this, Sorin!"

Sorin kissed Ariette, holding her hand tightly. Her lips were cold, and he could barely hear her breathing. He sat down on the provided chair and just stared at Ariette, Nicole continuing to berate him. He was too exhausted to care.

"Okay, Nicky," a voice said from the doorway. "I'm sure Prince Sorin has heard enough."

"Elizabeth," Sorin gasped. "I'm so sorry."

Elizabeth shook her head and sat down across from him, holding Ariette's other hand. Nicole sulked out of the room, muttering about going to see Liam.

"I know how Ariette is," she said. "Stela told me how she demanded to go with you. What happened, Sorin?"

He sighed, running a hand through his hair, and told her everything.

"Who's Nezeu? I've never heard of him."

"He's the god that created the first elf, vampire, and werewolf. I thought he was just a myth. Turns out he's real."

"And he told you that you're her best chance at living?"

"Something like that. He was really vague. I sincerely hope he didn't mean...."

"You're worried the only way to save her is to turn her into a vampire."

It wasn't a question and he stared at her.

"How did you know?"

"It's written all over your face. Not to mention, I've thought the same thing."

"I won't do it," he said, stroking Ariette's hair. "There has to be another way."

"You really love her, don't you?"

"Yes."

They sat in silence for a while.

"Is Liam here?" he asked, remembering what Nicole said.

"Yes. He came to help find you two and to see Nicole."

"I'll never redeem myself; not after this."

"Liam isn't mad, if that helps any. Nicole told me what happened when you got attacked on the way here. She's just worried about Ariette. She'll come around eventually."

"I just want Ariette to wake up. Who else is here?"

"Lucian and a few of the castle guards."

Someone knocked on the wall by the archway and they both looked over. It was King Taranis.

"Your father is asking you join him in the throne room," he said.

"No. I'm staying with Ariette. Tell him I'll be there when she wakes up."

"It's about the city. You'll want to hear this."

"Go," Elizabeth said. "I won't leave."

"Send word when she wakes up, please," he said, standing reluctantly.

"I will."

He followed Taranis out of the room, his shoulders low.

"Buck up, Prince," Taranis said. "She'll wake up."

"I wish I could be as confident as you are."

When they entered the throne room, his parents were standing with Ingvar and Sigrid. A wolf he didn't recognize stood with them, too. He had a pretty good idea of who it was, though. He shook hands with everyone.

"I am Seamus," the wolf said. "I'm sorry about your bride."

"She'll wake up," he said. "She has to."

"Laurent has said you wanted to wait to tell everyone what happened," Taranis said. "But Ingvar has given us some of what occurred."

"I saw Nezeu," Sorin said. "He said that Darius was desperate to find a way to get rid of thralls. Darius didn't like what Nezeu had to say, so he reached out to a demon. At the end, Darius begged for Nezeu to help, ultimately sacrificing himself to protect Talameh from the curse. I had to use my blood to break it. Before I woke up, I had a vision of Nezeu. He said that, if it hadn't been for Darius's sacrifice, we never would have been able to help."

"And what of Ariette?" Seamus asked.

"She's the last of a line of seers. She had to be there; it was the only way we'd find out what to do. I'm sorry I wasn't there to welcome you, Alpha," he added. "I had no idea we'd be in that place for so long."

"Ingvar explained the time lock," Seamus said. "You've done a great service for all of our races."

"Did you know who Nezeu is?"

"Yes," he said. "The tale of our father was passed down to each alpha."

Ingvar frowned. "Remus never told us about him!"

"And he's been reprimanded for it, believe me. The rift between the three brothers has weighed heavily on all of our races. Perhaps now, things will get better."

"What do you mean?" Laurent asked.

"The three brothers were of each race," Seamus said and gestured to himself, Laurent, and Taranis. "They fought, killed, and disappeared. Nezeu cursed us, as Taranis has told you. However, a great tragedy ended when wolves," here he pointed to Ingvar and Sigrid, "a vampire," he pointed to Sorin, "and an elf, dear Ariette, came together to end it. You put your differences aside to see the bigger picture."

"You know Ariette is part elf?"

"Yes. Do I think it will end this war? No. But I do know that this is all the reasoning I need." He looked to Laurent. "I will aid you."

Laurent and Sorin let out long sighs of relief.

"So shall we," Taranis said. "I don't know what we can give you. Our people are not made for war."

"The three of us coming together is all we need," Seamus said. "King Laurent and I are direct descendants of your brothers, King Taranis. Together, we can end what they started. Perhaps that will give us favor in Nezeu's eyes."

"First we need to deal with the mist," Taranis said. "The spell I had didn't work."

"Nezeu said that the secret to the mist is with Princess Fiona," Sorin said. "He didn't explain."

"Fiona?" Taranis repeated. "Perhaps, but I don't know what she can do to help."

"I don't either," Sorin said. "Frankly, my main concern is downstairs, unable to wake."

"She lost a lot of blood," Laurent pointed out. "It takes a while to recover it."

"Nezeu hinted that I was the one to save her. But if he meant turning her into a vampire, I refuse to do it. There has to be a better way," he repeated, frowning at the floor.

"Lucian has been with her since you got back. I had to make him go sleep."

"Please excuse me," Sorin said. "Alpha Seamus, thank you very much. Your allegiance means a lot to us."

He nodded and Sorin bowed to everyone before walking briskly out of the throne room. He wanted to know what things were like in Rosu, but he couldn't get his mind off of Ariette. Elizabeth was reading a book to Ariette when he walked in.

"I thought, maybe by hearing my voice, she'd wake up," she said. "It doesn't seem to be working, though."

Sorin sat down. He felt utterly useless. They sat in silence for a while, both holding Ariette's hands.

"The nomads are going to join us," he told her. "This war is all but won now. Do you know what things are like?"

"We were losing," she said. "There was another major battle and we lost a lot of men. The captain and lieutenants went back and stayed to fight. For now, the duke and duchess from the Priet province are watching over the kingdom."

"They're good people," he said. "It also helps that they are vampires, too. They know how Father runs things."

"King Laurent is getting daily updates. I don't know how, though."

"I don't care anymore. I'm so tired of all the mystery Talameh brought into our lives."

"We're leaving as soon as the mist falls. If it falls," she added miserably. "Taranis tried several spells."

"Princess Fiona is the one who is meant to break it," he said. "Though I'm not sure what power she possesses that can do it."

Elizabeth just nodded. Sorin closed his eyes and put his head on the table by Ariette's arm. He slowly fell asleep, waking briefly when some-one put a blanket over him.

***

At first, Sorin wasn't sure what had woken him. It could've been his aching back. But then he felt a weird fluttering on his head. It was al-most as if a bird were trying to find a place to land. He tried to ignore it. He just wanted to sleep until Ariette woke up. Then, something soft touched his forehead and his eyes shot open. Ariette was smiling weakly at him.

"Ari!" he breathed and hugged her gently.

"Glad to see we got out," she said, her voice hoarse.

"Lucian!" he shouted. While he waited, he hovered over her. "Are you thirsty? Cold? Uncomfortable? Can I do anything?"

"You can sit back down," she managed. "And tell me what's going on."

He pulled the chair as close as he could, holding her hand again.

"I fainted when we got back," he began.

By the time he was done, Lucian was sending for Elizabeth and Nicole. He checked Ariette over, frowning a little. He had her do a few tests and tried to help her sit up. Her body was too weak, though. When her mother and Nicole ran in, Lucian pulled Sorin to the side. Sorin moved as Liam barreled in shortly after the women.

"I'm worried, Sorin," Lucian said in an undertone. "She should have her strength by now. Color is back in her cheeks and her skin is warm, so I know she has her blood back. But I don't know why she's so weak."

"Maybe her body just needs more time to rest," Sorin said. "She is a human, after all."

"It could be," he conceded. "But I will feel better if we leave for Rosu as soon as possible."

"Send for Father. We'll see if they've gotten any progress with Fiona."

Lucian nodded and left. Sorin hovered on the outside of the group. Elizabeth was stroking Ariette's hair, crying. Nicole drilled Ariette with questions as Liam checked her over for injuries. He let out a long sigh of relief while he waited. He had been afraid she'd never wake up. As relieved as he was that she was awake, he was also worried. He was sure this was the time Nezeu meant when he said Sorin was her chance at life. But she came back on her own merit. If this wasn't the time, then when was it?

XXIX

Princess Fiona

Sorin stayed with Ariette as dinner was served. An elf brought in a plate with some meat and plenty of green vegetables and fruits.

"They'll help energize her," the elf whispered as Ariette snored a little in her sleep.

"Thank you," he said, and she bowed. He set the plates on the small table beside the bed that held the multitude of vials she had been given over the course of the three days. "Ariette, wake up."

He shook her gently until her eyes blinked open. She yawned.

"What time is it?" she mumbled.

"Around dinner," he said and helped her sit up, apologizing when her face twisted into a grimace of pain. "They said these will help you regain your energy."

"I can do it," she said but he pushed her hands away gently to feed her.

"Nothing is more romantic than a dinner in an infirmary," he said as he sat on the table beside her.

She laughed but it turned into a coughing fit. He rubbed her back until it passed.

"Is the mist gone?" she asked.

He set her empty plate down and picked at his own food.

"No," he said. "Princess Fiona is the only one who can get rid of it, though I don't know how. She must have immense power."

"What's her ability again? I can't remember."

"Wind. Perhaps she can create a sort of hurricane to diminish it?"

Ariette yawned again, her eyes half closed. "Maybe."

Sorin put his plate down and frowned at Ariette. She had fallen asleep again. He leaned over and kissed her before laying her back down. Lucian walked in as he was fussing with her pillow.

"Can't we move her somewhere more comfortable?" he complained.

"I was going to suggest it now, actually," he said. "Now that she's awake – for the most part – it's safe to move her back to your room. Ah, not you." Sorin stopped picking her up. "The king needs to speak with you about his daughter. I'll make sure she gets there."

Sorin hesitated but accepted defeat. With a final kiss, he left Ariette to his uncle. Peter was in the hall, struggling with a bandage on his arm.

"What happened?" Sorin asked.

Peter joined him as he walked up the stairs.

"I was trying to learn how to use a sword," he said bitterly. "I'm horrible. I think I'll just stick with daggers."

"Why were you trying to learn the sword?"

"I want to help more. I may not be able to go to battle, but I can at least keep you and Ariette safe."

"I appreciate it, friend, but you should focus more on recovering."

"It's been a month, Sorin," Peter reminded him gently. "I'm more than recovered now."

"Oh. Right. I forgot."

Sorin still had a hard time wrapping his mind around it. They had really been gone for a month. Even the land around them had changed, more leaves on the ground. He wondered what Rosu looked like; usually, it was starting to snow. Did the harvest go over well?

The royals were all in the throne room, Fiona at the center. She had been crying recently, and Taranis was pacing.

"I refuse to accept it," he said as Sorin and Peter entered. "There has to be another way."

"There isn't," Eratos said. He read over a piece of parchment in his hands, face extremely pale. "If what this spell says is true, then Fiona must-."

"I said no!" Taranis shouted. Sorin had never seen him this upset before. His usually straight hair was messy and his eyes afire with rage. "I don't care what that says! I will not allow it!"

"What's going on?" Sorin asked.

"We've found the answer we need," Eratos said.

"It is not the only answer!"

Sorin frowned between the two. Eratos thrust the parchment at him.

"I can't read this," Sorin said. "It's in Elvish."

"This is the spell Father used to create the mist," he explained. "In his... haste, he didn't read the full thing. It warns of the risks of casting the spell here at the bottom. To get rid of it, a sacrifice must be made. A blood sacrifice."

"Fiona," Sorin said and he nodded. "Does it have to be her life?"

"Perhaps not, but we're unsure. We've tried praying but none of us have gotten a response."

"That's why I sent for you," Taranis said. "You've seen him, you've spoken with him. You can appeal for me! Find another way! I won't give up my daughter like this!"

"I'm not sure I can do that, your highness," Sorin said. "I don't know why Nezeu revealed himself to me, much less if he'll do it again."

"Please try," Taranis begged. "If I had known, I never would have done that!"

"Can you tell me the words exactly?" Laurent asked.

Eratos read, "But know, should ye cut off completely, a sacrifice must be made to remedy it. Only the first-born daughter will be able to sac-rifice what is necessary."

Laurent stroked his chin.

"That doesn't necessarily mean her life," he said slowly. "It says she must sacrifice what is necessary."

"She's already sacrificed her voice and the love of her people!" Taranis shouted. Deirdre put her arm around Fiona as the princess started to cry again. "What more does he expect from her!?"

"If I may," Sorin said, "those weren't sacrifices. Those were taken from her. Princess, do you have anything else that is precious to you?"

She made strange gestures with her hands.

"She says just her family," Deirdre said. "This is the method she wanted to teach Ariette," she added when Sorin looked confused.

"Your ability is wind, correct?" Sorin asked. The princess nodded. "What if.... What if sacrificing your gift is what's needed?"

Fiona looked miserable and made the gestures again, her mother translating.

"She doesn't want to get rid of it. She thinks she's nothing without it."

"Ridiculous."

Everyone turned to the speaker. Sorin didn't recognize the elf, but his mother did.

"I thought you were in the dungeons," Stela said, glaring at him.

Sorin remembered what Ariette had said about the elf that she saw in her vision. The elf in the archway certainly matched the description. He was slightly taller than Sorin, his long blond hair pulled back with some vines. He was almost as muscular as Liam. This took him by surprise. Taranis had said his people weren't fit for battle, but the scars on this elf's arms suggested otherwise.

"King Taranis was kind enough to give me a pardon," the elf said. "I wasn't able to introduce myself properly. I am Ezekial."

He went to shake Stela's hand, but Sorin stepped in front of her.

"The king may trust you, but I don't," he snapped. "What do you want?"

"Fair enough," he conceded. "I've come for a few reasons. The first is to apologize. I had been so certain you and your kind would only bring more destruction. I heard about what you were able to accomplish, though. So, I also came to thank you. Though my brothers and sisters have not returned, at least their deaths weren't in vain." He balled his hands into fists, jaw clenched. "Originally, that was going to be all I was going to say. But now.... I've heard everything. Including your lie, Fiona," he added.

The princess looked away.

"What are you talking about?" Taranis asked.

"There is more that's precious to her," he said. "That is, if she was telling the truth."

It didn't take long for Sorin to understand.

"You're in love with him," he said, and Fiona hid her face. Taranis looked gob smacked. "Why lie?"

"Because she didn't want her father knowing," Ezekial said. "I know I'm not your favorite elf, your highness, but I do love your daughter. That's why I'm not going to let you sacrifice her life."

"That's exactly what I'm trying to avoid!" Taranis said. "And you expect me to believe you love her when you attacked the ship!?"

"I didn't know she was on it," he said. "The last I heard she was staying here. Knowing her, she lied to me so that I wouldn't try to stop her."

Taranis glared daggers at the elf. "How long has this been going on!?"

"Two years," he said. Sorin admired the fact the elf wasn't backing down. "We've been meeting in secret."

"Is this true?" Taranis asked, rounding on his daughter.

She nodded, crying more. Ezekial shouldered past Sorin and gently moved Fiona's hands from her face. She kept her head lowered in shame. Sorin pitied them. Just like Ariette, she had lived a lie to keep everyone happy. The stress of it must have made her miserable.

"I have an idea," Ezekial said as he embraced Fiona. "I, too, have the gift of wind. If there's one thing I've learned, it's that love can conquer any adversity."

"You're talking about combining your powers," Sorin said and the elf nodded. "But it says a sacrifice is needed. What if it hurts you?"

"Put yourself in my shoes, Prince Sorin. What if this was Lady Ariette everyone was talking about?"

Sorin searched the elf's eyes.

"I'd do whatever it takes to protect her," Sorin said finally. He sighed. "I guess it's worth a try."

"I just have one condition," Ezekial said.

"Seriously?" Eratos snapped. "First you rebel against my father, then you attack our ship, now you have the audacity to make a demand!?"

"Yes," Ezekial said evenly. "It's a simple one."

"What is it?"

"That, once this is done, you let Fiona come and live with me," he said to Taranis. "She and I will be married. If that's still want you want," he added.

Fiona was clearly terrified. She looked between her family and the elf she loved. Tremulously, she nodded. Taranis's shoulders deflated.

"Why didn't you tell me?" he whispered to Fiona. She spoke with her hands again. "I wouldn't have been angry! I would have tried to understand, at the very least!"

"You and I both know you wouldn't have accepted it," Ezekial said. "Do you accept it now, though?"

"If it means keeping Fiona safe and happy, then yes."

Ezekial gave a firm nod. "Good. Tomorrow morning, then. Excuse us."

He escorted Fiona out of the throne room, muttering words of comfort to her.

"I don't understand," Sorin said once his voice faded away. "Aside from the rebellion, what's so wrong with him?"

"Ezekial is a half elf," Deirdre said, running a hand through her hair. Her eyes were tired. "His mother was an elf, his father a human. His father was... not a good person. He forced himself on Ezekial's mother, causing her to get pregnant. He fled before facing the consequences of his actions. I don't know how he found out, but Ezekial has harbored a great hatred for outsiders ever since. He would get into fights a lot and built to be a warrior in case it happened to someone else."

"Where's his mother?"

"She died giving birth to him. He grew up here in the palace until he reached manhood. That would explain how they met," she added to herself.

"So his heritage somehow makes him unworthy?" Sorin asked, unable to hide the bitterness in his voice.

"It's not like that," Taranis said. "You saw what he did to us! I always feared his father's violent streak would show itself."

"When we expect the worst out of a person, that's all we see," Laurent said gently. "This Ezekial has made some mistakes, but I also think he wasn't exactly given the chance to do anything otherwise."

Taranis sat heavily in his throne.

"I just want my little girl to be happy," he said, dropping his face into his hands. "Ever since she was a child, no one wanted to be around her. They made up rumors, treated her like a pariah. I did my best to punish those responsible, but it just distressed her. She didn't like seeing others get in trouble, even though they didn't deserve to let their actions ignored. All this just because she's a twin."

Sorin felt bad for the king.

"I understand," Laurent said. "However, it seems like Ezekial is our best hope right now. If it truly is Fiona's powers that must be sacrificed, I can tell he would take care of her and love her regardless."

Taranis nodded. "I don't like it, but I also can't argue that point. We should all get some rest. Sorin, Ariette should be in your room now, if you'd like to go to her."

He didn't hesitate and rushed out of the room. He took the stairs two at a time. Peter and Sylvia were in the room, talking quietly with Ariette. When he walked in, they excused themselves. Ariette was sitting up in the bed, looking a little more awake than before. He kicked off his boots and got in bed next to her.

"How are you feeling?" he asked, holding her hand.

She leaned into him. "Tired as usual. I heard about Princess Fiona and that elf."

"It was quite the shock to her parents," he said. "You should've seen the look on the king's face."

"I feel for her," she said. "To have to keep that a secret for so long...."

"I'm sorry. I know you had to do that with Ingvar and Sigrid."

"It's different," she said but didn't elaborate. Before he could ask her to, she asked, "Will I be able to be there tomorrow morning?"

"Of course. I'll carry you there if I have to. Ingvar has finally accepted that Sigrid will not be marrying me, by the way," he said after some silence. "The treaty with the nomads will be signed as soon as we return to Rosu."

"Thank the gods," she groaned, closing her eyes in relief.

He chose his words carefully.

"That also means," he said slowly, "that we no longer have to pretend."

"Oh." Her voice was disappointed, and she turned her head away. "I had forgotten."

"I meant what I said, though. I want to do it the right way this time." He guided her face to look at him again. Her eyes were shining with tears. "I want to show you how much I love you. If you'll let me."

She swallowed thickly. He knew she was trying to speak. Finally, she nodded. He smiled and kissed her. At first, it was simple, just as before. However, the longer it lasted, the more his body reacted. And so did hers.

Ariette pulled herself closer to him and he wrapped an arm around her, gently pushing her onto her back. She deepened the kiss, not even getting scared when her tongue felt his fangs. He caressed her face, yearning for more but knowing better.

"I think that's enough for tonight," she panted, finally breaking from the kiss. Her cheeks were red and, not for the first time, Sorin wished he could read her mind. "We should stop before...."

"Before what?"

"Nothing," she said quickly, her blush spreading.

He smirked. "Before what, Ariette?" he teased.

She groaned. "Stop being an ass and go to sleep," she said, pushing on him to get him off.

Sorin laughed but got back into bed like normal. Once he was comfortable, though, he pulled her beside him. She didn't respond right away. Finally, she rested her head and hand on his chest, falling asleep quickly.

~~~

Ariette woke to Sorin's gentle prodding. She groaned and tried to hide under the pillows.

"I hate mornings," she grumbled when he laughed.

"Come on," he said. "You could use the fresh air. Besides, you won't have to walk over the bridge this time; I'll carry you."

She tried to get out of bed but almost fell. Sorin caught her, the humor in his face vanishing in an instant. She was still incredibly weak. Nothing she could do seemed to work. They had tried various tonics while everyone was figuring out what to do about the mist. Even the food that the elves used for this purpose wouldn't work on her. She was worried that she'd never get better. And, if Sorin was sincere about courting her, what kind of fiancé would that make her?

Everyone was waiting downstairs. She saw the elf from the attack and instinctively tightened her hold on Sorin's arm.

"I'm glad you're able to walk," Laurent said. "But are you sure you should come with us? It's quite the trip."

"I'll be here to help if she falls," Sorin said.

Laurent didn't look sure, but he nodded. They walked out into the morning air, Sorin and Ariette going a bit slower than the others.

"Sorry," she said. "I'm sure you want to be with your parents."

"I don't plan on ever leaving your side," he said quietly, making her blush.

Peter and Sylvia slowed down to walk with him, Sylvia asking Ariette if she needed any water every few minutes. When they got to the bridge, she groaned. Sorin picked her up and she buried her face in his neck. Even as they were suspended over a never-ending chasm, she noticed how strong his arms were, how pleasant the soaps he bathed in smelled. It made her heart skip and she checked that the necklace was
~~~

still around her neck. If Sorin could hear her thoughts, he would never let her live it down.

The trip to the main beach was two hours. It held a few ships and, according to Taranis, faced Rosu directly. Ezekial and Fiona were holding hands, standing in the middle of the beach. He was talking to her, presumably getting her ready.

"I wish I knew what they were saying," Ariette said, leaning into Sorin with a yawn. "Are you still unable to read their minds?"

"Yes. I haven't had a chance to ask Taranis about it yet."

She watched as Taranis approached the couple. Ezekial stood on the defensive, holding Fiona much the way Sorin did Ariette when someone threatened her.

"Are you ready?" Taranis asked.

"Yes," Ezekial said. "We've gone over the spell and think we know how to break it. Ironically, there are no words that need to be spoken."

"Very well. We have some elves here in case either of you get weakened. If you start to feel like you'll go unconscious, then stop right away. It isn't worth your lives."

Ezekial just nodded. Taranis backed off, holding Deirdre's hand tightly. Fiona and Ezekial faced each other. Ezekial kissed her and Ariette smiled. Their love for each other was apparent. It even made the air around them seem to glow. He muttered something then put his forehead on hers. Fiona closed her eyes, their hands clasped.

Nothing happened for a long while. No one spoke or moved. Then, Ariette noticed the wind pick up. It spiraled around them much as it had the night the royal family arrived on the shores of Rosu. The two elves were the focal point of the swirling air. It collected around them, causing their hair to fly straight up, as if getting sucked into a twister. Ariette was deafened by the roar of wind. Sorin pointed, and she followed his finger.

The wind was rising in a column above Ezekial and Fiona. She craned her neck to follow it as it went higher and higher. With a blast of wind that almost knocked them over again, it slammed into the wall of mist in the distance. Ariette gasped, gripping Sorin tightly. Fiona staggered and Taranis tried to get to her. He rebounded off of the wall of wind between them. Ezekial kissed Fiona again. She kissed him back and the air surged.

Several things happened at once.

The mist, once standing as thick and mystical as ever, vanished. People cheered. Then the cheers fizzled out, and dread fell with the wind. Fiona and Ezekial fainted from exertion. Ariette was worried about the princess, but something much more terrifying was on the horizon. Sorin was repeating the same swear word under his breath.

At least twenty ships, all with the Namhai flags, were coming directly for them.

XXX

Betrayed

"Get everyone back to the palace!" Sorin shouted, breaking everyone out of their shock.

Elves screamed and ran, two stopping two help Fiona and Ezekial. Ariette tried to walk on her own but just fell to her knees. Sorin scooped her up, panic rushing through every vein. They tore through the trees. The elves who had gone ahead of them were alerting those in the trees. Soon, the bridges were all creaking under hundreds of both adult and child elf feet. Sorin didn't stop until Ariette was safe inside. She had fainted and he looked for a place to put her.

"She needs to have her wounds redressed," Lucian panted, catching up with him. "I'll take her to the medical room. You need to talk to the king about defense."

Sorin passed her off then ran back outside. Taranis was directing elves into the palace, telling them where to hide. His parents were off to the side with the soldiers that had come with them, Generals Vasile and Marin included.

"We're going to have a fight on our hands," Ingvar was saying when Sorin got there. "There's no way to avoid it."

"They don't have enough ships to flee," Laurent agreed. "But we are grossly outnumbered."

Seamus gestured to the few wolves that accompanied him.

"We can help hold off the front lines," he said. "I doubt they sent many men here. I worry for the state of Rosu, though. If they got this far, they either took over or knew you were all here."

"Can you contact Duke Gregory?" Sorin asked his father. "Now that the mist is down?"

"I'll try."

Laurent shut his eyes and they waited nervously. Taranis was still trying to calm his people.

"Rosu still stands," Laurent said finally and Sorin groaned in relief, bending over to put his hands on his knees. "Apparently, this was a stealth mission on Namhai's part. He's organizing ships to be sent immediately. It will take them a long time to get here, though. We don't have the benefit of those blessed with elemental control."

"This doesn't make sense," Sorin said. "No one knew we were doing this! How did they know enough to be prepared!?"

"It's possible that they found out when we came to find you," Laurent said. "And, once they did that, they had the smarts to gather men to plan an attack."

"Damn it!" he shouted, his fangs growing. "If that's the case, then someone told them. Someone has been lying. But who?"

He paced the dirt, trying to focus. An elf had climbed the tallest tree and alerted them that the enemy was, at most, twelve hours away. That wasn't enough time to come up with a battle plan. They had no means of fighting back. Somehow, they knew that. Somehow, they knew they were coming to Talameh. Someone had-

He stopped. Pieces were starting to fall into place, and he grabbed Ingvar.

"Where is Sigrid?" he demanded.

"What are you doing?" Ingvar snapped, trying to push away Sorin's hand. "Let go of me."

"Where is Sigrid!?"

"I don't know!" he shouted back. "She was supposed to join us!"

"What has she been doing while we were together?" he asked.

"Are you accusing my daughter of something, Prince Sorin!?"

"Yes, I am! She's the only one who's known about everything from the start who is missing! Where is she!?"

Ingvar was indignant. "I may have accepted that she will not be your bride, but I will not stand here and let you insult her!"

"Just tell me where the hell she is!"

"I owe you nothing!"

"Ingvar." Seamus was beside them and Ingvar seemed to cower. "Where is your daughter?"

The duke swallowed thickly. "I don't know. She was there when we had breakfast. After that, she said she had to take care of something."

Seamus's eyes bored into Ingvar's. "And up until this point? Has she been acting odd?"

Ingvar thought. "I mean, a little. She was always mad about Ariette. She was sending a lot of letters to her friend back in Vin. The last one she sent was before we came here."

"You fool!" Sorin yelled and pushed Ingvar away from him. "She wasn't writing to her friend! I'd be surprised if that wench has any real friends!"

"Prince Sorin, contain your anger," Seamus said. "We don't know for sure what she's been up to, but it is suspicious indeed. Ingvar, use your power. Find her."

Ingvar's face was pale, but he nodded. He shifted and his ears and nose twitched. He turned on the spot a few more times before his tail straightened. Sorin followed the direction he was facing. It was right where the ships were. Ingvar shifted back. He no longer looked like the overconfident man he once was. He staggered and gaped up at Seamus.

"She's on the beach," he said in a hoarse voice. "She's-She's directing them to her."

"That bitch!" Sorin raged, fangs now fully exposed. His irises were red. "I'll kill her!"

"Calm down, Sorin," his father said. "Right now, we have to figure out how to protect Talameh."

"We have some weapons," General Vasile said. "Not nearly enough to fight off an entire fleet like that, though."

"King Taranis," Laurent called, and he rushed over. "Your hunters: Do they have a lot of bows and arrows?"

"I- Yes I believe so," Taranis said. "Why?"

"We need them," Laurent said. "And, if there's any among you that can fight, get them ready."

Taranis shook his head. "We're not made for battle!"

"We don't have a choice!" Sorin said. "Sigrid has been feeding our enemy everything we were doing from the very start." Taranis's eyes grew wide. "Which means she has told them that the defense here is weak! We have to find a way to keep everyone protected!"

"The bridges," Taranis said in a heavy voice. "We have to cut the bridges."

"You may not be fit for fighting with weapons," Laurent said, "but you do have your powers."

"This goes against everything I believe in," Taranis argued. "I know I said I'd stand with you, but I meant for supplies!"

"We don't have a choice now!" Sorin said. "They are literally just a few hours away! Get as many bows and arrows as you can. Gather the elves who are best at their craft and prepare yourselves."

Sorin was panicking. They didn't have any armor here except for what the soldiers and generals were wearing. A few elves dashed back across the bridges to gather as many bows and arrows as they could. Others were crafting more, felling a tree at the king's orders to make more. They worked surprisingly quick. Eratos had checked through as much of the castle as he could for anything that could give them more armor. Unfortunately, there was nothing.

Ariette had woken up about two hours later. Sorin was outside with some of the others, teaching elves how to use their bows to strike an enemy instead of just an animal. She stumbled out to him.

"What's happening?" she asked. "What's going on?"

He pulled her to a more secluded area and told her everything. Tears filled her eyes.

"We're going to cut the bridges soon," he said, pointing at them all with the arrow he was holding. "Father has made it clear that I will be in one of the windows to fight. I want you to stay with the other women below ground. I'm not going to argue this with you," he said when she started to speak. "You are in no shape to fight, even if you knew how. I'm not going to risk this, Ariette."

"I don't want you to fight!" she sobbed. "What if you get hurt!? You have no armor!"

"That's why I'll be in the windows!"

"And you think they're not going to have archers, too!? You're smarter than that, Sorin!"

"I know! But we can't just surrender, either! My father told you: Namhai doesn't take any prisoners! They will kill everyone here and destroy this island!"

"But why do you have to fight!? You're the only heir left!"

"It doesn't matter. I'm not going to abandon everyone."

"Please," she begged, grabbing his front, and pulling him close. She buried her face in his chest. "Please don't fight. Don't leave me. I love you."

The arrow fell to the ground with a light clatter. No one noticed. He was stunned and took her face, guiding her lips to his. He kissed her deeply, putting as much passion into it as he could. Her tears mixed in their mouths and he broke away to look her in the eyes.

"I love you, too," he whispered. "I'll come back to you. Besides, we have a secret ally."

"Who?"

"Nezeu," he said. "Remember? Seamus said that we may have gained his favor because of what we did."

"That's such a big risk, Sorin," she said. "I can't- I can't watch you go."

Somewhere in the distance, they heard a muffled explosion. He turned and swallowed thickly. Smoke was billowing up from the beach.

What caused it, he had no idea. Flames licked up the trees and the elves on the other side of the bridge screamed, fleeing back to the palace.

"They shot something at the beach," the elf above keeping watch yelled. "I don't know what it was. It's all in flames now."

"Please," Ariette tried one more time.

"Ariette," he said. "I know you're scared. I am, too. But we'll be okay. And, no matter what, I love you and I'll always be with you."

She tried to speak but, when their eyes locked, he pushed on her mind and she fell asleep. He caught her before she fell and called for Lucian.

"Take her with the others," he said. "Keep her safe."

Lucian nodded grimly. "I will. Sorin, be careful."

Sorin just strode over to the closest bridge. The lookout kept giving them updates. As the hours passed, the ships were getting closer and closer. Taranis sent both elves and vampires to each bridge, swords at the ready. Trees were being cut down on the other side as the enemy forced its way to them. When commanded, Sorin sliced at the ropes holding up the bridge. It took a few tries, but eventually they gave way. A dozen bridges crashed into the opposite wall, causing a small tremor in the earth. He sheathed his sword and fell back to his position on the second floor of the palace, bow and arrow at the ready.

The armies arrived not long after. They yelled in anger at the felled bridges. At the front, Sigrid was standing with Namhai's prince, no longer in her normal wolf pelt. She was in the armor of a Namhai soldier and anger burned through Sorin. Below, Ingvar yelled at her.

"Traitor!"

She held her head high, though, and didn't respond.

They all stood in tense silence. No one wanted to be the one to make the first move. Sorin's mouth was dry as more and more of the soldiers lined up on the ground in front of them. There were at least four hundred men gathered there.

~~~
~~~

Below, Ariette woke with a start. She was in the medical room, the queens, princesses, and women all gathered in small circles. Her mother, Stela, and Nicole were closest, and she grabbed them.

"What's going on?" she rasped. "How long was I asleep?"

"It's started," Stela said. "Laurent is keeping me updated. There are a lot of soldiers. Sigrid is with them." She sighed, covering her face. "I was a fool to let them come with us."

"There has to be something we can do," she said. "Something other than just-just sitting here!"

"This is how we help them," Elizabeth said gently. "By staying safe, they don't have to worry about us."

"I can't stand this."

Ariette pulled her knees up to her chin. She nibbled on her lip, trying to think of what she could do from this room. Sneaking out wasn't an option. She wasn't even able to walk on her own and the door was on the other side of the room. Instinctively, she held the pendent around her neck. Her father had given it to her, reminding her that he would always be with her. She hadn't had a chance to give it to Sorin. It felt like an omen.

Inspiration struck her. She looked at the pendent, her mind working quickly. Queen Deirdre had made these to make it so their peoples would never be disconnected from one another. She believed that Nezeu would provide for them. And now, Ariette had to believe the same.

She got on her knees and crawled to the back of the room, shooing away her mother when she tried to stop her. She got to a corner and looked around. She had never done anything like this before and wasn't sure if there were any requirements.

"What are you doing?" Nicole hissed.

"Deirdre," Ariette said when she saw the queens close by. "I need you to tell me something. How do you pray to Nezeu?"

"The same as you would any god," she said. "Sometimes with an offering, sometimes merely talking does the trick. Why?"

"So there doesn't need to be some kind of statue? Like the one in the city?"

"Not that I know of. Ariette, what are you getting at?"

"I'm going to pray to Nezeu," she said and sat cross-legged on the floor. Her face was determined. "If Sorin is going to lock me in here, I'm going to show him I can still help."

"You don't even know if Nezeu is real," Nicole said desperately.

"So what if he isn't? I can't just sit here, Nicky! I love him and the thought of him dying terrifies me!"

Her voice broke and she started to cry. Nicole cried, too, and hugged her. Before they could speak, there was a crash followed by the earth quaking around them. Ariette whimpered and wiped away her tears. She took a deep breath, closed her eyes, and tried to block out other noises. The women in the room were starting to get anxious, whispering to each other as more sounds resonated down to them. She wasn't sure when it happened, but suddenly, she was no longer in the medical room.

It was the silence that made Ariette open her eyes. The women had all stopped moving around, so she thought something had happened. She was sitting in water, though it didn't dampen her skin or clothing. The world around her was just dark purple and black galaxies. At first glance, she was alone. However, she could sense someone nearby.

"N-Nezeu?" she managed. "A-Are you there?"

"Ariette."

The voice made her jump. It was deep and resounding. She couldn't find the source, nor could she move.

"S-Sorry for bothering you," she stammered. "I just- The war- We're still in Talameh and we don't have any armor or anything. I'm so scared. Please. Isn't there something that can be done?"

She didn't get a response for what felt like an eternity. However, she had a feeling it wasn't long; time in different realms didn't work the same, as she had discovered. The water around her began to ripple, as if something large was walking towards her. She looked up in time to nearly faint in fear.

The being in front of her looked just as Sorin had described. He was immense and radiated power and respect. If she could move, she would've bowed low.

"I wondered when you would come," Nezeu said. "You fear for your loved ones."

"Yes. I don't want Talameh to be harmed, either. I- I may only be part elf, but I can still feel the ties I have to the land."

"What do you have to offer me?"

She blinked. "Well, I.... I don't really have anything. I mean, if you want some gold offerings, I'm sure the king would be willing to-."

"You misunderstand. What do *you* have to offer me?"

"Me? You mean... like how Fiona gave up something to lower the mist?" He didn't respond, which she took as a yes. "Erm.... I have...." She shook her head. "All I have is my life. But I thought that only demons dealt with souls."

"It is not your soul I desire. You are correct: demons resort to petty deals with souls. What I am going to ask from you is much more diffi-cult to give up."

She felt like crying. "Do I have to die?"

He smiled, his fangs glistening from the distant stars and suns.

"Of course not," he said. "Well, not in the sense that you think of dy-ing." He got on a knee, leaning down so that his face was more level with hers. "How much are you willing to give for this land? Are you ready to give up the life you knew? Are you ready to start a new life, one that may end up being lived in secret?"

"You want me to become a vampire," she whispered.

"I am afraid it is not as simple as that," he said. "You and Sorin have come a long way in ending this war. You have successfully brought to-gether my children once again. That was your fate. This is a pivotal mo-ment for both of you."

"Can you help us?" she asked.

"Yes."

"T-Then I will," she said, tears streaming down her face. "Whatever I have to do, I'll do it."

He nodded once and stood back up.

"If you do not uphold your end of the bargain, I will know," he said as everything began to fade. "Go to Sorin. He knows what must be done."

She couldn't speak. The world around her got so bright she had to shut her eyes. Sound rushed to her ears; women screaming. She opened her eyes again to see Queen Stela and Queen Deirdre trying to calm everyone down.

Filled with renewed purpose, Ariette got to her feet. Her legs shook under her, but she steadied them. No one noticed her in the panic. She wasn't sure how long she was with Nezeu. She did know one thing, though: She had to get to Sorin.

XXXI

Vampire

Ariette inched further down the hall. Her mother and Nicole were holding little girls, calming them with stories and songs. It was harder to get by the queens. They were right in front of the door.

"Everyone, please, just calm down," Deirdre said. "I'm sure everything will be fine."

"My husband is out there!" one cried. "I have to see him!"

Ariette's hand was on the door before anyone saw her. She slipped through and looked around. She heard shouting and screaming. On quaking legs, she made her way up the stairs. Sorin had to be near.

~~~

It was Namhai that made the first move. An arrow soared through the air and narrowly missed General Vasile. Laurent gave the command and Sorin, and everyone else with bows, shot their arrows. His landed squarely in the face of one of the soldiers up front. He didn't have time to pride himself on his shot, though. Their side was scattering for cover as arrows rained from the forest. Taranis shouted to some of his elves.
~~~

A line of them in the back got on one knee. As soon as their legs hit the ground, the earth quaked on the other side. A few elves raised their arms. Roots shot out of the ground and wrapped around the Namhai soldiers, crushing them as they tightened. From different windows, elves shot light into the eyes of the enemy. Water and fire spun together as they swept over the men.

It wasn't enough, though. Their first casualty was one of Vasile's men. A silver arrow landed in the man's neck, and he dropped instantly. Sorin jumped out of the window, landing catlike beside his father.

"We have to bring the land together!" he yelled over the sound of the battle. "We're out of arrows!"

Laurent nodded, dropping his bow as Sorin did the same. They drew their swords and shouted to Taranis. Many of the elves backed away as the vampires took up the front.

"Ready!" Laurent shouted over his shoulder.

"Now!"

It took a dozen elves to slam the earth back together. Sorin almost fell, but he steadied himself. He thought about Ariette and swallowed thickly. He'd have to break his promise to her. As the enemy got back to their feet, he could tell that they were ridiculously outnumbered. Seamus and Ingvar roared as they shifted, the other wolves doing the same. They snarled as the opposing generals got their men ready to attack. Sorin regripped his sword, trying not to think of the night Dalca died.

"I'm sorry, Ariette," he whispered and squared his shoulders.

The enemy gave a battle cry, then ran at them.

"Stand your ground!" Laurent shouted. "Wait!"

Sorin brought his sword up just as the first line of men got to them. The air shimmered with the heat of silvered weapons. They knew. There was no doubting it now.

"Use your fangs if you have to!" he shouted. "They know!"

No one needed to be told twice. Soon, the air was filled with not just screams of pain. Screams of terror mingled in with them now as fangs sank into skin. While they may have known, it was clear several hadn't believed their commanding officers. They made quick work of the first barrage, though several men were lost in it all. The second wave was just as bad, and Sorin realized they were being pushed closer to the palace.

Then something strange happened.

From the southeast, a fog lifted from the earth. It carried through the trees and to the battle. At first, no one paid it any mind. But then, one by one, the enemy started to scream in agony and fear. Sorin wiped blood out of his eyes and squinted them to see through the dancing air. He almost dropped his sword and staggered back as a body rammed into him. Among the fog, men and women in old Rosu armor were attacking the rear enemy lines. Leading them, somehow, was King Darius.

The fear these specters brought with them drove some of the Namhaians into a blind panic. They tried to attack, but their swords just went through the apparition and into one of their allies. The ghostly army were yelling and working in tandem. They couldn't seem to leave the fog, but it also didn't seem to matter. If the blades didn't kill them, something in the air certainly did. A few Namhaians fell to the ground, clutching their throats as their veins popped. Blood poured from their eyes and, when they hit the ground, they were dead.

Sorin didn't know what to think. What he did know, was that they were now winning. His eyes darted for the prince, but it was impossible to see him through everything. He kept fighting until he heard a blessed sound.

"Retreat!" a Namhaian screamed. "Fall back!"

"Don't let them escape!" Laurent yelled in response. Sorin tried to chase after them, but Laurent caught him. "Not you! Get to the women! Make sure everyone is safe!"

"Right," Sorin panted and sheathed his sword.

He couldn't believe their luck. He turned to run inside, but Ariette was already stumbling out of the palace, reaching for him. He met her halfway and embraced her.

"What are you doing out here!?" he shouted over the noise.

"I- I saw- Spoke to Nezeu," she gasped. "He s-said he'd help."

Sorin pulled her around to look at the ghost army.

"That's certainly help," she said. "Did we-?"

Her words were cut off as a blade went straight through her chest.

The world slowed down. Ariette gaped at the sword. She made a strange choking sound as it was yanked out of her. Sorin fell with her, speechless. Blood poured from the wound. The skin around it was burning as if something on the blade was eating away at it. He looked up.

"And to think," Sigrid said, wiping her blade on her leg. "All of this could have been avoided, if you had just swallowed your pride and agreed to marry me."

Sorin couldn't think straight. Ariette was gurgling, trying to breathe. He gathered her in his arms, only dimly aware of Ingvar tackling his daughter to the ground. He tried to get Ariette to look at him. He could hear Elizabeth screaming for Ariette somewhere in the distance.

"Ari," he gasped. "Ari, look at me."

"I just... wanted to help," she said. Her eyes were slowly going in and out of focus. "I'm sorry."

"No," he said. Tears were streaking down his face, leaving marks in the dust that had caked during the battle. "No, Ariette. Don't talk like that. You did great."

Her lips moved, but she didn't manage anything at first.

"I-I really wanted to marry you," she gasped. "I'm sorry."

He sobbed, holding her tighter. Elizabeth was running at them full sprint, screaming hysterically.

"Ariette, you can't go," he said. "You can't leave me. I need you."

"I love you," she whispered, her eyes starting to dim.

"Gods no!" he cried.

Elizabeth crumpled to the floor, reaching for Ariette.

"Keep close to Ariette, Prince. You are her only chance at life."

Sorin gasped through his sobs.

"No, don't make me," he moaned. "Please don't make me do this!"

Ariette's heart was slowing and he knew he was running out of time. He looked at Elizabeth.

"You can't just let her die," Elizabeth sobbed. "Please save my baby girl."

"I'll be killing her," he said.

"Save her, please," she begged.

"Ari!"

Nicole screamed and Liam ran with her. They dropped to their knees, both starting to cry.

"I'm sorry," Sorin said. "I'm so sorry. He said- I have to. Oh gods, I have to."

He moved Ariette's hair, revealing her neck. It was cold, too cold. He swallowed the lump in his throat and sank his teeth into her skin. Hating every bit of himself, he injected the venom. He drank some of her blood, feeling the convulsions start. His mother was with them, soothing Elizabeth as his father tried to calm down and restrain Nicole. Ariette's body stopped moving and he cut his arm.

"I'm so sorry," he repeated as he dropped his blood into her open mouth.

At first, nothing happened. It hit her teeth then slid down her throat. Her body tried to reject it, but soon his blood was running through her veins. Her back arched as she screamed, her body seizing. Elizabeth wailed into Stela's chest, gripping her desperately. Sorin held Ariette closer.

"You can do this," he said. "Please, Ariette. Pull through. You can make it. You're strong. I know you can do it." Her body stopped and everyone waited. Lucian, covered in blood, had also come. "Lucian, why isn't she breathing!?"

"It takes a while," Lucian panted. "You know it does. Give her more blood."

He obeyed but still, nothing happened. Sorin started to panic.

"Please, Ariette," he said again. He bent down and kissed her lips. He didn't bother to stop his sobs. "Please come back to me, Ariette. Come back to me, my little minx."

Just as he was about to give up, her eyes shot open and she inhaled sharply, her back arching. She screamed, fingers digging into the dirt. Nicole gasped as the wound in Ariette's chest slowly healed over. Sorin's sobs turned into relief as he cradled her in his arms. He whispered encouragement until her screams subsided.

"S-Sorin?" Ariette gasped.

"Thank the gods," he groaned.

He kissed her and, as one, they fainted.

***

Sorin woke in bed. Ariette was beside him, her body shaking as she cried. He sat up in panic. Lucian was monitoring her closely.

"Your blood," he said. "Give her more."

He bit into his arm and held it over her mouth. She was conscious, but her eyes were out of focus. As soon as his blood touched her tongue, they rolled back in pleasure. She drank deeply and fell back into the pillows. Sweat was dripping from her body and he waited before mending the wound.

"Everything's gone as it should," Lucian told him. "I have to go speak with your father about our next move. Stay here. The process will take another day."

Sorin nodded. When the door shut, he looked at Ariette again. Her eyes were fluttering.

"Ariette," he whispered. "I'm so sorry. I didn't want to. I'm so sorry."

"Don't... be," she said, taking deep breaths. "It had to happen."

"It's not going to be easy," he said. He gulped as her eyes filled with pain, her body twisting. "It's okay, though. I'm here."

As her body continued to die, he gave her the blood she needed. After several hours, she had finally quieted down. Tubs were brought in. Sorin didn't care anymore and helped lower her into the water, keeping his eyes focused on her face. Sylvia washed Ariette's body in shaking hands as an elf came in to clean the blood-soaked sheets. Sorin washed her hair, combing it carefully. Occasionally, she'd start to twitch, and he'd simply give her a bit of blood until it stopped.

That night, he stayed awake with her. He remembered the nightmares that plagued his sleep when he turned. He held her through them all. Just as he had dreamt of Charlotte, she seemed to be dreaming of her father. She would cry for him, begging for him to stay with her. It broke his heart. He kept her close to his chest. It didn't calm until dawn and he was able to get a few more hours of sleep.

When he woke again, Ariette wasn't in bed. He panicked, then found her by the window. She was staring into the distance.

"Are you okay?" he asked, hurrying to her. "You should be in bed."

"Sorin, look."

He did a doubletake. Slowly, he opened the window. The creature on the windowsill hopped out of the way.

It was a phoenix.

The feathers faded from dark red on the inside, to almost yellow at the edge. It was large, almost three feet tall. Its beady, black eyes were fixed on the two of them. Ariette hesitantly held out her hand. It hopped in one spot a few times before hopping the rest of the way. It put one talon on her palm. She gasped. Sorin saw her fangs and felt a pang of remorse. The phoenix whipped its head in his direction. It startled him. It spread its large wings and let out a trilling noise. It soothed his emotions.

It flapped its wings a few times before starting to sing. They could only watch in awe as it flew off, leaving a single feather behind. Sorin picked it up, turning it around in his fingers.

"It would seem the war is almost over," he whispered and put the feather behind her ear. He stroked her face. "I'm so sorry, Ariette. I never wanted this for you."

She nestled her face in his hand, holding it in place. She closed her eyes and leaned into him.

"I know. But it's not your fault. When I prayed to Nezeu, he said I would have to give him something for his help. He said I'd have to become a vampire and that you would know when the time was right."

"He told me something similar. He said that I was your chance at living. I had hoped this wasn't what he meant...."

"Sorin," she said, and he reluctantly met her eyes. "I'm not mad at you. You saved me. We're even now."

He couldn't help but laugh, and she did, too. He brushed his nose against hers.

"Does this mean you still want to be my queen?" he asked.

Her cheeks went red. "If you still want me," she said.

He grinned and kissed her.

XXXII

Return

Ariette was given a few days to recover. It had been the most painful experience she had gone through. Sorin was there for most of it, leaving only to discuss their departure. She had many nightmares and would wake up in a frenzy. Sometimes, she'd lose herself completely. A voice in her mind kept antagonizing her, especially when Sorin was gone. It would keep saying he was leaving her for someone else, or that he was going to get something to kill her with.

"It's your vampire," he explained the second time it happened. He had walked in to see her pulling at her hair and screaming. "She'll be very convincing for a while. You'll learn to ignore her." He let her curl into a ball, her face in his neck as she cried. "Do you still want to know how the meeting went?" She nodded and he got comfortable, wrapping his arms around her. "Well, Sigrid is dead. Ingvar killed her. I'm surprised to say that I feel bad for him. I think he really did just want what was best for everyone and was convinced Sigrid was the answer. Father wants to return to Rosu tomorrow if you're up for travelling. He also said we can stay here for longer if need be."

"I just wanna go home," she cried, feeling like a child. "I want to see my mother."

"I'll have my mother get her, don't worry. What is it?" he asked when she started to cry louder.

"So many voices!"

Dozens of voices had filled her mind, nearly driving her mad. Sorin held her tightly and put his forehead to hers.

"Imagine you're in the gardens," he said. "Remember all the lightning bugs? The roses and peonies?" She nodded. "Focus on those."

After a few moments, the voices started to dwindle. She relaxed.

"Those were the minds of the others here," he explained. "Oh, I was able to ask Taranis about the block. Apparently, when he cast the spell for the mist, it also cut off the telepathic link. Even though the mist is down, we still can't read his mind. It's probably for the best, though."

"Is Fiona okay?"

"She will be. It's as we thought, she no longer has the ability to manipulate wind." He ran his fingers through her hair as he spoke, her eyes slowly closing. "I spoke with Ezekial. It turns out her ability was the only redeeming quality she saw in herself. That's why it was a sufficient sacrifice for Nezeu. If Ezekial hadn't been there to help her, she would have died."

"Hmm."

He chuckled. "Am I boring you?"

"No," she said and nuzzled his neck, making him laugh again. "But I'm tired."

"Then sleep."

She just hummed and fell asleep quickly. The next morning, they had breakfast in the dining hall. Her mother and Nicole were fretting over her. That was probably the hardest part for Ariette. No one would let humans visit her until the process was done.

"It's too risky," Laurent had said as she raged through the door. "You're still turning, Ariette. It's very possible you could kill one of them."

She had called him a very unkind name and apologized at breakfast. He just laughed.

"I didn't know you had that word in your vocabulary," he teased, and she groaned, sinking in her chair.

Before they left, Nicole and Liam asked to speak with her alone. They went out to the gardens and Ariette showed them the fountain.

"How do you feel?" Liam asked once they were away from everyone.

"I feel okay," she said honestly. She touched her neck where the bite marks had faded. "It hurts sometimes, but Sorin says it'll pass. I don't remember a lot from when it happened."

Nicole shared a sad look with Liam.

"You were dying," she said, starting to cry. "That wench Sigrid ran you through with a poisoned sword. I've never seen Sorin that upset before.... He didn't want to turn you into a vampire. Honestly... I didn't want him to, either."

"I still can't believe vampires are real," Liam muttered.

"But then I saw you, barely breathing, and I didn't want you to die. Sorin kept saying no and how he didn't want to do it. Then he just apologized over and over again before he bit you. I felt sorry for him. It clearly killed him to watch you... you know."

Ariette hugged Nicole.

"I'm still me," she said. "I'm still Ariette. I love chocolate, I hate sprouts, and heels are the worst fashion choice ever made by men." Nicole laughed through her tears. "Nothing has changed. Except for a rather large extended life span."

Nicole sniffled. "Are you two going to get married?"

Blushing, Ariette nodded.

"I'll be havin' a talk with him first," Liam said darkly. "I didn't get a chance earlier before all... that happened." He gestured at her neck. "But he ain't gettin' away without one."

She laughed. "I'm sure he's been waiting for it."

"Excuse me," he said and strode to the palace with purpose.

The girls both laughed, linking arms. They took a more leisurely pace.

"I've missed Rosu," Ariette said.

"So have I. It was great to see Liam, but I miss my parents."

"I'm sorry for everything that happened," she said with a sigh. "I know I promised I would be okay, that nothing would go wrong, but...."

"I understand. But I don't think any of this is your fault. I'm a firm believer that everything happens for a reason. Sorin may not be my favorite person, but you are, so I'll give him some grace."

"I'm sure he'll be glad to hear that. He was sure you'd burn him alive."

"That's still a possibility," she said jokingly.

Ariette laughed. When they got back to the palace, neither Liam nor Sorin were anywhere to be seen.

"Liam came in and... escorted Sorin to the study," Laurent said when they asked, his eyes bright with laughter. "I'm sure they'll be out any second now." He raised his voice. "Or we're going to be late!"

The two men emerged from the archway a few minutes later, Liam looking satisfied and Sorin horrified. Ariette giggled and hugged him.

"Why does he scare me more than any vampire I've ever met?" he grumbled.

The ship was waiting at the beach and everyone saw them off. Ariette hugged Fiona tightly.

"Keep in touch," she said. "Now that the mist is gone, maybe you and Ezekial can come visit."

"That would be lovely, Lady Ariette," Ezekial said, shaking her hand. "Thank you for everything you did. I'm very sorry for what I did to you."

"Just make Fiona happy and we'll call it even," she said. "And remember: not everything is as it seems."

He smiled gratefully. "I'll be sure to remember that. Safe travels, Lady Ariette, Prince Sorin."

Sorin bowed and took Ariette's hand. Eratos was going to use his wind to get them home quicker. He didn't meet Ariette's eyes at all as they got ready to set sail and she frowned at Sorin.

"Did I do something wrong?" she asked. "He won't even talk to me."

Sorin snorted. "More like he's finally learned to keep his hands to himself," he said. "Oh! You forgot this."

He opened the rucksack on his back and took out a box. She opened it eagerly. It was the tiara the elves had made for her. He put it on her head and grinned.

"Beautiful as ever," he said.

She smiled and waved to the assembled crowd. They cheered as Taranis and another elf pulled the ramp up into the ship. Several elves had asked to join them so they could see some of the mainland, too. Sorin and Ariette stood near the front of the ship, leaning against the rail.

"Hold on!" Taranis called and they grabbed the ropes.

With a gust of wind, the ship lurched forward. Elizabeth, Nicole, and Liam joined them at the front.

"It scared me the first time," Elizabeth said as she watched the water rush by them. "But at least I was prepared for it."

"I wonder what it'll be like in Rosu. It's winter now."

"Lots of snow," Liam said. "It was already about six inches when we left."

"Was the harvest successful?" Sorin asked.

"Aye, your highness," he said. "We have plenty."

"Do you think Namhai will surrender?" Ariette asked.

"They'd be fools not to," he said. "But I think it'll take a while. They're proud and think what happened was a one-time thing. The prince got away, so they still have someone they can rally behind. Whether or not he'll be brave enough to go into battle again, though, is yet to be seen."

"I hate war," she sighed. "I just want it all to be over."

"Me too," everyone said in unison.

***

When they docked in Rosu, it was freezing. The ship had to cut through some ice that was starting to form in the shallows. King Taranis and Eratos followed them up to the front of the palace. Several of the citizens cheered when they saw Sorin and Ariette. Ariette waved to her friends, laughing when Ivan fled from his spot by the tanner's.

The castle was warm, and she relished in the relief. Luggage was carried in, gifts from the elves.

"It's good to be home," Stela said with a deep breath. "Let's try to avoid life threatening ventures for a while."

Ariette and Sorin laughed.

"We'll try to remember that," Sorin said.

"I'll be back soon," Nicole said, joining her with Liam. "I want to see my parents."

"No, go," Ariette said. "Take your time, okay? I'll let you know when we start planning for the wedding."

Nicole grinned. "I can't wait to see what your dress will look like."

Ariette waved. The king and queen were showing their guests to the provided rooms. Ariette stretched and gasped when Sorin picked her up off her feet. She laughed.

"But my room is there," she said, pointing as he walked by it.

He set her down outside of his room, brow raised. "You don't seriously think you're still my mother's lady-in-waiting, do you?"

She blushed. "Well, we never really discussed it," she said defensively. "Besides, I thought us sharing a room was because of the wolves."

"It was before, but now it's because I don't think I can fall asleep without you, to be honest."

She smiled shyly. "So...?"

He opened the door and gestured with his head. "Come on. I'm tired."

"Just keep your hands to yourself," she said.

A fire was going, and she hurried to it, rubbing her hands together. She was enjoying the heat when two hands slid from her hips to her stomach. She felt a different shiver run up her spine as Sorin placed long kisses on her shoulder and neck.

"You-You said you'd keep your hands to yourself," she stammered, trying not to get lost in his touch.

"I said no such thing," he said in a gruff voice.

She turned in his arms. His eyes were half-closed and brimming with lust. She stood on her toes to kiss him. He kissed her back, gripping her tightly. A myriad of emotions swept through her mind, but she couldn't focus on any one thing. When they broke from the kiss, her breath was heavy.

"I love you," they said in unison and kissed again, Sorin guiding her to the bed.

***

As the snow fell in Rosu, Namhai was experiencing unnatural heat. The king poured over the reports from the few men that survived the battle at Talameh. Elves were able to manipulate the elements!? And it would seem that the Rosu royal family really were a bunch of vampires. He spat in the pail by his desk. He looked at the document from his son. It was full of ramblings. Even now, he was down in the dungeons with the rest of the failures, babbling about roots coming to life.

He got to his feet and walked to his window. The capitol city was working harder than normal to train their boys to recover what he lost in that battle. He glared in the direction of Rosu and Talameh. He didn't care what he had to do. They would pay.

From the corner, an angry screech made him grimace.

"Shut up," he spat. "I can't think with you constantly screaming."

He yanked the blanket off of the cage. Inside, a blue phoenix flapped its wings against its steel prison. It swiped at him with a talon and he barely dodged it. He slapped the front of the cage, but the bird was unfazed. It had been acting up for the last two days, but he didn't understand why until now. On his desk, sat the only physical evidence of that blasted prophecy.

When the phoenix returns, Namhai will fall.

"Like hell it will," he growled and covered the cage again. "If they want to cheat and employ supernatural beings and powers, then so will I."

He opened a wardrobe door. His other secret treasure tried to hide. It was useless, though. He grabbed the jar and held it up to his face, grinning at the small being cowering inside of it.

"Time to see if wishes do come true," he said with a dark laugh. The fairy could only tremble in fear.

9 780578 981079